# THE OBSESSION

Also BY
# CATHERINE COOKSON

**NOVELS**

Kate Hannigan
The Fifteen Streets
Colour Blind
Maggie Rowan
Rooney
The Menagerie
Slinky Jane
Fanny McBride
Fenwick Houses
Heritage of Folly
The Garment
The Fen Tiger
The Blind Miller
House of Men
Hannah Massey
The Long Corridor
The Unbaited Trap
Katie Mulholland
The Round Tower
The Nice Bloke
The Glass Virgin
The Invitation
The Dwelling Place
Feathers in the Fire
Pure as the Lily
The Mallen Streak
The Mallen Girl
The Mallen Litter
The Invisible Cord
The Gambling Man
The Tide of Life
The Slow Awakening
The Iron Façade

The Girl
The Cinder Path
Miss Martha Mary Crawford
The Man Who Cried
Till Trotter
Tilly Trotter Wed
Tilly Trotter Widowed
The Whip
Hamilton
The Black Velvet Gown
Goodbye Hamilton
A Dinner of Herbs
Harold
The Moth
Bill Bailey
The Parson's Daughter
Bill Bailey's Lot
The Cultured Handmaiden
Bill Bailey's Daughter
The Harrogate Secret
The Black Candle
The Wingless Bird
The Gillyvors
My Beloved Son
The Rag Nymph
The House of Women
The Maltese Angel
The Year of the Virgins
Justice is a Woman
The Tinker's Girl
The Golden Straw
A Ruthless Need

**THE MARY ANN STORIES**

A Grand Man
The Lord and Mary Ann
The Devil and Mary Ann
Love and Mary Ann

Life and Mary Ann
Marriage and Mary Ann
Mary Ann's Angels
Mary Ann and Bill

**FOR CHILDREN**

Matty Doolin
Joe and the Gladiator
The Nipper
Rory's Fortune
Our John Willie

Mrs Flannagan's Trumpet
Go Tell It To Mrs Golightly
Lanky Jones
Nancy Nutall and the Mongrel
Bill and the
   Mary Ann Shaugnessy

**AUTOBIOGRAPHY**

Our Kate
Catherine Cookson Country

Let Me Make Myself Plain
Plainer Still

# CATHERINE COOKSON

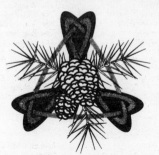

## THE
# Obsession

**BCA**

LONDON  NEW YORK  SYDNEY  TORONTO

This edition published by
BCA
by arrangement with Bantam Books

First reprint 1996
Second reprint 1996

Printed in England by Clays Ltd, St Ives plc

# PART ONE

## The Garden Party

# I

As he walked up the long, pine-bordered drive, so thick on
either side were the trees that they dimmed the sound of
voices and laughter coming from beyond them.

Approaching the end of the drive was like emerging into
daylight after walking through a tunnel. From the surroundings it was obvious why the house was called Pine
Hurst. This was the first time he had seen it, for it was
his partner's preserve. It was long but not too low, and
as his eyes travelled to the right they took in what looked
like a cottage attached to the end, yet, as was the rest, it
was mullion-windowed. In front of the main building was
a balcony from which shallow steps led down to a gravelled
area which in turn gave way to a large lawn.

It was a most attractive-looking house from its long front
up to its ornamental chimneys, of which, he noted, there
were several, suggesting the house was even larger than it
appeared to be from the outside. The neighing of a horse
coming from the far end announced there was a stable yard
round the corner. But he turned now from the house and
looked to where two freshly clipped topiary lions guarded
the low pillars that headed the four steps leading down to the
lawn, not into a rose garden as one would expect, but to the
large lawn on which was set a number of tables with bright

canopy umbrellas above them. Some people were already seated at the tables but more were walking about, and as he hitched up the small parcel under his arm he reminded himself that this wasn't only a garden party but a twenty-first birthday celebration for Miss Beatrice Penrose-Steel.

He noticed a man disengage himself from a group and walk towards him. This was, he surmised, the Lord of the Manor, as old Cornwallis dubbed him, and not a patch on his father, the late colonel.

Simon Steel greeted him, saying, 'Ah! Ah, you found us then. How is Doctor Cornwallis?'

'Not in very good shape today, I'm afraid; his leg is very painful.'

' 'Tis gout, but he won't have it, will he?'

'No, he won't have it.'

'Ah well, come and meet my daughter.'

He was now being led to a table at which sat a young woman, and immediately he noted the similarity between the father and daughter: they were of the same colouring, and both had light brown hair, grey eyes, the same-shaped mouth, wide but thin. Only the noses were different: his was beakish whilst hers was more inclined to be snub.

'This is Doctor Falconer, my dear, Doctor Cornwallis's deputy.'

John Falconer cast a sharp glance towards his host, and he had the desire to put him right and say, 'Partner', for the man *was* aware that there was now a partnership between Dr Cornwallis and himself.

'How d'you do? May I wish you a happy birthday?'

'Thank you.' Her voice was light and her smile wide, and as she took the parcel he held out to her he said on a laugh, 'I must inform you that this present is not of my choice; Doctor Cornwallis said you were partial to chocolates.'

'Yes, I am. Thank you so much.'

8

As two young women approached the table, she stood up and said, 'Oh, here are my sisters,' and indicating one, she said, 'This is my sister Helen . . . Doctor Falconer.'

He found himself looking at a young woman. Her hair was a gleaming brown, her eyes a darker shade; her skin was like alabaster, her mouth wide and full-lipped. She was tall, almost as tall as he: he was five-foot eleven, and she must be all of five-foot nine, and she carried herself so well . . . She was beautiful, unlike her sister.

His attention was jerked from her by Beatrice saying, 'And this is Marion.'

Marion, too, was tall, but very fair. She, too, was good-looking, not quite beautiful. She had a quiet expression, but her eyes twinkled as she said, 'I suppose you're standing in for his bad leg . . . not gout. No, not gout,' she added, mischievously, shaking her head; and he answered her in the same vein as he shook his head, too, and laughing back at her, 'No, not gout. Never mention the word gout.'

'It should be a lesson to you, Doctor, to shun port.'

'Yes, I'm learning that lesson quickly, Miss . . . Marion.'

They laughed together now until Beatrice put in again quickly, 'Helen, Leonard has arrived.' And on this the tall girl said, 'Oh! Oh, yes.' And then she made hastily for the steps and the tall, middle-aged man standing at the top of them.

Marion caught John's attention again, saying, 'As for me, I'd better go in and attend to the Army.'

John Falconer looked slightly perplexed until Beatrice said somewhat primly, 'She has a suitor, and just like Helen's, he is in the Army too.' Then she added, 'I'm sorry I'm unable to show you round at the moment . . . But ah, here's Rosie; you'll be shown very much around by Rosie, my youngest sister, every little detail. Rosie!' she called to a girl, who was on the point of running towards another group of laughing young people. The girl turned and, making towards them, said, 'Yes, Beatrice?'

9

'This is Doctor Falconer. Would you like to show him around and introduce him?'

'Oh yes. Yes.' And looking at John, she added, 'I've seen you before in the town. You are old Cornwallis's man, aren't you?'

'I am his partner.'

'Partner? Oh, I'm sorry. I thought you were just one of those, what d'you call them? locums?'

Her voice stern, Beatrice put in, 'Rosie! behave yourself. Please!'

For answer Rosie smiled widely at John and said, 'Come along. You'll get used to us all before you're finished.'

'I'm sure I shall,' he nodded at her. She was a very pretty girl, not more than sixteen or seventeen and sparkling with life, which showed in her step and her voice.

As they passed the steps above which were walking the tall, beautiful sister and the very smart and pleasant-looking man, he was informed in a whisper, 'That's her future. They're going to be married. He's oldish but he's a lovely man.'

'What!' He found he was surprised at his own tone.

'I said, they are going to be married, and he is a . . .'

'But she's very young,' he put in quickly.

'She's not, she's twenty. Of course, as I said, he's quite a bit older. Forty I think, which is old really, but he's nice. I'm nearly eighteen, and I wouldn't mind having him.' She laughed gaily.

He was shaking his head as if at a naughty child as he said, 'Well, I wouldn't have believed it. Twenty-four, I would have said.'

Casting him a sidelong, laughing glance, she said, 'Well, this is the rose garden. But you being a doctor, and clever, you will already have guessed that.' And she laughed again, a gay, girlish laugh, then added, 'And this is the topiary. I'm not fond of trees being cut and hacked about. Are you?'

He thought for a moment, then said, 'No, since you ask, I'm not. I think they're grotesque. They were never meant to grow like that.'

'You're right. You're right.'

She skipped on ahead now, saying, 'And this, sir, is the pine wood. You'll notice on each side of you there are pine trees.'

He smiled broadly at her. She was an imp, this one, but a loving, kindly imp, if he knew anything about character. Different from the rest. They were all different. He thought of the beautiful girl again who was going to be married, and to a man twice her age. He couldn't remember seeing anyone really like her before.

They emerged from the wood into a green area that ran down to the river. But he was brought to a stop by the sight of a very high wall. He looked to the right and couldn't see where it began for it was lost in trees. But he could see that it ended on the river bank. She was by his side now and he looked at her and said, 'That's a very high wall.'

'Yes; it used to be the kitchen garden. But it wasn't as high as that then, it's had another foot or so put on it.'

'Why?'

'Oh! Oh, Doctor, it's . . . a . . . long . . . long . . . story.'

'Well, I like long stories; I'd like to hear it.'

'Would you?'

She now threw her arm around a young sapling and he thought that she was going to twirl herself about it; but she leant her head against it and said, 'I call it the "Wailing Wall", rather like the one the Jews have in Jerusalem, or wherever it is.'

He smiled and said, 'Yes, wherever it is.'

'Well, I never was any good at geography. Anyway, that was the wall to our kitchen garden and, so I'm given to

11

understand, to the best piece of land in the whole sixty acres or so.'

'Really! sixty acres?'

'Yes, but not since that was cut off. Well, it all goes back to Grandpapa. He was in the Army, you know, a very soldierly man. But he was lovely.' Although she was still smiling there was a touch of sadness in her voice as she added, 'Oh yes, he was another lovely man. And Grandmama was lovely, too. Grandpapa was always shouting, bawling. And Grandmama would crook her finger at him like that' – she now demonstrated, wagging her first finger – 'and he would come like a lamb, and she would say, "The wolf's howling again," and he would answer, quite pettishly, "No, I'm not. No, I'm not." And she would often say with a smile, "Well, it must be just a dog barking." Sometimes he would yell, "Well, Needler is a fool." It was either Needler or Oldham or Connor, and Grandmama would then say teasingly, "It couldn't be James MacIntosh." You see Grandpapa was very fond of James MacIntosh.' She now nodded towards the wall saying, 'Robbie's his son.'

He wasn't enlightened, but he knew he would be presently.

They were walking on again as she said, 'Grandpapa, you see, was a lieutenant-colonel or colonel, or something like that, and he had a batman named Jamie MacIntosh, who went to India with him. That was the first time Jamie rescued him. It was in a skirmish or something like that. Grandpapa found himself in a fix: he was hemmed in and the brave Scots laddie,' – she had dropped into Scottish brogue now and was grinning at him – 'shot his way in. In fact, I think, being like Grandpapa, he yelled a lot. He must have frightened them to death which is why they ran. Anyway, that's how he got Grandpapa out. He was wounded; they were both wounded; but Jamie got him back. The second time was more serious. Jamie MacIntosh, I understand, was then a sergeant. They weren't in India this time but in some

12

other outlandish place, and Grandpapa was in charge of a company or something, and they had to retreat.' She turned now, her face bright and laughing. 'You always hear of the British advancing, never retreating, don't you?'

He bit on his lip but said nothing. And so she went on again, 'Well, in their retreat the Ghurkas or whoever they were . . . which side were the Ghurkas on?'

'It all depended,' he said, 'when all this happened.'

'Oh, but anyway, whoever it was, they shot Grandpapa in the leg. They thought he was dead and so they just tramped over him. But the great Jamie MacIntosh' – she had reverted to the Scottish brogue again – 'what does he do? He goes out to that field at night and sorts out my Grandpapa. But they were lying in wait and they shot Jamie's arm off.'

His eyes widened and he said, 'Really!'

'Yes, really, right from there.' She pointed above the elbow. 'He used to have a hook. He could do lots of funny things with that hook. Anyway, the great Jamie was decorated; quite a hero he was. And Grandpapa didn't lose his leg, but he always had to walk with a stick. Jamie MacIntosh, it's a wonder he didn't grow another arm. Anyway, there was our wonderful kitchen garden with the high wall all round it right down to the river. It was the best piece of soil, the gardener said, in the whole of the estate, and beautiful fruit trees grew on the side of the wall where the sun hit them, and the fruit and vegetables came up on their own. And at the head of that piece of land was a cottage. Well, it was bigger than a cottage, with eight rooms altogether, as well as offices, so it's bigger than a cottage, isn't it?' He nodded at her. 'And it had been empty for some time. So what does Grandpapa do? but get it fixed up for Jamie. And, moreover, he had to do this in secret. Of course Grandmama knew, but Father didn't. Father was nineteen at the time and very land-conscious; in fact, he still is. But Grandpapa passed over to Jamie all the land

13

beyond that wall. It was about ten acres of workable and planting land with a yard beyond for animals; or at least some. There were two meadows in which to run a horse and a couple of sheep. And, as all the men said, it was the best piece of land in the whole estate, because with so many pine trees growing all over the place, the roots riddled the earth, so they said, and they had to break new ground on this side to make a new kitchen garden. It used to be a flower garden with greenhouses and a vinery and things. It took hard work. I understand my father was furious, but he couldn't do anything about it because Grandpapa had passed it over as . . . ahem!' – she clicked her tongue before she asked as a question, 'deed of gift?'

'Yes. Yes, you can pass things over as a deed of gift.'

'Well, that's what he did. Then the war started. Well, it didn't really start until after Grandpapa died. But you see, the wall goes right down to the water and Grandpapa used to put on his high waterproof fishing boots and wade into the river and round the end of the wall. That was easy. I used to plodge round. The only other way in was to go on to the main road and through the front gate. That was a longish walk for Grandpapa and he used to take me by the hand from when I was very small and we would go to Robbie's. Oh, I forgot to tell you that Jamie had married Annie, and she had Robbie. He was ten when I was born. I was the last of the tribe. Mrs Annie makes lovely griddles in the pan and thickens them with butter and honey. And of course, I used to be sick and there was always trouble. I can remember from when I was three going plodging round there. Robbie was thirteen then or twelve or something like that, but I used to follow him around like Floss. He seemed old to me. Then there would be the days when Mary May and Henrietta, those were the cows, came round the wall and got into the garden and ate the shrubs. Oh my! Oh my! So, to keep the peace, Grandpapa arranged for some

14

railings and wire to be attached to the wall and extend into the river. Of course, it was further to plodge and get round; but there were still times when Mary May made the journey. Then she calved and little Mary May used to follow her.' She fell silent now and she gazed towards the wall and her voice had a deep, sad note to it as she resumed, 'They were wonderful days, beautiful days. Even when it snowed and sleeted and rained, the sun always seemed to shine, because Grandpapa and Grandmama were here. They were lovely people. Then two years ago everything seemed to happen at once.' She turned and stared him fully in the face, saying, 'Grandmama died, quite suddenly. Grandpapa was sitting with his arm around her and she died like that; and two months later, he died too: he couldn't live without her. From the day she died he never went into the water. He sometimes went along the road to Robbie's front gate, 'cos Jamie had died the previous year and Grandpapa missed him so much. But Robbie acted as a good second and would listen to all Grandpapa's tales of what he and Jamie got up to in the wars, and what a brave man Robbie's father had been. Then three months later Mama died, all of them in that one year. That was two years ago. Things have never been the same since.' She looked down at her feet now and said, 'Neither Grandmama nor Grandpapa wanted to die; their life together was so happy. But I think Mama wanted to die. Oh yes. Yes.' Her head jerked up and her voice was a whisper now as she said, 'I shouldn't have said that, should I?'

'Why not? It's in your mind and I'm a doctor, which is the same as being a priest, you know; I don't pass things on.'

'No?' There was a question in the word.

Then he asked, 'Why are things not the same now?'

She was walking on again, slightly ahead of him, as she said, 'Beatrice has taken over; she's now head of the house. She loves the house, you know. She glories in it. None of us have any feeling for the house as she and Father

15

have. She's very like Father. Then there's the war between Father and Robbie. If you come down here you'll see what I mean . . . down to the river.'

They walked by the wall and as they neared the river she let out a high exclamation, crying, 'Oh no! Mary May. Oh no! Mary May,' for there, coming round the end of the wood and wire entanglement was a cow.

He watched the girl now drop onto the grass, pull off her shoes, then quite unselfconsciously lift up her skirt, pull down her garters from below her knees, then her stockings, push these into her shoes, tie the laces together, sling them around her neck and dash into the water, saying as she did so, 'Take your shoes off if you want to come.'

'I'd rather climb the wall,' he shouted back at her.

'Can you?'

'Oh yes, yes; I'm used to climbing.'

He watched her now get a hold of the cow's ear and turn it about. The water was well over her knees and soaking the bottoms of her petticoats and what looked like the frill of her drawers. She was talking all the time to the cow while at the same time shouting, 'Robbie! Robbie!'

He glanced along the wall. Here and there a rough stone protruded from it. He made for one, and hauled himself up by it, far enough so that he could stretch and grab at the top of the wall. From there he could see he was right above a pig-sty with a grunter looking enquiringly at him. Then, looking down the path, he saw a young man, who cried at him, 'Hitch yourself along to the right. There's a ladder there.'

Glancing to the right he inched himself rather painfully along the uneven stone wall until he reached some espalier apple bushes trained along the wall. Then he saw the ladder.

By the time he reached the ground the young fellow was taking the cow from Rosie's hands and saying, 'You should have left her there.'

16

'And let Father shoot her? He will, you know. As sure as eggs are eggs he'll shoot her. He told you last time.'

'Just let him try. I've got a very good aim meself, and I've already promised him that.'

'Can't you put a barrier across the bottom so they can't get into the water at all?'

'Why should I? The river's a public pathway.'

'Don't be silly, Robbie.'

'I'm not being silly, Rosie. The river *is* a public pathway. You look it up.'

'Is it?' She had turned to John now who was dusting himself down and wondering whether the seat of his pants would last out until he got back to his lodgings, and he answered her, 'I've never heard of it; but if your friend says it is, then I'm sure it is.'

'Hello,' said Robbie.

'Hello, Robbie. I've heard a lot about you.'

'You're the new doctor?'

'Yes, I'm the new doctor.'

'Well, I hope you answer calls quicker than your boss.'

'He's not my boss, Robbie, he's my partner.'

'Oh, you're partners. Oh, partners? You've bought in? Good! Good! Well, I'll be pleased to see you at any time. Wait till I lock this one up, then come up to the house and have a cup of tea.'

'We are . . . at least I am a guest at a birthday party.' He thumbed over the wall.

'Oh aye. Well they won't miss you for an extra few minutes, so come and meet my mother. She's always grumbling about aches and pains; she'll be glad to see you.'

As John walked up the long path towards the pretty house at the end of the land he could understand this being a productive piece of ground, judging by the way the plants were sprouting up all around him, and also, why the present owner next door hadn't wanted to lose it. Oh yes. Oh yes, he

17

could see that all right. But in a way he was glad that this forthright young man was following in his father's footsteps. He sounded like his forebear: a man it would be good to have with you in a tight corner.

Mrs Annie MacIntosh seemed to him to be well named: she was round, plump, rosy and cheery.

'Oh, you're a welcome visitor, Doctor,' she immediately said to him. 'We'll likely get a bit of attention now. You've got to be dead and ready for your box before the old 'un will put his neb in the door, and then it's only to see if you're screwed down all right.'

John laughed, thinking it was odd why everybody referred to his partner as 'the old 'un', when he was only in his fifties. Admittedly though, he did look a bit worn. The battle had taken its toll, and in more places than his leg.

As he sat in the kitchen tasting Mrs MacIntosh's griddle cakes, hot off the pan, the young fellow was saying to Rosie, 'Get your shoes and stockings on again; anything less like a young lady I've never seen.'

'Oh you! Then you should keep your animals in order and I wouldn't have to strip off so many times.'

John and Robbie exchanged a knowing glance at this and only just managed to suppress what could have been a bellow of laughter at her words.

'You have a very nice house here, Mrs MacIntosh,' said John now.

'Aye, it isn't bad; and all due to the Colonel, bless him. May he rest in peace. And I'm sure he does, and his lady alongside him. He's a great miss. He is that, isn't he, Miss Rosie?'

'Yes. Yes, he is, Mrs Annie. I miss them both every day, because they were lovely people.'

'You're not the only one, lass. You're not the only one. Well now, another griddle, Doctor?'

18

'No. No, thank you. I'm expected to go and eat some birthday cake. Isn't that so, Rosie?'

'Oh yes, I suppose so,' she replied, bending to fasten the lace of a shoe. Then she stood up as she added, 'and we should be there now, so come on.' Her tone was casual as if she were addressing an old friend.

'How are you going to get back? I'm not going over the wall or through that water. You can, but I'm going down the road.'

'Who said I was going through the water? I'm going down the road, too.'

'Well, look out,' said Robbie now to Rosie. 'There'll be squalls if you're caught.'

'I've never been caught yet.'

'Well, don't act too clever. Go on, get yourself away.'

John was amused at the attitude between them. They could have been father and daughter, or brother and sister. But if his guess was right, there were different thoughts in Robbie's mind with regard to this girl, although he didn't know about her, for she was so young; in fact, childlike in her unconscious gaiety.

Five minutes later they had made their way through a gap in the railings in the pine wood to emerge onto the lawn and were walking side by side, as if they had just done the rounds. And Rosie's next remark brought his attention back to her sister: 'Look!' she said; 'Beatrice has already started on your chocolates. She's got a thing about chocolates. She's always nibbling chocolates, but she never gets fat. It's a good job her fancy isn't towards wine or beer, isn't it? That would be something. Just think of the effect. Oh my!'

As her laughter joined his, he thought, she's like a breath of fresh air. It's to be hoped she'll remain so, at least for a while.

# 2

John was to look back on the garden-cum-birthday party as the beginning of his new life. His medical training seemed to be far away in the past. Two years spent walking the wards were as if they had never been. His mother was the only thing that remained prominent in that past. This reminded him that he should have gone to see her today. But a visit would mean a rush there and back and today was his day off and he felt he wanted it to himself: to get away from the town and people, to walk in wide open spaces, to climb hills, if not mountains. He just wanted to get away. Yes, just get away. Which is what he did, with a knapsack on his back and freshly baked buns and sandwiches from the bakers' and two bottles of ale.

It was the middle of July. The sky was high, and there was a slight breeze blowing that tempered the heat. The ground was hard beneath his feet and, having taken off his cap, the wind blew coolly through his hair.

Avoiding hamlets, he made for the hills. He knew this route: it led slowly upwards towards a near vertical outcrop which brought him to a small plateau from where, in the far distance, could be seen Durham Cathedral rising from its perch on the bank of the river Wear. To the left was Gateshead, and beyond it, across the Tyne, was Newcastle.

He had only recently got to know the North country. His mother was a Sussex woman and his father half-French. But his mother's sister Ada lived in Middlesbrough which is where his mother was staying at the present time, and not liking the situation at all. And as her rheumatism was worsening with the years he felt, if not through love, which he had for her, then duty bound, he had to bring her nearer to him.

But today he wouldn't think about it, today he was free: there were no bowel troubles to see to, no biles, warts, sore feet, headaches, all of which were on the lighter side. The incurables were another matter.

He now stretched himself out on the hard turf, his hands behind his head, his cap shading his eyes, and it was no surprise to him that his mind immediately touched on Pine Hurst. He was again at the garden party and he could see himself almost frolicking with that young sprite, Rosie. Then came the picture of the sister Helen, the one who was shortly to be married. And he wondered, yet again, why her face should have made such an impression on him. Yes, she was indeed beautiful, but he had seen beautiful girls before, beautiful women of all ages. Yes, of all ages, because every age had its beauty. But hers was of a different kind. And then there was Marion. Marion puzzled him. She, too, he had learned, was going to be married. His thoughts, of a sudden, jumped to the father. He was glad he wasn't on his list; he couldn't stand his type; bumptious, arrogant. If anyone played the Lord of the Manor, he did. And yet, he understood, the man's father had been just the opposite. He recalled Rosie's description of her grandfather which fitted in with what he had heard from Cornwallis. As Rosie had put it, he must have been a lovely old man. Lovely seemed to be a special word she used in describing those she liked. But where did the girl Beatrice come in this family? She was running it now. In a way he felt sorry for her. He didn't know why, but he did. She wasn't like any of the others. Although she was quite pretty, she had no particular attraction.

Ah well, he sighed, they were all down there in the valley and he was up here, at peace with the elements and God. Yet was he? Why did he keep thinking, in the back of his mind, that he had arrived too late? Too late for what?

. . . Was that a rabbit scurrying across the sward? Would one have scaled this tor? Why not? Necessity, through time and circumstance, made life.

When a dream voice said, 'I'm sorry,' he answered it in return, saying, 'You couldn't help it. You weren't to know. I came a year too late. I'm sorry, too. These things happen out of the blue.' Then a warm, soft, comforting blankness came over him and he let himself sink into it.

How long he had slept he did not know. But he knew that his face was hot. His cap must have slipped off it, and the sun was very bright in his eyes. He'd be red tomorrow; his skin burnt easily. But then it didn't turn a nice tan, but a rough brown. His mother used to say it was attractive. That reminded him, he must see about his mother. He must ask for a few days off.

When he opened his eyes slowly and blinked into the sunlight he saw a face, and it was smiling at him. So he closed his eyes tight again.

'You've had a nice sleep.'

He sat up so quickly that his back went into a cramp, and he grimaced as he stared to the side and saw Helen Steel sitting there.

When he went to get to his feet she put her hand out and said on a laugh, 'Don't jump up! Doctors say it's bad for the heart. You could give yourself a turn.' She was nodding at him.

He covered his face for a moment, then muttered, 'I'm sorry. How long have you been up here?'

'Oh, let me see.' She put up a hand to cover her eyes, and,

her head back, she said, 'Since time and circumstance made life, and you were sorry for something.'

'How long ago was that?'

She turned her fob watch around and after a moment said, 'Forty-two minutes, to be exact.'

'And you've been sitting there all that time?'

'Well, like you, I needed a rest after that stiff climb. But I judged that you needed it more than I, you having been up half the night.'

His eyes widened and he ran his hand through his hair, endeavouring to flatten it, before he asked her, 'How do you know I've been up half the night?'

'Needler told me.'

'Needler?'

'Yes; he was taking Pansy to be shod and you were returning the horse you had borrowed from Ben Atkinson, the blacksmith, because Isaac Green's place is a good four miles out and it was three in the morning and Nancy was having a very bad time.'

'I think both Needler and Ben Atkinson should start up a newspaper business.'

She laughed now as she said, 'Was it a boy or a girl?' And when he answered, 'Both,' her mouth widened and she said, 'Not twins!' And he nodded at her, saying, 'Yes, twins. That makes eleven.'

'Good gracious! And she's also lost four.'

His eyes widened still further. 'How do you know she's lost four?' And then, both their heads bobbing, together they said, 'Needler.'

She was laughing out loud now as she went on, 'Needler said that Isaac took Nancy for a rabbit and they both ate the grass together. He also said that Isaac read the Bible every day and stuck to it to the letter.'

His body was bent forward now and they were again laughing together; then, turning his head to the side as he

23

rubbed the water from each eye, he said, 'I think Needler forgets he's talking to a young lady.'

'Are you shocked?'

'Shocked? Me! No. But it's a surprise to find young ladies so well informed on certain matters.'

'Oh, we're all well informed. Grandpapa saw to that, and good for Grandpapa. He used to take us next door, you know, when the pigs were being born, and he and Mr Jamie used to talk about things. And then there was Robbie. Rosie's trailed Robbie since she could walk, or crawl under the fence, or paddle round the wall. And like us all, her education was extended through a couple of cows, the five goats, and the pony which gave birth to a beautiful foal, but which died the same day; and on that day I can tell you there was a lot of wailing in our house that even Father couldn't stop. Of course, you will know by now about the war between Father and the MacIntoshes, having talked with Rosie.'

He nodded at her, saying, 'Well, I did learn quite a bit, yes. He seems to be a very enterprising young man, that Robbie MacIntosh: it's a miniature farm he has behind the wall.'

'Yes.' Her face lost its smile now as she said, 'And it still remains a bone of contention. Anyway, here we are.' She leaned back on her hands and stared up into the sky, saying, 'Isn't this the most wonderful spot?'

'Yes. Yes, it is.'

'How did you come across it?'

'Oh, well, I'm a bit of a climber.'

'Really? You climb mountains?'

'If I can find one handy, yes. But that last sixty feet almost vertical up to here keeps me in very good practice. How on earth did you make it?'

'I, sir, like climbing, too. I've come up here for . . . oh, years and years. Even in the winter. It's an amazing sight from here in the winter: everything stands out unblurred.'

He now watched her pass her tongue over her lips, which caused him to ask, 'Are you thirsty?'

'Yes. Yes, I am. I generally bring something with me but I didn't today; I came out in rather a hurry.' Her face lost its laughter again. And now he said, 'Well, I can quench your thirst, but will you be able to drink it? it's beer.'

When she said, 'Old or mild?' he let out a hoot of a laugh, reached back, gripped his knapsack and, feeling for a bottle, he said, 'Oh, it'll be mild, I think. And it'll be warm; I should have put it in the shade.'

'Well, that would be difficult to find up here.'

'I could have hung it down the rock if I'd had any sense; there's a stump of a tree over there,' he nodded. Then he poured out a cupful of the beer and handed it to her.

When she emptied it on the second go, then handed him back the mug, he had to quell the sudden urge to grip her hand and pull her to his side.

He remained quiet as he poured out a drink for himself; then, taking the cardboard box from the middle of the knapsack, he said, 'Nothing in here comes from Mrs Pearson's.'

'Is she as bad as all that, her cooking?'

'Worse. And the trouble is, if you're polite and say you like something, you get it five days in the week.'

'Oh, Cook's like that, too. I once said I loved her plum duff and she's made me special ones since. The others can be having trifle, or apple dumplings, or anything, but I have plum duff.' She now imitated Cook's voice in saying, ' 'Cos Miss Helen's partial to packin'.' She shook her head here and added, 'I've never been partial to packing. But I've got a good ally in Janie.' She nodded as she explained: Janie Bluett, the parlourmaid, you know. And Flossie and Biddy, the dogs, always know when it's packing day for they bark their thanks when they see me.'

He kept his eyes on her as he said, 'Cheese, tomato or . . . their best ham.'

'I'll take their best ham, sir, thank you.'

He handed her the box and joined in her mood as he said, 'At your service, madam. They're on the right, that will be your left.' Again they were laughing.

He finished one bottle of beer and opened the second. And as she took the mug from him, she held it to her lips and laughingly said, 'Wouldn't it cause a sensation if I went rolling in the front door and Father demanded, "Where have you been, girl?" and I replied with a wide grin, "Out with the doctor. Sitting on the top of Craig's Tor." . . . Oh my!'

She drank the beer; then as she handed him the mug she said, 'I'm going to lose my ladylike manners again and say I've thoroughly enjoyed this afternoon. I can't tell you when I've had such fun.'

He stared into her eyes; they seemed to be waiting for his gaze. He asked quietly now, 'When are you going to be married?'

Her voice was as low as his, as she said, 'Next Easter.'

'Where are you going to live?'

'In Hampshire at first. We've rented a little house there.'

'Oh!' Their gaze never wavered as he went on, 'I hope you'll be very happy.'

'I'm sure I shall. Yes; yes,' her nodding was emphatic, 'I'm sure I shall.'

Suddenly he sat back and pulled out his watch and exclaimed in a loud voice, 'Good heavens! Do you know the time? Half-past four and I've got a surgery at five. I'll have to get down there quicker than I got up.' . . . Why had he said this? He had no surgery today.

After pushing the box and empty bottles into his knapsack, he rose hastily to his feet and, looking down at her where she remained sitting, her hands around her knees, he said, 'You won't be coming down yet,' not as a question but in the form of a statement, and she said very quietly, 'No; if you don't mind. Anyway I'm not going back home, I'm

26

going over there.' She pointed. 'Can you see the top of that house down in the valley?'

'Yes. Yes, I can just see it.'

'I have a friend lives there. That's really where I was making for when I was tempted up here.'

'It looks a long way off.'

'Not as the crow flies. Three miles from here, perhaps, about five or so from the town.'

Pushing out the palm of his hand towards her, he said, 'Don't get up. Just sit there like that.' And she stared up at him, her face unsmiling, then said quietly, 'Thank you for a lovely afternoon. I'll always remember it.'

'So shall I, always,' he said and turning quickly, he let himself over the edge of the plateau.

After his head disappeared she stared towards the house in the far valley. Then she brought up her knees again, put her hands around them, and laid her head on them. And so she sat; and she said to herself, Time and circumstance make life.

# 3

'Is Wallace's farm a big one, Robbie?' asked Rosie.

'Well, it's all a matter of what you call big. No, I wouldn't say it was big, anything but. Yet it isn't just a smallholding like this. He keeps half a dozen cows on it and a few sheep. And he also goes droving at times. That used to be his permanent job, a drover. Why do you ask?'

'Oh, no reason.'

'You never ask questions without a reason. Now, why d'you ask?'

'Well, I saw the son, Jackie . . . isn't he called Jackie? And he was in our pine wood the other day.'

Robbie stopped what he was doing and turned to her and said, 'In your pine wood? What was he doing there? He'd better look out for your father, hadn't he? Especially if he's got his gun with him.' He smiled.

'Well, that's what I thought.'

'Was he picking up wood?'

'No; he was just walking, and he jumped the railing and went into the field . . . Is Mrs Wallace a nice woman, Robbie?'

'Huh! Well—' he gave a bit of a laugh as he said, 'it all depends on what you mean by nice. To be nice looking, nice character . . . kindly?'

'Well, just nice.'

'Well, she's pretty, and lively in a sort of way. But what's put her into your mind?'

'Nothing.'

'Nothing?' His eyes narrowed as he looked at her. He knew his Rosie: if she asked a question it was after some thought. She was fast growing up; she wasn't so much of a tomboy now. In fact, that phase seemed to have lessened during these last few months. He resisted putting his arm around her shoulder and saying, 'Come on, spill it. You know me, I'll get it out of you.' That was a tactic he had used when she was running wild; but now she was turning into a young lady. The youngest of the Steel bunch, the last of them. What was he going to do about it? What *could* he do about it? He knew what would happen, he'd get a bullet in the back some dark night. He always told himself he wasn't afraid of anybody on God's earth, that he was like his father, but that was when you were facing an enemy, one you knew, to a certain degree, what he was about. But you never knew what Simon Steel was about; he worked in the dark. Aye, and in more ways than one. It wouldn't be that she had got wind of . . .?' He swung round and looked at her; but he couldn't see her face, for she was bending over the calf and saying, 'As it's a bull, you won't have to shoot it, will you?'

'Shoot it?' His voice was loud. 'Good gracious! no. Fatten him up and let him out for breeding, more likely.'

'I'm glad of that; I can't bear the thought of it going to market.'

'Mine never go to market.'

'The hens and ducks do.'

'Oh, well' – he wagged his head – 'only when they're very old.'

'I don't know how you can kill a chicken, or a duck, or a goose, when you love animals so.'

'Oh, Rosie! I'm not feeling inclined to give you a lecture on life and the sustaining of it. But what I do want to know is why are you glum these days? Anything wrong over the wall?'

'No; only that Helen will soon be gone and then Marion will follow, and I'll be left.'

'With only me?'

She turned now and laughed at him and at the face he was pulling, and she said, 'Yes; and isn't that prospect awful? Only you!' Then she thrust her hand out towards him as if pushing him away, saying, 'Oh, you'll always be there, or here.'

It was a moment before he answered her, when he said, 'Yes, Rosie, I'll always be there, or here . . . Where you off to now?'

'I'm going home; it will soon be teatime. But I'm not going by the front road or the river track, I'm going to cross the fields and up the pine walk. Be seeing you.'

He didn't answer but stood watching her walk to the far end of the grounds, climb the fence, then cross the field. And he remained so until she had disappeared from his view.

There was something wrong with her, something on her mind. He knew his Rosie. Oh yes, he knew his Rosie. But his Rosie didn't know him, not yet at any rate.

Instead of going straight to the house, Rosie made for the gazebo that lay beyond the tennis court, and there she sat down. She wished she had someone to talk to. But whom could she confide in about this thing that was on her mind? Because she might be wrong. But then again she knew she wasn't wrong.

She put her fingers between the slats in the seat and gripped the wood. Life wasn't nice; but it had been until recently. Although she knew her father hated Robbie, and Beatrice, too, disliked him almost as much, that had been

30

something else, and she had lived with it. But this other thing was something new and nasty.

She turned her head quickly now as the sound of approaching footsteps came to her from behind the gazebo, with Helen's voice saying, 'Let's stand behind here, Marion, because you know Beatrice: she's got eyes at the back of her head, at least when she's on the west end of the balcony. And if she sees us walking and talking she will want to know what it was all about . . . You say you would like us to have a double wedding, Marion?'

'Oh yes, I would, Helen. Anything to get away. I had a letter from Harry yesterday. He said there's every possibility of his being sent to India early next year and he wants to come down and see Father. And you know, up till recently I didn't really know how I felt about him; but after his letter I . . . well I know now that I love him. And the thought of going away to India with him, or to follow him out or just to be married to him, has become exciting. I could see a new life opening out for me.' There was a pause. 'Do you love Leonard?'

There was another pause before Helen's answer came, 'Who could help loving Leonard? He's so kind, so good, so caring.'

'Yes. But do you love him, Helen?'

'Oh. Oh, yes, I love him . . . Yes!' – the voice was louder now – 'I love him. I'm going to marry him, aren't I? I love him.'

There was another silence before Marion asked, 'Would you put it to Father about us having a double wedding? I'll be nineteen next month, so it isn't as if I'm a child. And I know something and I think you know the same thing, that Beatrice will be glad to see the back of both of us.'

Rosie now turned and stared at the wooden partition that separated her from the others as she heard Helen say, 'But what about Rosie? She'll be left.'

31

'Oh. Well, it mightn't suit Rosie, Helen, but it'll suit Beatrice, 'cos if Beatrice likes any one of us, it's Rosie. Odd, but I always thought she's treated Rosie as the child she'll never have. She'll not let Rosie go easily. And Rosie, somehow, is still so young for her age.'

'Oh, I don't know so much about that; she's on eighteen. And remember the garden party and Teddy Golding? He's very smitten with her, and she likes him, too. And don't forget he's been down four times since. Of course, the last time he didn't see her when she supposedly had measles that turned out not to be measles after all. And he would get Father's permission all right, because the Goldings are very well off and equally so connected. What's more, he's in the Diplomatic Service. That sounds good at the tea table or in the Gentlemen's Club. Anyway, what do you think we'll do? Leonard did suggest we be married in February, but I pushed it on to Easter. He thinks he will be sent abroad and that's why he wanted to make sure I would be with him . . . Oh, I think it will be all right for both of us. But wouldn't it be better still if three of us were to go up the aisle on the same day? And that would be possible I'm sure if it wasn't for our dear older sister.'

'Yes. Yes, it could be.' This was Marion's voice now, and she added, 'Oh, how she gets on my nerves about the house. The house. Father's got a mania for land and she's got a mania for the house. She's like an old maid. I wouldn't be surprised to see her going round with a feather duster one of these days. How different it was when Mama was alive, and different again when Grandpapa and Grandmama were still here. Life was good then, wasn't it, Helen?'

'Yes. Yes, Marion; looking back, life was good then. And we all seemed so young and untroubled. Even after Grandpapa went, we could still laugh about him and Robbie next door. But it didn't seem to last for long.'

Hearing a rustle in the grass, Rosie almost sprang out of

the gazebo, landed on her toes for a moment, then made a grating noise with her feet as if she were coming down the gravel path. But when she rounded the gazebo the sisters were no longer there. Helen was walking towards the house and Marion was making for the rose garden.

When she had first sat in the gazebo she had felt sad and worried, but now a sense of desolation was added to these feelings. Helen and Marion wanted to get away. Well, they weren't the only ones; she, too, wanted to get away. Oh yes, she did, even more than they, but for different reasons. She had made arrangements to meet Teddy on Saturday and should his manner be anything like her sisters had predicted, she would in no way repulse him. Oh no! And it wouldn't only be to get away from here, but because she liked him. Did she love him? Yes. Yes, she thought she loved him, too, and she would give him an indication of it on Saturday. Oh yes, she would. She would.

# 4

The church bells had been ringing for the past half-hour. People were passing the surgery window on their way to the church, many of them intending just to stand outside to see the Steel girls emerge after their double wedding. It was quite an event, two sisters being married together, with the youngest sister acting as bridesmaid.

When the bells had stopped ringing, John lay back in his revolving leather chair and closed his eyes tightly. But even then he could visualise it all: Helen was walking slowly up the aisle now on the left arm of her father, with Marion on his right. The grooms were waiting, standing beyond the first pew.

He glanced at the clock. It was half-past ten in the morning. On an ordinary day there would still be patients waiting in the other room, but today there was just one. He knew it was Ethel Hewitt, for her stick was beating its usual tattoo of impatience on the floor. He forced himself up from his chair and opened the door. 'Good morning, Ethel. Will you come in?'

'Not before time an' all, Doctor, and the place empty.' As she hobbled past him and took a seat at one side of the desk, she added, 'It's a wonder you're not along there with the rest of the daft 'uns. They don't know what's coming to them, they don't. A bed of roses, they think. But just you wait, they'll get their eyes opened. Rich and poor alike, it's all the same.'

'You're a born pessimist, Ethel.'

'I'm not from there, Doctor. What makes you say that? I was taken for a Lancastrian once, but I'm Durham born and bred.'

Another time he would have laughed, but not today. 'How's your leg?' he said.

'Well, I've still got it on,' she said.

'That's fortunate.'

'Why aren't you along there?'

'Well now, I ask you, if I was along there how could I see to you. And anyway, Doctor Cornwallis had to be there; he brought those two young ladies into the world and—'

'Aye,' she interrupted him, 'and he's going to see them out of it, but in a different way, 'cos they're going into another world. You know that, don't you? But then you don't because you've never been married . . . have you? I have three times. You can't tell me anything about marriage. If I had that kind of brain I could write a story.'

'Without . . . that kind of brain, you could still write a story, Ethel. Anyway, come on, let me have a look at your leg.' . . .

Fifteen minutes later he escorted Ethel to the surgery door with the usual warning, 'Keep off it as much as you can. Rest it; if not you're in for trouble. I've told you.'

'Yes, and I've heard you. What d'you expect me to do? Hop around on one leg, with eight grandbairns coming in at all times of the day and sometimes the night?'

'You're a lucky woman, you know.'

As she was about to step into the street she paused, turned her head round towards him and her thin wrinkled face

35

took on a smile as she said, 'Aye, I know I am blessed in a way, 'cos to speak plainly, all the bairns like me. One or two of them better than their mams and dads. 'Tisn't that I'm soft with them either. I scud their backsides, then end up makin' them taffee.'

He could hear her still chuckling as she hobbled down the empty street that led to the church.

Doctor Cornwallis was in the habit of iterating how, at one time, there hadn't been a house or cottage between the church and this his family home, that could go back for almost three hundred years. When John had first heard this remark he had laughingly replied, 'Well, it's time it was seen to here and there, don't you think?' but afterwards knew he had made a grave mistake when his superior had no conversation with him other than about medical matters for almost a week.

The surgery and waiting room were cut off from the main house by a long passage and as he locked the door of the surgery, there appeared at the end of the passage the figure of a woman. Her appearance made him stiffen slightly, and before she could approach him he said, 'You're too late, Mrs Wallace; I've an urgent call.'

She walked towards him, saying now, 'It's just something for me stomach, Doctor. I . . . I can't go, you know.'

'Well, I couldn't see to you in any case, Mrs Wallace; you're Doctor Cornwallis's patient.'

'Yes, I know. But the old fellow's at the wedding isn't he?' She grinned at him. 'And I thought you might oblige. You see, I haven't been for days.'

'Another few hours won't hurt you. And as I said, I've an urgent call.'

She was standing right in front of him blocking the way out.

'I could go to Mrs McDougal, but the doctors don't like that, do they?'

36

'Well, that's up to you, Mrs Wallace. You know what happened the last time you went to Mother McDougal. She certainly made your bowels work, didn't she?'

The woman made no reply for a moment, but hitched up her breasts with her forearm and, her manner changing from its fawning style and her voice now without its pleading note, she said, 'You know what you are, Doctor?'

'No! What am I, Mrs Wallace?'

'You're a nowt. You're a snot and you're out of place here. You ought to go back to where you came from, because you don't fit in. Never did and never will.' And on this she pursed her lips and wrinkled her nose so much that, for a moment, he thought she was going to spit at him. Then she turned and flounced along the passage, leaving him standing where he was. And in this moment he felt she was right, for he didn't fit in, and he longed to be back where he came from, to where people did not come out with mouthfuls of dirt. But he had burnt his boats, for added to the weight of the practice was this great hollow inside him that had resulted from two short meetings, the first of which had been on a mere introduction.

He squared his shoulders and went out into the street and walked in the opposite direction from the church.

It was his weekend off, and so he took the train to Middlesbrough; and from the station a two-mile walk brought him to his aunt's cottage, where his mother was waiting for him. She was standing outside the gate and she called to him over the distance: 'Look! No sticks.' As she lifted one hand from the support of the railings, she wobbled and laughed; and when he reached her and put his arms around her, he said, 'No, only a length of railings. But you're looking fine. Feeling the same?'

'Yes. Physically I'm heaps better, although mentally I'm much worse.' She was laughing at him.

37

'Go on with you.'

He had his arm around her waist now as he led her up the path towards the ivy-covered cottage. 'I'm bored to death, Johnny,' she said quietly. 'If we were in the town it wouldn't be so bad; but what do I see here? Cows, sheep, goats, a stray fox. Oh!' – she wagged her head now – 'great excitement last week. There was a travelling fair. I didn't even see that, really, but I heard the hurdy-gurdy from here.'

Inside the cottage, he looked about him and said, 'Where's Aunt Ada?'

'Oh, she decided to go into town. She wanted something special for your dinner, something different. And by the way, I've got news for you, she's selling this place. She's going to live with George down in Devon.'

'No! Live with George? But what about George's Vera? They're like cat and dog when they meet.'

'She knows that, but I think the cat and dog business is between him and Vera now, and she wants to be near him. And I can understand it.' She turned now and patted his cheek none too softly. 'I would go to Halifax or the Klondike if it meant being near you. And don't think I'm going soft in the head because I've said that openly for the first time.'

He kissed her again and said, 'Well, you had the chance to live near me, practically next door, but you didn't like Fellburn.'

'Then I hadn't seen Fellburn, had I? and we had only just left beautiful Sussex, hadn't we? Remember?'

'Yes; and I also remember your first impression: you wouldn't be found dead in the place, so you jumped at Aunt Ada's offer to live here.'

She pulled herself away from him, saying, 'Well, I'm prepared to be found dead in Fellburn from now on. And what d'you think? She wants me to buy this place. She reminded me I was glad enough to come here, and that I was supposed to love the country and gardens. But look out

38

there. How big is that? Are those gardens? It would take four of that garden to make a small allotment. No, Doctor Falconer, I have decided,' her voice dropped to a soft note now as she ended, 'very definitely, lad, that I want to be near you. At least near enough to catch a glimpse of you dashing backwards and forwards with your little black bag, even if it's only out of the window, at least once a day.'

He was holding her again. 'Well, that's the best news I've heard in a long time, for you know what, I was getting fed up with Fellburn myself, and why on earth I ever decided to buy a partnership in the practice that's going to keep me there for another five years, I'll never know.'

Her voice loud now, she said, 'It needn't keep you there for five minutes longer if you don't want to. Look, I've told you, we're pretty warm now. What with look, lad, pet, and hinny, I'm getting as bad as these Northerners. Anyway, I got much more than I expected for the house, and then your father's shares have doubled in value in the last year or so. You could go and put your share back on his table tomorrow and tell him . . .'

'Shut up! Mrs Falconer. We've been through all this before; it's got hairs on it. What's yours is yours and what's mine will be when I work for it. And anyway, you've spent enough on me already. So forget about that. Shut up! No more!' He wagged his finger in her face. 'But I tell you what. I feel like dashing back now and seeing if there are any rooms to let.'

'Oh no! No' – she shook her head – 'I'm not going into any rooms. I want a house and I'm going to have a house, and in a decent part. And . . . with what I call a garden. If I've got to look through a window, I want to see something worth looking at, not a brick road or a cobbled street or ancient houses drunkenly supporting each other, which seems to make up the main part of Fellburn.'

He was smiling at her now. 'There is always Brampton

Hill, and the houses there have lovely gardens, some of them two to three acres, and six to eight bedrooms, servants' quarters, butler's pantry, the lot.'

'Well, I could afford one of those, Mr Sarcasm. And I just might, if you can't find me anything decent in the town or near you . . . well, not in the town proper, you know what I mean.'

He came to her again saying, 'Yes, *old lady*, I know what you mean. And now, as we have to wait for dear Aunt Ada to come back with the special something for my lunch, do you think, in the meantime, I might have a drink of tea or coffee? A drop of the hard stuff would be even better.'

She hobbled from him now towards the kitchen, saying, 'It's going to be tea. Doctors shouldn't drink, not hard stuff, in the mornings. You should have learned that already from your partner. By the way, how is he?'

'When he's not putting it on he's bad, when he's putting it on, for some reason or other, he's on the point of death. But seriously, that leg of his is going to be the finish of him if he doesn't watch out.'

'Well, then you could buy the practice.'

'*Mother!*' He sounded shocked. 'Give over, wishing him dead! He's a decent old fellow really.'

'He's a selfish old devil. Don't talk to me about people being decent. The majority only do what suits them: if they go out of their way they want something.'

'I don't know whom you take after, Mrs Falconer. Your cynicism is bitter. Grandma and Granddad were the sweetest couple.'

'Yes, I know, and everybody loved them and thought they were a pair of old dears. That was in company and when they were being made a fuss of; but let me tell you, like everybody else, they had selfish streaks, some broader than an arrow on a convict's back, and would go for each other, like cat and dog at times. I was often woken up by it; all that sweetness and light business made me sick.'

He sat down near the kitchen table and started to laugh as he watched her making the tea. He knew that her rheumatics, as she called her arthritic pains, were likely giving her gip and that she, herself, was putting on an act for him. Oh, he was glad she was coming to be near him, for he needed her company even more than she needed his: there was a great emptiness in him. But if she were available he could see life taking on a lighter pattern; she was so good to be with. Funny, yet so sensible, and kind. And these qualities he needed very much at the moment.

Simon Steel stood before the hall mirror adjusting his cravat. Beatrice was at his side holding a thick overcoat and a tweed hat with side flaps.

She watched her father now wet the end of a finger and rub it along each side of his narrow moustache. He was a handsome man, and she was very proud of him. As she now helped him into his coat, she said, 'It's very cold out. How far are you intending to walk?'

'That all depends upon how I feel, Beatrice. If I reach town I might stay and have a bite.'

'Why don't you take the carriage, Father?'

He turned on her now, saying, 'I'm not an old man, Beatrice: I don't have to ride in the carriage every time I want some fresh air. I hope that necessity doesn't happen for the next twenty years.'

'Of course not, Father, of course not. I was only . . .'

'Yes, you were only playing the mother again. And you play it very well, dear, very well indeed. You're to be congratulated.' As he took his hat from her with one hand he was feeling in his pocket with the other and he said, 'Oh, have you any loose change?'

'Loose change, Father?'

'Yes, that's what I said. Let me have a couple of sovereigns, perhaps three.'

'But . . . but, Father' – she stepped back from him – 'I . . . I have only enough of the housekeeping money to see us through the week, until . . . until the end of the month. And then there are the bills, Father.'

He closed his eyes as if attempting to be patient and he said, 'You needn't remind me of the bills. They will be settled at quarter day and that is in three weeks' time. Now can I have some small change? You are the housekeeper; I would have thought that, like most good housekeepers, you manage to keep a little on the side.'

'I . . . I do, Father; but it's eaten up with' – she had almost added, 'with your demands for small change.' Grim-faced, she now turned about and walked down the short corridor to the office. Taking a tin box from a drawer she looked down on it in apprehension for a moment before selecting two sovereigns. A few minutes later, when she handed them to him, he looked at them and the only remark he made was through a statement that cast her down: it was, 'You have the makings of an old maid.' Then he marched across the wide hall, pulled open the front door and closed it none too gently behind him, the while she remained standing where he had left her.

She loved her father. She thought she understood him. He was a wonderful man, kind, generous: he was always helping people, wanting money to give away. But at times he said hurtful things. Yet she understood that as well, because she was the only one in the family who took after him: she, too, said hurtful things when she was annoyed. And she was annoyed now, for there was Rosie coming down the stairs, all dressed up for going out, and she cried at her, 'Where are you going on a bitter morning like this?'

'Why are you asking the road you know, Beatrice? I'm going next door, the only place I have to visit.'

43

'Well, all I can say is you've got very poor taste. I've warned you, haven't I? If Father knew you went there so often there would be the devil to pay. And you know what he has threatened to do with those animals should they stray round that fence. And he'll do it.'

Rosie stood at the foot of the stairs. She was half a head taller than her sister and she looked down on her as she said quietly, 'If he didn't do it, you would, wouldn't you, Beatrice?'

There was a pause before Beatrice said firmly, 'Yes. Yes, I would, because he's on land that doesn't belong to him.'

'But it does belong to him; it was his father's. Grandpapa gave it to his father. He saved . . .'

'Oh, don't go over that again. I'm sick of listening to it. But I'll tell you this much: Father's going to see if something can't be done; there might be a loophole in this deed of gift business.'

Rosie fastened the button on the collar of her coat under her chin, as she said slowly, 'Oh, you would like that, wouldn't you? to see them turfed out, to see his livelihood taken away. Well, if that was the case and I wasn't going to marry Teddy, I would go with him.'

Beatrice laughed sneeringly at this, saying, 'Don't talk stupidly. Anyway, you can't do anything for nearly another three years: you're under Father's jurisdiction until you are twenty-one. He could have you brought back from wherever you were and made to look foolish. So, get that out of your head. It's a wonder he allowed you to become engaged to your dear Teddy. I was surprised.'

Rosie leaned towards her now and quietly said, 'Well, I'll tell you why he permitted it, it's because Teddy is in the Ministry, the Diplomatic Service, and knows lots of people in high places, and Father is a snob of the first water. And you take after him.'

As Rosie walked towards the door Beatrice gaped at

her open-mouthed. There went someone who had suddenly changed. Rosie was no longer her favourite, the only one she liked among her sisters. She had been the little girl who could be scolded, then pampered; she had been the child to whom she could play mother. But the child had gone; in fact, the young girl had gone. She rested her hand on the bannister as if for support. She knew what both Helen and Marion thought of her; but Rosie had always been on her side. Even when she had chastised her about her visits next door, she had never turned on her and retaliated as she had just done.

Of a sudden she felt a loss and she cried out against it. Rosie had been a kind of companion, with little to say but such a good listener. And she laughed easily. Even when she had upbraided her she would laugh.

She turned her head to look towards the door. It had closed on her sister, not loudly, not with a bang, as it had done on her father, but it had just closed as if it had put an end to something, softly. But what?

She told herself she must not go for Rosie any more, at least in connection with those next door. No matter what she thought, she would keep it to herself: she couldn't lose Rosie, too. Before she had become engaged to Edward Golding, she herself had had fears at times of what might happen between Robbie MacIntosh and her, for it made little difference that he was ten years older. She herself had been against the idea of her becoming engaged to Edward, but the alternative was unthinkable.

She gazed about the hall. She should be happy, very happy, for now she was mistress of this house, this beautiful, beautiful house. She'd always loved her home, but now it had become an obsession with her. She ruled it. She didn't own it, but she ruled it. Now and again, though, a particular thought would frighten her: What if her father decided to marry again? In her mind she had screamed at

45

what she saw as the consequence. She would go mad. She couldn't bear another woman ruling this house. It wasn't so much she could not think of her father taking another wife, but it was another woman being mistress of this house.

She took her hand abruptly away from the bannister and her skirts seemed to dance from one side to the other as she briskly made her way towards the drawing-room to check Janie Bluett's work of the morning.

Instead of taking her usual way by the wall and the water to get into the smallholding, Rosie walked through the main gateway of the house and proceeded along the road.

She found it strange that by whichever way she entered this place it was as if she were moving into a different world: she took deeper breaths, and she always had the desire to sit down, even to lie down somewhere and stretch her body to its full extent and relax.

Today, Annie MacIntosh hailed her from that part of the garden where the animal enclosure was railed off and she called to her, 'Isn't it a snifter! But I love these mornings. I'm coming in, don't come down.'

Rosie merely nodded at her, then went into the cottage and straight to the kitchen, where immediately the warmth met her like a wave.

After loosening her coat, she flopped down into the basket chair to the right of the large open fireplace, and she emitted a long drawn-out sigh. If the kitchen had been that of a huge farm it could not have represented it more fully, for from its oak-beamed ceiling hung legs of smoked ham and bunches of herbs. A long white-topped kitchen table ran down the middle of the room. The china-decked dresser stood against one wall, and flanking another was a padded settle, at the end of which a door led into the long, cool larder.

Rosie always felt this to be a comforting room, so unlike the one in the house, and at the present moment she was feeling in need of comfort.

The little woman came bustling in and as she dropped a heavy basket of sprouts onto the table, she said, 'Me finger ends are dropping off.'

'Where's Robbie?'

'Oh, he's gone into town with a load. The cabbage is finished, and the carrots. There's only the sprouts left and the last of the clamped taties.'

She stopped in the act of pulling her mittens off and, looking hard at Rosie, she said, 'What's the matter, girl?'

'Oh, everything, Mrs Annie. I've just had words with Beatrice. The house is awful these days. Oh! I wish I was married and away.'

Annie MacIntosh took off her short coat before reaching up to the delft rack to lift down two cups and saucers. Then, putting these onto a tray she asked quietly, 'You want to be married so much?'

'Yes. Oh, yes, Mrs Annie.'

'You want to be married just in order to leave the house?'

Rosie did not answer immediately: she stared at this dear friend of hers while she seemed to consider, then she said hesitantly, 'I want to leave the house, but I do like Teddy.'

'You *like* Teddy? What does that mean, girl, you *like* Teddy? You like me, you like Robbie, but if you're going to marry somebody you've got to more than like them.'

'Well . . . well, yes. Yes, I more than like him, I'm very fond of him.'

'Very fond of him.'

'*Yes*.' Rosie's voice was loud now.

'Does that mean you're in love with him?'

'In love with him? Yes, I suppose so.'

'You suppose so.'

Annie went to the hob now, a teapot in her hand, tilted

the spout of the sizzling kettle over it, then brought it back to the table, put its lid on and then covered it with a tea cosy. And what she then said had nothing to do with love or emotions: 'I've made up a new recipe, a kind of currant bun. I had a go at it last night. D'you want to try one?'

Rosie was breathing quickly. She didn't answer but stared across the table at the elderly woman; then of a sudden, she burst out laughing, spluttering as she said, 'You're the funniest person I know, Mrs Annie.'

'Well, so far you don't know very many, hinny.'

'Oh yes, I do. But they never say anything funny.'

With her head now thoughtfully to one side, she added, 'Come to think about it, the people around here are dull. They just talk about the weather, or birthdays or deaths. All, that is, except Doctor Falconer. I like him; he made me laugh the other day: he said, "You know, last night I dreamt I was a worm." And I said, "What on earth made you dream that you were a worm?" "Well," he said, "I was called up to The Hall, and it was the way the butler looked at me. They call him Lemas, so I made a funny rhyme up about him." ' She started to laugh again. 'I can't remember it now, but it was funny. Yes, I like the doctor.' As she took the cup of tea from Mrs Annie's hand, she added, 'I'll meet a different class of person altogether when I'm married.'

'Oh, well,' said Mrs Annie quickly, 'I hope they suit you. But let me tell you, girl' – now she wagged her finger at Rosie – 'you've got a lot to learn, and from what you're saying now it'll be painful. I myself would say, fancy talk and highbrow conversation doesn't make for happiness: it often hides meanness and many other things. And you haven't got to go very far to find people like that.' As she now stamped around the table Rosie got to her feet and laid her cup down, and, her head bowed, she said, 'I wasn't meaning anything nasty, Mrs Annie. I'm just . . . oh, I don't know . . .'

When her voice broke with the tears, Mrs Annie was

48

around the table again and holding her in her arms, saying, 'There now. There now. I understand. You have a pretty gloomy time next door; you always have had, as your mother did before you.'

'What?' Rosie's head came up from Mrs Annie's shoulder and she blinked and swallowed, and said again, 'What? What do you mean, as my mother before me? My . . . my mother was very happy.'

'Your mother, girl, let me tell you, appeared to be happy in order to keep you girls happy. She wasn't a happy woman. Now that's all I'm going to say. There'll come a time when you'll know more about your mother.'

'Well, who's to tell me if you don't?'

'Well, I'm not saying any more, so there. I've said too much already. But it was your attitude made me do so. I can tell you this much though: your sisters can't enlighten you either. So it's no use asking them. Now drink up your tea because I'm off for the outside again: Mary Ann's not like her mother with her litter; she's not letting them suckle properly. Let's go and talk to her; she likes to be talked to. Wrap up again.' She now lifted her hand and said, 'I can see by your face you're going to ask questions. Well, girl, it's no good. I'm not going to say anything more. I'm sorry now for what I've said. But I'll add this: your mother, as you know, paid me many visits when your grandfather was alive, and we talked. And some day I may tell you what we talked about. But not today, or tomorrow, or the next day, so come along.'

Rosie followed the bustling little body out of the door, and down the garden and into the animal enclosure, where the sow, with her twelve of a litter, was rubbing herself uneasily on the frozen ground as the youngsters tried to find her teats.

'Now, now, Mary Ann,' said Mrs Annie. 'Lie still and let them have their feed. Now be a good girl.' She put

49

her arm over the low wall but could not reach the pig's head, so, without removing her arm, she said, 'You try, Rosie.' And Rosie pushed up her sleeve, leant over the wall and quite easily laid her hand on the sow and began to talk to her, saying, 'What's the matter, Mary Ann? Got a pain in your tum-tum? Be a good girl now and let them have their breakfast.'

When the pig grunted, Mrs Annie smiled and said, 'Keep at it, girl, she's answering. You might do more than the vet man can do, because I was thinking of getting him the day, although I hate paying him good money for what I used to do myself, but seemingly I've lost the touch lately. But she's talking to you. There she goes again. Oh, and look, they've all got one. That's good. Is your back breaking?'

Rosie muttered, 'No, no. I'll stay like this until they have their feed.'

'Funny if I had to call on you every time they wanted a suck,' Mrs Annie said, then added on a giggle, 'I would have to go to the back door though, wouldn't I? and say, please tell Miss Rosie to hurry up, Mary Ann's refusing to give her bairns their dinner.'

Rosie's body shook and she muttered, 'Don't make me laugh, these bricks are sticking in me; in another minute I'll be down there beside her.'

'Well, take your hand away now and see what she does.'

Slowly Rosie removed her hand and painfully straightened up. Then they both stared down at the sow who remained passive and allowed her litter to get on with the job. And Mrs Annie smiled and said, 'I'll tell Robbie. He'll be pleased, because he's been worried about her. He tried all ways yesterday to let her give them a full belly, but she was no sooner down than she was up. Thanks, lass.'

'You're welcome, madam. That'll be two and sixpence.'

'Will you have it now or will you wait till you get it?'

They turned from the sty and went over to the cowshed,

where the two cows were peacefully chewing their cud.

'I haven't let them out the day, the grass is so stiff it would cut their throats.'

In the yard once more Mrs Annie pointed to the chickens trying to scratch the earth and said, 'Oh, I had to laugh, the young ones couldn't understand why they couldn't mount the bank, they were sliding down on their backsides. Some of them were persistent, and it was funny. Robbie brought me out to see them. He cleared the steps, but they won't take the steps, they've been used to the grass.'

Rosie looked towards the mound. It wasn't very high, and yet from the top of it, there was an amazing view of the surrounding country.

Mrs Annie seemed to have sensed her thoughts, for she was saying now: 'Things will be standing out sharply from up there, this morning. I can't understand why people say that frost flattens everything; to my mind it brings things to life. It gives the land another picture, different again from when the snow's lying.'

'I'll go and take a look,' Rosie said.

Standing on the uneven top, she shouted down, 'Oh, yes, it is different. It's beautiful. I've never seen it like this before. And away to the right the countryside looks pink, not white; must be the sun slanting on it that way.'

She turned about, then cried, 'Good gracious! I can see Col Mount, the chimneys and the roofs. That must be nearly three miles away.'

'All of that,' Mrs Annie called back to her. ' 'Tis an extremely hard and bright frost. Frosts are not all alike, you know. Nature's got her moods through sun, wind and rain. Oh yes, yes, she has.'

'Good gracious! I can see Wallace's farm as if it was almost next door. Good Lord! We never see it from down below. I suppose the wood cuts it off.'

She kept her eyes on the farm. There was something she

51

should remember about it. She could now see some movement over there. Someone coming into the field. She was puzzled for a moment. That field adjoined their property. In fact, if she wasn't mistaken, it led to the wood. She shook her head, then walked carefully down the cleared steps, and Mrs Annie said, 'Come on back to the house and get warmed. Robbie should be here any minute.'

She had been about to follow Mrs Annie, but the mention of Robbie halted her. In some way he was associated with the earlier conversation of her wanting to leave this place and get married. And he had a habit of probing and questioning, and getting things out of her. He always had. She could hear him saying, 'Come on you, Rosie Steel; I don't want any painted lies, varnished truth is what I deal with.' And she could hear herself responding, 'You think you are clever, Robbie MacIntosh, because you read books. Well, anybody with any sense can pinch words and sayings out of books.'

No, she didn't want to meet Robbie this morning. She couldn't explain why. Yet, she had explained why: he'd get to the bottom of what was worrying her. *But what was worrying her?* Oh, she answered herself, just living by herself next door now the girls were gone. But she shouldn't say that: there was Beatrice and her father. Oh, let her get away. She'd go for a walk. And so she said, 'No, I've got to get back. I think Beatrice wants some help . . . in fact, I don't think it, I know it. She's house mad, you know. There's the two girls working like slaves, polishing, polishing, and she would have me going round with a duster. Can you believe it?'

'Oh yes, I can, dear, of Mistress Beatrice. From what I gather, she takes a great pride in ruling the roost. I think Cook has her belly full of her at times.'

Rosie laughed at this and said, 'We all have our bellies full of her at times, I can tell you. Yet, at the same time I don't know, I feel sorry for her, and in a way I'm fond of her.'

'Of course you are, dear. Of course you are. But off you go if you're going to have that walk through the wood; get yourself away now. If you look up, you'll see the sky is changing. I shouldn't be a bit surprised to see snow, although we generally have a thaw after frost like this, and then the snow. But, of course,' she laughed, 'since I've stopped running things, the weather's got out of hand.'

Rosie pushed her gently on the shoulder and she, laughing too, said, 'I'll go out the top way, because there's no way I'm going to climb that wall this morning; I'd slip off those stepping stones that Robbie's fixed. They give very precarious footholds as they are. If I wasn't such a good climber I would have been on my back before now.'

'Likely. Likely,' said Mrs Annie as she accompanied her to the field gate leading to the road.

After patting Rosie on the cheek, she stood for a while watching her until she disappeared through a gap into the wood. And as she did so she thought, she'll make a lovely woman, and she's jumping out of girlhood. If only . . . oh, if only . . .

It was beautiful in the wood. The path stretched away like a silver river for some distance, but then, as if curved, it was cut off by a great barrier of frozen pines.

There was a silence all about her. It was deep and thick and comforting. Even the sound of her footsteps on the frozen ground did not intrude.

She was now passing a section of the wood where the trees thinned out a little, with low scrub between them, and under which, surprisingly, the earth was bare of frost.

She was brought to a sudden stop by a sight that widened her mouth and brought a gleam to her eyes, and she uttered two words, 'Oh lovely!' as she turned swiftly to the object that had attracted her. It was an unusually tall fungus that could have been eight inches high. She bent over it; then, as she had seen Robbie do, she sat back on her hunkers and looked at part of nature's bewildering beauty. It was a fairy house. She hadn't seen one for some years. Toadstools, oh yes, big ones, fairies' umbrellas, they called them, but not a fairy house. Her hand wavered towards it, then stopped. It was so delicate that likely the slightest touch would push it over. She thought it was the biggest and the most beautiful fungus she had ever seen.

From its round base there rose striped columns supporting its circular roof, an enormous deep pink umbrella all of six inches across. The ridged supporting columns were either dark green or cream in colour, and the whole was surrounded by a spiked fence of silver grass an inch or so high.

As a child, she had always imagined such a house to be full of fairies and she used to talk to them, telling them not to be afraid and that she wouldn't tell any of the others where their house was in case they should come and knock it down. She had a vague memory of a sister kicking one down and of herself screaming at her, and of her mother having to put her to bed with hot milk and cinnamon.

Reluctantly she rose and stepped back from it, telling herself that once she got home she would draw it, then paint it. She would never forget this morning and this beautiful, beautiful fairy house. It had lifted her heart. It was a delightful morning, oh such a delightful morning.

She looked about her; then bending over her fairy house and with the very last trace of childhood that, in a moment, was to be torn from her, a moment she would remember for the rest of her life, she said, 'Goodbye, dear people, until next year,' and straightaway turned into what was to be the full realisation that life was made up of bitter reality, and with no fairies.

She stepped onto the rooted pathway, and from there, in the distance, could make out a boy who seemed to be acting strangely. He had emerged from the wood on the opposite side and he was looking towards where, just a few yards ahead, the path again curved sharply away out of sight. He had his head to the side as if listening.

She remained still; she was curious. Then her eyes widened when the boy jumped from the path and into the cover of the wood again and, at the same moment, a figure came striding round the bend. Her mouth now dropped into a gape: it . . . it was her father.

But it couldn't be; he'd said he was going into town – As she had stood on the landing she had heard him tell Beatrice. But this was definitely her father. There wasn't another man like him.

She was on the point of going forward and hailing him when she stiffened as the sound of snapping timber filled the silence. Then she let out a scream as she saw a huge branch fall across her father's path. The sound and sight had caused her to screw up her face and to close her eyes, and when she opened them she became aware of two things: the boy whom she knew to be the Wallace boy was fast disappearing round the bend with something trailing behind him, and that the branch hadn't fallen across her father's path but directly onto him.

She was now running while crying out words which were unintelligible, but all bordering on, 'Help! Help!'

When she reached her father she was unable to see his face for blood. She looked along the length of the branch: it was thick, more like a tree itself. Oh, dear God! What was she going to do? She looked about her. And that boy, he might have gone for help. No! no! What was she thinking? That was a piece of rope dragging behind him. He had been on the look-out for her father. Oh dear Lord! She tried to lift one end of the branch, but without success, all the while crying, 'Father! Father!' Then, of a sudden she was flying back the way she had come and yelling at the top of her voice, 'Robbie! Robbie!'

When she reached the road it was to see Charlie Fenwick,

55

the coalman, about to hump a sack onto his back from the dray cart, and she yelled, 'Mr Fenwick! Mr Fenwick! Come quickly! Please! My father's been hurt! A tree fell on him. My father's been hurt!'

'What is it, miss?' The two coaly hands came on her shoulders. 'What d'you say, your father's been hurt? Now, now, now; where is he?'

'In the wood! In the wood! Please come! He's all blood!'

Still keeping hold of her, the man turned and yelled, 'Mrs Annie! Mrs Annie!' And when Mrs Annie came hurrying to the gate, she exclaimed, 'Oh my God! What's the matter, girl? Have you had a fa . . .?' She didn't finish her sentence because the coalman interrupted her, saying, 'She says her father's been hurt, that a tree fell on him. He's in the wood.'

'A tree . . . fell . . . on him?'

'Yes! Yes!' Her eyes screwed up again, Rosie was yelling, 'Yes! Yes! Mrs Annie. He's all blood! I couldn't lift it.'

'It's all right, girl, it's all right. Let me get me coat. Leave that Charlie and let's go and see what's happened.'

When they reached the blood-covered prostrate figure under the branch Charlie Fenwick exclaimed, 'Oh my God! What's happened here? Dear! Dear!' and he said, 'Let's get this off him.'

Together, as gently as possible, they lifted the entwined and broken branches away from the man's head. And, seemingly reluctantly, Mrs Annie knelt down on the frozen earth, and after turning the head slightly she too muttered, 'Oh my God!' Then looking up, she said, 'There's a bit of a branch sticking in him. We'd better not touch it. We'll have to get the doctor, and . . . and some men from the house. I'll shout over the wall and get them. There's bound to be somebody near,' and turning to where Rosie was standing, her hand across her mouth again and her eyes wide, she said, 'Come, me dear. Come. Charlie will stay with him. Come on. Come on.'

It seemed as if Rosie were rooted to the ground, because Annie had to pull her away while repeating, 'Charlie will stay here with him. Come on now. Come on.'

Rosie allowed herself to be led away. She felt cold, strange. She wanted to be sick, really sick. Her chest was heaving and she felt faint.

Annie just managed to get her into the kitchen and to the shallow stone sink into which she actually vomited, and she urged her: 'That's it, dear! Get it up! Then sit by the fire; I've got to get help. You understand? You understand, girl? Well, do what I say, sit by the fire.'

Annie now went out of the house and to the wood shed, where she grabbed a short ladder and, trailing it, she made her way to the wall. From the top rung she could just see over the coping; and now, her voice as loud as she could make it, and that was very loud, she screamed, 'Help! Help! Somebody come! Help! Mr Steel's hurt in the wood.'

It was Willie Connor who first heard her shouts. He didn't know who it was, just that somebody was calling for help somewhere in the shrubbery at yon end of the garden.

When he reached the wall and saw Annie's face above it and heard what she was screaming at him, he said, 'Oh God in heaven! We'll be there.'

Her last words to him were, 'Bring something to carry him on. And get the doctor.'

Rosie was still in Annie's kitchen, and she was being yelled at by Robbie, standing in front of her as she sat on the settle with Annie's arm about her holding her tightly.

Annie looked at her son and didn't interrupt a word he was saying or check him for his manner, for now he was actually growling at Rosie, 'Forget it! You didn't see Jackie Wallace in the wood. You saw nobody in the wood. You were just going to meet your father and then the tree crashed down on him. It's . . . it's rotten anyway, the whole branch was

57

rotten. So how could he have had anything to do with it?'

'He did! He did! I saw him running. He was waiting for Father, he was waiting for Father. I tell you, I tell you. And he had something trailing behind. I know what it was now, it was a rope. I tell you . . .'

'You'll tell me nothing, girl. Now listen to me, Rosie. If you open your mouth and say that you saw the boy there, you're going to cause such a stink in your house that you've never smelt before. And you'll never get it out of your nostrils.'

Rosie turned to Annie now, saying, 'He was waiting for Father. I saw him beforehand, he was waiting for him. He . . . he must have pulled that branch down with the rope. I tell you I saw him. I . . .'

Robbie had his hands on her shoulders now. 'It's no good hoodwinking you any more, miss, or letting you keep your eyes closed. Very likely it *was* Jackie. All right, and he had a reason, because you know where your father had been? He had just come back from being in bed with Jackie's mother. Get that into your head. Listen!' He now caught her face between his hands and held it stiffly as he stared into her eyes. 'Your father had just been in bed with Jackie's mother. That's where he often went, and the boy had had enough. She supplied men when her poor man was away, droving. And all Jackie does is try to frighten them off. He's set fire to haystacks, he's left gates open, he's done all kinds to frighten men off his mother. But his mother is a whore. Do you know what a whore is? You don't know what a whore is, do you? A whore is a loose woman who'll let any man go with her for money, never for love, just for money. And your father was a rotten man. Ask Mam here. Your poor mother went through it for years, but she had to put a face on it, to bring you all up respectable like, not looked down on as the daughter of a woman-chaser.'

Now Rosie was struggling in his grasp, but he did not let go of her. He was now holding her hands as he said, 'You're

going to sit there and come to life, come out of the little girl.
I thought you had when you took up with fancy Mr Golding.
But even that didn't bring you into reality. Well, now you're
in it. Your father was a stinker in every possible way. And I'll
tell you something else. Charlie Fenwick, the coalman there,
he wasn't delivering this morning, not to your house, 'cos the
bills haven't been paid for months and months. Oh! That's
opened your eyes more than the immorality has done. You
can't believe it, can you? He owes everybody in the town.
He's gambled and whored for years. Your grandfather paid
his debts just because of your mother. Then there was a
point when he, too, had to stop. He appeared to be a jolly
man, didn't he, your grandfather? Well, let me tell you, he
had lived under a cover for years, just to preserve something
called class respectability. Now, now, my girl, you mention
Jackie Wallace's name and all this will come out, and you'll
have to live under it. And do you think your fiancé, Mr
Golding, will be big enough to take it? He's in the Civil
Service, isn't he? the Diplomatic side, and they're a very
snooty lot, they are. They don't like scandals. They may
have them among themselves, but they're well concealed.
In a way, they're like your mother, for some of them will
put up with anything rather than have their class sullied.'

When she did not answer but he felt her slump within his
hold, he let go of her and, straightening up, he said quietly,
'Think on it, Rosie, and as you're thinking, remember that
that young lad has gone through hell trying to keep things
from his father. Yet, his father is aware of a lot. He is the
butt of jokes in the bars, but he's a good man. A quiet
hard-working man is Dave Wallace. He didn't deserve her.
And that lad has seen for years what his mother is and
has attempted to keep it from his father, just by trying
to frighten off her visitors. And he managed it with a
lot of them. Oh yes, he did.'

Rosie leant back against the head of the settle and Annie's

arm went around her, holding her close; but she was cold, right to the very heart of her. She felt she would never be warm again. She couldn't believe it, but yes, she did believe it. It all explained that old probing feeling she had had for some time about her father. And now she recalled how often her mother had colds that made her eyes water. She recalled many things, and one in particular, the time that Wallace woman passed her in the market and had laughed as she looked at her. She had thought she must be strange, for her hat wasn't on straight, and she had left unbuttoned part of her blouse below her breasts. But no! not her father and that woman.

When suddenly she disengaged herself from Annie's hold and said, 'I'd better go; Beatrice will need me,' Robbie said, 'All right. I'll see you along as far as the gate.' He had not added, 'Because your father's not there to greet me any more.'

# 6

The light from the carbide lamp picked out only the road directly ahead as John pushed his bicycle slowly up the hill. He was tired. He'd had a long day; he hadn't stopped from half-past eight when he took his surgery. Every other person seemed to have either a very heavy cold or bronchitis, among the minor ailments. And then there had been the business of Steel.

It was just on seven o'clock now and, following on the thaw this afternoon, the ground was freezing again. He'd have to watch out; he had almost skidded into a ditch a little way back, and only his grabbing at a small tree had saved him.

He raised his head as a swinging lantern appeared over the brow of the hill; and the bearer, when he reached him, stopped and said, 'That you, Doctor?'

'Oh. Oh, hello, Mr Wallace. It's going to be another freezer.'

Dave Wallace did not respond but said, 'You haven't seen my lad about, have you?'

'Jackie? No. Well, what d'you mean? Just lately, this last couple of hours or so?'

'Any time. He's been missing all day. I had thought the darkness would bring him back.'

'Has he been playing truant?'

'No, no. He hasn't been to school for a week or so, but it was because he wasn't feeling well.'

'Oh; oh now,' John put in. 'Yes, when I come to think of it, I have seen him. But it was . . . oh, let me see, it must have been round about four o'clock, over by Bishop's Meadow. I wondered what he was doing down there, unless he was looking for stones from the old farmhouse. I remember telling myself, he wouldn't be looking for wood because what the fire didn't take the children did.'

'Bishop's Meadow? Oh, thank you, Doctor. About four o'clock?'

'Yes, it would be that. Has he ever been away this long before? I mean, kept away all day?'

'No, never! Never!' Dave Wallace paused before he said, 'I haven't been all that long back from a drove. I hear' – another pause – 'that Mr Steel has died. He was hit by a falling tree, I understand.'

'Yes. Yes. Quite a tragedy. A rotten branch. Well, you know what they're like in this weather. They can snap with the speed of lightning. The most dangerous place on earth is in a wood when there's the kind of frost there was this morning.'

'What time did it happen?' asked Dave Wallace.

'Oh, about the middle of the morning.'

'And in the wood?'

'Yes. Yes; not far from your place.'

When there was no response to this statement and the man turned sharply away, John stood watching the swaying lantern, indicating that Wallace had jumped a ditch which would take him into a field and to Bishop's Meadow. He wanted to say, 'Hold your hand a minute, and I'll come along with you;' but he was tired, and he was hungry. There came to his mind the odd accidents in the past which had happened to that woman's visitors; or at least, to their property. And

62

Steel had been coming from the direction of the farm; and the boy had been missing all day, and Dave Wallace was a tormented man. It all seemed to link up. And so it was no surprise to himself when he heard his voice yell out, 'Hold your hand a minute, Davey; I'll come along with you.'

After removing the lamp from his bicycle he pushed it into the ditch, and jumped over it.

Dave Wallace did not slacken his pace, but when John caught up with him, he said, 'There's no need, Doctor. Thanks, all the same.'

They had to climb a stone wall to get into Bishop's Meadow, and then they were walking down the gentle slope towards where the burnt-out farmhouse had stood. As they approached it, John raised his lamp head-high, and it showed up a doorless scarred wall. But most of the roof had gone too, the slates likely now patching some other farmer's house. When he brought down the lamp again, Dave Wallace had already stepped through the opening, and John could see what his lantern had revealed: the boy crouched in a corner. He made no movement, but his eyes were staring out of his head and his mouth was agape.

Within seconds they were both kneeling by his side and Dave Wallace was saying, 'It's all right, son. It's all right. It's all right. D'you hear? It's all right.'

John now took one of the boy's wrists and began to check his pulse. The fingers were stiff and dead cold, and so he chafed the hands. The boy's face was deadly pale, except for a blue tinge.

'I . . . I didn't mean it, Dad.'

'It's all right, boy, it's all right. Don't talk.'

'But he's . . . he's dead. I . . . I didn't mean it, Dad.'

'I know you didn't; I know you didn't.'

'Just . . . just to frighten . . . just to frighten him. The branch was rotten. Wouldn't . . . wouldn't hurt, not . . . not really. Didn't mean it, Dad.'

'Come along. Get up.'

When they both now attempted to help the boy to his feet, his legs buckled under him, so they laid him down again and began to rub the frozen limbs.

'Did . . . didn't mean it.'

'Shh! Be quiet now. Be quiet. Your father knows you didn't mean it,' John said.

It was as if for the first time the boy had become aware of the doctor, for his mouth opened wide and he gasped, 'Don't . . . don't take . . . don't take me away.'

'Nobody's going to take you away. The only thing is' – John was patting the boy's cheek now – 'listen to me. Don't talk about it. Do you hear? Don't talk about it. What did I say?'

'D–d–d . . . don't t–talk . . . about it.'

'That's right. That's right. Nobody knows but you. Your dad doesn't know, and I don't know, only you, so don't talk about it. It was a rotten branch. Everyone knows that. Do you understand?'

'Don't . . . d–d–don't talk about it. Y–yes, Doctor. I'm hot. I . . . I was cold. I was cold for a long time, Dad. I was cold.'

'You'll soon be home, son. Come on now; get on your feet.'

They lifted him up again, but his legs still wobbled as they supported him out of the derelict house, then up the slope. But ten minutes later when they reached the farm, the boy was walking unaided, although his head was drooped and his breath came in short gasps.

After Dave Wallace pushed the cottage door open with his foot, John realised he was no longer the quiet man.

The room led into the kitchen and there was his wife standing at one side of the table, and her head wagged as she said, 'So you've found him, have you? Causing trouble, as usual. And the doctor with him. My goodness! We have

64

company this evenin', haven't we? What have we done to deserve this?'

Dave Wallace made no response to his wife's quip; it was as if he hadn't noticed her. But he guided his son and John past the foot of the stairs in the middle of the room, and through a door into a bedroom.

Here he thrust the lantern onto a low chest of drawers before leading his son to the bed.

If the boy had been capable of saying anything he would have remarked that this was his father's and mother's bed; but he wasn't and so allowed his father and the doctor to strip his clothes off him, then rub him down with a rough towel before putting him under the bedclothes.

When, in a low voice, John said, 'I'll have to go back to the surgery; he'll need some medicine,' Dave Wallace said quietly, 'Before you go, would you stay with him for another five minutes? There's something I have to do.'

'Yes. Yes, Dave. Go on.'

Dave Wallace walked slowly from the room and closed the door behind him. Then, moving calmly to the table where his wife was still standing, and without saying a word, he drove his fist between her eyes; then as she fell back screaming, he gripped the front of her blouse, pulling her towards him until their breaths fanned each other. Then he growled, 'You filthy, dirty, common slut! You're not fit to live. For two pins I'd send you along with him. You'd served him well afore the tree hit him. Well, better than the gun I was going to use on you both, for it saved me own neck. Now, you dirty whore, get up them stairs an' get your fancy dibs together, and out. No waitin', no talkin' it over this time. No promises. *Out! Out!*' It was his voice that was screaming now. He thrust her towards the stairs and, her back hitting the bannister post, she almost slid to the floor. Then, her hand over her brow, she said, 'You . . . you can't do this. I've nowhere to go.'

'What! You've nowhere to go? What about your clients? Their wives would welcome you, especially Gladys Knowles. She would tear the hair from your head if she knew that you had started to serve him again. Now get up there before I kick you up.' His foot went out as if he was about to carry out his threat, and she stumbled up the stairs. And he followed her.

Half the landing was taken up with a large cupboard, the doors of which he pulled open, and from it he dragged a two-handled canvas bag and threw it at her feet, saying, 'There you are! Get your fancy dibs into that, and what it doesn't hold you can hang around your neck. But do it, and do it now. And if you don't look slippy I'll throw the whole damn lot out of the window an' you after them.'

She stood for a moment defiant, her bottom lip trembling as she said, 'Big fellow all of a sudden.'

'But not before time,' he yelled at her. 'No, by God! Not before time. If there's anybody been a bloody fool in this world, it's been me. Now get packin'.' This time he did lift his foot and kicked at the bag, saying, 'I'm warning you, I'm only givin' you minutes.'

Furiously she now grabbed up blouses, skirts and underwear. Then as she went to get some oddments from the lower shelf, she said, 'The bag's already full an' I want me bits and pieces from downstairs.'

'Oh yes, your bits and pieces. Your cheapcrack jewellery and your powders. Oh, you'll get those all right; you'll need 'em in your trade.' And he leapt down the stairs, and from the back of the kitchen door he grabbed a bass bag and rushed into the bedroom. The lantern on the chest of drawers he pushed to one side, and, with a curved arm, he swept a number of fancy boxes into the bag. Then he pulled open the top drawer and tipped up its contents into the bag.

During all this John had not turned from the bed, where he was chafing the boy's limbs. However, he was aware of

66

the woman's voice yelling, 'I'll get me own back on you, Dave Wallace, you'll see. An' . . . an' what's more, I haven't any money.'

'Didn't he pay you this morning? Get out! *Get out!* else before God I'll do for you.' There was the sound of the door being banged closed.

Dave Wallace did not return immediately to the bedroom, for he felt as if he had just emerged from a long physical battle. Instead, he slumped against the door, his head drooping to his chest; and so he remained for some minutes. But the minutes were long and brought John to the bedroom door, then across the room towards him. And he put his hand on his shoulder as he said, 'Come on; sit on the bed. The boy needs you there. He keeps asking for you. And I'll get away; but I'll be back shortly. Just keep him warm – put an oven shelf in the bed and give him a hot drink.'

Dave Wallace spoke no word of thanks, but just allowed himself to be led to the bed. And there he put his arm around his son and brought his face up to his.

It was almost an hour later when John returned to the cottage, entering it very quietly.

Dave Wallace was still sitting at the side of the bed: he was holding his son's hand and it was evident that the man had been crying.

# 7

Perhaps it was because of the fresh fall of snow that the funeral had been so sparsely attended. Very few of the mourners returned to the house, but what was noticeable to the family was the presence of four very well-dressed gentlemen who weren't known to them, but who drank the mulled wine and seemed to enjoy the meal that was provided.

But now it was four o'clock in the afternoon. The drawing-room fire, heaped with logs, was burning brightly. The gas chandelier filled the room with light, although no such illumination was registered on the faces of the small assembled company. There was Beatrice, her skin taking on the patina of alabaster against her heavy black garb, her eyes wide-stretched, her lips tightly closed. Then there was Helen, tall and looking more elegant than ever in her mourning clothes. Next to her sat her military looking husband. And lastly there was Rosie. She was not sitting straight up in her chair as were the others, but leaning on the side, her head resting on her hand, her elbow on the arm of the chair. And she did not raise her head when the solicitor, Mr Coulson of Coulson, Pratt & Sanders, who was sitting behind the sofa table, said, 'There is little to read as there are no bequests, but just a simple letter. Your father left no will.' He was looking straight at Beatrice now. 'There had been a will of sorts, but that was before your mother died. After he mortgaged the house . . .'

'What?' Beatrice was sitting on the edge of her chair now. 'What did you say?'

'I said, Miss Steel, after your father mortgaged the house, and I may add, although there is no will to read, there's a great deal to be told.'

'Mortgaged the house? This house isn't mortgaged.'

The solicitor's sigh was audible to all of them and patiently now, his eyes still on Beatrice, he said, 'This house, Miss Steel, is mortgaged to an amount of ten thousand pounds. That is a great deal of money. But the security for it did not rest with the house alone. Numerous articles in it had to act as security, including a number of the pictures which are listed here.' He tapped a document on his desk. 'Five pictures in all, I think, which he imagined were of great value. But only two were authentic, one a Boucher. Unfortunately, the Rembrandt was a copy.'

His words were checked by Beatrice, who almost screamed at him, 'What are you talking about?'

'Be quiet! for a moment, Beatrice,' put in Helen.

Beatrice turned on her now and yelled, 'It's all right for you, sitting there po-faced! You're out of it, nicely out of it; I'm left with all the responsibility, and here I'm being told . . .'

'Do you wish me to continue, Miss Steel? Or shall I leave the matter to one of my partners, and you can come to the office?'

Beatrice bowed her head for a moment, her knuckles showing white where her hands were gripping each other and pressing a dent into her black skirt. There was silence in the room before Mr Coulson resumed his address: 'I will now read this private letter. I don't know its contents; I only know that the deceased gentleman' – he seemed to stress the last word – 'left it in our care to be opened after his death.'

He slit open the envelope, took out a single page, then stared at it for a few seconds before he raised his head and looked from one to the other of the small company. In a low voice he then read:

> I leave my estate to my eldest
> daughter, Beatrice Steel, and express
> the wish that she find some means of
> maintaining it.
>       Signed, Simon Arthur Steel

Those assembled were all looking towards Beatrice now; even Rosie had straightened herself up. Beatrice's lips were no longer set in a line, her mouth was opening and shutting like that of a gasping fish.

It was Leonard Morton Spears who broke the silence. His voice too was quiet, and he looked at the solicitor and said, 'What is the income?'

'Very little, sir, very little. In fact, it's negligible now.'

'It's not! It's not!' Beatrice was shouting again. 'There are bonds, securities; Father received the interest every quarter.'

'Your father, Miss Steel, had for the last six months received a loan from a company that charges exorbitant interest rates. The bank had not allowed him a second mortgage, and he was reduced to borrowing.'

'But Mama's bonds, and investments, and . . .'

Her voice now trailed away to a whisper, and the solicitor, with pity in his eyes and his voice, said, 'Your mama, I'm sorry to say, Miss Steel, had to sell a number of her interests and bonds to meet—' he paused here, swallowed, then glanced at the others before adding, 'your father's debts.'

It was in a whimper that Beatrice asked, 'But . . . but what debts? He only went to Newcastle to his club twice or three times a week, and very rarely to London.'

'You don't need to travel far, Miss, to spend thousands of pounds when you're addicted to gambling.'

'Father addicted to . . .?' Now Beatrice turned appealingly to Helen; then her eyes lifted to the man at her sister's side. But neither of them could find anything to say to comfort her.

Beatrice was looking at the solicitor again and she said, 'He . . . he could not have lost all that money on gambling; he . . . he must have won sometimes. He must.'

'Yes. Yes, he won at times, a little. But from what I gather, that was only an incentive to lay on more money, sometimes hundreds.'

Then the company was startled by Rosie's words stabbing like a wasp's sting: 'And then there were his women, Beatrice, there were his women. You know nothing about that, do you?'

Helen now rose from her chair and went to Rosie and, putting an arm around her shoulders, she said, 'Shh! Shh! Rosie, please!'

But for answer she got, 'No, Helen! Let it all come out. Mr Coulson is too polite. And I'll tell you something else, Beatrice. The morning he died he had just been visiting one of his lady friends, just one of them. But he had to pay them, hadn't he? And you had to give him two pounds out of the housekeeping money.'

They were all on their feet now.

'You're . . . you're insane, girl, insane!'

No-one responded to this remark for a moment. Then Mr Coulson, sitting down again almost with a plop, said, 'No, Miss Steel; regrettably she is right. But I was too polite to put it as boldly as she has. Your home and land is in the state it is today because of your late father's weaknesses.' His voice becoming brisk, he said now, 'There is one small item of business to be discussed, but it *is* important. So will you please be seated.' He now drew towards himself

71

a large number of sheets of paper which had been lying to the side, and tapping them, he said, 'There are many outstanding bills, not only from the local shop-keepers, but from certain . . . we'll call them gentlemen, who are here today. Two are directors of the loan company, the others are from a gambling syndicate. Now their demands are substantial. But there is a point here. As there is no money in the estate, I don't know whether, legally, these men can call upon you to pay your father's debts. I'll have to look into this. The interest on their money alone will take some finding. To that, I'm afraid, has to be added the interest on the mortgage. If I may advise you, and if there is any possible way you can manage it, I would see to the local debts immediately; and also think about reducing your staff. Consider too what you intend to do with the property, because, as I see it from here, it will be impossible for you to continue living here under the conditions I have stated.'

As he picked up a leather case and began to return the papers to it, Leonard Morton Spears said, 'Leave the bills for the local debts, I shall see to those.'

'Oh, that is kind of you, sir. And . . . and you know, there is still hope. There is still something you can do.' He was now looking across the table at Beatrice who was staring at the floor. 'You still have about fifty acres of land here, some of it unused, I should imagine; well, I mean, it's just rough woodland. I think you should sleep on the idea of selling a strip of it. You can get a good price for building land today; that is, for good-class houses. I'm sure the bank would support you in this.'

Beatrice's head came up. 'Sell the land? Father would never . . .'

'Shut up!' Again they were looking at Rosie, unbelieving now, as she went on, 'Don't bring up what Father would do and what he wouldn't do. To my mind and everybody else's, he's done more than enough, and he's

72

hoodwinked us for years. And from what I understand, he led Mother a terrible life.'

Helen now took Rosie by the shoulder and forced her towards the doors. 'Come along, dear! All right, all right! Be quiet now, be quiet!'

Beatrice's mouth was again agape. Rosie. How dare she! How *dare* she! It didn't matter what Father had done, she had no right to speak to her in public like that. She had no right! She had no right!

As if a voice had yelled at her from inside, Shut up! she suddenly stopped, then sat down heavily.

Her brother-in-law went to her, put a hand on her shoulder, and said, 'Try not to take it too badly, Beatrice. These things happen. They'll work out though, you'll see, they'll work out. We'll do what we can.'

She should have raised her head and thanked him, but she couldn't. He and Helen: he doted on her . . . blatantly. Life was unfair. Oh, how unfair it was.

She got up and left the room without even a nod towards the solicitor. And now Leonard turned to Mr Coulson, saying, 'It's a dreadful business. He really was an utter swine. I've known it for some time. But you don't talk about such things, not to womenfolk, especially his daughters. Are things indeed so black?'

'Well, from my point of view, sir, they could not be worse. What should happen is that the house and land should be sold, and what is left after the bank has been paid, would, I imagine, enable Miss Steel to get a little place of her own. But I can see that it would be quite impossible. Oh, yes, yes.'

Leonard nodded at the man, saying, 'My wife's always said that Beatrice had an obsession with this place, which is why she always expects to be addressed as Beatrice Penrose-Steel. Even as a child, it used to be a place for everything and everything in its place. She used to be what they call 'the little madam'; but now she's an infuriated woman. And

73

the hardest part for her, I'm sure, will be to accept her father's revealed character, because, in a way, from the little I have seen of both of them, they were very alike under the skin, except of course, morally.'

'Yes, of course, except morally. Well now, sir, I will make my way home. The rest of the business will have to be attended to at my office.'

As he rose to his feet and took up his case, he said, 'It hasn't been a happy funeral.'

Leonard thought it was a most strange remark to make. But he had to agree that it had not been a happy funeral.

# 8

Turning to Helen who was standing near the foot of the bed, John said, 'She'll sleep for a good twelve hours, I hope. What brought this on?'

Helen moved from the bed towards the window and stood looking out into the thinly falling snow before she answered, 'The disclosure of my father's misdeeds, principally; that the house is choked with mortgage, with debts to a large number of local tradesmen; also money owing to fellow gamblers and to money lenders who charge exorbitant interest. And he left no will.'

'None at all?'

'Only a letter. Very brief; two lines to Beatrice.' She did not repeat what the two lines were, because they seemed so incredible in their subtle demand for Beatrice to clear up the impossible situation he had created.

'And that caused Rosie to become hysterical?' His tone held a note of incredulity and she turned to him, saying, 'No, not just that: she seemed to have been aware of all his misdeeds before the solicitor brought them into the open. And it wasn't just the money alone.' She walked past him now towards the door and he stopped her opening it by saying quietly, 'Well, his liaisons were not only public knowledge but food for parlour jokes, so I understand.'

He was standing close behind her now when she swung round to him and, in a low voice, exclaimed, 'I don't know how she got to know this. Nor do I understand why we were kept in the dark so long, because, apparently, my mother suffered at his hands, too. Yet, looking back, it seemed to be a happy house. There was always so much gaiety among us girls, and with mother, too . . . Yes, that is strange, for she alone seemed to set the tone of our lives: she kept us happy and it wasn't until she died that things changed, when one by one we expressed our desire to leave the house; except, that is, for Beatrice. Marion got away at the same time as I did. She's in India now, you know, with her husband.'

He made no comment but kept his eyes fixed on her face as she went on, 'And Rosie's going. She won't be able to get away quickly enough from now on.' She moved her hand slightly in order to look towards the bed and, sadly now, she added, 'She was the happiest of us all. A tomboy, a chatterbox. Never still. But I was amazed at the change I saw in her when we arrived three days ago. She acted strangely, on the point of tears all the time and didn't want to talk. But now we know the reason why. What is more, she must have been very unhappy for some time. This I gauged from her letters.'

'Are *you* happy?'

'What?'

'I said, are *you* happy?'

She returned his deep, piercing look for a moment before she said slowly, 'Yes, I am very happy. I . . . I have a wonderful husband. He is a lovely man . . . a lovely man.'

'I'm glad.'

Their look held until the movement she made to turn and open the door caused him to step back. And without further words he followed her out and onto the landing and down the stairs, to where Leonard was waiting for them and said to her, 'Teddy's just come. Teddy Golding. He couldn't get here

76

for the funeral but he felt he had to come and pay his respects. What's more, he has to be off again this evening . . . How is she? Can he see her for a moment?'

He was now addressing John. And John shook his head and said, 'I've had to sedate her; she was near hysteria. She'll be all right tomorrow morning, but I'll have to keep her quiet for a day or two until she gets over the shock.'

'Where is Teddy?' Helen asked her husband.

'Beatrice has him in the drawing-room. We'd better go in and see him, dear, to explain things, because I don't think Beatrice is in a condition to entertain anyone at the moment, unless it is through blurting out her worries and blaming the world for her father's misfortune.' He now turned to John, saying, 'I'm sure you could do with a cup of tea or something before you go out into that' – he jerked his head back towards the window. 'It's getting thicker. Come into the study; there's a fire there and the girls will bring you a hot drink.'

John hesitated to follow him; in fact he was about to make an excuse that a patient was awaiting him, when he caught Helen's eye: it was as if she were saying, 'Please be friendly. He's a lovely . . . lovely man.'

A few minutes later he was seated in a deep leather chair on the opposite side of the fireplace from Leonard, although he found it impossible to open the conversation. Then there was no need, for the tall, good-looking soldier rose from his chair, saying on a laugh, 'I asked if you'd like a hot drink, then forgot to ring for it.' He now pulled a cord to the side of the fireplace before sitting down again and saying, 'We've never really met, have we? What I mean is, we've never had the chance to talk. Yet, through Helen I seem to know a lot about you.'

He found himself repeating inanely, 'Through Helen?'

'Yes. Yes, she thinks you're a splendid doctor with the right personality and all that goes to make . . . well, not exactly the bedside manner, but the sort of fellow who

77

gives a patient confidence and assures him he's not going to die from a tickly cough.' They both laughed, somewhat embarrassed now.

After a short silence Leonard said, 'I suppose it's stupid to ask why you went in for doctoring? No; I take that back, because I know only too well what some of you go into it for, especially the surgeons; just for the money. Here and there you get one who sees it as a vocation, a duty to mankind. And this is the type we seem to get in the country.'

'You talk as if you'd had great experience with doctors.'

'Yes. Yes, I have, unfortunately.'

'Oh.' John's eyebrows moved up slightly. 'You've been ill?'

'Oh, earlier on, the usual things that one picks up from abroad; malaria, fevers, this and that. But I've seen doctors treat men like cattle, while others, through fatigue, have fallen asleep across the foot of a patient's bed. But I have a good one now.'

'Oh, how long have you been in the Army?'

'Since I was eighteen.'

They were laughing together as John said, 'I take it from that there is a love relationship between you.'

'Oh, definitely, definitely. Add a little hate here and there and you'd be nearer the truth. I asked you why you went in for doctoring. You didn't give me a reply. But I wondered if it was the same way I got into the Army, because my father had been in it and you feel you must follow in father's footsteps. Was your father a doctor?'

'No. No. He was a stonemason.'

'A stonemason?'

'Yes, a stonemason. He should have been called a sculptor because he could do anything with stone. But he never seemed happy unless he was hanging on by his teeth to a church tower, when he was replacing a block of stone or a

78

gargoyle, or adding to a coping in the manner it had been worked two hundred years before.'

As the door opened and Janie Bluett entered the room, Leonard said to her, 'Do you think we could have a tray of tea, Janie, with a few eats too?' He asked this in a confidential, loud whisper, and she smiled at him as she said, 'Of course, Mr Spears, and in two shakes of a lamb's tail.'

The lamb's tail took five minutes over its shaking, but then Janie brought in a large tray holding a tea service, and behind her, Frances Middleton carried a tray on which was an assortment of scones and biscuits.

After Leonard had thanked them both warmly, John smiled at him as he said, 'With regard to a bedside manner, I am often accused of being too brusque, as I know I am with lead-swingers.'

Leonard was about to take the cosy from the teapot when he stopped and said, 'I hated my father at one time for encouraging me into the Army, but the day I got into my uniform he gave me a piece of advice: 'You'll see men,' he said, 'kicked around from dog to devil by their superiors. The bigger the bully, the louder the mouth, and the more hate they engender. Be firm. Don't be familiar with men out of your class; that is the way to lose their respect. But when you deal with them, deal with them fairly, remembering they are human beings. Remember that but for my position, and my father's, and his father's, you could today be one of them.' I learnt more from that little speech than from all my years at public school, and from the floggings.' He now pointed to the tray of food: 'See what it's done for us in this case.'

John sat looking at him. He was a likeable fellow; there was no doubt about it. And Helen saw him as a lovely man. It was a term Rosie had a habit of using too; at least she had up to now. He was the kind of man a woman would find very attractive. But did Helen love him? She said she was happy. But it would be a very odd woman who couldn't be happy with a man like this.

At this point, the door opened again, and when Helen entered, Leonard cried, 'See! one can't get five minutes alone.' But he put down the teapot and went to her and, his arm about her shoulders, he led her to the seat he had vacated near the fire. Then, looking from one to the other, he said, 'Oh, this is nice. It's like escaping from the war zone.'

As John observed them he wondered why he was able to sit there and listen to this fellow whom, secretly, he had envied and, indeed, at times hated.

# PART TWO

*Beatrice*

# I

Beatrice sat behind the desk in her study. Spread out before her were papers of all shapes and sizes. She leaned her elbow on the desk and cupped the side of her head in her hand and stared at the glass cabinet opposite, the while telling herself there was nothing for it but to do as the solicitor had advised: she must sell some of the land; perhaps as much as twenty acres. As prices were now it would realise enough to pay the interest on the mortgage and clear the debts that her father had accumulated; or at least the one from the loan company. The gambling debt was questionable; a matter of honour, Mr Coulson had called it. He had also suggested that she cut down her staff by half, but she had stood out firmly against that: the small staff represented prestige, and that was all she had, the house and its prestige, and she was going to hang on to it. Oh, yes; yes, she was.

She began to look through the bills again. Leonard had settled a number of them straight away. But since then, others had come flooding in, all back debts. There were two amongst them that caused her teeth almost to draw blood from her lips, for they were from a fashionable shop in Newcastle. Two separate bills for ladies' gowns, and they were dated eighteen months previous. Although she knew she had inherited many of her father's traits, had he been here at this moment she would have done him a physical injury: she could see him standing at yon side of the desk and hear his voice saying, 'You know, you are rather extravagant regarding the housekeeping bills. You'll have to learn how to manage better.'

Over the past weeks she had learned a further hard lesson: so-called friends backed discreetly away from the word 'scandal' and all that was attached to it. It was now well known in the vicinity that her father had left no will, but instead a mountain of debt. On top of this, what the solicitor was kind enough to call his weaknesses had also been exposed, proof of which had straightaway shown itself when Dave Wallace's wife arrived at the inn in a very dishevelled state and with two rising black eyes.

She now sat back in the chair. The house was very quiet: she was alone; she did not consider the staff as occupying the house.

Rosie had gone into Newcastle, there to meet Edward Golding, who had come up from London to do business. He would be here for two days. Apparently, he had something special to say to Rosie, probably about the post he was hoping to get in Newcastle and where they would live.

Something had happened to Rosie since she had been made aware of the real nature of her father. Although she herself was shocked and sickened by it, it had not affected her to the same extent. But then, of course, Rosie was always child-like and would never face up to real life. Airy-fairy was the word for her. But, nevertheless, Beatrice was glad that when she did marry she would be living near at hand, because without her she would feel isolated altogether. And in spite of her light character, she was fond of her; in fact, she liked her more than she did either Marion or Helen. Oh, yes, Helen got on her nerves, and that doting man of hers too. Yes . . . yes, he had been kind in paying the bills, but then he had plenty of money with which to do so. Yet she had earlier understood he wasn't a rich man. Oh, there were different degrees of wealth. But Helen herself: oh no, she couldn't stand Helen, never could. There was that something about her which gave off the impression that she was superior. Perhaps it was just because she was taller and quite good-looking. But, nevertheless, there was something that got under her skin and irritated her every time they met.

There was a tap on the door and she called, 'Enter!' and Frances Middleton came in carrying a silver salver and saying, 'Second post, miss.'

'Put them there.' Beatrice pointed to a corner of the desk. She gave the girl no thanks but went on writing.

It was later and with some reluctance that she opened the letters. The first one, she knew, was another bill – bills had special envelopes. She had come to recognise that. But the second envelope she scrutinised more carefully. Before reaching here it had been delivered to two other addresses. She slit open this envelope and saw immediately, from the heading, that it was from a firm of solicitors. It began:

Dear Colonel Steel,

Swiftly now she looked back at the envelope. It was addressed to Colonel Steel, not to her father, but to her grandfather. She went on reading.

I have to inform you, sir, that your sister, Alice Benton Forester, died on the 17th February, at the amazing age of ninety-eight. We have had difficulty in tracing your address, as the only thing she seemed to have remembered was your name. She left no will, and the annuity that kept her in the home, of course, died with her. Her possessions were few: a bracelet and a pendant, neither of which is of great value. But I will send them on to you, if you so wish.

85

I met the lady on a few occasions but that was some years ago. She appeared to be a gentle creature, as apparently she did to the nursing home staff, who informed me that her records showed that her illness had changed since she was forty years old, when her previous high spirits and hysterical outbursts, during which her one desire seemed to be to disrobe, and her fits, too, had gradually diminished. Apparently she had been a favourite among the staff.

She is being buried in the local cemetery and, as it is not expected you will be able to attend, I shall follow your orders as to what is to be done with the few trinkets.

I await your reply.

Yours respectfully

Thomas Harding.


Her eyes flicked to the top of the page to read: 'Harding & Bright, Solicitors'. There was a Falmouth address lower down and to the side of the page.

It *would* be somebody who could leave them only a few trinkets; she thrust the letter away from her in disgust. This was the Aunt Ally of whom the family remembered her grandmother would talk and to whom her grandfather would make the long journey to Cornwall.

She turned her head to the side as her mind disdainfully repeated the word 'disrobe'. Well, they could keep their few trinkets. She wasn't going to answer the letter, she had enough on her mind without taking on anything more, because the next thing she would have would be a bill for the funeral. She knew solicitors. She had had enough of them with Mr Coulson. Solicitors were supposed to be helpful and arrange one's business, but all he could advise was that she sell the land. Then, of course, there had been the advice from Helen, that she could let off the annexe, which was really a separate house. Well, let her take her own advice and take lodgers into *her* home.

Suddenly she rose from her seat, declaring, 'I can tackle no more today,' and marched out of the room.

In the hall, she hesitated. She had intended to go into the drawing-room, but coming from there was a busy sound, telling her that one or other of the girls was at work. So she went upstairs. On the landing she again paused and peered over the balcony and down into the hall. How was it that the house seemed so empty today? Likely it was because Rosie was away. What would she do when Rosie was married? Of course, she could be living nearby, but that wasn't the same as living in the house. Still it was preferable to Marion's choice, to go to India, and Helen's to live in Hampshire. Of course, Helen would choose *that* place in order to live near her husband's titled cousin. Her reason had been that all the men liked sailing . . . And she liked to be among the men, didn't she?

She entered her bedroom and going straight to a side table she lifted the lid of a box of chocolates, picked one out and put it in her mouth. And as she went to turn away she hesitated, then grabbed up the box and went to the seat by the window, where she ate one chocolate after another. Whenever she felt distressed there was a feeling in her to eat something sweet, and as far back as she could remember chocolates had been a source of comfort.

Suddenly she stopped chewing and pushed the box away. She wished Rosie was back.

She looked around the room. Everything was shining; but the sight brought no satisfaction to her present mood, for this was new and somewhat strange: she had never imagined she needed people. She had always kept her distance from company; chatter and laughter irritated her.

She turned to look out of the window again: the rooks were making their nightly journey home. She was on her

87

feet now. She hated rooks and their constant cawing. She'd take the gun out tomorrow. Although her aim was never as good as her father's, she was always able to account for a few of them. But the last time they moved their nests they picked on a tree that was nearer still to the house.

The sound of the front door being banged turned her about, and she almost ran out of the room and down the stairs, to see Rosie drawing the pins from her hat; and she approached her, saying, 'Oh, you look cold.'

'No, I'm not' – Rosie was smiling widely – 'I took the horse bus from the station and walked the rest. It was lovely.' As she pulled off her coat she said, 'I'd love a cup of tea, Beatrice.'

'I'll ring for it now. Come along to the little sitting-room, the girls are giving the drawing-room a turn-out.'

As Rosie flopped down onto the sofa, Beatrice asked, 'Did you have a nice meal with Teddy?'

'Yes. Yes, wonderful. I've got news for you. Come and sit down here.' Rosie patted the sofa cushion near her; and when Beatrice was seated beside her, she gripped her hand and said, 'I'm so excited,' and shook her head before she went on, 'I can't believe it. I can't believe it: I may be going to America.'

After a long pause, Beatrice said, 'What? America?' Her eyes were screwed up as if she were endeavouring to imagine the distance to America.

'Yes. Yes, America. You know Teddy was going to take the opening in Newcastle, but he was called into His Majesty' – she flapped her hand – 'that's what he calls the head one. Well, he is a very important man and as Teddy said, you don't always get invited upstairs unless you're going to get pulled over the coals, which he had thought was going to happen to him.' She giggled now. 'And what do you think? It was to ask if he'd like to go to America. Apparently one of their men over there collapsed and died.' The smile went from her face as she added, 'He was only a young man, and . . . and unmarried. And that's the point' – her face had lost its beam – 'that's the point. They like their young men to go out there unmarried, but they do make exceptions, and before Teddy put it to them he wanted to be sure I would marry him.'

Rosie bit on her lip to stop herself from grinning widely. 'He's staying over in Newcastle for two or three days because he's coming to see you. Well, Father being gone, he would like to ask your permission as he would have done of Father. He's very proper, is Teddy, even though he's so young. Well, not so young, being twenty-four. He's staying at the George Inn and he would like us to go there to dinner the night before he leaves. Oh' – she closed her eyes tightly and hugged herself – 'I'm so happy I could burst. America! America!' Suddenly opening her eyes she looked at her sister, then said, 'You're not pleased for me? I know, I know it's awful leaving you. We shall have all left home then, but . . . but you must understand. I've been very unhappy lately, since . . . since Father's business, and to be able to get away . . .' She was now gripping both of Beatrice's hands: 'You could come out there for a holiday. It's easy now; the boats are so quick. It only takes eight days, and you've never been away from here. None of us have. Well, Marion's now in India, and that's marvellous. In her last letter she said it was simply out of this world. But you still have Helen near at hand. She'll visit you if you'll let her.' She now drew the hands within hers to her breast and held them there. 'You've never got on very well with Helen, but if you'd only try, Beatrice. She's so nice. And she thinks about you, she's concerned for you. She told me so.'

Beatrice practically tore her hands from the gentle grip, and she was now on her feet looking down at Rosie and saying, 'I don't want any condescension from Helen or from anyone else. No-one need be concerned for me; I can see to myself. As for you and the news you've thrown at me: going to America! You're not thinking about me, are you? I'll be left here on my own, but that doesn't matter. No, it doesn't.' She turned towards the fire now. 'I still have the house, and . . . and that's all that matters to me. Understand that, having the house and being able to keep it.' Even as she spoke she knew that it wasn't all that mattered to her at the moment: she needed company, she needed Rosie. Of course, she wanted the house. It was the main thing in her life, but she wanted to share its comfort with . . . well not just anybody, but with one of them who had grown up in this house and could appreciate it and love it, and foster it, as her . . . She had almost thought, as her father had done. But she didn't want to think about her father these days.

Rosie was standing beside her now, her voice pleading: 'You'll see him, won't you, tomorrow afternoon? He said it would be tomorrow afternoon.'

'Yes. Yes, of course I'll see him. In any case, as things stand legally, I'm your guardian, I could object.'

'But you wouldn't do that, would you, Beatrice? You know how I want to get away.'

'But why? Why? This is your home.'

Rosie now almost jumped back from Beatrice as she cried, 'It isn't my home! I don't look upon it as a home any longer. To tell you the truth, I'm much more at home yon side of the wall.'

'Oh, yes, yes; I can almost believe that, with that common pig-breeder and his mo—'

'Don't you dare call him a common pig-breeder! If ever there was a real farmer, he is one. Only he hasn't got enough land. Now if he had this' – she swung her arm wide – 'you would see what he could make of it!'

Beatrice was staring at her wide-eyed now: she was looking at a young woman, no vestige of the child or the girl here; no-one she could dominate any longer, and that was a necessity as much as was the need for company. Although she might not have been aware of it, she needed to use her questionable power on someone.

As Rosie marched down the room her voice was still loudly indignant: 'I'm going to America and there's nothing you can do about it.'

Her left arm thrust out, her hand gripping the mantelpiece, Beatrice became taut as she thought, No, there was nothing she could do about it. Then, her whole body slumping, she dropped onto the couch again and, her hands covering her face, she groaned aloud. She had the unusual desire to cry.

She straightened up, wiped her face with her handkerchief, then took in a number of deep breaths which seemed to signify resignation to the events that were about to happen . . .

Ten minutes later, in her study, she set about busily tidying her desk. The last thing she did was pick up a number of opened letters that she had not yet answered, and tap them into tidy formation. It was as she did so her eyes fell on the letter she had received from the solicitor, telling of the death of that unknown woman in the nursing home.

She was well acquainted with quotations from the nursery days: A stitch in time saves nine. Big oaks from little acorns grow. Her eyes remained riveted on the paper as her mind quoted, Desperate situations require desperate remedies.

She now lifted the sheet from the rest and read the letter again, her eyes dwelling on the words:

'her high spirits and hysterical outbursts
in which her one desire seemed to be to disrobe, and
her fits . . .'

Now she had her fingers spread flat over the letter as if she were pressing it into the table. She looked back down her young sister's life. There was a thread there. Definitely there was a thread there. She wouldn't be lying. She now grabbed up the letter, folded it, searched until she found its envelope, which she had thrown into the waste-paper basket, then stood up, and again she took in three long breaths, but for a different reason now.

# 2

Rosie was sitting at one side of Annie's table. Annie was facing her and Robbie was standing behind his mother, his hand on the back of her chair. They were both staring at Rosie as Annie repeated, 'America?'

'Yes. Isn't it marvellous! Oh, please, please' – she put her hand out across the table towards them – 'don't say "it's a long way away" and "we're going to miss you", because you won't miss me half as much as I shall miss you. But I . . . I want to get away.' The last words had been spoken in almost a whisper and, her voice still low, she said, 'And somehow this seems to be an answer to my prayer. I don't just want to go into the next town, or Newcastle, or Durham, I want to get away, miles away, from that house.'

'What does Beatrice say about this?'

'Oh, she was up in arms and threatened that she could stop me going, because I'm not yet twenty-one. But now I think she's accepted it. Teddy's coming to tea at three o'clock, and I heard her ordering Cook to make some dainties which' – she smiled now wanly – 'pointed to the fact that she wasn't just going to greet him with "good-afternoon", and "goodbye". She's gone into Newcastle to see her solicitor about selling the land. It's the only thing she can do if she wants to keep the house going. But she said she'd be back about one o'clock. I'm all churned up inside, Mrs Annie. And oh—' she glanced up towards Robbie, saying, 'don't look at me like that. Please! I shall hate having to leave you. I shall, for you mean so much to me. I mean, you both do. Without you these past years, I think I would have done something desperate . . . perhaps even asked Jimmy Oldham to marry me. He's only about forty. But then they would have had to get another yard man. Still, he's always been nice to . . .'

'Shut up! Stop talking like a town slut!'

She gazed open-mouthed to where Robbie was marching out of the kitchen; then she turned to his mother. Annie's eyes were cast down at the table on which her fingers were beating out a rhythm, the sound of which seemed to increase loudly in Rosie's ears as she stared at her and waited for an explanation. And when it came it was simply a statement: 'Robbie's very fond of you,' she said.

'I . . . I kn–kn–kn– ' now she was stammering – 'I know that and I'm fond of him, very. But I was just trying to put a lighter side on to why I want to get away.'

'I know, lass, I know.' Annie thrust a hand out across the table and gripped Rosie's as she said, 'But it's a funny thing, lass, we never seem to see the things, the important things, that are right under our noses. We should be able to smell their meaning, but we never do. It takes something, I don't know what, a hurricane, an earthquake . . . a personal earthquake, or just something, before we get our eyes opened.'

Rosie's face held a perplexed expression and she told herself that Mrs Annie couldn't be implying what she thought she was implying, because Robbie was twenty-eight years old, and . . . and he had always been like a big brother to her; at times, almost like a father. And he was rough with her in his voice and manner; he never spoke to her softly as Mrs Annie did. Well, not now, he didn't. He used to when she was little. He would give her piggy-backs then. But during this last year or so there had been times when he had hardly opened his mouth to her. And she knew he had gone dancing with Peggy Morgan and Mary MacKenzie. But of course, Mary MacKenzie was married now. And she remembered a young woman who used to call pretty often and Mrs Annie used to tell lies and say he was out. She was a grocer's daughter, and Mrs Annie said she was after Robbie's blood. She used to think that was a funny thing to say.

But nothing in life was funny any more. For a moment she was sorry that she was going to America because she would miss these two people. She loved them. Yes. Yes, that was the word, she loved them, like she hadn't loved anyone in her own family, not since her mother had died anyway. But she was fond of Helen. Oh yes, she liked Helen . . . Why was she sitting here, her mind muddling all her thoughts?

Annie said suddenly, 'Go on, have a word with him.'

'He'll go for me, the temper he's in.'

'Well, what d'you expect, lass?'

'I expect him to wish me to be happy and to get away from next door. He hates that house as much as I do. In fact, he's hated it longer. I thought he'd be happy for me.'

Annie rose from the table and turned to the stove and she repeated, 'Go on; have a word with him.'

Slowly Rosie rose from the chair and left the room. She knew where he'd be, and she made for the cowshed.

When she opened the door he was standing at the far end, rubbing down one of the animals with a bundle of straw.

'Robbie.'

He turned to look at her.

'I'm . . . I'm sorry if I upset you by saying such silly things.'

'Forget it.' He turned and went on with the job in hand.

'I can't forget it. I . . . I'll likely be going away sooner than ever I thought I would. And no matter what happens I'll . . . I'll miss you. You don't know how I'll miss you.'

'Then why are you doing it?' He had swung round, thrown the straw to one side, and now was close to her, his face almost touching hers. And he demanded again, 'Why are you doing it?'

Of a sudden she couldn't answer him. Her throat was full. The tears spurted from her eyes and she gulped as she gasped, 'You . . . you know why. You know why. I just must get . . . get . . .'

'If you want to get away, there are other means of doing so.'

'No . . . no . . . nobody else had asked me to marry . . . them.'

'Oh my God! girl.' He now had his arms about her, holding her close. 'Don't cry, love, don't cry. I understand. I understand.' Then in a whisper he said, 'Nobody had asked you to marry them? Good God! Bloody blind fool! Don't, love, don't cry like that. It's all right, I understand. Yes. Yes, I understand.'

Her tears subsiding, she drew herself from him, saying, 'I'm sorry . . . I'm sorry.'

He looked into her eyes, his voice still quiet. 'All I want is for you to be happy, Rosie. All I've ever wanted, my main aim in life even, since I dragged you down from the tree, was that you should be happy and keep that youthful spirit that made you different from everybody else. And it's still there, I know it's still there. It's concealed at the moment; growing up always does blanket it down for a bit, but it'll come back. You'll see. Wherever you are, in America, or Timbuktu, it'll come back. Come on now! Don't start again, 'cos Mam will knock me block off for upsetting you. You've had enough upsets lately. You want a little happiness. Believe that, Rosie, believe that's all I want for you, to be happy.' He now just stopped himself from adding, 'And me along with you. Oh yes, and me along with you.'

He put an arm around her shoulders and led her out of the cowshed and back to the house. And in the kitchen once more he said to his mother, 'You haven't guzzled the last of that hard stuff, have you?'

'What d'you mean?' she came back at him; 'I don't guzzle any of it. But I could put me name to who does.'

'Well, let's drink to America, eh? Let's drink to America.' He smiled at Rosie, then turned to his mother, and he thought for a moment that she too was about to burst out crying, and he bawled at her, 'Don't stand there like a stuffed dummy, woman! Go and get the bottle.'

As Annie lifted the half bottle of whisky from the dining-room sideboard, she bit tightly on her lip and said to herself, 'Annie MacIntosh, you've got a son in a million.'

The sight of Beatrice entering the drawing-room wearing her best dress brought Rosie to her feet, saying, 'Oh, you do look nice, Beatrice. I've always liked that frock; it suits you. And thank you for getting dressed and for the tea. My goodness! In the kitchen, you would think there was a party, the things that Cook's done. What time is it?'

Beatrice looked at the clock. 'Ten minutes to three,' she said. 'I hope he's a gentleman who keeps to time.'

'Oh yes, he is. That's part of his work, making appointments and arranging board meetings and such. He says he feels like a Parliamentary Secretary at times. He made me laugh yesterday when he said he's always the bridesmaid but never the blushing bride.'

'Your hair's hanging over your cheek.' Beatrice put out her hand and, with a finger, she lifted the strand of curling

97

hair from Rosie's face and placed it behind her ear. It was such a tender action that Rosie leaned swiftly forward and kissed her sister on the cheek. Then sitting down, she murmured, 'I'm nervous, you know. This is going to be a formal meeting, isn't it?'

'Well, sort of.' . . .

Three o'clock came.

Half-past three came.

And now Rosie, making for the door yet again, said, 'He must have missed the train, or perhaps he was unable to get a cab from the station. I told him to take a cab.'

'There is plenty of time. Sit yourself down. There's nothing spoiling; Cook won't brew the tea until he comes. Come and have a chocolate.' Beatrice held out the box of chocolates, and Rosie dutifully took one, although she wasn't very fond of chocolates. But she held it in her fingers as she watched Beatrice eat the cream, then pick up another before she laid the box back on the table. And she forced herself to say, 'You'll lose all your appetite for tea if you go on eating those sweets.'

'It's odd,' said Beatrice, 'but they never interfere with my appetite . . . Do come and sit down, dear. You're getting on my nerves, walking around.'

It was ten minutes to four when there was a ring on the bell, and they both rose from the couch. And as Beatrice stroked down the skirt of her velvet dress and adjusted the waist, she put out her hand and checked Rosie from making for the door, again saying, 'Frances will see to it, dear. Now, calm yourself.'

They heard voices coming from the hall; then the door closed, and presently there was the tap on the drawing-room door, and Frances entered carrying a salver on which lay a letter, and she looked from one to the other before handing it to Rosie, saying, 'It's for you, Miss Rosie.'

Rosie took the letter, broke the seal, then read:

My dear Rosie,

It is most unfortunate, but I have been called back to London and must leave straightaway. I don't know what this means in regard to my future in America, but I shall let you know later what has been decided.

I hold you in the deepest affection.

Believe me. Always.

Teddy.

She stared at the sheet of paper.

No 'my dearest'. No 'I love you'. 'I love you'.

No 'how I hate having to leave you'.

She couldn't understand it. This wasn't like Teddy. She had kept his letters: they were warm, loving, even passionate. In a way, they had, she felt, kept her from utter despair during these last few months.

Automatically, she handed the letter to Beatrice, saying, 'I . . . I can't understand it. I . . . I really can't! Yesterday—' She stopped speaking. She could not describe his attitude of yesterday, at the thought of their being married and going to a foreign country: he had been as excited as a young boy and full of talk about America and the life there. But, of course, as he had warned her, they didn't like young men getting married before taking up a post there. However, he had felt sure it would be all right. But as he hadn't yet put that question to his superiors, this recall to London could have nothing to do with his request to be married before leaving the country.

After Beatrice had apparently read the letter twice, she said, 'To say the least, I think it's very bad manners.'

'It . . . it must have been urgent, else he wouldn't be recalled.' Rosie had risen to Teddy's defence immediately. 'He's not the kind of man to be rude. In fact, he is too formal. That is part of his position. He meets so many people he has to be formal. He explained it all to me.' She suddenly sat down on the couch. And now she asked herself how long she would have to wait for an explanation. He wouldn't see his superiors until tomorrow, then he would have to write to her and she wouldn't receive the letter until the next day. That was two full days to wait after she got over today. She didn't know how she was going to bear it.

She looked at Beatrice wearing her best dress; and she had gone to all that trouble about the special tea, and she knew of the special effort she would have had to make to be nice. She said now, brokenly, 'I'm sorry, after all the trouble you've gone to . . .'

'Oh' – Beatrice's tone expressed her concern – 'please, please, don't worry about me, just because I put on a decent dress. With regard to the tea . . . well, we have to eat anyway. It was all nothing. But I'm sorry that you are disappointed. It's very odd. Sit down and I'll ring for tea.'

'No, no. Please don't, Beatrice. I couldn't eat anything at the moment; not even drink tea. I'll go out for a while.'

As she turned away Beatrice said, 'Where are you going?'

Rosie did not answer. She walked slowly towards the door until her sister's voice came at her, the tone more recognisable, 'You're not going next door to tell them, are you?'

Rosie turned and looked at her. 'Yes. Yes, that's just what I'm going to do. I was going there in any case, after tea, to tell them about the arrangements, so I'll go and tell them there aren't any arrangements.'

'You know I don't like you going there so much, so why do you do it?'

'Because they are my friends. They have always been my friends, and always will be, no matter what happens: and, I'm sorry to say, Beatrice, you can do nothing about it. I'll always visit them as long as they're there to visit.'

After a pause during which they stared at each other over the distance, Rosie turned and went out, closing the door quietly behind her. And now, going to the hall cloakroom,

100

she gathered her old coat and woolly hat, and from a rack at one side of the room she picked up her overshoes. This was the outfit that she always wore when she had to scale the wall. Yet she knew she wasn't going to scale the wall today, she was going by the front way . . .

Five minutes later, when Annie heard the tap on the kitchen door, then saw the figure standing there in what she termed 'her old disabelle', she exclaimed loudly, 'Why, what's the matter, girl? I thought you were—' but her voice was cut off by Robbie's. He had risen quickly from the table where he had been eating his tea, and he cried at his mother. 'Will you get out of her way and let her in? What's the matter with you, woman?' Then turning to Rosie, he said, 'Something gone wrong? I thought . . .'

'May I have a cup of tea?'

'Yes. Yes, hinny, two, three cups. Come and sit down by the fire.'

There was no more conversation until Rosie had drunk a cup of tea. Then looking from one to the other, where they were sitting on the settle opposite, she said, 'He didn't come, but he sent this.' She took the letter from inside her blouse and handed it towards them.

It was Robbie who read it first, after which he lifted his head and looked at her but said nothing, then passed the letter on to his mother. But after she had read it she said immediately, 'Odd business. Do you usually get letters like this from him? I mean, in this sort of tone?'

Rosie's head drooped before she said softly, 'No.'

'Well, there must be a reason for it all,' Robbie said; and he repeated, 'Well, there must be a reason and, as he says, he'll let you know in a couple of days. It was likely written when he was worked up and found he couldn't come and see you. You say they've got an office in Newcastle or some connection there anyway. And it's also distantly connected with the Government, isn't it? You never know about these things, the intricate business that goes on.' He got up from the settle and dropping onto his hunkers before her, he took her hands in his and said, 'It'll all work out. If I know anything, that fella thought the world of you. Yes, he did. So, as I see it, it's nothing to do with his . . . well, personal wishes, it's something that's come up in his business.'

'You think so?' Rosie looked into the deep brown eyes that held a tender expression in them and, her voice breaking, she said, 'The worst of it is, I was getting Beatrice on my side. She had put on her best dress, and had ordered a lovely tea. And she was putting on . . . well, trying to be very pleasant.'

'That's unusual for her.' Robbie grinned at her now.

'Yes. Yes' – she nodded at him – 'Which makes me feel all the worse, that her good intentions and efforts were to no avail.'

He rose from his hunkers, saying, 'I'll have to be away down. Betsy's foal's coming.'

Rosie's voice and expression changed as she said, 'But it isn't due for a fortnight, you said.'

'Yes, I know. But she came in this afternoon and I knew there was something wrong. Well, she practically spoke to me, so I think that she needs help. I might have to get the veterinary man, too.'

'May I come down with you?'

It was Annie who put in, 'You've got your good frock on, lass,' at which Rosie turned to her, a half smile on her face as she said, 'But I've got my old coat with me, if you've noticed.'

'Yes. Yes, you have.'

Robbie helped her into her coat; then handed her the woollen hat and for a moment his hands indicated that he was going to put it on her head; but they paused half-way and he handed it to her.

Annie said nothing the while she watched her son pull on his coat and cap, then put his hand on Rosie's elbow as he led her out of the door. And a strange thought ran through her mind as she combined two quotations and put them into her own words, 'God's slow but He's sure, and He takes a number of sideroads His miracles to perform.'

It was three days later when Rosie received the letter. She took it up to her bedroom to read, and its contents so stunned her that, after reading it for the third time, she let it flutter to the floor. And she sat on the bed staring ahead of her, until a tap came on the door. It was opened by Beatrice. 'What is it, dear?' she said. 'You've had news?'

Rosie looked at her, but she couldn't speak for the moment. She pointed to the floor, and Beatrice picked up the letter. But before she began to read it she walked to the window as if to see it in better light. Then, after a moment, she said, 'Oh, dear me! Dear me! I'm so sorry,' but instead of turning about to look at the dejected figure sitting on the side of the bed, she addressed the window again, saying, 'Dear me! Dear me! What a thing to happen.'

Only then she turned towards Rosie, saying, 'What are you going to do? But then, what can you do? I . . . I never expected this of him.'

She handed back the letter to Rosie who, after glancing at it again, folded it into four and put it back into its envelope. Then she too rose and walked past her sister and out onto the landing. And this very action puzzled Beatrice, because her sister wasn't crying.

As she followed her along the landing, she said, 'Where are you going, dear?'

She had received no answer before they reached the bottom of the stairs, but there, she added, 'Let us have a cup of coffee, and . . . and talk this thing over.'

For the first time Rosie spoke. 'What is there to talk over? Nothing could be more final than this letter.' She lifted it up almost in front of Beatrice's face. In fact, Beatrice retreated a step in something of alarm, as she muttered, 'You . . . you mustn't take it too deeply. These . . . these things happen. Come and . . .'

Her words broke off as she saw Rosie walk towards the cloakroom, and she cried at her, 'No! No! You are not going next door, not in that state.'

She now rushed across the hall and attempted to pull the old coat from Rosie's hand, at the same time crying, 'It isn't right! Have some dignity, girl. One doesn't go and spread one's troubles far and wide like a common individual.' Her voice now dropped as she continued more rapidly, 'You expect that from the servant class. But remember who you are; and you belong to this house . . .' Beatrice could not have sprung back quicker had a gun been pointed at her, for Rosie's voice was menacing as she yelled, 'Damn the house! Blast the house!'

Then Beatrice found herself almost tumbling back against the grandfather clock as Rosie's arm thrust her away. It was characteristic of Beatrice that she turned and steadied the clock with both hands, then looked up into its brass face as if for assurance that it had not been damaged, before she turned again on her sister, who was now at the front door. But such was her astonishment and more so her amazement when her emotion was streaked with fear and she asked herself if it could be possible. But her mind refused to explain why it was asking this . . .

When Rosie neared the cottage, it was to see Robbie leading the horse and cart through the gate, but he didn't notice her until he left the animal to go back and close the gate.

He looked at her open-mouthed for a moment before he said simply, 'Rosie!' Then going close up to her he looked into her face. He didn't ask any questions, but said, 'Go on

104

in; I'll be with you in a minute, after I've put her in the stable.'

In the kitchen Annie greeted her in a similar way. On a high note, she said, 'Rosie! What is it?'

Annie watched the girl drag off her coat and hat and throw them across one of the kitchen chairs, then go and sit in the corner of the settle, from where she stared into the fire.

When Annie sat beside her, Rosie did not turn to her, and so, in an embarrassed and troubled fashion, Annie muttered, 'I think what you're in need of, girl, is a cup of tea.' And at this she got up and went about the process of making it, and nothing was said until Robbie came hurrying into the room and to the settle where, sitting beside her, and in a manner quite different from that of his mother, he said, 'Come on now; spit it out! What's happened? You've heard from him?'

For answer Rosie put her hand into the pocket of her house dress and, without looking at him, handed him the letter.

What he read was:

My dear Rosie,

I don't know how I am going to begin this letter, for my mind is in such a turmoil, so I had just better state facts. I have been told by the powers that be that they do not allow their younger members to marry before they have established themselves abroad. On the other hand, I know that they couldn't really stop me from marrying. But should I take this step, then I would be deprived of promotion. Moreover, I could be sent to some outlandish country, and in a very subordinate position. From what I understand, they have already made arrangements for me to go to America to fill in this particular post that has become available by the unexpected death of a young member of the firm.

105

So, you will see, my dear, the position I'm in. By the time you receive this letter I shall be on my way to America. But I can assure you, it is with a sad and heavy heart, for you know, Rosie, I have always held you in deep affection. But now, under the circumstances, it would be unfair and unwise to hold you to any promise. As I've explained above, I don't know what my future holds in this new country. Try to understand my situation, Rosie. All I can say is, I am too troubled to write any more, but will always hold you in the highest affection and will never forget our friendship. Forgive me and think kindly of me, if you can, my dear Rosie.

Teddy.

Robbie sat there, the letter still in his hand, until Annie's voice demanded, 'Well, what does it say?' And at this he handed her the letter. After reading it, her response was the same as his; silence, until she suddenly burst out, 'The dirty swine of a man! I've heard plenty of tales about jilting but never read one. He's a . . .'

'Mother!' It was a deep throaty demand, of which Annie took no notice, for she cried at him, 'I'm not going to keep me tongue quiet, not for you or anybody else. I'll say again, he's a swine!' She now hurried to where Rosie was sitting, her head bowed, and thrusting her doubled fist under Rosie's chin, she brought her face up with a jerk and, looking down into it, she said, 'He's not worth your spit.'

'Shut up! Mother, will you?' Robbie was on his feet now, pulling her away from Rosie's side. 'And listen to me for once. I feel there's something wrong here. There's more in that letter than meets the eye. I've met that young bloke, and that letter and he don't match.' He now turned to Rosie who was staring up at him and he demanded, 'How was he when you last saw him? I mean, in his manner.'

How was he? She turned her head to the side as if thinking. He had been wonderful, excited. After they had eaten they had walked in the park and he had pulled her into the shadow of some bushes and had kissed her. Oh, how he had kissed her. But nevertheless, besides all that, she knew he was ambitious. She knew he wanted to go to America, his heart was set on it. He had told her that one star had dropped from heaven into his hands and that was her. And now another had been presented to him, an opportunity he imagined would never happen for years. A position in America was a goal that those in the office were all aiming for. They would be jealous, he had said; there would be a lot of talk. But God had spoken: he had raised his head and wagged his finger and had said, 'You're to go to America, Golding. Fitzsimmons has unfortunately died and you are to take his place as soon as possible.'

She looked back into Robbie's eyes, as she said, 'He . . . he was as usual, kind and—' her head bowed again as she muttered, 'loving.' Then as if her tongue had become loosened, she turned to Annie and went on, 'And I was excited, too. Oh, Mrs Annie, I was excited at the thought of leaving next door. Never having to live there again. To get away from Beatrice. And yet' – she shook her head quickly now – 'she's . . . she's been quite good over it. More kind than I ever thought she would be. But' – her voice sank – 'nevertheless, she's still Beatrice, and she has her house. Oh, yes. Yes' – her voice rose as she nodded from one to the other – 'her house. She's mad about the house. I told you, didn't I? Her and her feather dusters, and one mustn't do this and one mustn't do that. It isn't done. It isn't done. What isn't done?' She got to her feet now. 'It isn't done to be happy; it isn't done to want to be loved; it isn't done—' Her voice rose to a crescendo, and then there came a sound like a wail from her lips and the tears spurted from her eyes.

107

They had their arms about her pressing her down onto the settle again, sitting one on either side of her. And through her tears and sobbing, she cried, 'I . . . I want to die. I . . . I feel dirty, used. He said friendship.' Her head was wagging on her shoulders now and neither of them could keep her still. 'It wasn't a friendship, it was a courtship. It was, it was, it was a courtship.' She turned her face towards Robbie, and he nodded back at her, saying gently, 'Yes, dear, it was a courtship all right, a very good courtship.'

A knock came on the door and a voice said, 'Anybody at home?' And when it was opened Annie sprang up from the seat, saying, 'Oh, come in, Doctor. You're very welcome at this point, I can tell you.'

'What is it? What's the matter?' John laid his bag on the table and pulled off his overcoat as if he were at home, then went to the settle and sat down next to Rosie. And, looking across at Robbie over Rosie's bent head, he enquired, 'What's happened?'

'Oh, quite a deal, Doctor. Rosie's had . . . well, a great disappointment. I'd like to talk to you about it.'

'No! No!' Rosie's tear-stained face came up now and, looking first at one then the other, she said, 'Let it rest! It's finished! It's my business! Yes, it is, it's over.'

'Yes. Yes, dear, it's over. Don't worry. All right, we won't talk about it. Come on, dry your eyes. Could you do with a cup of tea, Doctor?'

'I could that. Two cups, in fact. I've not been near the surgery since I left it this morning. I've been looking for a place for Mother, as I told you, and my feet are worn down to my knees. I'm going to get a horse and trap. All right, all right, you did tell me I should have one ages ago.' He rose from the seat now and walked behind the settle to where Annie stood at the end of the table pouring out the tea, and he jerked his head backwards, and in answer Annie reached out and picked up the letter from the end of the table and silently handed it to him.

As he read she watched his expression alter in disbelief, and then he shook his head slowly and muttered, 'No, no! Not him.'

'Aye, him.'

'I can't believe it.'

'Nor can I. Worst of all, nor can she.'

He put the letter back on the table, then went and sat by Rosie again and, gently turning her face towards him, he said, 'Had you any inkling at all of this?'

Her crying had eased but the dry sobs in her throat checked her speaking, and she brought out slowly, 'No . . . no, Doctor. None . . . none.'

'He did send her a note three or four days ago to say that he couldn't come to tea,' said Robbie. 'He was to ask the head of the house' – there was a sneer in his voice now – 'for her hand, but instead he sent a note to say he had been called back to London and would write . . . and now he has written.'

They both turned to look at Annie, who was standing before Rosie now, saying, 'Come on, lass, into the sitting-room; there's a fire on in there. I don't know why I put it on, it being only Saturday. Just to keep the room dry, I suppose, or I must have known it would be needed. Come on.'

Obediently, almost like a child again, Rosie allowed herself to be led from the room, which left the two men facing each other.

'What d'you make of it, Doctor?'

'I just don't know. I can't make it out, only that it's very strange. It seems a funny business.'

'You said it there; a funny business. But I mean to get to the bottom of it. That fellow was in love with her as much as . . .' Robbie stopped and walked towards the fire, and John said quietly, 'You were going to add, "as much as I am".'

Slightly indignant now, Robbie said, 'I wasn't going to say that.' But then he asked softly, 'Does it show so much?'

'Well, I've been here nearly two years and I guessed I would have been a blind man if I hadn't seen how things were with you. If you had had any sense you would have spoken before now.'

Robbie swung round on him. 'She was a child. I'm ten years older than she is. I've carried her around since she was a baby, when her grandfather used to bring her over here every day to talk with my dad, but leave her to me. She looks on me as a brother; sometimes, I've even thought, as a father, but in no other way.'

'You've never given her a chance. The Scot in you has put bristles on your tongue, like all your clan. Oh' – he flapped his hand – 'don't get on your high horse.'

'I wasn't getting on any high horse, Doctor, but . . . but I didn't think it showed like that.'

'Well, it doesn't to anyone else. You have very few visitors here. The Mackays, too, look upon her as a child. The Robsons . . . well, if I'm not mistaken and he dared risk it, Harry would have showed his hand before now. But there was you to get over, and then the lord of the manor, next door. And now he's gone, you feel the lady is worse. Her one aim in life is to achieve prestige. And yet, you know, I feel sorry for her. She's got another side altogether. I've found that out of late, too. Quite a softer side, at least where Rosie is concerned. She is fond of her and if it wasn't for her mania for the house and its surrounding grounds, she could be quite attractive and interesting.'

'Well, I've yet to find that out, Doctor.'

'Yes, and so have other people. But we've all got two sides, you want to remember that. One of yours you've kept dark for too long.'

'And what d'you want me to do about it now?' asked Robbie. 'She'll never get over him, or if she does the insult

110

will remain with her the rest of her life. She'll feel inferior. Women that are let down always feel inferior.'

'Then you'll have to bunk her up, as you call it, won't you? and stop making her feel inferior.' The doctor's tone changed now as he said, 'Give her time, and let her see how you feel in little ways.'

'I doubt if there's any chance of that, Doctor. She'll see me as her brother, her big protective brother until she dies. We've been an escape hole for her and we always will be. I'll see to that. Anyway, what's brought you here today?'

'Something else that you're blind to. Your mother's cough. Oh, yes, she says it's just a tickly cough, but that could easily become bronchitis, I'm telling you, and in this dreadful climate of yours. Of course, I don't suppose it's as bad as Scotland, but it's bad enough in the winter.'

Robbie's tone had changed to one of deep concern. 'Mam's got something wrong with her chest?'

'No, not something wrong, but she certainly will have if she neglects it as she has been doing. She's got a bad cough and she wheezes. Haven't you heard her? What's more, she goes out in all weathers. Well, that's up to you, you'll have to see that she doesn't. And I'm leaving some medicine and stuff to rub in and you've got to see that she takes that.'

Robbie bowed his head before saying, 'Funny, things that are under your nose you never notice unless they smell.'

'Well, there's something I smell, too, and it's about that letter. I have a cousin in the administrative Civil Service. It is just possible he could throw a little light on the matter about marrying and so on. Meantime, my advice to you, Robbie, is to forget about the brother and fatherhood and make yourself even more indispensable to her than you are already. You follow me? If you don't you must be blind.'

Robbie gave a 'huh!' of a laugh and said, 'You're about as tactful as a charging rhino, Doctor, but I'm partial to charging rhinos.'

111

# 3

'I hate doing it, but I've got to let the annexe . . . Did you
hear what I said?'

'Yes, Beatrice, you've got to let the annexe. All I ask now
is why you didn't let it before you dismissed Connor and
Taylor?'

'I dismissed them because they're unnecessary now. Since
the land has been sold it's taken away a lot of the bottom
ground, and William Connor was well into his sixties and
really past his work, as was Luke Taylor. Anyway, in my
opinion, he has been unnecessary for a long time. As far as
I can gather he spent his time trimming trees.'

'But you were against cutting down the staff.'

'Yes, yes; I know I was, but circumstances have altered
things.'

'Then why didn't you get rid of one of the girls when
you were at it? You don't need both a housemaid and a
parlourmaid, there are only two of us to be waited on.'

Beatrice's voice was near a bark as she cried, 'I can do
that, too, and put you in their place with a duster. You need
to do something.'

Rosie had been sitting on the couch in the drawing-room,
but now she was on her feet, crying back at her sister and
vehemently, 'You'll never get me working inside here. You

and your house! That's all you think about, the house. And don't say to me what you're going to put me to. You'll put me to nothing more. For two pins, if it wasn't leaving you on your own I'd go to Helen's. I'd be welcome there.'

'Oh, yes. Oh, I know you'd be welcome at Helen's. If Helen could do me a disservice, she would do it.'

'Helen wouldn't do anybody a disservice. You've been jealous of her all your life. You hate the idea of her being happy and living above the level you've always aimed at, lady of the manor. She's a natural lady of the manor.'

'One of these days . . .' Beatrice looked to be on the point of choking; then she flung round and hurried from the room.

Rosie sank back onto the couch again. She couldn't stand much more of this. She asked herself why she was putting up with it; but she knew: being made as she was, she knew that if she left Beatrice here on her own she'd be worrying about her all the time, for she had no-one in the world to care for her. She hadn't kept a personal friend over all these years. It seemed that, except for her father, she had never needed a friend. And now, since he had gone, she was adrift. Oh, what was she going to do about it? She was sick at heart; sometimes she felt she was of no consequence. Teddy . . . oh, don't let her think of Teddy, it would drive her mad. Months now and she hadn't heard a word from him. That indeed had been a letter of rejection. That was the word that bored into her all the time: rejection. What she would have done if she hadn't had Robbie and Mrs Annie, she didn't know. And the doctor, too. Yes, he was nice. She had met him a number of times when he visited next door. Funny, calling Robbie's place 'next door', when it was in all ways a thousand miles away from this house. When she was there she had to force herself to return here.

Well, that's where she would go now.

The thought brought her swiftly up from the couch and she went from the room into the hall. But as she went to pass the main door, which was wide open, she saw coming up the steps the man she had just thought about. And she went towards him, saying quietly, 'Have you come to the wrong house?'

'No, I don't think so.' His voice was as quiet as hers, almost a whisper. He was smiling at her. 'I've come in answer to the advert.'

'What? You mean, for the annexe?'

'Yes, for the annexe. I couldn't believe it. Is she really letting it? It does mean here, doesn't it?'

'Yes, it means here all right. And you are the first applicant, I think. Come in. Come in.'

As he stepped over the threshold his eyes lifted to where Beatrice was now descending the stairs, and there was certainly no welcome in her expression, nor in her voice as she said, 'Good-afternoon, Doctor.'

'Good-afternoon.' He did not add, Miss Beatrice or Beatrice.

She was now asking plainly, 'Did someone call you?'

'Yes. Yes.' He moved his head twice, his manner now as stiff as hers. 'A newspaper advert called me. I understand you are letting part of your house?'

He watched her expression slowly change, then resume its former stiffness as she said, 'Not part of my house, Doctor, merely the annexe.'

'Well, your annexe.'

'Do you want to take it, the annexe?'

'Well, it all depends.'

'Yes, yes.' She nodded at him now. 'But I must tell you straightaway that I would not allow a surgery to be held there.'

'I had no idea of setting up my surgery in there, Miss Steel' – his tone now matched hers – 'or of living here

114

myself. I've been looking for a house or private apartments for my mother for some time now.'

'Oh, well, I'm sorry.' Her words were apologetic. 'I merely thought . . . well, you understand.'

He did not come back politely to say that he did understand, but turned to look at Rosie where she had been standing the while, and she said, 'It really is nice, a house on its own,' and Beatrice's glance towards her sister was almost soft as she said, 'Yes, as Rosie says, it's a house on its own: it has a private entrance and a conservatory, rather small, but leading to its own garden.'

He was looking at Rosie now and he seemed to see the appeal in her eyes, as there surely was, for she was thinking, If his mother comes there and she's anything like him, it will be someone else to talk to. And he'll be popping in. I hope he'll take it. She looked at Beatrice now, saying, 'Will you go through the house or shall I get the key for the front door?'

'Oh, we can go through the house.' Beatrice was even smiling now. And as she walked ahead, saying, 'Would you like to come this way?' John and Rosie exchanged glances and followed her.

He had never been in this part of the house and he was amazed at the size of it. They were in a broad corridor now with doors going off one side and tall windows the other, facing out onto the garden.

When they entered the small hall with a flight of stairs going off it, Beatrice pointed to them, saying, 'That leads to the servants' quarters, but this is the side door to the annexe. Of course, it can be locked permanently from the other side.'

They had now turned down a short passage at the end of which was a grey panelled door, and as she pushed it open she stood aside to allow him to enter. But he put his arm out for her and Rosie to precede him.

115

He now found himself in a quite large, square, tiled hall and Beatrice was saying, 'It's a very compact little house. There are only eight rooms altogether; three are bedrooms upstairs.'

He put in here, 'I'm afraid my mother would have to sleep downstairs as she suffers rather badly from rheumatism.'

'Oh, that could be easily arranged, because this was once used for children and there is a small bathroom downstairs.'

She led the way to a room across the hall, saying, 'This is the sitting-room.'

He stood in the middle of the room looking about him. He was really amazed at the furnishing and the comfort it expressed.

'It's a lovely room,' he said.

Beatrice made no reply but said, 'Come and see the dining-room.'

The dining-room was much smaller but the table was large enough to seat six. Again he was amazed at the quality of the furniture and the curtains.

Next, as she thrust open another door, she said, 'This would make a lovely bedroom for your mother. You see the long windows open out to the conservatory and there's the garden beyond. And the three bedrooms above, which I will show you, needn't be wasted, because she could have her friends to stay.' Beatrice's smile was broad as she turned to Rosie, saying, 'That's what Grandpapa built it for . . . well, I mean to house a family.'

It was Rosie who put in now, and she was smiling, too, the sad plaintive smile he had come to know, 'Mother's cousin used to love to come and stay. But they had four children and they were four too much for Grandpapa, because there was no controlling them.' She turned now and looked at Beatrice, saying, 'Remember? they used to slide down the bannisters and into the hall. We were all younger than they were but we emulated them as much

116

as we possibly could. And Marion nearly broke her neck. Remember the day? Pandemonium.'

'Yes. Yes, I remember.' The sisters were nodding pleasantly at each other. 'I remember distinctly Grandpapa laying down the law to Grandmama.' Beatrice turned to John now, saying, 'You see, they were here for nearly two months in the year. And Grandmama's brother-in-law was an architect, and it was he who set the ball rolling. And Grandpapa took it up like a new toy.' Now she added on a laugh, 'The only toy he had that wasn't of the Army.' Then, her tone changing, she said, 'It cost quite a bit to build, but the sad thing about it, at least the annoying thing about it to Grandpapa was that it was used only for two years after it was built, for my great-uncle, I understand, got another bee in his bonnet: it was called emigration and he whipped the whole family off to Canada, of all places.'

John was laughing now, as he said, 'And it's been unused ever since?'

'Oh no. No.' That tone of dignity was back in Beatrice's voice. 'At one time when we were young—' she glanced towards Rosie; then on a forced smile she said, 'well, children, there were lots of parties. Grandmama seemed to have friends and distant, very distant relations in all parts of the country. You find that when you've got a big house and there is free hospitality. Some of them, I recall, stayed for weeks on end. And that's why the kitchen was added. Come.'

She turned about and Rosie and John followed her into the hall and to the far end where a door led into what was quite a small kitchen, but one that was adequately fitted.

'As you can see,' Beatrice began, 'it isn't very large. My cook would turn her nose up at it. But it's adequate.'

John noted that Rosie had turned her head away. Whether it was the words 'my cook' or not, he didn't know. Beatrice had gone to the small range and was saying, 'It's very cosy in here when the fire's on. Even when the fire isn't on, it's a nice little room with its cupboards and such and all the kitchen utensils. And now, I suppose, you would like to see the garden.'

He admired the garden, having walked through the conservatory to reach it, and as he looked to the wall of fir trees at the far end, he thought to himself, She would love this, it's the very thing. He turned and, looking straight at Beatrice, he said, 'Well, we had better get down to business, hadn't we?'

'You like it?'

'Oh, yes. Who couldn't like it? I'm sure my mother will.'

Beatrice paused before saying, 'She will have her own furniture, I suppose? But that will prove no difficulty, as we can store everything here up in the attic.'

'Oh, I'm afraid she hasn't any furniture; it went with our house when she sold it. You see, she had the idea she was going to live with her cousin for the rest of her days. But I'm afraid that didn't work out. And so for some months now she has been living in a guest house, while I have been trying to find a suitable place.'

'Well then, would you take it as it is?'

'As it is?' His voice rose. 'Oh, yes! Yes, definitely.'

She seemed to be relieved at this and her smile was wide again as she said, 'Well then, I'll be pleased to lease it to you. It will be on a lease, of course.'

'Oh, of course.' His head was bobbing.

'The only proviso is that your mother must come and see it first.'

'Oh, indeed, yes. Will tomorrow be suitable?'

'Any time. Any time. Would you like a cup of coffee?'

'I would. Thank you.' Then turning to Rosie, he said, 'You don't know what a relief this is. For months past I have been in and out of people's houses, not including the empty flats, all advertised with pleasant outlooks which, in

118

most cases, meant the front street, or' – he pulled a face now – 'a cul-de-sac of course, where there was no traffic.'

They were all smiling as they returned to the main house again, and as he took in his surroundings, he was thinking that this was the kind of place he himself would have liked, but without the surgery of course. Anyway his mother would surely love it and it would be a refuge for him at times. He wondered what she was asking for it and so he put it to her now, saying, 'Well, we had better get down to business, hadn't we? What are your terms?'

He saw her wet her lips and give a little cough before, hesitantly, she said, 'It . . . it would work out, that is on a lease, at two pounds ten shillings a week.'

He kept his eyes on her while being aware that Rosie's head had jerked round towards her. 'But if you are taking it as it stands,' she went on, 'I . . . I would have to ask another ten shillings a week, for, as I said, there's . . . well, as I said, as you can see, it's ready to be lived in, even to the linen. There are plenty of sheets and towels in the linen cupboard on the landing. And all that is needed to bring in . . . is food.'

He raised his hand and smiled as he said, 'It's quite all right. It's quite all right; I'm agreeable, and I'm sure my mother will be. You see, it will be in her name.' But even as he spoke he was thinking, Three pounds a week. He could have mortgaged a fine house just outside the town with four acres of land and it wouldn't have cost him much more than three pounds a week, if that. But still, it was a lovely place and he could see it would be ideal for his mother.

He not only saw Beatrice sigh but heard her sigh, then she said, 'Well, let us get that cup of coffee.'

Once more she was leading the way and before Rosie followed her she turned and looked at him and gave a small shake of her head which said quite plainly, You're being robbed; but as he would say to her later, 'I couldn't afford it, but my mother can. She's pretty well off.' Then he let her know he understood the meaning of her look by patting her shoulder and pursing his lips at her.

They were now in the drawing-room of the main house, and as he looked about him in admiration he was not to know that the decision he had just made would change the course of his life.

# 4

'Three pounds a week!'

'But wait till you see it; I keep telling you.'

'Yes, you do, but it's part of a house – an annexe is part of a house. I wanted something private.'

'This is as private as you'll ever get in this town or hereabouts, unless you go right into the country.'

'That means more than one hundred and fifty pounds a year. At that rate you could buy a decent house within three years. And if it's as grand as you say . . . well, I don't want anything grand, just comfortable.'

'Mother.' He turned to her as they walked up the side drive, having left the cab at the gate. 'I'm telling you, if you don't take this you'll have to take on the house-hunting yourself, because I haven't the time or any more patience trying to find exactly what you want.'

Her voice was now apologetic as she said, 'I'm sorry. I'm sorry, dear. I know I've put a lot onto you lately, but I just wanted something . . . Oh! why don't I shut my mouth until I see it, as you've been saying all along. You say it has its own private entrance not connected with the house?'

'Yes. Yes, and this is the private drive to it. Woman—' he again stopped in his slow stride and, looking down into her face, he said, 'if she had asked five or six pounds I would

121

still have thought it was worth it and exactly what you need and it will be a way to get some of that money out of the bank's coffers. Anyway, the interest alone on some of your bonds will pay for the rent, and more.'

'All right, all right; let's see this wonderful place.'

As they went through an ornamental gate and into the garden, she stopped and said, 'Oh, well, this part's all right; very nice indeed.'

He said nothing more but led her round the corner and to the front of the annexe, and there her impression was definitely favourable.

After unlocking the door he stood aside and let her enter the hall. And as she muttered, 'Oh, yes, very nice, very nice indeed,' the sitting-room door opened and there stood Beatrice, a vase of flowers in her hand. And she spoke immediately, saying, 'Oh, I'm so sorry. I thought you wouldn't be here for a while and I . . . I was arranging a few flowers to brighten things up, and . . .'

He stopped her embarrassed prattle by saying, 'This is my mother . . . Mother—' he extended his hand towards Beatrice as he added, 'Miss Penrose-Steel.'

'How d'you do?'

Beatrice quickly put the flowers down on a side table and, coming forward, she held out her hand as she said, 'I . . . I'm so pleased to meet you, and I do hope you will be happy here. I can assure you that you won't have any unexpected visitors popping in. I'm so used to coming through the house, but you can lock the door on the inside.'

Mrs Catherine Falconer surveyed the young woman. She was seeing her as quite a bonny piece with a nice speaking voice. She was looking older than the twenty-four-year-old that John had suggested she was; in fact, old enough and capable enough to be in charge of such a splendid house, and she smiled at Beatrice as she said, 'Well, from what I've seen so far, Miss Steel, er . . . Miss Penrose-Steel, it has

122

been very impressive and exactly what I would want . . . especially the garden. And I see there's plenty of woodland round. I've always made syrups and jellies from the wild fruits.'

'Oh, that's interesting. Well, you'll find plenty of hips, haws, crab-apples, blackberries and sloes hereabouts. But now' – she looked at John – 'I'll leave you. But would you like a cup of coffee? I'll have one of the girls bring it in from the kitchen. Afterwards, I can assure you, you won't be troubled by anyone from the house.' She smiled widely as she added, 'Not more than you wish.'

'Well, we'll see. We'll see.' The answer was slightly non-committal. But Beatrice, still smiling, turned about and went out.

John now led his mother into the sitting-room, the sight of which brightened her face still further, as did the dining-room and the study, which was to be her bedroom. In the kitchen she put voice to her pleasure, saying, 'Well, I never! I never thought you would come across a place like this for me. Talk about home from home. It's lovely. It's a beautiful little place.'

'Yes' – he nodded at her – 'it is lovely.'

Quickly now she said, 'There's three bedrooms upstairs, so I understand. Why don't you come and park here then?'

His answer was quick: 'No, Mother. I've told you, my business is in the town and I must be near it. What's more' – he smiled now – 'I don't know whether or not lodgers come into the lease. Anyway, you know I'll pop in every day to see you. And by what you've already said, you're not going to be lost for an occupation with all that material to hand.' He motioned towards the window. 'There's only one more thing I've got to say and then it's finished. You'll have to have someone to come in at least two or three times a week to clean for you.'

'I can do that . . .'

123

'No you can't! and you're not going to. There's many a woman in the town who would be only too glad of the offer of a part-time job, when she knows she'll spend most of her time drinking tea and nattering over the kitchen table to the mistress. But one thing I'd advise you, Mrs Falconer, don't go on extolling the virtues of the South to any of these Northern ladies, whoever they are, or you'll likely find yourself in their black books and asked why you don't go back there. I've been told that numerous times.'

'You haven't!'

'Oh yes, I have. When the old boy's been laid up they've looked at me and said, "I want me own doctor. I'll wait until he's about again." They're a hardy lot around these quarters, I'm warning you, and that goes for the mistress of this house.'

'Oh, she seems very nice.'

'Yes, she is at times.'

'You're qualifying it. Have you had a do with her?'

'No, not what you would call a "do", but she can be a madam when she likes.'

'Is her other sister the same then?'

He laughed now. 'Rosie? Oh, no, they're chalk and cheese. And the other two are much the same as Rosie. Yet they are all different; but the lady of this manor is as different again, very unlike the rest of them.'

'Well, from the little I've seen of her, I get the idea we'll get on together.'

'Let's hope so.'

'You seem to have doubts?'

'No. No, Mother. No, I have no doubts, merely just expressing an opinion, because, you know, you're a rough old bird, too, when you can't get your own way.'

There was a tap on the door and it opened and the maid came in with a tray. She smiled from one to the other, then, addressing Catherine Falconer, she said, 'Me name's Janie

124

Bluett, ma'am. I'm the parlourmaid. And may I say, welcome to the annexe. I'm so glad you've taken it, being Doctor's mother.' She cast a smiling glance at John now before she added, ' 'Tis nice to have somebody along here. I've always liked the annexe; it's homely like, ma'am.'

'Yes, Janie, I know what you mean, and I may say I'm very pleased to be here. And thank you very much for the coffee.'

'You're welcome, ma'am.' Janie bobbed her head from one to the other, then turned and went out, her smile wide.

'Now wasn't that nice?'

'Yes, very nice, Mother, but don't expect that every day. You're on your own here. This is a private house and I'm sure Miss Beatrice would like it kept like that.'

'You talk as if I was some nosy old woman,' said his mother now.

'And that's what you are. Oh, come on, drink up this coffee.' He handed her the cup. 'And get that look off your face, because I've got to be away and if you want me to take you back and get your things together, then just don't sip at it as if you were in the drawing-room.'

First, she sipped at the coffee while staring at him; then she said, 'There's times when I wonder why I ever want to be near you.'

'The same here, Mrs Falconer, the same here. Come on now, finish it and let us get off, because there's a lot to do between here and tomorrow, when you start your new life in your private section of the mansion.'

# 5

As Beatrice was about to leave her office, having given the cook her orders for the day, which varied very little from the day before, she had straightened the papers on her desk, then risen from her chair and was about to walk towards the door when it was flung open by a very excited Rosie, holding out a paper towards her and gasping now, as she said, 'Robbie's just shown me. It was in yesterday's paper. Look! Look!' She pointed to the column on the folded sheet, and Beatrice, taking the paper in her hand, read:

'A tragedy occurred yesterday when Sir Frederick Morton Spears and his son Michael were both drowned in a squall in Plymouth Sound. Sir Frederick was a well-known figure in the sailing world, as was his son. Mr Michael Morton Spears, aged twenty-five, was unmarried, and as Sir Frederick leaves no other male descendant, the title falls to his cousin, Major Leonard Morton Spears.

Major Leonard Morton Spears and his wife, Helen, were both staying with Sir Frederick and they, like all Sir Frederick's many friends, are devastated by the news.

The bodies were recovered late last night, and the funeral is arranged for Wednesday, the 3rd October.'

When the paper went limp in Beatrice's hand, Rosie took it from her, saying, 'Isn't it awful! Awful! Helen was always talking about them. She said they were lovely people, and the son, Michael, she thought, was soon to be engaged. She told me so in her last letter.'

'In her last letter? What do you mean?'

'Well' – Rosie tossed her head now – 'you always get angry when she writes to me, so I took it out of the post.'

'How could you, Rosie! How could you! It's to me, the head of the house, she should be writing.'

'Damn the house!' Rosie actually jumped back a step when this exclamation broke from her, and she dared to go on, 'You and the house! That's all you think about. Two people have been drowned. Leonard will be feeling awful, because he told me that he and Sir Frederick were more like brothers than cousins. They were very fond of each other. And now he's gone, and his son's gone, and all you can say is, why doesn't Helen write to you because you are head of the house? Well, I'll tell you why she doesn't write to you. It is because of your reception of her when Father died, and the fact that you've never got on together. But now, what's not going to please you is that, if Leonard inherits the title, Helen will be *Lady* Helen Morton Spears. That will endear her to you more, won't it? Oh, I can never understand you, Beatrice. Never! Never!' On this she swung round and left the room, leaving Beatrice leaning against the side of the desk, her hands gripping the edge.

*Lady Helen*. Her, Lady Helen. Why was it that she should be so lucky? There will be no holding her now. She'd be in society, perhaps presented at Court. Why did all the good things happen to her? Why did nothing exciting come her own way, something that would make her happy? She

127

was only twenty-four, and she considered she had looks, interesting looks. It wasn't fair. Her hands slackened on the edge of the desk and now she almost groped her way back to the chair and sat down. As she laid her head back she told herself to be calm, because when she got herself worked up in such a state, inside it made her feel awful for days. And it became evident in her expression, she knew that.

She now asked herself a question, even quietly, Why did she dislike Helen so much? Her dislike almost amounted to hate. Was it because she was so beautiful? Not entirely. No, not entirely. It was something about her, that ease, that off-hand manner, that laugh of hers. The way she talked, and she would talk to anybody, always the same, to servants, trades people, anyone, just as Rosie did, while she herself couldn't act like that. For one thing, her father wouldn't have liked it. Her father had a sense of class. *Class*. She almost sprang up from the chair now. Why did she keep seeing the good side of him? He had deceived her for years. She used to pride herself on being like him. Now the one wish in her life was that she could be someone different, free and easy in her ways. But she had been more free and easy of late since Mrs Falconer came, and the doctor. Oh yes, the doctor. She could even joke with him: they would laugh together as he teased his mother, especially about the wine making. Mrs Falconer was teaching her how to make wine. She never knew there were so many different kinds that could result from the fruit in the hedgerows: sloe, elderberry, rose-hip syrup, besides all that could be made from vegetables, such as rhubarb and potatoes, and a wonderful wine from parsnips. Cook had been a bit uppish about making jelly from rose-hips, but her ruffled feathers had been soothed when Mrs Falconer had given her a bottle of damson wine and sent her in tasters from the others, too.

Altogether, she had felt happier of late, until Rosie had dashed in with her news. She was finding Rosie an irritant, more so as time went on. Yet, she needed her. She couldn't think of living in the house alone and eating alone.

The only comfort in all this was that Helen and her husband were miles away, and that they were not likely to move . . .

It was later in the day that John visited his mother and the first words she said to him were, 'Have you heard about the sister becoming a lady?'

'Yes, Annie told me.'

'What do you think of it?'

What did he think of it? In a way it had put the final seal on his emotions: it had buried, as it were, all the tender thoughts of her that he still harboured.

'I think she'll carry the title very well. But then she was a lady before, and will always remain a lady.'

His mother stared at him hard. 'You liked her, didn't you?'

He came back at her quickly now, saying, 'I liked them all. They are four unusual sisters.'

Catherine stretched out her feet towards the blazing logs; then, turning her head to look at John sitting on the other side of the fireplace, she said, 'You know, although Mrs Atkinson is a very nice woman, and good at her work, just look at this place; and she says she would stay with me any time I wished, I must admit I would have been a bit lonely at this end if it hadn't been for Miss Beatrice coming in, and with her interest in the wine and things. I think she's what they call up here a canny lass. And I can tell you this, I feel she is lonely under that prim exterior of hers, because when we get talking and she loosens up, there's a warmth there that hasn't been tapped.'

'I'm glad you find her so companionable. What about Rosie?'

'Oh, Rosie's a lovely girl. There are no complications about Rosie. I think she's got over that jilted business,

129

although,' she paused, 'at times she becomes quiet, and there's a sad look comes into her eyes, as though she is lost. At those times I forget she's a young woman and I think I'm dealing with a child, but a hug and a cup of tea usually bring her around. She says I'm like her Mrs Annie next door; she says I'm comfortable.'

He laughed now as he said, 'Yes, that's Rosie. She needs comfortable people.'

'She's a bonny girl and she's always talking about that Robbie. Is there something between them?'

'If Robbie has anything to do about it, there will be some day. But she still looks upon him more as a brother. I don't think she'll come to her senses with regard to him until she realises she might lose him.'

'Yes, that's often the way. Do you know something? I'm looking forward to Christmas.'

'That's weeks away.'

'I know it is, but I can still look forward to it. I think it'll be lovely here: the trees and the garden all covered with snow and a big log fire.' She flapped her hand towards the grate as he laughed and said, 'Don't bank on it. It'll likely be pouring with rain, then the nearest you'll get to it is sleet and a wind that'll cut the face off you.'

'Oh, you are a dampener, aren't you? You're not going yet? You've only been here an hour.'

He looked at his watch. 'I've been here two hours and fifteen minutes, Mrs Falconer, and I could have seen half a dozen patients in that time. Now don't you get up: I'll see myself out. If I can I'll slip along this evening.'

'Do . . . do that' – her voice was soft now – 'and we'll ask her in for a game of cards. She enjoyed that the other night.'

'Yes, all right. I'll do that on one condition, I'm not sticking my winnings in the poor box. You understand?'

'Yes, Mr Scrooge, I understand.'

She waved to him as he went out laughing.

He was in the hall putting his coat on when the communicating door opened and Beatrice appeared. She hesitated, saying, 'Oh, I'm sorry, I didn't know you were here; I didn't think you were expected until this evening.' As she made to step back, he put out his hand and pulled her forward, saying, 'Don't be silly. Anyway, I think she's waiting for you,' and he jerked his head towards the sitting-room door. He was still holding her hand when he put his other hand on top of hers, saying in a low voice, 'Thank you for being so kind to her. She's very grateful for your company, and so am I.'

Her face flushed pink and her eyelids blinking, she wetted her lips before she said, 'It's nothing, the thanks are all on my side. She's taken some . . . well, she's given me a purpose in life and taken some of the loneliness away.'

They stared at each other; then in a very small voice, she said, 'Rosie spends a great deal of her time with the MacIntoshes. As you know, I've never approved of them but,' she swallowed deeply now and added, 'we all need something, don't we?'

His voice was as low as hers as he agreed, 'Yes, Beatrice, you're right, we all need something. And you have my deepest thanks and regards for your kindness to my mother. I have been very concerned about her for some time. You see, her arthritis is worsening and there will likely come a day when she'll need a nurse. She makes herself walk about now, but it can't go on for much longer. Of course, she fights the fact all the time, because she used to be a live wire: she could ride a horse as well as any man, and row a boat, too. She used to go out deep-sea fishing from Rye, when we lived down south.'

'Really?'

'Really.'

'She never speaks of it.'

131

'No, of course she wouldn't. She's still angry inside that it all had to come to an end. Half her time she should be in bed, so you can understand how grateful I am for your attention to her.' His hand slid away from hers; then he was exclaiming almost in horror, 'Oh, my dear! Don't cry. Please!'

'No, I'm not, I'm not. I was just . . . just being silly. It isn't very often I . . . I am thanked for anything I do.'

'Well, if you want my opinion, that's bad manners on the part of many people, I should think. But don't, please, please don't upset yourself.'

'I'm not; I'm just grateful. Now I don't want your mother to see me like this; if you'll excuse me.' She backed from him, her lips quivering as she pulled open the door and went back into the house again, leaving him standing very perplexed.

Well! well! As his mother had said, there was another side to Miss Beatrice Penrose-Steel. Indeed, indeed there was. Her loneliness was a cloak about her, a cloak that she had likely never lifted to allow her sisters to see the person beneath. He put on his hat and went thoughtfully out of the house. Life was full of surprises. Was this why she insisted on being called Penrose-Steel? He was well acquainted with the ailments that attacked the body; but not so much thought was given to the secret ailments that attacked the mind, and so often loneliness was one of them.

# 6

'It'll do you good to get away, lass,' Annie was saying.

'Yes, it'll be nice to see Helen again, and she wants me to see the house before it is sold. It's much too big for them, she said; but it's a lovely place on the river.'

'And you're travelling with her friend, you say?'

'Yes, I remember her. A nice young woman. Helen used to spend a lot of time at Col Mount. I once went there on an errand years ago. I don't suppose it's changed all that much. But it's a beautiful place. Gets its name from being in a pass between two hills.'

'Is she coming here for you?'

'No, we're meeting at Newcastle station. I think she's moving, too. She lost her husband a little while ago.'

'How long will you be staying?' put in Robbie.

Rosie turned to him, where he was sitting at the end of the table, and said, ' 'Til the New Year, which will make it about a fortnight altogether.'

'What did Miss Beatrice have to say about that?'

'Oh' – Rosie now looked from one to the other – 'not as much as I had thought she would. She doesn't, of course, like me going down to see Helen, and I was expecting to be faced with a battle. But she just said, "Well, you know what I think, but you don't take any notice of me." '

'Is that all?' Annie's eyebrows were raised.

'Yes, that's all, Mrs Annie. But she's been different of late, I must say. She's got a new interest now since the doctor's mother has taken the annexe. In fact, she's never out of it.'

Annie's lips formed the words, 'Oh! Oh!'

'What do you mean, oh, oh?' Rosie asked, with a smile.

'Just, oh, oh. Is there not an ulterior motive there?'

'You mean the doctor?'

'Yes. Who else would I mean?'

Rosie did not answer for a moment but she looked at Robbie and then shook her head and said, 'Oh, no,' which wasn't convincing even to herself, and Robbie put in, 'Why not? How old is she now, twenty-four? And he's what?'

The question was put to Rosie, but she shrugged her shoulders and said, 'I don't know about him. Thirty or so, I should say. But I can't imagine . . .'

'Now don't you say you can't imagine anybody falling for her,' – Annie was wagging her finger at her – 'men do strange things, especially to people who are kind to their mothers.' And she laughed now as she looked at her son; then on a high note, she said, 'Isn't it about time you did some strange things, too? What about cocking your cap at Battling Bella? She's just been widowed for the third time.'

As they all laughed at this suggestion, Robbie flapped his hands towards his mother and said, 'Surprise you if I did, wouldn't it? Desperate men do desperate deeds. And she's got five bairns, and two of them are ready for work. Yes, it needs thinking about. Just think of the help I'd get in the yard.'

As Rosie looked at these two friends and listened to the silly back-chat, she thought, I'd really rather stay here for Christmas. But then, no, it's too near Beatrice; and it will be lovely to see Helen again. Then a strange thought interrupted her thinking: Beatrice and the doctor? No. No. He's too nice. He . . . he wouldn't want her. Then again a thought: But she

134

had been different of late, hadn't she? Nicer, kinder. And . . . and if it did come about, it might make all the difference to life in the house. And if it made her happy . . . But the doctor, he's . . . he's really too good for her. And why should she have someone like him when she herself had been jilted by Teddy? Oh! Teddy. The name now no longer revived a feeling of love, but more one of hate. She had received no word from him, nothing more since that final letter. There were times, even now, when she could hardly believe it and thought she must be dreaming. But no, she wasn't dreaming. She had been spurned. That was the word, an old-fashioned word, she had been spurned, rejected, thrown aside. And it had done something to her, for she would never again feel young or gay. She did laugh at times, especially when she came over here: this house was a refuge; these two people had saved her life. Well, if not her life then her sanity.

'Do you visit the doctor's mother often?'

'Yes. Yes, I'm always popping in on her. She's a very nice old lady, very jolly, but she's crippled with arthritis, yet she still gets about. She's made piles, I mean, bottles and bottles of wine these last weeks. She said they're all going to get drunk at Christmas. She's shown Beatrice how to make the wine. She wanted to show me, but . . . well, I wasn't interested.'

'You're catching the ten o'clock train in the morning; so I'll run you in.'

'Oh, that's nice of you, Robbie. Thank you.'

He turned about now and without another word pulled his cap and coat from the back of the door and went out.

As she herself stood up to leave, Annie remarked, 'You'll meet a lot of different people at Helen's. That'll be another kind of world. Who knows, you might come across the one you like.'

It was almost with a bark that Rosie turned on her, saying, 'I won't! I won't and I wouldn't. I . . . I'll never

135

believe anybody again, not in that way. Never! D'you hear Mrs Annie? never!'

'Never's a long time, lass. Never's a long time. I know how you feel, though, but stranger things have happened. Time will tell. It seems it could be happening to Robbie; there are two lasses after him again.'

Startled, Rosie said, 'What! After Robbie?'

'Why look so surprised; he could marry any day if he had the mind,' to which Rosie said nothing, she only stared wide-eyed at the older woman.

# 7

Frances Middleton set the large tray down on the table with a clatter, saying, 'Well, they've done justice to that I must say. And they're as merry as church bells; laughing their heads off.'

'Well, so will we be,' said Cook, 'when we get through these three bottles,' she pointed to the dresser, 'because it's good stuff the old lady makes, although she did warn me it's very new and needs to stand for some time. My! I slept like a log last night after those couple of glasses.'

'It's because you mixed them, Cook,' said Mary Simmons. 'Me dad says that's what makes you drunk, mixing them, more than the amount.'

'These are home-made wines, miss know-all, not the stuff your dad drinks.'

The kitchen maid bowed her head slightly, but Janie Bluett winked at her, saying, 'Well, we'll see what happens later, at least to me, because I'm havin' one of each, and the sooner the better. So, let's get cleared away and settle down to a night of it because the missis is quite set in there, I can tell you.'

'There's a change, if ever I saw one.' Frances Middleton nodded her head. 'I've never had a thank you out of her since she took over, until these last few months. And now she

137

actually asks you to do something, not tells you. When I took tea in this afternoon for her and the old lady, she was laughing her head off. It was a sight to see, I can tell you.' . . .

At this moment Beatrice was again laughing her head off as she said, 'Oh, I can't believe that, Mrs Falconer.'

'You can, my dear, you can. He there, sitting grinning like an idiot now, went upstairs and wrecked his room. He even threw his toys out of the window, all because I wouldn't let him go on a day's outing with—' she now shook her head and looked at John, saying, 'what was it? the Boys' Brigade, or the Band of Hope, or something? He was only six at the time. It was no use trying to knock into his head that you had to be invited, that it was only special children that went. We lived in Tunbridge Wells at the time, and the trip was to Hastings and he had been to Hastings a number of times before that. And then there was the time he was sent home from school for kicking a boy on the shins, and the parents came to the school and complained. But I was for him that time; he wasn't ten and this young lout was twelve or so, and a bully.'

'Mother! Mother! Will you shut up? And put the corks in those bottles, or I shall start reminiscing, or perhaps recalling the story of a young lady who dived off the end of Hastings pier in little more than her knickers.'

'I didn't! I didn't! It wasn't like that at all.'

'Yes it was. And what you need now is a very strong coffee.'

'Oh, I'll tell the girls.'

'You'll do nothing of the sort.' John stabbed his finger down at Beatrice who was about to rise from the couch. 'I'm the only steady one on my feet; I'll make it. And Mother—' he turned now and his finger was again wagging to where she sat in the deep armchair to the side of the fire, and he said, 'No more tasters, d'you hear? I'm on duty in the morning at half-past eight, and I know what

138

your potions do to my head. I've had experience of them before. So, leave the corks where they are. Now, I mean it.'

'All right, all right. We'll see about it after we've had the coffee.'

After he had left the room there was silence for a moment or two. Then Catherine Falconer said quietly, 'It's been a lovely Christmas, hasn't it? I've never seen him so relaxed. I think it's because he's got me settled in this lovely little house.'

Beatrice did not answer for a moment. She raised her eyes and looked at the ceiling and in a thoughtful voice she said, 'It's the nicest Christmas I've had since . . . well, since I was a child. Even when they were alive, my mother and father, there was always Helen and Marion and Rosie. They were always so gay and laughing, and somehow I was never able to join in. I don't know why. At times I felt I had no-one belonging to me, except Father. And then to find out all that.'

'Now, now forget it, my dear. Forget it.' Catherine pulled herself painfully to the edge of her chair, saying again, 'Forget about the past. You can never cure the past. Just think of the future. You're a bonny young woman . . . a bonny lass, as they say up here.'

Beatrice quickly pulled her head up from the back of the couch, saying, 'You think I'm bonny?'

'Yes. Yes, I do. You're very presentable.'

'I'm . . . I'm putting on weight; I eat too many chocolates.'

'Well, the cure for that is to stop eating chocolates. Ration yourself, and look to the future; you're young and have all life before you.'

'Yes, I will. I will.'

'What will you do?' John was asking the question as he appeared carrying a tray with three cups of coffee. But it was his mother who answered him, saying, 'Never you mind. Just let's have the coffee, and we can pull out the corks again.'

'Oh no, you can't, Mother. I mean it.'

'We'll see, we'll see . . .'

They drank their coffee. They had one more glass of wine, parsnip this time. They talked, at least Catherine did, recalling the days in Tunbridge Wells, and Rye, and Hastings, and trips to Eastbourne and Brighton. Then after a time, when she sat for a while with her eyes closed, John said, 'I think you're for bed. Anyway, I want to see you tucked up before I leave.'

'Yes, I think you're right. It's been a long day and a lovely day.' She looked from one to the other and repeated, 'A lovely day.' And as he helped her to her feet and handed her her sticks, she said, 'Now leave me alone; I can manage.'

Beatrice was on her feet too, saying, 'May I come and help you?'

'Oh no!' The protest was loud. 'That'll be the day when I need somebody to help me to take my clothes off. Goodnight, my dear. See you in the morning.'

'Good night, Mrs Falconer; and thank you.'

'You've nothing to thank me for, my dear, the thanks should be from me. Now you sit yourself down.' She jerked her head towards her son. 'Give me fifteen minutes and I'll be all tucked up.'

'Very well; fifteen minutes.'

They both remained standing watching her hobble from the room; then John, turning to Beatrice and holding out his hand said, 'Come and sit down.'

He did not actually touch her but she looked at him a moment before taking her seat again at one corner of the couch while he dropped down onto the other end and, lying back and stretching out his legs, he said, 'I've never seen her so happy and contented for years. She missed my father terribly, and I couldn't fill his place.'

'Oh, you fill her life now.'

140

He turned to look at her. She, too, was lying back and looking relaxed. He had never seen her look so relaxed and, could he say, happy? Over these past months he had got to know her in a way he would never previously have imagined. The young madam he remembered appeared to have never been. Yet, he was well aware it must still be there, but her better nature, which hadn't been given rein, had now come to the fore and made her into an attractive, pretty young woman. Yes, and she *was* pretty. She hadn't a figure like her sisters, for both Helen and Rosie were sylph-like; Marion perhaps had been inclined to plumpness, as was Beatrice herself, but it was a rounded and attractive plumpness. Above all, he would never have imagined he could grow fond of her, but he had. She had been so kind and thoughtful to his mother, too; and his mother's opinion of her was that she was a first-class girl.

She broke into his thoughts by saying quietly, 'I don't think I'll ever experience another Christmas like this.'

'Why not?'

'Oh, I don't know. It's been exceptional, in all ways. I imagined there would be just Rosie and me, and she would be spending most of her time next door, and . . . and I'd be on my own. When Grandpapa and Grandmama were here, and Mother and Father, and Helen, Marion and Rosie, I used to think I wouldn't mind being on my own. The house always seemed packed with people. Sometimes I longed to be on my own, but . . . but not lately.' Her voice was very low now, and she brought herself upwards to the edge of the couch and pressed her joined hands on her knees. And, her head turning slowly towards him, she said, 'Do you know what it's like to feel lonely? Not only lonely, but one alone, and out of it?'

He, too, had hitched himself upright and, after a moment's thought, he said, 'Not lonely in that way. But, you know, Beatrice, there is a feeling of what I call aloneness in most of us. There are parts of us that are empty and need to be filled—' he shook his head now, he couldn't voice the word love, but in a hesitant way he went on, 'until it's filled with something, companionship, affection. I'm . . . I'm sorry, Beatrice, you have felt like this. I never guessed. Then no-one knows what goes on in another's mind. But don't be sad, or you'll spoil the day.' He put out his hand and laid it on hers now, and he recalled that he had done this once before and that it had made her cry; and it was doing the same again, for her eyes were bright with unshed tears. Hitching himself closer to her, he exclaimed, 'Oh! my dear, dear Beatrice. Please! If Mother sees you've been crying she'll kill me.'

'It's all right. It's all right. It's . . . it's just because I'm happy. I . . . I feel needed now' – her eyes were looking into his – 'I . . . I have a friend in you.'

'Oh yes, Beatrice, you can rely on that.' He was shaking her two closed hands between his own now. And when a voice from deep within him said, Careful, careful, he answered it loudly, Why? She takes care of Mother. She's kind, and I'm fond of her. Yes. Yes, I've grown fond of her. And what else is there for me? The past is dead. Very dead. In fact, it was never born; at least, it was never given birth; it was strangled by time in just being too late. So what is there for me? Who do I meet at old Cornwallis's dinners? His married contemporaries and their wives, with dizzy young daughters, sometimes a settled spinster. And he must say he preferred the spinster to the dizzy ones, especially the sixteen-year-old one, who had developed all kinds of ailments to take her to his surgery, until he had the option either of actually being rude to her or of putting the case to Cornwallis. He chose the latter, after which her visits ceased, only to learn that the young lady in question said she hated Doctor Falconer, and that he didn't know his job and nobody should go to him. Such were the passions of youth.

But here he was facing a different case altogether. Beatrice was a very presentable young woman. Moreover, she was the

142

owner of this beautiful house, even though it was mortgaged to the hilt. But apart from what she could offer, there was herself. She was thoughtful, as her attention to his mother had shown. And she was good company. She was surprisingly well read, which must have developed from her loneliness and feeling apart from the others. Of course, she still had the traits of her father showing in her; and she had a feeling for land, and definitely for the house.

'I've . . . I've embarrassed you.' Her voice came to him softly, and he shook his head and vehemently denied her statement by saying, 'Embarrassed me? Don't be silly, dear. It's the reverse, you've . . . you've made me think, and . . . and of the future. But there' – he dropped her hand and shrugged his shoulders – 'I know what my future is: I may have my own practice one of these days and that's as far as it will ever go. No honour or glory for me. Anyway, you only get those when you start cutting people up and you take out the right parts and manage not to leave any instruments inside.'

They were both laughing now, their heads almost together. But her next words took the smile from his face as she said, 'I wouldn't mind if you hadn't a penny, now or at any other time.'

There was a long pause before he said, 'Oh, Beatrice.' Her head was drooped right down on her chest now as she muttered, 'I . . . I can't help it. It's . . . it's the way I feel about you. There.' Her head came up and the tears were splashing down her face now, and her voice was thick, as she muttered, 'This kind of thing is never done by young ladies. But . . . but as I said, I can't help it. I . . . I don't suppose I would have had the courage if it hadn't been for—' she gave a wry smile and pointed her thumb towards the table on which were a number of bottles and glasses. 'But . . . but please, forget it. At least we'll both forget it by tomorrow morning. As . . . as long as you'll be my friend, that . . . that will be enough.'

143

He had his hands on her shoulders now and his voice was quiet, as he said, 'Beatrice. Look at me.' And when she looked at him, he said, 'Would you marry me?'

Her eyes were screwed up tight: the tears were streaming from her eyes and she was unable to speak as his arms went about her, and she fell against him.

'It's all right, my dear, it's all right.' As he stroked her hair he felt a surge of feeling sweep through him. He couldn't put a name to it. It wasn't passion. Was it love? It was something. Compassion, perhaps. Yes. Yes, compassion. But even more than that. Pity? . . . Well, no, no. She wasn't the kind of person you could pity. She was too strong and . . . and she loved him. It was good to be loved. Oh yes, it was good to be loved. He held her closer, and when she actually moaned, he lifted her face from his shoulder and put his lips on hers. And at this her arms went round his neck and she returned his embrace with such fervour that he felt humbled at the feeling she was expressing. A moment later they were standing apart and he was wiping her eyes, as he said, 'Well, if Mother's weakness has brought this about, let us drink to it, eh? We'll have parsnip this time; it isn't so potent.'

As he was about to move from her, she said, 'You might be sorry in the morning.'

'No, no.' He shook his head. 'I'm not drunk. It takes a lot of that stuff to get me over the top. I've been seasoned to it from a boy. I admit it damps down the worries of the day, but drunk? No. And tomorrow morning I'll just feel the same.'

'Oh John. You'll never know what you've done for me.'

'You'll likely have to pay for it, my dear. I'm bad tempered, I'm taciturn, I'm unstable, at least in my times, coming and going: as my mother has always told me, I'm never to be found five minutes in the same place.'

She now dabbed her face with her own handkerchief as she smiled and said, 'I'll put up with all that, dear.'

144

And she knew she would. No matter what his foibles were, she would welcome them, because he would be hers. Her husband. She would be a married woman, a wife. She suddenly thought of Helen and a wave of emotion, not untouched with fear, swept over her. Yet, at the same time she knew an elation. Helen was married to a man twice her age, and she knew now as she had known then, that her main object in marrying Leonard had been to get away from here, and from her. Yes, from her, because there had never been any love between them. But now *she* was marrying someone younger, good looking, attractive and a doctor.

As she watched John pouring out the parsnip wine she had a great longing for it to be morning, for his reactions next day would confirm that it was no dream and he wasn't regretting what had happened tonight. On this thought she stiffened. She wouldn't let him forget. He mustn't, he had given his word, he had. She closed her eyes for a moment and told herself to be calm.

'To us.' Her eyes sprang wide. She took the glass from him and smiled as she repeated softly, 'To us,' while the words in her head were loud, ringing. 'To us. To us. Oh yes, to us.'

# 8

Looking back, Rosie remembered the shock she received when, in the New Year, she had returned home to be met by a radiant Beatrice. She recalled how first she had been surprised by the happy expression on her face, and of the gaiety in her voice as she had welcomed her back. Then later, in the study, Beatrice had poured out her news. At first she had made no response to it, and the old Beatrice showed itself when she cried, 'Why are you looking like that? Why shouldn't I be engaged?' and she had spluttered, 'N–n–no reason at all, only it's . . . a shock, a surprise.'

'That John . . . the doctor, should love me?'

The doctor love her? Rosie recalled she had almost said the words out loud, except that she would have changed the word, 'her' to 'you'. She had again stammered, as she said, 'We – well, it – it's so unexpected. I mean, I never knew you loved him.'

'There's lots of things about me you don't know.'

'Yes. Yes, Beatrice, you're right there.' She had nodded at her, then added, 'But I am glad for you.'

The rest of the conversation had been stilted and she had gone upstairs and changed her clothes. And when Beatrice saw her in her old coat and hat, which meant she was going next door, she had looked at her and said flatly,

146

'What has happened makes no difference to my opinion of our neighbours and your constant visits there,' to which she had answered briefly, 'It makes no difference to me, either, Beatrice.' . . .

Both Robbie and Annie had welcomed her back so warmly that she felt she was really home. But when Mrs Annie said to her, 'Now give me your news of Helen,' she had replied, 'I'll deal with my visit and Helen later; first, I'll give you the doorstep news.' And when she had told them, they both stared in disbelief and said, 'The doctor and Beatrice?' with Robbie further remarking, 'He's such a sensible fellow. When did this happen?'

'From our brief snatches of conversation, I understand it was on the evening of Christmas Day.'

'He must have been drunk.' Annie had bobbed her head. 'That's it. And let me tell you, lass, you can get drunk, more drunk on home-made wine than the real stuff. I should know.' And she had bobbed her head again as if there were a story behind her words.

'Well, there's one thing for sure,' Rosie said; 'she'll be no longer on her own and needing me; and so I shall get myself work of some kind.'

'Work?' Robbie had turned on her. 'Work? What kind of work can you do? You'd have to go to one of these secretarial colleges or something like that to learn.'

'I wouldn't go to a secretarial college, I would go on a farm. I've had enough experience here, haven't I? She looked from one to the other. 'I have dealt with horses, cows, pigs and all the lesser breeds, haven't I? for years now. So, don't you think I'm qualified to get a job on a farm?'

Robbie and his mother had looked at each other, and Robbie then said, 'Aye, yes; you've had plenty of experience, with a couple of horses, a couple of cows and a couple of pigs.'

And at this she had put in, 'And don't forget your main

trade, cabbage, onions, carrots, leeks, the lot on the ground, besides the stuff clinging to the wall.'

The response to this had been that both Robbie and his mother laughed loudly. And after a moment Rosie's voice joined theirs; and then she said, 'Well, you see what I mean?'

'Yes. Yes, lass, I see what you mean.' Annie sat down at the other side of the table and she said, 'I'm not making this up.' She glanced over at her son now, asking, 'Am I?'

'If you're going to say what I think you're going to say, no, you're not making it up, Mam.'

Again Annie had looked at Rosie, then said, 'Only yesterday, he there' – she nodded towards her son – 'was making enquiries in the market to see if there was any young fellow he could take on as a helper, an apprentice, sort of, you know. That's right, isn't it?' She had again looked at Robbie, and he nodded at Rosie, saying, 'Yes, that's quite right. We're not making it up; in fact, I've got two young fellows coming to see me today. If you stay long enough you'll meet them. But what Mam's trying to say is, there could be three applicants. D'you get me?'

Rosie, so to speak, got him, and her face brightened and she said, 'Really?'

'Yes, really. You see, as I've only the two horses and they're inside most of the winter, that field down there, half of it at least, is wasted. So, the idea was to grow more. The town's spreading: they'll take as much as I can give them and pay my price. The land that's being built on now used to be allotments. Well, what d'you say?'

'Oh, I'd love that,' said Rosie. 'Oh, yes.' And she thrust her hands across the table towards the older woman and, gripping them, she said, 'It would be a relief to be out of the house all day and just have to go back there at night. And she surely won't put up much resistance to it now. Anyway' – she shrugged her shoulders – 'she's different. It shows in her face. I know she's twenty-four, and an oldish twenty-four; but today she seems younger than me.' And now smiling at Robbie, she said, 'And will I be paid? Well, of course I'll be paid, but how much?'

'Huh! It's started' – he nodded at his mother – 'the money business. That's what one of them said to me in the market, "How much?" Well, miss—' his eyes on her again, his face took on a dark stern look as he said, 'it all depends on your capabilities, Miss Steel. If you come up to expectations you'll get ten shillings a week to start with and your grub. And I'd like to bet that's twice as much as your sister pays her cook.'

Rosie did not come back at him with any jocular remark but, looking down towards the table, she said, 'You know, I've never had any money of my own; everything used to be bought for me. I was sometimes given a shilling, but that was for a birthday, to spend on sweets. However, since Father died, there has been nothing. She . . . Beatrice, reluctantly paid for my train fare to Helen's and I had nothing with which to buy Christmas presents. I felt awful. But Helen was kind. Helen is kind, always was. I . . . I would have loved to stay down there, and I could have, only they are going to Switzerland: Leonard is not well, he's had to come out the Army, and he has to spend some months there. And you know what?' As she now looked from one to the other her eyes were moist as she said, 'Helen gave me five pounds before I left and they had given me so many presents at Christmas.'

'Don't cry, lass. Don't cry. Anyway, you'll always have Helen. And although we are poor substitutes, you've got us.'

Rosie's lids blinked rapidly and she said, 'Oh, yes, I've got you both. And you know something? I wouldn't be here without you; I would have run away, done something quite stupid. You know I used to be airy-fairy, mad-hatter, more

149

like a boy than a girl, but a dreaming one, I was always dreaming. But no more, no more.'

When her head drooped again Annie said briskly, 'Well, if you're going to start work, miss, there's no time like the present, and we're not going to pay you for sitting there guzzling tea and eating me best scones. They were for the tea, anyway. Now, come on, get yourself up and let's get outside.'

That had happened on the day she had come back. But now this was another day: Beatrice's wedding day, and John's wedding day.

John stood facing Doctor Cornwallis. They were each dressed in a dark suit with a carnation in the buttonhole. It was Doctor Cornwallis who spoke, saying, 'Well! day of execution,' and he took two steps towards John and, putting his hand on his shoulder, he said, 'How d'you feel?'

'Oh, fine.'

'I don't mean physically, I mean mentally; how d'you feel about all this? It was a surprise to me, you know, that you were going to take her on, because I've always found her a bit of a madam.'

'Everyone has two sides, sir.'

'And you've seen the good side?'

'Oh yes. Yes, I've seen the good side.'

'And you're quite happy about all this?'

'Yes, of course.' A stiff note had entered John's voice now.

'Well, that's something to know. And, you know, you're doing yourself well. I know the place is up to its neck in debt, but nevertheless, it's a very fine house; it'll be worth your paying off that debt, boy. It's the best house around here for miles except perhaps for The Hall, and that place is about as warm as a beer cellar. But one thing I would ask you: why didn't you have a church wedding?'

'She didn't want a church wedding, sir; she wanted it done

150

quietly.' He did not add, 'And quickly.' She had seemed so anxious to get it over and done with. And he had wondered if it was because she sensed the doubt in him. However, he had pushed this thought aside; she was a nice girl, a good girl, and he was very, very fond of her. And he had to marry sometime, for he wanted a family. Yes, he wanted a family. And that house was made for a family. He could see it swarming with children. Yes, he wanted a family, and she wanted children. Oh, yes, she had stated that quite openly: she would love children and she didn't care how many.

'Well, time's pressing, so let's away.' Doctor Cornwallis thrust out his hand, saying, 'I wish you all the best in the world, John. We have known each other long enough for me to be able to say two things I like about you: you're straight and you're a damn good doctor. And' – he poked his head forward – 'an uncomplaining one when Betsy Ann' – he pointed to his leg – 'decides she wants a rest; and so, thanks for that.'

'Well, sir, I've . . . I've been very happy here and hope to go on being so and working with you for a long time with Betsy Ann.' They both laughed as the older man pushed him in the shoulder, saying, 'Go on. Get yourself away to a lifetime of worry, frustration and regret.'

As John led the way, he repeated the words to himself, 'A lifetime of worry, frustration and regret.' Oh, no! he hoped not. It would be a happy house, and what was more, his mother was settled for good and delighted about the arrangements, for she had taken to Beatrice and Beatrice to her. Yes, that was one of the main advantages, they had taken to each other . . .

As Rosie looked at and listened to the man behind the desk uttering the words that were marrying her sister to John Falconer, the lovely doctor, as she thought of him, she could not take it in that this was a marriage: everywhere

151

was so bare, so stingy looking and all without God. It was a queer thing to think, but it jumped into her mind: there was nothing religious or holy happening that was tying these two people together for life. It seemed to be over in a few minutes, and then she was kissing Beatrice and then John. And John put his arms about her and again she thought, He's such a lovely man. She did not at that moment add, 'What does he see in our Beatrice?' but the thought was wavering somewhere in the back of her mind . . .

The dining table was beautifully set, but there were only ten people seated around it. Yet, the talk was loud and merry, dictated mostly by Doctor Cornwallis. Then, at three o'clock the coach was at the door and they were waved off to spend their honeymoon at St Leonards, which was a part of Hastings, so well known to John, and which had been suggested by his mother. Apparently Beatrice had no preference for where they spent their honeymoon: as she had laughingly said to his mother, 'It wouldn't matter where it was spent, even in Bog's End, as long as I was with John.' This had caused a great laugh between them as Bog's End was known as the lowest part of Fellburn and ruled by the riff-raff.

# 9

It was half-past seven in the evening. John came through the communicating door from the annexe to meet his wife in the hall. Her face was straight, her tone tart. 'Why must you always go next door before you come home?' she demanded.

'I thought it was all my home.' His voice was weary.

'Don't be silly. You know what I mean, the meal's been waiting since half-past six.'

'And don't you be silly, either, Beatrice,' he said in a sharp tone. 'You know I've told you again and again that I can't walk out and leave a full surgery if the old man is not able to do it.'

'You have an assistant.'

'Well, the assistant's surgery was full, too. And what's more, I had a call.'

Saying, 'Calls. Calls,' she led the way now to the dining-room. He did not follow her, but said, 'Would you allow me to go into the cloakroom first?'

After washing his hands he gazed at his reflection in the mirror. His face had changed over the past eighteen months, he told himself. Had he been married for only eighteen months? It seemed like eighteen years; at least, the last year had. The first six months had been enjoyable

. . . well, up to a point. He had thought he knew it all; at least about sex and marriage. He dealt with the effects of it every day. But he hadn't experienced his own. During the first few months, he had to admit, he had been flattered by her constant desire of him; then it had become a little wearing, finally wearisome; sometimes he would describe her as ravenous. He knew now that she had certainly inherited her father's trait; the one that had led to his death.

Finally, he had turned on her and said, 'No more. No more tonight. I'm . . . I'm a tired man. I do a twelve-hour day, and I can't keep this up.'

He could see her now, her face a beetroot red, and she had jumped out of the bed and walked the floor until he had got up and calmed her down, imploring, 'Try to understand there's moderation in everything,' while at the same time thinking how awful it was having to say this to a woman, and she his wife. But she was eating him up and now blaming him because he hadn't given her a child. He had often thought, rakishly, that her antics should have produced litters not just one or two. He daren't tell her that he hadn't come straight from work that night, but had called in next door to see Annie who, like his mother, was having trouble with arthritis; although not in her state, not to that extent. But Annie had found of late that she had great pain in her left arm from her shoulder downwards and it had put a stop to some of her hard labour. Luckily, Rosie was proving a marvellous helper. He had never seen Rosie looking so happy; well, not exactly happy, that girl would never really feel happy again unless she were to realise how Robbie felt about her. But she loved being in that house. Sometimes he did not see her for a week or more because when she came in she generally went straight up to her room, and he was either in his office working, or with his mother . . . and Beatrice. That was another thing, Beatrice hardly ever allowed him to be alone with his mother. And what was also beginning to trouble him now was the fact that his mother was seeing another side to her daughter-in-law. Only yesterday she had said to him, 'Things aren't right, are they?' and he had answered, 'Oh, just the usual marriage pains,' to which she had replied, 'She's changed . . . changed in all ways. I've never seen her like this.'

'No, of course you haven't, Mother, because you didn't know her before you came here.' He could have enlarged on this by adding, 'You first met her just when she was setting her trap,' for he knew now from his inner knowledge of his wife that she had worked up to that proposal. Oh, yes, it was quite clear to him now. Still, it was done and the thing to do was to make the best of a bad job. Life must go on.

At this moment he was asking himself, 'But how was it to go on like this?' for he was feeling angry inside . . .

They were half-way through the meal when he looked across at her and said, 'Why couldn't you tell me that Helen had moved back here?'

He watched her gulp on her food before she answered, 'Because I didn't think it would be of any interest to you.'

'Not that your sister had come to live here again, and could call?'

'She won't call.'

'No, I suppose not, knowing the welcome she would get.'

'May I ask how you've just found out? You must have been over to the piggeries and talked with Rosie.'

'Yes, I called in to see my friends . . . and Rosie, whom I haven't seen for over a week, informed me that she had told you about Mrs Sylvia Davison selling Col Mount and that Helen and Leonard were buying it.'

'Then can you tell me why she has bought it when he was ordered to Switzerland, from which one could have assumed that he had consumption or some such, and surely this end of the country is no help to a consumptive? Answer me that: why did she buy it?'

'You had better ask her when you see her, or at least I will.'

'You won't!' She had half risen from her chair. 'You won't go and visit them.'

'Why not?'

He'd really had no intention of visiting them; the thought of seeing Helen again would be too much. But he had said, 'She is my sister-in-law, and I liked Leonard very much. Out of courtesy we should visit them; we could go together.'

She banged down her knife and fork on the table and her lips hardly moved as the words came through, 'You know how I feel about Helen, so don't you dare suggest that I . . . that we visit them.'

He was on his feet now, his anger showing, as he cried at her, 'Don't you dare tell me what I can or cannot do. I intend to visit them, so get that into your head, and anyone else I wish to see, when and where I like. I've had enough of your niggling. I think that the less we see of each other for the time being, the better. So from now on I'll make it my business to sleep in the guest room . . .'

Before he could finish she was round the table, crying at him, 'Oh no! No, you won't! You won't show me up in front of the staff.' But then her commanding voice changed to a plea as she said, 'Please John, don't do that. Don't do that to me. I promise you, I . . . I won't be . . .' She drooped her head; she could not put a word to the demands she made on him, that feeling that consumed her, that made her want to bury herself in him, possess him, make him hers alone. Oh, yes, hers alone. Even his feelings for his mother were intruding into her emotions now; he spent too much time with his mother. If she wasn't careful she would come to dislike her.

He put out his hand and touched her shoulder, saying, 'All right, all right. Don't get upset. We'll see. Just leave it. I'm . . . I'm going into the office; I've got some work to do now.'

156

'Please! Please finish your dinner.'

'No, I can't. I'm not really hungry. Ask Frances to bring a cup of coffee in to me.'

She bowed her head again and stood still, and he walked past her and out of the room.

In his office he sat staring down at the neat array of pads, papers, pencils, pens and ink, everything in its place and a place for everything. He closed his eyes, put his elbow on the table and leant his head on his hand. Helen in Col Mount, not twenty minutes away.

His elbow seemed to slide away from him and his head came up with a jerk as he asked himself, What difference does it make? She's married, I'm married, and don't forget she's married to . . . a lovely man. He could hear her voice saying it. And who was he married to? A termagant, and an obsessive one, and an enigma: she was two or more persons – the housewife at which she acted the madam; and at times the talkative, pleasant young companion, a facet of her character which had disappeared long ago into the hungry, passionate, even indecent creature of the night, ravenous at times.

He wanted love, he wanted bodily satisfaction, but there was a limit. He couldn't imagine that this feeling had been inspired in her just by marriage; and yet, she'd had no man before himself. He'd heard of such women, but had never thought to experience the effects of one. He wished he could talk to someone about it. But he couldn't imagine himself bringing up the subject with Cornwallis. It must surely be an inherited trait, one which led back to her father.

But Helen was back and into his mind, too, and he could see himself sitting with her on the top of Craig Tor, and her pointing across the valley to her friend's house. And the sad thing about it then was that they had both been aware they had met too late, just a little too late.

He raised his eyes to the ceiling when he heard muted footsteps going across the floor. She was in the bedroom.

157

He rose quickly and went quietly out, through the hall, down the long corridor and into the annexe.

His mother was in bed. He tapped on the bedroom door, calling, 'All right?'

'Yes, all right, dear. Come in.'

Catherine looked at her son and said, 'Been getting it in the neck again?'

He pulled up a chair to the side of the bed as he said, 'Sort of.'

She stared at him and watched his head droop, and then she said softly, 'Would you like to talk about it? There's something happening and I can't get to the bottom of it.'

He lifted his head quickly and looked at her, Yes. Yes, he'd like to talk about it. And he could talk to her: she was a wise woman was his mother. He asked quietly, 'Have you heard of or had any experience of knowing women who are . . . well, very highly sexed?'

He watched her eyes become hooded, and then she said, 'I was right, then.'

'What d'you mean?'

'I guessed it was something like that. Oh yes, lad, I've heard of women who can eat a man alive. Yet, when you see them during the day they are so pi that you'd think butter wouldn't melt in their mouths. It's only when someone speaks about it that you learn of these things. It's natural with some men; but when it's a woman I understand it's worse. You might not believe it, but your Aunt Ada's sister-in-law was one such. He had to leave her. I suppose you could say it's not really their fault, it's the way they're made.'

There was a long pause before he nodded.

'And it's odd' – her head was wagging now – 'it's generally the quiet ones, the demure ones that turn out like that. Under other circumstances they would likely be on the streets . . . as prostitutes.'

'Oh, Mother!'

'Now don't say it like that, son, but it's true. D'you remember Farmer Braithwaite, and how everybody condemned him because he walked out and left his poor little wife with the farm and three children? Well, he had something on his side as well, he told your father all about it. His work and everything else had suffered because of her.'

'Mrs Braithwaite?' His eyes were wide.

'Yes, Mrs Braithwaite.'

He looked to the side. She had been a smallish woman, not unlike Beatrice in figure and ways; a housewife, bossy. The things you knew and the things you didn't know.

'I would sleep in another room for a time.'

'I told her that, but she got into a state.'

'Well, it might calm her down. She should be taking a sedative, you know, one to knock her asleep.'

'I can't see that ever happening.'

'No, nor can I with her.'

'You know, I thought the world of her at first. But, there you are, you don't know people until you live with them closely.'

She put her hand out. 'I'm sorry, son.'

He stood up and went to the window and looked out into the twilight as he said, 'Helen has come to live at Col Mount, and she knew it and never told me. I got it from Rosie.'

'So did I.'

He swung round and looked at her. 'You knew?'

'Yes. Yes, I knew, and I also know other things, so I thought the less you knew, the better for your peace of mind.'

'Oh, Mother!' He sat down again. And as he muttered something, she repeated it, 'Yes, it's a hell of a life, but it's got to be lived, and you've got to put your foot down. Move to that other room.'

'No,' he shook his head, 'I can't do that yet. She was in a state.'

'Well, it's up to you. But looking at you now, I think what you need most is sleep. So, give me a kiss and get yourself away.'

He kissed her and they held on to each other for a moment. Then he turned and went out and back into his office.

It was after twelve when he went upstairs. She was lying on her side and she appeared to be asleep. And when he lay down beside her she did not turn towards him. And he sighed a deep sigh, but it was some time before sleep overtook him and gave him enough rest to face another day.

For the past two days John had been attending a course of
lectures at a London hospital, and he had just left Trafalgar
Square and was walking towards Regent Street when a
figure he had noticed darting between two cabs came to a
breathless stop in front of him and gasped, 'I . . . I thought
it was you, but I wasn't sure.'

John saw a tall, well-dressed, tanned young man, and for
a moment he did not recall who he was, until the young man
added, 'You're a long way from Fellburn. I never expected
to see anyone from there down here, and . . . and it's my
last day. Well, I leave tomorrow.'

Until that moment John had been unable to recall who
the man was. And then the name hit him. This was Teddy,
Rosie's Teddy; Edward Golding, whom he had first met at
the garden party, on Beatrice's twenty-first birthday. But
this wasn't the Teddy who had ruined Rosie's life. He
had changed. The other Teddy had been more like his
name; young, very young. This one was a mature man.
And now he was being asked if everything was all right
back in Fellburn. And he answered stiffly, 'Yes; when I left
three days ago, things were much as usual.'

His voice low and his face now unsmiling, the young man
said, 'How is Rosie?'

The nerve of the fellow, to ask how Rosie was; so he answered bluntly, 'She's very well and apparently enjoying her work.'

'Rosie working? Is she better then?'

John put his head to one side, saying, 'Better? I have never known Rosie to be ill, except with a cold.'

'You what? You . . . you *are* her doctor, aren't you?'

'Yes, I am her doctor.'

'And . . . and you say she has never been ill?'

'Yes, that's what I said.'

John now watched the young fellow look towards the traffic that was passing thickly on the road, then put out his hand as if to rest it against the shop window, as if he were changing his mind. And now speaking briskly, he said, 'There's . . . there's a coffee shop further along. Would . . . would you mind if . . . if we talked for a moment?'

What John answered now was, 'I have an hour before my train goes. All right.'

Neither of them spoke again until they had entered the coffee shop and taken a seat in the far corner. They had the place almost to themselves; there were only two other customers seated. It was John who ordered the coffee and while they waited for its coming John watched the young man run his hands through his thick hair before he said again, 'You said that Rosie had never been ill?'

'That's what I said, except . . .' but John was interrupted by the young man saying, 'But . . . but twice when I called she had what was supposed to be measles. And then after her father died, I met you and . . . and you wouldn't let me see her.'

'No, I wouldn't let you see her because I had given her a sedative. She needed one. She had just learned the truth about her father's character. He had left them up to the eyes in debt through his women and gambling.'

'But . . . what about the problem she had inherited?'

162

'Inherited? Inherited what?' John watched the young man now grip his forehead with his stretched hand and say, 'The grandfather's sister, the one who died in the asylum. I . . . I saw the letter and . . . and it had been passed on and I couldn't . . .'

'What in the name of God! are you talking about?' John now hitched himself forward on his seat and Edward Golding swallowed deeply as he murmured, 'Beatrice, she . . . she came to Newcastle and . . . and showed me the letter. It related how the old aunt had died in the asylum, the grandfather's sister. It . . . it explained her mania.' He stopped for a moment, wetted his lips, then seemed to be troubled with swallowing before he went on, 'She . . . she apparently had fits and . . . and what I imagined was a . . . well . . . a sort of hysteria that caused her to disrobe . . . I recall that word the solicitor had used, she disrobed, he said and well . . . went tearing around the place. And . . . and Beatrice said that,' he now put both elbows on the table and gripped his head for a moment until John asked very quietly, 'Said what?'

And still in the same position, but in a whisper, the young man said, 'Rosie had inherited . . . and that's why I couldn't see her when I called on those two occasions. She . . . she suggested that because the news would have to be broken to me sooner or later she felt duty-bound to tell me then. As she put it, it would be dreadful for both of us if this happened in America; here, she could have treatment and understanding.'

He now stared at John across the table, but John felt unable to make any comment, and the young man went on, 'You . . . you will remember that Rosie was very gay; in fact, when I first saw her she was up a tree. And she danced about and sang.' Again he closed his eyes. 'It all seemed to fit into the pattern. I . . . I was devastated. I loved Rosie deeply then' – the words had been muttered – 'And I . . . I still do.

163

My heart has been sore for her these past years.' Then, his voice becoming almost demanding, he leaned towards John and said, 'Why? Why? Why would she have done this?'

The reply John could have given him at that moment was, 'Because she's an evil, deceiving woman.' What she had put to this man about Rosie was an evil thing; what she had done to himself was a deceiving thing: she had ensnared him into marriage with a soft side, a part of a character that didn't belong to her. She had played on her loneliness. She was afraid of being lonely, which very likely had been the cause of her determination to separate the young couple and so keep Rosie with her.

The young man was speaking again, saying, 'She made me promise never to tell Rosie the reason for breaking off the engagement, because this would only increase her trouble.'

Suddenly John put his hand across and gripped the young fellow's wrist as he said, 'Come back with me; Rosie is there. She has never got over you, I'm sure. It was a dreadful thing you did, but I can see now that you're not to blame.'

Once more Edward Golding drooped his head and he said, 'I . . . I can't. I'm married. I . . . I had a daughter only a month ago.'

John's grip slackened and fell away and he sat back in his seat and stared at the bent head opposite, and he repeated to himself, 'Married, and has a daughter.' Well, it was a natural thing to do to seek solace with someone else.

'That woman!' The young man was sitting up straight and taut now. 'I could go to her now and throttle her, really throttle her. Why? Why did she do this?'

'Simply because she couldn't bear to be left alone. Likely if you had married Rosie and lived in Newcastle, you would have heard nothing about this, but the thought of Rosie going so far away, and with her other two sisters already cut off from her, apparently she couldn't bear it. But oh, that is no excuse. It was an evil thing to do. Dear God! I'll say it was.'

164

Now, Edward Golding was leaning across towards him and in an intense whisper asked, 'Will you tell Rosie? Will you explain to her? Tell her I . . . I've thought about her every day in sorrow for her—' he gave a shake of his head as if throwing off the word he was about to say, 'disease. At times it was unbearable to think about it. She was so beautiful, so . . . so gay. That was it.' He nodded. 'That's what she stressed, Beatrice, her gaiety, which had been the symptom of the other poor woman.'

'Did you actually read the letter?'

'Oh yes. Yes. She handed it to me first before she said a thing. I tell you I nearly went berserk. But I see now that she had it all planned out. I wasn't to see Rosie. And the fact that I would have to get permission to marry and take her with me all worked in to her plan. And then there was something else. As Rosie seemed so unhappy, Beatrice suggested that . . . well, she was aware of her condition and that's why she wanted to get away from home, thinking that marriage would cure her. The other poor woman had never been married. She . . . she even suggested that her grandfather was slightly unbalanced, which was why he had given the land to his batman or sergeant, or someone. You know, the fellow next door whose son now has the place.'

John closed his eyes and for the moment his thoughts centred entirely around his own condition. He was married to her and she would never let him go, unless he divorced her. And on what grounds could he get a divorce? That his wife was an evil woman, a schemer?

'Will . . . will you do something for me?'

'Yes, if I can.'

'Will you tell Rosie? Will you explain to Rosie? That would ease my mind a lot if she knew the truth of why I seemed to scamper off like a cur. And I can tell you I felt like a cur of the lowest order.'

165

There was a short silence between them before Edward Golding spoke again. And then he asked, 'Is Beatrice still there, in the house? I know she had no money.'

At this, John buttoned the top button of his coat, put his hand along the seat and picked up his hat and case; then, getting to his feet, he said, 'Yes, she's still there. I married her eighteen months ago. The outcome of another of her plots.'

'Oh, my God!' The young man, too, was on his feet now, and he was stammering, 'I . . . I'm . . . I'm so . . . sorry. But . . . but I didn't know.'

'Please! Please! Don't worry yourself more than you have to. I found my mistake out some time ago. Come on, let's get out of this place.' He thrust his hand into his pocket, brought out some loose change and placed it on the bill that had been left on the corner of the table. Out on the street again, they stood facing each other until John asked quietly, 'Are you happy in your marriage?'

There was a pause before Edward Golding said, 'Yes. Yes, in a way, for she is . . . well, she is a lovely girl.'

A lovely girl . . . a lovely man. He could hear Helen using Rosie's words, 'He's a lovely man.' What did it mean; a lovely man, a lovely girl?

He held out his hand now, and when it was grasped, he said, 'You've got your life before you. Forget this end of it. I think that Rosie will eventually find happiness with Robbie . . . Robbie MacIntosh. He's the fellow next door. She's looked upon him as a brother for years, but he doesn't see her in that relationship. And they've been working close together for some time now. So, try not to worry about her any more. Get on with your life. You owe that to your wife and child.'

The young man seemed to find it difficult to speak. When he did, his words were halting. 'In one way I'm glad we met up. But in another, not, because the burden is on you now. I . . . I didn't know, you see.'

'Please! Please! Think no more about that. I'm used to dealing with problems; I'll deal with this one.' As he finished his words, a voice loud in his head cried, 'By God! I will. Yes, I will!' for the anger in him was rising, but it had yet to reach its height.

John arrived at the house in the early evening and took the side drive to the annexe.

His mother was in the sitting-room, reading. Seeing him, she threw the book aside, started to say, 'Hello, dear,' then changed it to, 'What's the matter? What's happened?'

He drew in a long shuddering breath as he stood looking down on her, saying, 'A great deal. First of all, I'm going to lock the inside of the communicating door. I don't want her in here with you, and neither will you when you hear what I have to say.'

'Dear Lord! Sit down, man. Sit down. What is it?'

Very briefly, he gave her the outline of his meeting with Teddy Golding. And when he finished she was sitting with her hand across her mouth, muttering, 'No! No! She wouldn't!'

'She did! Now stay quietly there, and don't distress yourself, at least try not to.'

'She's . . . I told you, she's been different of late.'

'She's always been different, Mother. As she planned Rosie's future, she also planned mine. And I've said this more than once. But there's a limit.'

'John! John!' She called to him as he went to the door, and when he stopped and looked back at her, she pleaded,

'Please! Don't lose your temper with her. Please! Remember, I'm still here, and . . . and I need you.'

He said nothing, but went out and through the grounds and into the front door of the house. Seeing Frances going towards the kitchen door, he called to her, 'Where's your mistress?'

'Oh, it's you, sir. You're back? Oh, well, she's gone down to the bottom land. She's very angry, for the gypsies have gone into the field again. You know, they used to do it, but they haven't been back for some time. She had already been down and warned them, but they took no heed and went into the field and . . .'

She broke off but he didn't wait for her to go on; instead, he hurried down the corridor and into Beatrice's office. And there, pulling open one drawer after another of her desk, he rummaged through the neatly stacked papers. But when he didn't find the letter he was about to leave the room when he noticed a deed box on the top shelf of the alcove near the fireplace. Then he returned to the desk, the middle drawer this time, where he knew her keys were kept, and within seconds he had the box on the table and was taking out one parchment deed after another until he came to a long white envelope. The heading of the letter inside told him it was what he was looking for. After he had read it, he understood how easy it had been for Beatrice to ruin her sister's life.

He returned the letter to the envelope and put it in his pocket, put the deeds back into the box, and returned it to the shelf.

When he entered the hall, Frances was still standing there, and she hurried towards him, saying, 'Doctor, sir, I . . . I didn't tell you—' She didn't add that he hadn't waited to be told, but went on, 'the mistress took a gun with her.'

'What!' He jerked his head in her direction as if he had just become aware of her presence.

'She . . . she was angry, and she took a gun.'

169

He left her at a run, went straight across the lawn, through the gardens and wood to the field that bordered the river. But before he reached it he could hear the yelling.

A yellow caravan, one horse between the shafts, another tied to the back, was being urged back towards the gate by an elderly man and a woman, with two youths and other children all yelling at the figure standing by the tree with the gun poised.

He had approached Beatrice so quickly from behind that he was able to knock the gun upwards before she was hardly aware of him. And then he was wrestling with her. He had no compunction in using his fist to knock her flying up against the tree trunk, where she stood stunned for a moment, her eyes wide and glazing, her face scarlet.

He was in possession of the gun now, and he yelled to the man to stop, then he called, 'Get back! Stay as long as you need. You won't be troubled again.'

They were all silent now, staring at him. 'Thank you, master. Thank you,' the man called. ' 'Twill only be for a day or so. Thank you, and God's blessing on you.' Then one of the younger men led the horse and caravan on to the road, turned it about, and they all re-entered the field.

He stood watching them until they reached the place where the spring water ran into the horse trough and spilt over into a pipe that led to the river. He had heard from Robbie that until the grandfather died the same family of gypsies had come each year, and that he himself had watched some of the children grow up. If he remembered rightly, the old man had had six sons and there used to be three caravans. Now there was only the one, and two box carts which were likely used as sleeping quarters. The old lady was a fortune teller, and they eked out a living by making clothes pegs and baskets, the younger ones going round the doors selling them.

He now turned back to Beatrice and saw her standing away from the tree, her hand on the back of her head.

170

'How dare you!' she yelled. Then again, 'How dare you!'

'Get up to the house!'

Her eyes widened, the colour deepened, if that was possible, then she muttered, 'What did you say?'

'I said, get up to the house! Because if you don't, I'll bring this across your back. Before God! I'll bring this across your back, that's if I don't throttle you.'

She backed away from him: he looked like a madman. All at once she knew a deep fear of him. But when he made another step towards her, she moved, and she was about to make for the wood when he grabbed her arm and dragged her along by the bottom fence until it opened abruptly into another field edging the river. As he made towards the bank, still dragging her, she cried, 'You're mad! You're mad!'

He did not release his hold on her until they reached the river, at which point, lifting the gun by the end of its barrel, he swirled it around his head before letting it fly and into the water. She could not have been more startled if he had tried to drown her. 'That . . . that was Father's.'

'*Shut your mouth*! and get back to the house and upstairs.'

'What?' She was stepping back from him now, one step at a time as if she were measuring the ground, or perhaps to give her enough distance to turn from him and run. And this is eventually what she did do. She ran up over the field and into the wood, and he hurried behind, keeping her in sight all the way.

When he entered the hall, the two maids, Frances and Janie both turned sharply and on the sight that he presented they, too, stepped back; then with awe-filled gaze, they watched him take the stairs two at a time. And when the door clashed overhead they looked at each other before moving to the foot of the stairs and, with their heads cocked to the side, strained their ears to hear what the doctor was yelling. 'You evil, wicked, horrible creature! If your great-aunt's madness was passed on to anyone, it was you.'

171

Beatrice was standing near the head of the bed now, her hands clutching her neck. Then her eyes sprang wide and her mouth became a gape as the light dawned on her: it wasn't her attitude towards the gypsies that had made him mad, but . . . Oh no! Oh no! She was shaking her head now and he came back at her, 'You can shake your head, woman; and at this moment I'd like to shake the life out of you. You're evil. I repeat it, you're evil. To ruin your sister's life. Yes, open your mouth wider. It's unfortunate for you that I ran across Teddy Golding in London. His first enquiry was about Rosie. Was she still at home or – he didn't actually say – in the asylum? For that's where you suggested, like the one mentioned in this letter.' He now pulled the envelope from his pocket and said, 'That's right, sit down on the bed; you're going to need all the support you can get. And why didn't you, when you were on, burn the evidence of the letter you got from the solicitor, eh? You took it to prove to him that your lying, filthy scheme had some foundation.'

He suddenly stopped yelling; the sweat was running down his face. She was staring at him, her eyes stretched so wide they seemed to be popping out of their sockets. Then he broke the heavy ominous silence by saying, 'Marion got out of your clutches. Helen did, too. And Rosie wanted to follow them, to be rid of you, because they knew you for what you were, your father's daughter. And you *are* your father's daughter, aren't you? Because if any woman has inherited whoring instincts, it's you. You should have been on the streets, eating men up like you've tried to do me. You inveigled me into marrying you. I see that now as plain as the scheme you planned to keep Rosie by your side, because you were afraid to be left alone in this mausoleum of a house you're obsessed with. Did you ever think of turning it into a whore shop? Or becoming a madam? because let me tell you, that prim exterior of yours must have been ready to burst by the time you hooked me. It's a wonder you weren't up in the

172

loft with Needler or Oldham. Now I'm asking myself why young Arthur Winter suddenly gave in his notice. I can recall seeing you with him one day in the harness room. When I pushed open the door it nearly knocked you on your face, and the fellow looked not only embarrassed, but frightened. I thought nothing of it at the time, but I have done since. Well, from now on, let me tell you, you'll have to look for someone else to ease your bodily cravings, for I wouldn't touch you again if you were dying at my feet. You smell, you stink. If it wasn't that my mother was in such a bad state and that you inveigled her on the side – oh yes, on the side; I knew nothing about it, or I would have put a stop to it, to pay in advance for a five-year lease on the annexe – I'd be out of here tomorrow. But from now on I live there and don't you dare come near it, or God knows what I may be tempted to do to you; at this moment I want to drive my fist into your mean, scheming face.'

He drew in a long breath, then swinging about, he marched into the dressing-room. Pulling out one drawer of the tallboy after another, he threw his clothes here and there on the small settee and the armchair. He next went to a wardrobe from which he grabbed at his suits. Then pulling open the door leading into the corridor, he let out another yell: 'Frances! Janie! Come here!' It was as if he knew they would still both be at the foot of the stairs. And when, white-faced, they appeared at the door, he said, 'Take as many of these suits and coats and underwear as you can, and leave them at the communicating door leading into the annexe.'

As each girl, with trembling hands, picked up a number of garments, he pulled two suitcases from the side of the wardrobe and began stuffing the remainder of his shirts and underwear into them.

It was some minutes before the girls returned, and when he saw they were visibly trembling, his voice was quiet now as he said, 'Will you take these, please, and put them

173

with the others? I'm just going to collect some books from the guest room. I'll take what I need at present; I can collect the others at any time.'

Neither of them spoke, nor did they make any motion with their heads; and he went past them, into the corridor and along to the end to the guest room where his books were stored on several shelves. They were mostly medical books and the reason why they hadn't been put in the library downstairs was that most of the shelves there were filled with leather-bound volumes; and he had been quick to discover that Beatrice didn't like them out of order, that the whole contents of the room were mostly for show, as were a number of first editions behind glass-fronted cabinets. The old colonel, it would appear, had been a collector but not a reader. And so, his own tattered volumes had been relegated to the shelves in the spare room. He now picked a book out here and there until he had his arms full, then went downstairs.

The house was very quiet. It was as if a death had just occurred. And yes, a sort of death had really taken place, for their marriage was certainly over. And, too, she might as well have killed Rosie as do what she did to her. Although it was now a long time since that happening, Rosie still bore that look of rejection, even behind her laughter. Once his things were inside that annexe, he would go to Rosie and lift that look from her face . . .

It was not more than twenty minutes later when, hurrying along the road towards Robbie's, he saw Rosie approaching. She was smiling as she came up to him and said immediately, 'You're back, then. I thought you wouldn't be home till later. I'm going in to pack a case. I had a letter from Helen today: they'll be back from London tonight and she wants me to go and stay with her for a while. She's very worried about Leonard; he seems to be no better.' She paused, then said, 'Is something the matter? What is it?'

174

Before he answered her question, he said, 'Leonard? What about Leonard?'

'Well, you know he's been ill. That's why they went to Switzerland. For his consumption. But . . . but what is it? Why are you looking like that? Has something happened in town?'

He took her arm, pulled her round gently and walked her back towards Robbie's, saying, 'Yes, something happened in London and . . . and it concerns you.'

'Me?'

'Yes, you. That's what I said.'

'But how? Why?'

'Wait until we get inside. I think Robbie would like to hear this, too.'

She remained silent but her step quickened to keep pace with his. And then, without knocking, he was opening the kitchen door and pushing Rosie in before him to meet the surprised gaze of Robbie and his mother.

It was Annie who repeated Rosie's words now as she looked at John, saying, 'Is there something the matter? What is it? Has something happened?'

'Yes, Annie, you could say something's happened. Let's all sit down.'

Robbie pulled a chair out for Rosie, then sat next to her; but he didn't ask any questions, he just kept his eyes on John. And John now leaned across the table and gripped Rosie's hand as he said, 'You can take that look off your face from now on and out of your heart as well: Teddy never rejected you.'

'What?' It was a small sound, almost a whimper.

'You heard what I said. Your dear Teddy never rejected you. The simple truth is that he was warned off by your dear sister to prevent him from being saddled with a wife who would eventually go mad as did your great-aunt, who apparently danced about naked.'

175

Rosie now drew her hand from his and put it up to her throat and whispered, 'She wouldn't! She wouldn't! Not that!'

'She did, and in detail.'

From then on, John described how he had met Edward Golding and what had transpired.

When he had finished there was utter silence at the table. Even Annie made no comment. Then Rosie asked quietly, 'Where is he now?'

'In London, but he returns to America tomorrow.' He paused before he added, 'He has a wife and a young baby now.'

John watched Rosie's eyes widen, then her gaze drop to the table to where her hands were joined, and her voice sounded steady as she said, 'Well, that doesn't matter any more.' And suddenly lifting one hand, she put it on top of Robbie's, where it was gripping the edge of the table; he grasped it, but said not a word, leaving the expression on his face as he gazed at her to declare his thoughts. Then he turned and glanced at his mother, but the words she muttered were unintelligible.

Then the three of them were startled as Rosie bounced to her feet, saying, 'In a way, she's done me a good turn, but I'll never forgive her for what I've been through. No! I'll never forgive her. She's wicked! Wicked! She always was. I knew she was. That's why I wanted to get away. There was always something in her. If anyone has inherited Aunt Ally's traits, it's her.' She was nodding at John now as he said, 'Yes. Yes, you may be right there. In fact, I think you are right.'

Then she gave a shake of her head as if she were just recognising a fact and said, 'But you are married to her, John.'

'Yes, I am married to her, dear. But you leave me to manage that. I'm going to live in the annexe with Mother until I can find a suitable place, although, as you know, she inveigled her into signing a lease for five years. Payment in advance, of course. In every way, she's a scheming devil.'

176

Rosie now turned to Annie, saying, 'I was about to go and pack my case, as you know, to go to Helen's. Now, if you don't mind, I'll bring the rest of my things here, because I'll not live in that house again with her. I'll . . . I'll stay with Helen for a time and . . .'

'Oh, lass, why d'you need to ask? This is your real home, always has been. Go on and get your cases; Robbie'll go along with you.'

'No. No.' Rosie turned now and looked at Robbie. 'I'll go on my own.'

For answer, Robbie went to the back of the door, took down his coat and his cap, and for the first time he spoke, saying, 'I'll not go in. I have no desire ever to enter that house, but I'll be there to carry your things.'

Rosie stared at him; then turning to John, she said quietly, 'It's you I'm sorry for now; I . . . I feel free. It's . . . it's as if I'd lived all my life under that feeling of rejection and not knowing why, only that rejection makes you a lesser being to yourself. But . . . but you, you are tied to her.'

'Don't worry about that. But get yourself away and finish the business, and then start your new life.' John looked from one to the other.

It was Robbie who answered him: 'Yes, John, we'll start a new life, and not before time. But there's still years ahead of us and we'll make up for it,' and he took hold of Rosie's arm, saying, 'She knows how I feel . . . at long last.'

When they had gone, Annie put out her hand and took hold of one of John's and, shaking it, said, 'I can say in all honesty, John, this is the happiest day of my life. My lad has come into his own at last, and if anybody has worked and waited for it, 'tis he.'

At the front door of the house, Robbie said quietly, 'Try to keep calm. The least said is soonest mended, and this could be the last time you need ever see her,' and Rosie answered him with a small nod of her head, then went inside.

Frances was coming down the stairs and Rosie waited until she reached the bottom before she asked, 'Where is Miss Beatrice?'

Frances's voice had a slight stammer to it as she said, 'Sh . . . she's in her st . . . study, miss, and she's in a bit of a tear.'

'Will you come and help me pack?'

'Pack?'

'Yes, Frances; I'm leaving home' – she looked about her – 'this house for good.'

'Oh, miss; not you an' all, not you an' all.'

'It's got to be, Frances. Will you?'

'Oh, yes, miss. Yes, miss,' and she turned and followed Rosie up the stairs, where, as had happened only a short time before, drawers were pulled open and clothes rammed into cases. And when at last three cases were full, Frances picked up two of them and Rosie the third, and with loose garments hanging over her free arm, without a backward glance she left the room that had been her own since she was ten years old.

Frances had placed the cases at the foot of the tall fellow from next door; then she was stepping back into the hall to take the other case and loose garments from Rosie when, from along the passage, her mistress appeared.

Beatrice's hair was dishevelled and there was a wild look about her. The spring she made across the hall towards Rosie bore out her appearance, for she yelled, 'What d'you think you're doing?'

She pushed Frances to one side and glared at the man standing outside the door, the cases at his feet, before banging the door closed. Then her back against it, she cried, 'What d'you think you're up to?'

'You can see what I'm up to: I'm leaving.'

'Oh, but you're not. Oh, but you're not. I've gone through too much for you to . . .'

178

'Shut up! What you have done is tried to ruin my life with your lying and your schemes. You're evil. You always have been.'

At this Beatrice turned and yelled at Frances, 'Get away! Get away!' And the girl actually ran now, down the hall and through the door leading to the kitchen.

But she didn't close it, and she could hear her mistress yelling, 'That husband, or supposed husband of mine, is a liar: he's told you half-truth. What I did, I did for you, because . . .'

'You didn't do it for me. You did it because you couldn't bear to be left alone in this beastly house. You weren't married then and there was no hope of anyone ever taking you. And I wondered why John had stepped in. But now I know it was through pity for you. Anyway, I have no pity for you at this moment, but in a way, I should thank you for what you did. I have been haunted by the thought of rejection, but now I know where my true feelings lie. I know that I've always loved Robbie MacIntosh, and what's more, I'm going to marry him and' – she was almost screaming now – 'live next door! Do you hear?'

A scream which outdid Rosie's came from Beatrice as she sprang again on her sister, almost knocking her off her balance as she yelled, 'Never! Never! I'll see you dead first. Married to that coarse, ignorant . . .'

'Leave go of me!'

'I won't! You're not going. I'll see you dead first.'

When Rosie's doubled fist came up between Beatrice's hands, which were gripping her sister's shoulders, and landed on her mouth, she was released instantly. But Beatrice did not fall back, she just staggered a little and put her hand quickly up to her face. And when she looked at her hand and saw the blood, she gave a gasp of astonishment. Then it was with frenzied rage that she again attacked Rosie, and it would seem that she was intent on tearing the hair from her head

179

when the front door was thrust open, as also was the kitchen door, and Frances and Janie Bluett rushed into the hall, there to join Robbie as he was endeavouring to pull Rosie away from Beatrice's frenzied, clawing hands.

'Mistress! Mistress! Stop it! Stop it!' The girls were holding on to Beatrice now. Blood was running from her mouth and over her chin onto their hands as they continued to hold her back for, still consumed with rage, the sight of Robbie MacIntosh was infuriating her further, and she screamed at the top of her voice, 'Get out! Get out, you! Out of my house!'

But he, one arm around Rosie's quivering body, her case in the other, her coat over his shoulder paused and, casting a withering glance at Beatrice, cried back at her, 'Yes, I'll get out, and your sister with me for good and all. And I'll say this to you, woman: if there's anyone inherited insane traits in your family, it's yourself!'

This statement, one would have expected, would have torn Beatrice from the servants' hold; instead, it had the opposite effect, for they felt their mistress going limp under their hands, and then her body beginning to shake as if with ague.

Tom Needler had appeared on the drive and Robbie called to him, 'Would you mind hauling the rest of her luggage down, Tom!' And Tom, his eyes wide, hurried forward, saying, 'Yes, laddie. Yes. Don't worry about it; I'll bring the lot to the gate.'

Rosie's face was bleeding from two nail scratches down the side of her right cheek. Her body, too, was shaking, but this was due to her shuddering crying.

When they reached the gate, Robbie called back to Tom, 'Just leave them there, Tom. I'll come back for them.'

'From what I saw of her,' Tom Needler called, 'she won't be on the look-out to see what I'm up to for some little time. So leave the lot and I'll get them along to your place.'

Rosie was awake, but she hadn't yet opened her eyes. She knew that she was lying in Robbie's bed and her mind was perfectly clear as to what had transpired last night. She could recall that she had been unable to stop crying. Mrs Annie had held her and Robbie had held her, but still she couldn't stop. Then John had arrived and he had seen to the scratches on her face. He had said soothing words to her about her future, and of how happy she was going to be. But still she had been unable to stop crying. Then he had made her drink something and she must have gone to sleep. But now, when she felt a hand lift hers from the counterpane, she opened her eyes and looked at Robbie. He was bending towards her, and he smiled softly as he said, 'You've had a good sleep. D'you feel better now?'

She did not answer for some time. She didn't know whether she felt better or not. Her face was paining; and she put up her other hand to it, asking quietly, 'Is it much?'

'It's enough,' he answered in his blunt way. 'But John says it isn't very deep, which is a good thing. It will soon heal.'

She found it painful to turn her head to the side in order to see him the better; and then quietly she said, 'It's over.'

'Yes, love, it's over.'

She watched him lower his head for a moment, then look at her again and say, 'I heard it all from outside. Was it true what you said?'

There was no coyness about the answer, just a plain, 'Yes, Robbie, it was true.'

'And not as a brother, or a . . .?'

'No, not as a brother, or anything else. But as it should have been years ago, if I'd . . . if I'd had any sense.'

He lifted her hand and brought it to his chest.

'How long have you felt this way . . . about me, I mean?'

181

'Oh, for some time. But I . . . I don't think I could ever have told you, because I was still carrying that dreadful feeling of rejection.'

'Oh, my dear. You must have known you would have found no rejection in me, because I've loved you all your life. When you were a child I loved you. Then I loved you as a young girl, and that was a painful time, because I knew how you viewed me. But not so painful as when you became a young woman and were about to marry.'

'Oh, Robbie, Robbie.' She had raised herself from the pillows now and, bringing her face close to his, she said, 'You know something? You have never kissed me. Patted me, hugged me, but you've never kissed me.'

'Oh, Rosie, Rosie.' His face looked on the point of laughter; then his lips fell gently on hers and he held the kiss for some time. Now, pressing her face from him, he said, 'That's merely an introduction. When your cheek is better I'll do it properly.' And attempting to smile now, she murmured, 'Oh, Robbie, Robbie. I love you. I do, I do. I . . . I never felt like this with . . . well, I can say, with Teddy. Looking back, that seems like a girlish dream, something that all girls have to go through. You . . . you believe me?'

'I believe you, love. Oh, yes, I believe you. And all I want to know now is, how soon d'you think it will be before we can get married?'

She brought a deep gurgling laugh from him when she said, 'Make it tomorrow, or a week at most. In any case, as soon as we can. But I would like it to be in church.'

'So would I, dear; although the lady downstairs' – he laughed – 'will call me a hypocrite. But there's something in what you say, 'cos the quicker it's done, the quicker we'll get the winter cabbage in.'

The bed shook through their mingled laughter and Annie MacIntosh, who had been about to enter the room, stopped

182

with her hand on the door knob, hesitated a moment, then turned about and went slowly downstairs again. But when she reached the bottom, she lifted her eyes to the ceiling and said, 'At last; thanks be to God. But not afore time.'

# 12

When he first saw the house from the drive, John was asking himself why he had offered to bring them in the trap. Robbie could have brought Rosie on the cart. She wouldn't have cared how she had got here so long as he was with her.

Robbie's voice came softly at him now, saying, 'It's a bonny house. Lovely.'

'It's better inside,' Rosie said, and he smiled at her but made no further comment.

John drew the horse to a stop at the foot of four shallow steps; but before moving from his seat, he looked to where Helen was standing almost at eye-level at the top, and his heart jerked against his ribs, reviving the old pain and making him chastise himself.

She ran down the steps, hugging Rosie to her, before she turned to Robbie, saying, 'How nice to see you, Robbie.'

John still hadn't left his seat and she looked up at him, and her voice changed as she said, 'Hello, John.'

'Hello, Helen.' He forced himself to smile as he pointed to the horse's head, saying, 'Where am I to put this?'

'Oh, Henry will see to it. Look, here he comes.'

A small, thick-set man appeared, and she pointed to the horse, saying, 'Stable him, will you, Henry, please?'

'Yes, ma'am.' There was a broad smile on the man's face; but then his head turned sharply as John, descending from the trap, said, 'Oh, I won't be able to stay long. Just put him under shelter because I fear' – he looked up at the sky – 'we're in for a shower, or a thunderstorm.'

'Good enough, sir. Good enough, sir,' and the man led the horse and trap away.

Walking side by side with Robbie, John followed the two sisters and for the first time he entered Col Mount.

He recalled the day that Helen had pointed it out to him from Craig's Tor, and it came to him that the name didn't really suit the house. It was a harsh-sounding name whereas this hall, with its rose wallpaper, gilt-framed pictures, polished floor, scattered rugs and soft pinkish upholstered chairs and curtains appeared anything but masculine. Perhaps panelled walls and a broad oak stairway would have better suited the entrance to such a named house.

They were in the drawing-room now and here the femininity was even more emphasised. But at the moment it did not impinge upon him for he was staring at the man who had pulled himself up from a chair and was shaking hands with Robbie. And he could not believe that this was the man whom he had continued to envy over the years, thinking of him always as a tall man with a military bearing. This man was still tall, but he looked emaciated.

'Hello, Doctor, so nice to see you again. It's a long time since we met.'

'Yes, sir. Yes, it is a long time since we met.' He stopped himself from adding, 'How are you?'

'Well, don't let us stand here like stooks, as Cook would say. Sit yourself down . . . Hello, my dear.' He had turned to Rosie but didn't kiss her or put his arms about her. Instead, his hand went out and gently touched her cheek.

185

John had not sat down, and Helen repeated her husband's words: 'Do sit down, John.' He had been asking himself why he hadn't sat down and was still standing like a stook, and he put it down to the change he was seeing in this military man because he recognised impending death when it stared him in the face, even from a distance.

As he sat down, he heard Helen say, 'I'll ring for some tea,' and he realised that she was very ill-at-ease; also that she too had changed: she looked older, yet even more beautiful.

Afterwards, he couldn't remember what he had eaten for that tea. All he recalled of it was that Leonard joked with the two maids who brought it in, Hannah and Betty, and that they were rosy-cheeked, bright-eyed, middle-aged women. After the tea had been cleared away, a silence had fallen on the five of them until it was broken by Rosie excitedly saying, 'I'm . . . we're going to be married, Robbie and I.' She put her hand out and gripped Robbie's hand. 'But . . . but it all happened quite suddenly, and I'm going to let John tell you about it.' She now turned to him, saying, 'Tell . . . tell them, John, everything. Please! Every word.'

He felt his face flushing. He had not expected this. He had thought that she would do the telling, and in her own way, and he said so: 'It . . . it should really come from you, Rosie.'

'No. No. Please, John. I couldn't. I mean . . .' She drooped her head and at this he looked from Helen to Leonard, then after a long pause, he said, 'Well, it was like this. I was up in London for four days, on a two-day course of lectures and we bumped into each other in the street.' He stopped here, then said, 'I'm referring to Teddy Golding . . .'

'Teddy Golding?' Helen's voice was high with surprise, and at this, her husband put out his hand and, patting her knee, said, 'Shh! Listen, dear.' And as John went on, so she sat and listened. And now and again she would turn her head and glance towards Rosie, her look saying, 'I can't believe it.'

When John neared the end of the tale he left out the scene between Beatrice and himself. But what he did say was, 'I know I could have kept this to myself, but I also knew how Rosie was still feeling. As she herself said, the feeling of rejection was unbearable at times, more so, I should think, because she did not know the reason for it. Teddy's rejection of her had seemed to be so casual, and knowing what had previously transpired between them, she had found it impossible to come to terms with it. And another reason why I felt she should be told was that if she ever married, or I should perhaps say, allowed herself to be married, the feeling would have remained with her, for she had lost her trust in men.' He now looked across at Rosie, to see her gazing at him, her eyes moist. 'And it had prevented her from showing her real feelings for Robbie.' He now drew in a long breath and said, 'The rest Rosie can tell you herself. But I think her expression speaks for her.'

Helen rose from her chair and went to Rosie and, drawing her up from the couch, put her arms about her, but seemingly found it difficult to speak, so Rosie said, 'It's all right, Helen. I'm . . . I'm all right now. Since John told me the truth that feeling of stigma has been lifted off my mind, and I no longer feel inadequate. Yet, it all happened at a cost to John. It's upset his life.'

At this John remarked promptly, 'You needn't worry about that, Rosie; it was upset some time ago.'

'What are you going to do?' Helen's question did not bring an immediate answer from him. And when he gave it, his gaze was directed away from her. 'I'm leaving her. In fact, I've already done so. I have moved into the annexe

187

with Mother. And,' there was quite a long pause before he added, 'I'm applying for a legal separation.'

There followed another embarrassed silence, until Leonard altered the course of the conversation as he looked at Rosie and Robbie and asked, 'When is it to be; the wedding?'

'Oh' – Robbie jerked his chin – 'for myself, it could have been next week. But this woman here' – he glanced at Rosie – 'fancies a church wedding.' And Rosie, smiling now, added simply, 'The banns go up on Sunday.'

'Good. Good. I'm happy for you both. And that goes for Helen, too, doesn't it?'

Helen answered briskly, 'Oh, yes. Yes. But it should have happened ages ago. You're a stiff-necked Scot. D'you know that?' – she stabbed her forefinger towards Robbie – 'You should have made your feelings clear years ago.'

'Helen! Helen!' Leonard, catching hold of her skirt, tugged her gently towards him, saying, 'Every man has his reasons, and Robbie certainly had his. Not everyone is like me, rushing in where angels fear to tread.'

John did not feel envy, but just a slight pain in that special place below his ribs as he saw the exchanged glance between them. Then Leonard again changed the subject by looking at him and saying, 'Do you play bridge?'

'Oh, bridge?' John shook his head. 'Haven't done for years; not since college days.'

'Whist then?'

'Oh, yes, whist. I've devised a two-handed game with my mother. It's a bit complicated. You've got to do as much thinking as one would at chess.'

'You play chess?'

'Yes. Yes, I like a game of chess, whenever possible. But I seem to have so little spare time.' He was about to go on when Helen, getting to her feet, said suddenly, 'Come on, Rosie, let's show Robbie how to grow vegetables. We've got a good patch, too, you know.' And Robbie, smiling

188

at her, said, 'I'm out to learn, Miss Helen,' only to glance quickly towards Leonard and apologise, 'Oh, I'm sorry. It's . . . it's habit. I meant . . .'

'Never mind what you meant,' Helen put in quickly, 'just drop the miss, for you will soon be my brother-in-law.' She smiled widely at him now. Then after a short pause, she ended, 'And that will be most welcome. But come on, both of you, before it starts to rain.'

Left alone, the two men looked at each other and it seemed that one was waiting for the other to speak.

It was Leonard who spoke and there was bitterness in his voice as he said, 'This is a stinking disease, isn't it?'

John found himself blinking rapidly, and he wetted his lips before he could answer. 'I understand they are researching hard for a break-through.'

'Yes, that's what they tell me. But in the meantime one is sent to the South coast, or to Switzerland. And what does it do? Just prolongs the agony.' Then, his tone altering, he said, 'You likely know Doctor Peters?'

'Yes. Yes, we've met on several occasions.' He made himself smile as he said, 'Yes, he has his patch and Doctor Cornwallis our patch.'

'Have you many TB patients?'

'A few. It seems to run in families.'

'Do you find them ostracised?'

John raised his eyebrows as he repeated, 'Ostracised?' Then after thinking a minute, he said, 'Yes, I suppose they are to a certain extent. But it isn't deliberate; it must really be through fear.'

'Yes, fear.' Leonard's head now was nodding. 'We've experienced that. But I wouldn't give a damn for myself; it's . . . it's Helen.' He moved forward in the chair, then turned and looked towards the window as he said slowly, 'You know, when we were first married and used to come here visiting Helen's friends the place seemed to be swarming

189

with other visitors, all desirous of giving us a good time. It was the same up in town, especially after I unfortunately came into the title. But when I developed this' – he tapped his chest – 'except for one or two here and there, the others melted like snow under sun, especially those who had young sons or daughters. But it's' – and he smiled wanly now – 'I suppose it's natural. I've asked myself, would I not have done the same? But—' he deliberately turned and looked at John again as he said, 'I'm not concerned about company for myself, it's Helen. She hides it, but she has felt the rejection of friends. There were the Maldons, and the Oswalds, and the Fenwicks. They had known her for years, long before I came on the scene. In fact, I understand that the older members had been regular visitors at their house. But now the only ones she sees are the Conisbees and the Maguires, and, of course, Dashing Daisy. Oh, I don't know how she would get on without Daisy. You'll have to meet her.' He gave a mirthless laugh now as he said, 'Lena Conisbee's as deaf as a stone, and he has a voice like a roaring bull. You know, I look forward to their visits, because one can't help laughing at them, especially when she answers the question he has never asked. And then she yells, and he yells at her, and she yells back "I'm not that deaf." The Maguires are different: they are quiet, too sympathetic. But there again, they never bring their two sons. I understand all this, for myself I do, but when I realise that I brought all this on Helen . . .'

John put in sharply, 'You shouldn't think about it like that; I'm sure Helen doesn't. She's deeply concerned for you, that's all, she won't be thinking of herself. And I feel sure that you are the only company she wants.'

Leonard stared at John for a long moment before he said, 'Would you come over now and again for a game of whist or chess, or what have you?'

'Yes, I would like to; but then, it must perforce be a matter of timing. You see, I do surgery most evenings; I have one day off a week, and a full week-end a month. The afternoons would be my best time between half-past two and five.'

'That would be fine. Yes; yes. But what do you do after you finish surgery? Oh, I forgot. I'm sorry, one becomes selfish. You have your mother with you, and I understand she is rather poorly.'

'Oh, well, she's not poorly in what you could say a sick way, but she suffers badly from arthritis in her legs and finds it difficult to get about.'

'Would she mind meeting me?'

'Mind . . . meeting you?' John had spaced the words; then repeated them quickly, saying, 'Mind meeting you? Mother? She'd be delighted. But unfortunately I could never get her up into the trap, it's too high.'

'What about a carriage? I mean, *our* carriage. It has two detachable steps. Is she a big woman?'

'No, anything but.'

'Then she could be lifted into the carriage. It's very comfortable.'

John thought for a moment; then smiling, he said, 'She would like that. Oh, yes. She never gets out. Yes. Yes, indeed, she would like that.'

'We'll do something about it, then, eh?' and Leonard returned John's smile, his gaunt features stretched and John saw a glimpse of the man he had once known as he said simply, 'Thank you.' And when Leonard said, 'I'm so glad you came; I feel it's going to make all the difference,' John could not see in what way his visits would achieve that, but then he couldn't know this man's wishes were to cut into his pattern of life in the same way as had the taking of the annexe for his mother, and with even more dire results.

191

# 13

〰️

'So you've come back at last, Miss Simmons?'

'Well, Cook, 'tis me half day off,' replied the kitchen maid. 'And I was, sort of' – she grinned widely now – 'detained.'

'Detained?' This came from Frances, who sat at one end of the kitchen table drinking a cup of tea. And she turned her head towards Janie Bluett, sitting opposite, and repeated, 'Detained? She was detained.' Then looking at the young girl, she said, 'And who were you detained by?'

Mary now slowly took off her short jacket and unpinned her straw hat before, brightly, she said, 'The bride.'

When she did not go on, but turned to hang her coat on the back of the kitchen door, Cook, with an exaggerated gesture, pulled out a chair and said, 'Won't you sit down, miss?'

And when, quite coolly, Mary sat down, the two maids burst out laughing; and Cook, gazing down on her young assistant, said, 'You're askin' for your ears to be clipped, aren't you? Well . . . go on.'

When Mary did not go on, Frances, leaning forward on the table, looked at her and said, 'Tell us about the wedding. How did she look?'

Immediately Mary's small show of defiance was swept away, and following Frances's action, she too leaned forward and, joining her hands tightly together, as if to give emphasis to her words, she said, 'She looked lovely. Beautiful. And he was as smart as smart. It was lovely. Her dress wasn't exactly white; not white, you know, just like a creamy colour, and it had three skirts, and the bodice was all tucks. And she had elbow sleeves and the frill on the end was embroidered with tiny pink roses. It was the same on the panel in the front of her bodice. Oh, she did look lovely.'

'Was the church full?' Cook had now seated herself, and Mary answered, 'No. No, it wasn't really full, and they were mostly Robbie MacIntosh's people. There seemed a lot of them; but Miss Rosie only had the doctor and Miss Helen. He gave her away. Oh, he looked smart an' all. And Miss Helen. Eeh!' – she put her hand across her mouth – 'I always call her Miss Helen – I don't think of her as Lady Spears – but she looked lovely an' all. She always did look lovely, didn't she? And the organ played lovely and when Miss Rosie walked back down the aisle, her arm linked in Robbie MacIntosh's, I could have cried. There were crowds outside and they followed them across to the George and Crown where the reception was being held.' She now looked from one to the other as she said, 'I forgot to tell you that she arrived in the coach with Miss Helen and the doctor. The husband didn't come; Miss Helen's, that is. They say he's bad.'

'Well,' put in Cook, 'where did this, your being detained, come in?'

'Well, you see, Cook, it was like this: I went with the crowd across the road, and I can tell you I nearly went on me back once with all the rice that was lying about. Anyway, gradually people thinned out, you know, when they couldn't see any more, and I was left. Then up came this fella. He startled the wits out of me. He grabbed my arm and he said, 'Come on back, the bride wants to see you.' And I was for saying, 'Well, I can't go in there. I'm not togged up,' but he said, 'She wants a word with you. Come on!'

And he actually pulled me up the steps and into the hall and then into a room where there was a crowd of folk. And he pushed his way to where Miss Rosie was standing, and she took my hand. And you know what she said?'

They waited, all staring at her. And now there was a break in Mary's voice as she went on, 'She said, "It's lovely to see you, Mary. Tell Cook and the girls I wish they could have been here." Yes, that's what she said.'

There was silence around the table and Cook's reaction was to pat her lips quickly with her fingers. But both Frances and Janie groped for handkerchiefs behind their apron bibs and dabbed at their eyes.

It was a full minute later when Mary went on with her tale. 'Miss Rosie then said, "You must stay and have something to eat." And then there was a lot of talk and laughter and pushing and shoving, and there was waiters going round with trays with glasses of wine on them, and Robbie MacIntosh took off one and handed it to me. Well, me hand shook so much that I nearly spilt it; and then he bent towards me and whispered, "Don't waste that stuff, Mary; it cost a lot of money." And at this Miss Rosie laughed out loud, and she pushed him, he who's her husband now, and their glasses nearly spilt. And there we were – I couldn't believe it – the three of us laughing our heads off; and then his mother came up and spoke to me, and she started to laugh, and that seemed to set off everybody else. Most of them didn't know what they were laughing about. Eeh! It was lovely. And then the doctor came and told Rosie that they were waiting for her to sit down. The tables were arranged like a horseshoe. Anyway, I was making for the door when the doctor was back again and saying, "Where are you off to, Mary?" And then he didn't wait for me to tell him, but he took my hand and pulled me through all the bustle to the bottom of one side of the table. And he pulled a chair forward from against the wall and said,

"You sit there, and enjoy yourself. It's Miss Rosie's special day. You understand?" He looked solemn for a moment and I said, "Yes, Doctor." Then he laughed and again said, "Enjoy yourself." Then amid all the noise and chatter he went up to the top table, and the meal began. It was very nice, very nice. But I thought you, Cook, could have done better.' Tactfully now, she nodded to her superior; then she went on, 'After that there was speeches and a lot of laughter. I couldn't hear what they were laughing at; I was too far down, you see. Robbie MacIntosh didn't say much, and it sounded very solemn, until the end when he went into broad Scots. There was a lot of laughter then. And then' – her voice was slowing up now – 'they cut the cake. His hand was on top of hers. That finished me; I was all choked up.' Her lids blinking rapidly, she looked from one to the other, then dropped her head onto her folded arms on the table and she began to cry, and the others, rising to their feet, commiserated with her. And it was Cook who said, 'Come on now. Go up to your room and wash your face and pull yourself together. Then come down and have a cup of tea.' . . .

They had been sitting in silence when Cook again spoke, saying quietly, 'I've been thinkin' about her along there all day. She must be goin' through hell.'

'She's gone through two boxes of chocolates that I know of,' said Janie now. 'She must spend a small fortune on them. Yet, she's cutting down on the store cupboard and us, isn't she?'

'I can't help but feel sorry for her, too, Cook,' Frances said; 'but she's asked for all she's got, if we only go by the bit we've heard and seen. She was a different woman altogether when she first used to go into the annexe. And Mrs Falconer and she got on so well together. And look how she used to come into you, Cook, and get you to make the old girl special dishes.'

'Yes. Yes, we all know about that,' Janie put in now. 'But, if you ask me, it was all a sprat to catch a mackerel, because, there's no gettin' away from it, she trailed the doctor: for him she put on a different face from the one she used for Miss Rosie; she was all butter and sugar when he was about. And I'll tell you something else' – she now leant down the table towards the cook – 'As I've said to you, Cook, I've heard things upstairs, things here and there, that seemed very odd at times. And knowing her now makes me think she is one of those women who eat men alive.'

'Oh! Oh! Janie Bluett. Be quiet!' Frances had turned on her workmate now. 'The things you say.'

'The things I say? What have you been sayin' all along? Anyway, me mind's settled. I'm going to look out for a change. And if you had any sense you would do the same, 'cos to my mind, she's going up the pole. I'll tell you something you didn't know. I was putting her linen away the other day in the top drawer and I managed to feel something hard. I pulled it out, and it was one of the doctor's scarves, and it had knots in it from beginning to end, tight, tight knots.'

'No!' Cook was now biting on her lower lip and Janie turned to her, saying, 'Yes, Cook. Tight, tight knots. Don't you think that means she intends to do him an injury? And I don't want to be here when it happens.'

A bell attached to a board on the wall rang loudly, and Frances, rising with a sigh, said, 'Here we go again. What now?'

# PART THREE

*Helen*

# I

~~~

Leonard was saying, 'I should have been there. I was quite capable . . .' when Helen cut him off by bending over him and putting her lips to his brow as she said, 'You weren't quite capable and you know it. So, don't let's be silly.'

'If there's anyone silly in this ménage, it isn't me. I could have made it, couldn't I, John?'

'No, you couldn't.'

'Well, well.' Leonard put his hand up to his thin gaunt face and shook his head: 'Not a friend in the world,' he said.

'Poor soul!' When Helen again kissed his brow he caught her hand and said, 'They looked so happy when they came in, didn't they? Joy personified.'

'Yes, dear, joy personified.' Helen bit on her lip and her eyes became moist as she said on a shaky laugh, 'They're looking round the kitchen garden again, would you believe it? She's so interested in their future. And I can see them making quite a business of their bit of land, more so than it is now. Odd,' – she straightened up and looked at John – 'she was never happy unless she was over there: she loved that house and his mother.'

'You say Robbie's mother's having a ceilidh tonight?' Leonard said.

'Yes, she's entertaining all his friends. Her cousin and his

199

wife are staying with her for the four days, and they are Scots, too.'

'I always thought that a ceilidh was an Irish pastime.'

'No; it's a Gaelic name for a do. Of the two nationalities I wouldn't lay bets as to who makes the more noise, or drinks the more whiskey, or which one of them finishes up without a fight. But I doubt if the latter will happen with Robbie's mother about . . . You're not going now?' Leonard pulled himself up slightly from the back of the long lounge chair as John got to his feet.

'Yes, because if I stay five minutes longer I'll be invited to dinner.'

'Well, you haven't a surgery tonight; you said so.'

'Yes, I know, but I've got a mother. I've had a number of late nights during the last few weeks, don't forget. Your gambling sessions have got me hooked.'

Leonard lay back and smiled his gaunt, wide smile as he said, 'Oh, yes. I reckoned up yesterday, you must have lost all of fifteen shillings; but what you shouldn't forget is that you've also had tuition for that amount.'

Helen had said nothing during this jocular exchange, for she was used to such banter, but now she went from the room, saying, 'I'll call that pair in to say goodbye. Anyway, it's almost dark and they won't be examining vegetables in this light.'

Left alone for a moment, Leonard put his hand out towards John and beckoned him closer. And when John bent over him, it was to hear Leonard say, 'I would like to have a talk with you, in private.'

'Private?'

'Yes. Yes, private. She's arranged to take them to the theatre on Monday; at least, I forced her hand in it, so they'll be leaving here any time after five. Could you make it?'

'Yes. Yes, of course.'

200

They stared at each other for a moment, then closing his eyes, Leonard said, 'I'd be grateful.'

John could say nothing to this, but if he had voiced his thoughts, he would have said, 'The gratitude, really, is on the other foot; a visit here is the only light in my life now,' to which, in all honesty, he could have added, 'When, not only do I see Helen, but also enjoy this friendship which has surprisingly grown up between us.' There was a time when perhaps thoughtlessly he might have wished this man dead. But not any more. The thought of his impending end was painful. He had found Leonard Spears to be not only a good man, but also a gentleman of the first rank, in all ways.

He straightened up, and assuming his doctor's manner, he said, 'Now behave yourself. Do as you're told and no attempting to go outside until the sun starts to behave itself, too.' He nodded sharply down at Leonard now; and when there was no response, he turned abruptly and walked from the room.

Helen was in the hall. She seemed to be waiting for him, for she had his coat in her hands, and silently she helped him into it. Then, handing him his hat and gloves, she said, 'I'm going to the theatre with Rosie and Robbie on Monday night; I'm . . . I'm being got out of the way.' Her voice had a break in it. 'I suppose he's asked you over because he wants to talk to you in private?'

'Well . . . yes.'

She gathered the front of her dress into her fist as if she were cold; then, turning to him, she peered at him through the twilight as she said, 'I don't know what I'll do when he goes. He is my life. He has been my life for a long time now. You understand?'

'Yes. Yes, I understand.'

'It wasn't so at first.' She swallowed deeply. 'I liked him then, admired him, and he was a quick escape route. But . . . but that soon changed. He . . . he's a wonderful man.'

'Yes. I agree with you.'

She turned from him now, muttering, 'Why? Why?'

'Used in this context, that is the hardest word to give an answer to,' John said quietly.

Her voice became a slight croak now as she said, 'How long do you think he has?'

He paused for a moment before he said, 'His . . . your doctor would surely have given you an indication.'

'No, he hasn't. He thinks it would hurt me. Anyway I have eyes. And you know that this is the worst possible climate for him. But he won't budge, he likes this house. He says he wants me to be . . . settled here,' and her head bounced back as she said, 'When he goes, I too go far away, miles away, across oceans . . .'

As her voice broke, he put in softly, 'Don't! Don't! He'll notice immediately and that'll upset him more. You've put a face on things up till now; go on doing so. And I can say at this moment, Helen, that there is no-one who hopes or would even pray for his survival as much as I would.'

At this point he happened to glance into the corridor where Bertram Johnson, Leonard's valet-cum-nurse was hovering. Strange, he thought, but the man always seemed to be hovering in his vicinity. He had never taken to the man. He couldn't tell why, for apparently he was good at his job and was very necessary to Leonard.

'I must be going,' he said now and made a motion to take her hand, although it got no further than a motion; then he went out into the night and towards the stables where he knew Henry would have his horse and trap ready for him.

One thing John was to remember about Rosie's wedding day had nothing to do with that happy girl or her groom, but was something his mother had said to him the previous night.

Both she and Mrs Atkinson had been somewhat surprised to see him back so early. And when he told Mrs Atkinson that he wasn't going out again and that he was sure she'd be glad of an early night, she thankfully took him at his word.

His mother wasn't in bed. In fact, as she said herself, her legs had taken a holiday and left her substitutes, and she had been walking around most of the day. She also insisted that she had no intention of retiring until she had heard all his news.

They were settled in the sitting-room and she was saying to him, 'I was vexed this afternoon because I knew I could have been there, as I've said, I've been on my pins all day. What d'you think's given me this relief?'

'Oh, don't be silly.' He jerked his head impatiently. 'You know you have your good days, and that they are followed by bad ones.'

She smiled now as she said, 'Say that again. I didn't quite get it.'

He closed his eyes for a moment as he smiled widely; then she said, 'Well, go on, tell me. Right from the two of them going up the aisle.'

'Oh, I told you that bit when I popped in before the reception.'

'All right, then, start from the reception.'

And so he started from the reception, even bringing in young Mary's appearance, which had pleased Rosie greatly. And he finished on a laugh when he related that the young couple had gone out to examine the kitchen garden once again, in deep twilight!

'It's been a good day then, for all concerned?' She had stopped here; then, her head slightly bowed, she added, 'That was the wrong conclusion,' and she thumbed now towards the wall, adding quietly, 'She's been on the rampage. Twice I heard her yelling at the girls. Then Mrs Atkinson had a word with Tom Needler. He said that the mistress had given Jimmy Oldham . . . that's the yard man, isn't it? Well, she had given him orders to clean the carriage, get

203

it ready for outside. And the carriage, you know, is Tom's business. Anyway, as he said, it hadn't been used now for some time, and what's the use of a carriage without a horse.' She paused now while staring at him; then said, 'I used to love living here. But the way things have turned out, I wish I had never come. And you know, if I hadn't, you wouldn't have been in the mess you are today.'

He had got quickly to his feet, saying, 'We've been through all this. Come on, get yourself to bed.'

She did not move, but went on, 'How did you leave the patient?'

'Leonard?'

'Yes, Leonard.'

'Well, he's not my patient.'

'No, I know that, but you're across there enough times as if he were.'

Looking down at her, he said, 'Mother, he likes company. And, as I told you, and he has said himself, their so-called friends have faded away like snow in sunshine, apart from one or two. Only one does he find amusing. And not one of them plays cards.'

'I'm . . . I'm not questioning you, John, or blaming you, only I . . . well I get worried. What I saw of him I know he's not long to go and there's going to be a great gap in that girl's life when he does. But what I'm going to say won't please you. Nevertheless, I'll say it: she's not the kangaroo type; she won't jump into somebody else's arms the minute that he's gone.'

'Mother!' He took two steps back from her. 'Really!' The word might have been an instant reprimand, but her gaze remained steadfast and her voice calm as she said, 'I'm not blind, and I'm your mother. I remember your telling me about that garden party, and you could talk of nothing else, and the fact that she was intending to marry a man old enough to be her father, or so you thought. And then

204

you purposely didn't go to her wedding, and you were like a bear with a sore skull for weeks on end. Oh yes, you were.' She held up her hand. 'Remember I had to put up with your moods when you were a boy, the long silences when something troubled you and you wouldn't speak of it. Well, she's something you wouldn't speak about. And now it would seem you've got both on your mind,' and she thumbed towards the wall.

'I haven't got both on my mind, Mother. There'll be no-one more upset than I'll be when Leonard goes. He's become my friend. I . . . I like him; in fact, I more than like him.'

'No doubt, no doubt. I'm glad of that. And he's a fine man. But that still leaves the question of when he goes, what will she do?'

'From what I understand from her own lips, she's going to travel, get away.'

'Oh! Oh, well, although you won't agree, I'll say, thank God for that, because you're still married and she's your wife's sister. And what's more, you can look at me with your face blazing, but, you know, I'm just bringing out into the open what's on your mind. Anyway, you were saying that he wanted to talk to you on Monday night, private. Now, I wonder what that'll be about?'

'Well, Mother, I can tell you that whatever it is, you won't get to know.'

'No? Well, that's up to you. But remember the old adage, actions speak louder than words. So now, lad, if you can bear to touch me, you can give me a heave out of this chair and then leave me to myself; I can manage.'

He heaved her up from the chair. Then, when she independently pulled her arm from his hold, she said again, 'I can manage. Give me fifteen minutes; that's if you wish to come and say good night.'

She hobbled on her sticks across the room to the door, and he had not rushed to open it for her as he usually did, but watched her transfer the right-hand walking stick to the left hand and lean on the two before she pulled the door open. But as she made to go out she turned her head over her shoulder and said, 'Thank you very much, Doctor, for your help' – there was a smile on her face now – 'and, speaking of medicine, as you do most of the day, I would advise you now to take a dose in the form of a double whisky, neat.'

He stood stiffly, his head bowed. Then he turned about and dropped into the chair he had recently vacated and, leaning his head back, he closed his eyes and he could hear her saying, 'When he goes, I go, too, far away, miles away across oceans.' And he knew this is what she meant to do.

He had heard them laughing about Dashing Daisy. She was apparently one of the few visitors who had no fear of visiting a man dying of tuberculosis. She was the widow of a District Commissioner from Africa, who, he understood, had caused her husband more trouble than any rebel chieftain or witch-doctor.

John had never met her, but now he was about to have the experience. He learned from Johnson, who had met him in the hall, that Lady Helen and the young couple had left at six o'clock, and that Mrs Freeman Wheatland had called and was with Sir Leonard in the drawing-room.

In the drawing-room, the woman sitting near the bamboo chaise-longue twisted her body round towards him as Leonard said, 'Oh, hello there, John. By the way, this is Mrs Freeman Wheatland,' but before John could acknowledge the introduction the lady cried loudly in a rough-toned voice, 'Don't be two-faced, Leonard. Tell him what you usually call me, behind my back, of course. Dashing Daisy May, that's what he calls me, Dashing Daisy May. I was stupid enough to tell him that's what Tommy used to call me. He . . . he was my husband. Sit down!' Her command was imperious.

John looked at Leonard. Leonard's face was stretched

with laughter; his own, he knew, was full of amazement. He sat down and looked at the visitor . . . Dashing Daisy. Yes, the title seemed to suit her. He could imagine her sitting on a horse going hell for leather over the fells. She was a gaunt woman, probably sixty. She was big-made, all bone; as his mother would say, no meat on her; all gristle. Her face looked fleshless, yet pixiefied. Yes, that was the word, pixiefied. An odd name to put to her looks because, taken over all, she was ugly. She had very long fingers which looked absolutely fleshless; and then there was her body: her shoulders looked broad, and likely, when she stood up, he would find she was tall, because there seemed a good length of leg under her long skirt, at least from her knees down to the caps of her sturdy brogues.

She startled him somewhat by saying, 'I've heard all about you, you know, and not only from him,' she nodded towards Leonard, 'but down in the town. They have their censors, you know. There's more for you than against you. How do you put up with old Cornwallis? There's an old shyster if ever there was one. You know, he's got that bad leg of his insured to make sure it doesn't get better.'

'Daisy!'

'Yes, Leonard, dear?'

'Give him a chance.'

Her head back and her mouth wide open, she let out a roar of a laugh. He noticed, as far as he could see, that she had all her teeth but that some were very discoloured.

She now turned her round bright eyes towards him, saying, 'My nanny used to say to me when I wouldn't eat my oats, "If you don't like it you can lump it. You'll go to it before it'll come to you." '

He was smiling as he returned her gaze. If you didn't like it you could lump it. That was plain enough. He turned now to look at Leonard, who had his head back into the cushion of the chair-bed. His eyes were closed and his teeth could be seen nipping at his lower lip.

'Have you ever been in Africa?'

'What?' The question almost swung John round in the chair, and he repeated, 'Africa? No. No, I've never been to Africa.'

'Well, in my opinion you haven't missed much. I lost all my flesh there, you know. I used to be round and plump. You wouldn't believe that, would you?'

He did not know whether to say, 'Oh, yes,' or 'Oh, no.'

They both turned to Leonard now, who still had his eyes closed but was saying, 'Tell him, Daisy, about the disinfectant bath.'

'Oh, go on with you. Why should I entertain your guest and him a doctor?' She turned a quick glance on John now, saying, 'I never had much room for doctors. Witch-doctors can beat them any day in the week.'

'I have no doubt of that.'

'Go on, Daisy, tell him about the bath,' repeated Leonard.

'Why? You've heard it all before.'

'I'd like to hear it again.'

John was watching her face. Her eyes were on Leonard now, and he noticed a softness, like a pale cloud, pass over her dry and wrinkled skin. And she blinked her round bright eyes for a moment before, returning to her former manner, she said, 'Well, you've asked for it.' Then turning to John again, she said, 'I don't know whether you want to hear this or not. But it should happen that at one time I was a spanking lass. That's what they would have called me up here, a spanking lass. Can you believe that?'

'Oh yes. Yes.' He had not hesitated with this reply, and repeated, 'Yes, I could imagine you being a spanking lass.'

As she looked at him now there was cynicism in her eyes as she said, 'Huh! The Colonial Office weren't alone in breeding their diplomats. Anyway, there I was being quite happy as the sixth daughter not counting the four older brothers of a very busy father and I was the only one unmarried. But I was in love with a horse, so it didn't matter . . .'

When Leonard made a coughing sound in his throat, she stopped for a moment to glance at him, then went on, 'Then to my mother's dismay and my father's joy there rode into my life one Thomas Freeman Wheatland, who was on leave from Africa. Apparently he had gone out as Assistant Commissioner, and when his superior retired, he got the job. He was a good age, but that didn't matter, he liked horses, and he asked me to go to Africa with him. It was a toss-up between Brutus and him. Brutus was my horse. I'd had him since he was a foal. As for Africa, I knew it was on the map somewhere and that it was hot, and, that there was a lot of sand, and it was full of camels and sheiks and dung and flies and some such. Anyway, I found myself married, and all I remember of my wedding day was that my father got mortallious, or nearly so, even before the ceremony, with relief at getting rid of me, and when I woke up the next morning on a boat in the middle of some ocean I knew I didn't like marriage, and to make matters worse, I was sea-sick.'

As John watched Leonard press his hand across his mouth, he wanted to do the same. His eyes were wet, his lips were tight pressed; that was until the next moment when she said, 'You've likely dealt with drunks, Doctor, including ones that have been in a brawl. And I'm sure the expression "being kicked in the guts" isn't new to you. But that's what Africa did to me, right in the guts. And it was some time before I could straighten up, metaphorically speaking, that is.'

He did not see her put her hand on her stomach, for he was wiping his eyes with his handkerchief, and when he muttered, 'Oh, Mrs Wheatland,' she responded with, 'Call me Daisy; I like that better.'

He did not call her Daisy, but Leonard was saying, 'Go on, Daisy. Go on.'

She turned to John again, and, her voice serious, she said, 'Can you imagine being dropped into the middle of a forest? No path, nothing, and just left there day after day. Not that the house wasn't comfortable, and the clearing roundabout good, and there were roads and paths leading off to this tribe and that tribe. But inside my mind I was in a forest and, at times, was frightened to death. Especially when Tommy had to go on these treks and I was left alone there. Oh, there were servants galore. Oh, yes. But only one could speak a smattering of English. Sometimes we had visitors, but what did they do? They sat on the verandah and drank, and talked about this head man, or that witch-doctor. That was when I was there. But I've good hearing, and when I was supposedly out of the way, bits of scandal would emerge; this one had left her husband, or a certain lady was being visited by so-and-so. I didn't know then that the certain lady being visited by so-and-so was the woman that Tommy had wanted to marry. But she had turned him down, and to ease his lacerated feelings he had taken leave and come to England and found a girl who was going cheap from the dregs at the bottom of the barrel.'

'Oh, no! no!' Leonard had pulled himself up a little in the chair now, and he said again, 'No, no; never think that of yourself, Daisy. That isn't your character.'

'You know nothing about it, Leonard. You've never reached desperation point and been number ten and nobody wanted you. Anyway' – her voice was loud now as she turned back to John – 'everybody has to go through an apprenticeship in life. And those first few months were my apprenticeship. And then I met *the man* from the leper colony.'

She nodded now at John, repeating, 'Leper colony. I'd never heard of it, never heard anybody speak of it. Well,

210

would I now? Would I hear such a thing from the few people I had conversation with? The word leper was taboo.

'I had gone beyond the compound. I was out walking. It was a sort of main road and there, coming towards me, was this man who looked like a down-and-out priest: he wore a flat hat and a long black gown. But I'm not being sentimental or ridiculous when I say he had the face of an angel. And he was an angel. When he introduced himself as Doctor Frank La-Mode, he laughed and swept his hand down his gown and said that it was hardly a recommendation for his name. That was our first meeting. He seemed to know who I was. Over the course of the next few weeks I met him on that road three times. He always had two carriers with him and they always seemed loaded down with parcels and boxes.

'Then one night I said to Tommy, "Do you know Doctor Frank La-Mode?" The name made him sit up straight in his chair, and he said, "What do you know about Frank La-Mode?"

' "Nothing, only that I've met him two or three times." And this made him jump to his feet, demanding, "You didn't go there?"

' "Go where?" I asked. "The leper colony, of course" was his reply.'

John watched her sit back in the chair, and when she didn't speak for a moment, he whispered, 'A leper colony?'

Now she turned her head towards him and, nodding, repeated, 'A leper colony. My husband, Tommy, was a phlegmatic kind of man. Perhaps it was the lack of passion or any kind of real emotion that had lost him his true love. But at that moment I was confronted with another Tommy, who was actually yelling that I must not go near that man, and I must not go near the leper colony.

'I remember thinking, where is the leper colony, anyway? So vehement was he and so altered was his whole personality as he went for me that I realised he was afraid of the leper

211

colony. He was afraid of leprosy. And that did something to me. As for me, I thought, I'm not afraid of the leper colony or lepers.' She pouted her lips now and smiled a sad smile before she went on, 'Oh I knew nothing about lepers, except that they were untouchable people, and once you had leprosy it was a death warrant and you were hidden away somewhere. Yet, there was that man, Frank La-Mode, looking so serene and peaceful. Yes, that was the word, peaceful. And the person I had to live with never looked peaceful, nor did any of his acquaintances. They drank too much to be peaceful. When he yelled, "Do you hear me? Do not speak to that man again, and not on your life, go to that colony. Do you hear me?" . . .' and now she looked towards Leonard, saying, 'I can still hear him yelling at me, Leonard, no matter how many times I relate it. And the more he yelled the more defiant I became inside.' Her head was back against the cushion now, her eyes turned ceilingwards, as she continued, 'It was a fortnight later when I met Frank again, and I said to him straightaway, "I would like to visit the colony, your colony." And he said, "Oh, dear me! Have you your husband's permission?"

'And I said, "No; but I mean to go there and see for myself, with or without permission." And after a while he muttered, "Very well. Can you come now?"

' "Yes," I said; "I have nothing else to do." ' She now brought herself upright in the chair and, looking at John, she said, 'It was a very strange journey. The main road seemed to peter out into a forest and we walked and walked. I don't know for how long. It was a narrow track and wouldn't take two abreast. And then, there were the wooden palisades. It was like I had imagined a fort in the Americas, you know, to keep the Indians out. My first introduction to leprosy was when the gate was opened by a man who had one finger on his hand, the rest resembling a bundle of knots. And then we were passing through little groups and everybody who

212

could seemed to be busy, that is, those with hands. And then there were those who shambled towards Frank, their twisted faces alight with love.

'His house was made of bamboo with a number of rooms. And then there was the surgery, and in it I met two women, English women. I couldn't believe it. One of them was big and robust, and the other had marks on her hands and arms. But the expression on both their faces was the reflection of that in Frank's. Well, I won't go into any more, except that I stayed there until my emotions told me I had to get away else I would shame myself. Frank, himself, saw me to the edge of the forest and onto the main road again. And there I was met by three of the servants. They wouldn't come near me, but they dashed away along the road to inform their master that a leper was approaching, because that's how they now looked upon me.

'Tommy was waiting for me in the middle of the compound and he was so full of emotion and rage that he spluttered; then he ordered me into the bath house, and I said to him, "Why the bath house?" Such was his rage he forgot himself and spoke in the vernacular, yelling, "Get in there and strip off!" Not undress, strip off.'

Now she put her hand up to her face and began to laugh.

' "Why?" I asked him. "Because you're going to take a bath," he said.

' "Oh, is that all?" So away I went into the bath house and I stripped off, but when I put my hand into the water and it stung – I don't know exactly what was in it, but something besides carbolic – but there I was standing in my bare pelt when he came to the door and the very sight of me like that caused him to close his eyes. It did. It did.' Her head was bobbing now. 'Then he ordered me to get into the bath.

' "Not on your life," I said. "That isn't only carbolic. I don't know what you've put in it, but I'm not getting into that."

'I went to grab my clothes, but he was there before me. He didn't touch them, though; he had a stick in his hand with which he whipped them aside. Then what d'you think he did? He started to poke me with the stick.' She stopped and covered her face with her hand for a moment before she said, 'I can laugh at it even now: that dignified, pompous individual, poking me with a stick. But it had an effect when he poked me in a certain place and I lost my footing and over I went with a terrible scream. But I didn't go under, only waist-high, and there he was, standing above me, yelling at me, "Duck your head! Duck your head!" I did not duck my head, and I wasn't going to duck my head, but instead I thrust out my hands, and you can see they are quite large hands, and they were always very strong. Horses don't only strengthen your buttocks but they have the same effect on your hands and your arms, too, so when my hands gripped his trouser tops and pulled at them, which action must have been painful to certain parts of his anatomy, he lost his footing and the next minute there he was in the bath, fully clothed and face down.'

Her mouth now opened in a gape as she drew in a long breath before she went on, 'I . . . I was stinging and burning in every pore. I started to laugh and when I pulled myself from under him, he, struggling in the slimy water, went down again. And then I was out and within seconds he was out, too.' Her head was again back and when she spluttered, 'No swain could have thrown off his clothes quicker to get to his bride than did Thomas Freeman Wheatland that night.'

John roared, and Leonard held his ribs tightly and the tears, ran down his face before he could entreat her, 'Please! Please, Daisy!'

'Oh. Oh, I'm sorry, Leonard.'

John was on his feet now, his face still awash with tears, his mouth wide, and leaning over Leonard, saying, 'Are you all right?'

214

'Yes. Yes,' Leonard gasped; 'just give me a tablet,' and he pointed towards the side table.

A minute later, seeing the concern in Daisy's face, he said, 'It's all right, Daisy. You're . . . you're a marvel. But now tell John the rest. That'll quieten us down.'

'Sure you're all right?' said John. 'Shall I call Johnson?'

'No. No. A laugh like that is the best medicine in the world. You should know that, a doctor.' He turned to look at the big, gaunt face again and said, 'Go on, Daisy. Finish it.'

Sitting back in the chair, Daisy put her forearm under what must have been her withered breasts and heaved them upwards slightly before, looking at John, she said, 'The following day there was a letter on my breakfast tray. It was to the effect that if I wished to remain his wife and not be sent home in disgrace, or words to that effect, then I must promise to obey him, in all ways – oh yes, he added those words, in all ways – but mostly I must promise never to go near the leper colony or to speak with Frank La-Mode again. He ended by saying that he would be up country for the next four days and that he would expect my answer on his return.'

There was a pause before she said, 'Well, I wrote him my answer. It was to the effect that, before the leper incident, I had intended to return to England, my wish being that he would divorce me, as I knew our marriage had been a grave mistake. But now, since my acid bath, or whatever it was, and by the way' – she now nodded at John – 'it left me feeling skinned: for weeks I looked as if I had been boiled, and when my body started to peel it was a very painful process. Anyway, I said that it was a toss-up whether I returned to England or went to work in the leper colony, but that after much thought I had decided on the latter course. And I finished the letter with the words: "Some people are afraid of the death they'll never experience, but die they will some day." And so I went into the leper colony as a helper, and I was there for seven years.'

'No!' John was shaking his head. All their faces were sombre now, and Daisy said, 'Yes, and I can honestly say they were the saddest yet at the same time the happiest days of my life. And you know, it was very strange, but in the second year there I began to get parcels of medicine and first-aid materials from people in other districts of whom I'd previously known nothing.'

'Why did you leave after seven years?' asked John quietly now.

'Frank insisted on it. My flesh began to drop off me, literally. I had been a big woman and I became skin and bone, as you see me now.' She held out her hands. 'Yet, I never contracted the disease. It was strange.'

'What did your husband do about all this?'

She remained silent for a moment before she said, 'What could he do? He'd lost face, which was an awful thing. I was sorry about that, because the natives talk. He wasn't moved from his position – I was glad of that – but he died from malaria the year after I came back to England. At least, that's what it was put down to. But he had never got on with a certain tribe and had made an enemy of the witch-doctor. And the servants, I understood, said this man had put a curse on him and prophesied he would die on a certain day and had sent him word to that effect. And he did die, so I'm told, on that very day. It was his assistant who spread the story. But I don't think it *was* a story. I realise now that Tommy was terrified of death and I've always blamed myself for the words I put on the end of that letter. Yet, at the time I was suffering bodily agony from whatever chemical he had put in that bath. It obviously wasn't really acid or I wouldn't be here now. But even Frank, who happened to be a doctor' – she nodded now at John – 'he couldn't put a name to what might have been mixed in with the carbolic. Carbolic is bad

216

enough, you know, but I don't think it would have left me the way it did, or him. But it was his face and hands that caught it most. His clothes and the speed with which he got rid of them had saved him from anything worse, I should imagine.'

'You're a wonderful lady, Daisy.'

'Now don't you try to soft soap me, Sir Leonard Morton Spears.' She turned towards John, saying under her breath, 'You never get offered a drink in this house, only soft words. D'you know that?'

At this Leonard laughed and put out his hand and rang the little bell on the side table, which brought Johnson into the room, and Leonard said to him, 'You know the tastes of our friends, don't you, Johnson?' And the man, looking from one to the other, smiled, but stiffly, as he said, 'Port for madam, and whisky, plain, for the doctor.'

'And what about me, Johnson?'

His man now shook his head as he said, 'You may have a choice, sir, of orange juice, apple juice or a blackcurrant cordial.'

'Yes. Yes, you needn't go through them again, I'll have the last one. It's got some colour about it, anyway, and one can use one's imagination.'

When the man had left the room, John said to Daisy, 'Do you still ride?'

'Oh yes. Yes. I've got a beautiful mare. She's called Fanny, for short. She's nine.'

'Well,' said John, 'if she's Fanny for short, what is her real name?'

'Fanackapan.'

'What?'

'Fanackapan, Fanny, Fan . . . ack . . . a . . . pan.'

John was laughing again. 'That's a very odd name to give a horse.'

'Yes. Yes, but the day I bought her there were a number of women among the dealers, and one, looking at mine

217

as she was led round the ring, said, "Oh, that's a Fanny Fanackapan." I'd never heard the expression before and I've never heard it since, so I bought her. She was a yearling, and oh, have we enjoyed ourselves. She can take a farm gate like a ballet dancer.'

Before the drinks were brought in Daisy looked at Leonard. His eyes were half-closed and, getting to her feet, she said, 'You know what I'm going to do? I'm going to throw off that port in one gulp and get myself out of this. I've just realised I've left her standing in that cold wind. Why don't you have your barns made like any other sensible man, with four sides on them and a door, not just a roof?'

Leonard opened his eyes and smiled at her, saying, 'Give Fanny my apologies. I'll still the wind for her the next time she comes.'

Johnson came into the room with the drinks and, as she had intimated, Daisy threw the drink off in a gulp; went to the chair-bed, bent over Leonard and said, 'Smell my breath; it will do you good.' Then, her voice dropping, she added, 'Be a good fellow.'

His voice was a mere whisper now as he said, 'Come again soon, Daisy. Please!'

'I will. I will. Good night, and all the gods be with you.' She straightened up now, turned to John and said briefly, 'Good night, doctor.'

'Good night, Daisy. It's been a pleasure.'

She made no reply to this but went out of the room, followed by Johnson. And John, about to sit down again, was stayed by Leonard saying, 'Bring a chair up near me,' and he pointed to the side of the chair-bed. And when John had done this, Leonard said, 'A remarkable woman.'

'Yes, indeed, a very remarkable woman. And one who can laugh at herself.'

'Every word she said was true, but she didn't go into other details that are more surprising still. She's been through the

218

mill, oh yes; and ground down finely, I can tell you. And she's been a very good friend to us.'

'Yes; yes, I should imagine so.'

'But now, after all that, how am I going to say what I want to say? It will sound so mundane, but I must say it. And there's not a lot of time left, now is there?'

John made no reply for a moment, and then he said quietly, 'It's up to you. The will is a mighty machine: if it knows you have an incentive strong enough to guide it, it'll work for you.'

Leonard's head was turned away and his voice was low as he said, 'What d'you think has been working for me for weeks past? I have to call on the incentive every time I look at her because of what will assuredly happen to her when the time comes. Of one thing I am sure: our so-called friends will all gradually find their way back here. The thread that ran through Daisy's husband runs through them all. Daisy will be the only one besides yourself whom she'll have as a real friend. And it is about this I want to talk. Rosie now has a husband and a mother-in-law, and a business in which she's very interested, and she is a woman. But Helen . . . well, Helen is a man's woman.'

John looked somewhat startled, for his eyes had widened, and his mouth was slightly agape, which brought a smile from Leonard as he said, 'What makes you look so surprised? Surely you know there are women who need men's company and men who need women's company, more than they do that of their own sex. Not that they need men, plural, but man singular I would say. Oh, dear me, I'm putting it very technically and badly. And so what I want to say I had better say straight out. Will you continue to be her friend? She'll be a widow, and as you are not her doctor, your visits might cause a little talk. But would you risk that and continue to be her friend, if nothing more? *Oh! Oh!*' – he screwed up his eyes now and held up his hand

219

– 'Don't protest, don't protest. I know something and you know something: if I hadn't come on the scene when I did, then I would never have got her. Had you two met earlier, that would have been that. Oh, I knew that. Please! Please! John, don't look so embarrassed. I've known it all along. She kept talking about you after your meeting on that hill; and then you avoided our wedding. After that, she never again mentioned your name. And then there came the time when she grew to love me. Oh yes, she grew to love me, so very much. Never as much as I loved her, but she loved me, and from the moment she loved me she began to talk about you again, although in an off-hand way. But when you married Beatrice, that was that. She just couldn't believe it and you went out of her life completely, and I was very, very happy. But life plays strange tricks with one. Anyway, this is something rather difficult that I'm asking you to do, because you're still married to Beatrice and so any visits to her sister would not go unnoticed and there would be talk. I'm asking this of you for very selfish reasons: there is a man I know who will, as soon as I'm out of the way, make a bee-line for her. Not that, under normal circumstances, she would think about it in any way, but loneliness is a very strange thing. I've experienced it, so I know what I'm talking about. Perhaps you too have waited for the gold and it has passed you by, so you have taken the dross by way of comfort. I've learned that you cannot blame people for what they do shortly after a bereavement. Now, I know Helen is not of a weak nature and so could be easily influenced, but I want her to have the right company. If you had still been living with Beatrice, I would not have put this to you. Do you consider it strange that I should be asking this of you?'

John paused a moment before he said, 'Yes, in a way, Leonard, I do. I can only see myself and my reactions as if I were in your shoes. But I'm not as big as you in any way, for I would be jealous of the thought of anyone like

Helen finding solace, any sort of solace in another man's company. And now let me say something, Leonard. I was jealous of you. Oh yes, very jealous of you, for a long time; and then we met and I realised how wise she had been in her choice. I could never have hoped to live up to your high standards. I know myself, and over the weeks during which our friendship has grown, my admiration for you has grown too. And I say again, I wouldn't be big enough to act as you're doing now, not in any way.'

'You have a very poor opinion of yourself, John. It is quite different from that which others have of you. There are not many who would have wrecked their own marriage, as you did through helping Rosie.'

'Oh no! No!' John shook his head vigorously. 'My marriage was on the rocks before that. But you're quite right about us not knowing what goes on in another's mind, especially in a lonely mind, and of the results of that loneliness. Marriage with Beatrice proved that to me. If ever there was a double personality in a human being, it is in her. I can't go into it, but long before Rosie's affair our marriage was ended. I was already considering a legal separation.'

Following John's statement there was silence between them. Then, as if aiming now to dismiss the conversation, Leonard said, 'Those pills are marvellous, you know' – he nodded towards the table – 'they put new life into me.' He smiled now, then added, 'Going back to what we were talking about earlier, man's woman, and woman's woman, you wouldn't think Daisy would fall into the former category, would you? But she does. With her looks you would think she was out of the running altogether; but even at her age she could have a number of men friends tomorrow. She's had three permanent men in her life.'

John's face showed surprise, and Leonard said, 'Oh, yes, you can raise your eyebrows. And she's known the grand passion. Just once, as she said, but it has remained with her.'

'Well, you do surprise me, Leonard. I must say you do, for she seems the most unlikely person to . . .'.

'Come! come!' said Leonard now somewhat briskly; 'You a doctor and admitting that anything you hear that is off the beaten track about another's life should surprise you. Tut! tut! But yes, I can see your point: the first meeting with Daisy can be a little mind-boggling. Her Tommy divorced her on the grounds of desertion while she was still in the leper colony. So she had no monetary support and she was almost penniless when she returned to England. It was when she found herself in hospital that she first saw her dear Stephen, Stephen King, which she doesn't think was his real name. But she understood he visited old people who were without friends. And apparently she was without friends and from the first time they met up, it was done. It was the same with him, I think, from what she says.'

'But what about her family? She said she was one of ten.'

'Yes, she was one of ten, John, but they were all married and had children. And were they going to rush to meet this weird Aunt Daisy, who had spent seven years in a leper colony and was likely contagious? Without exception, all her family held the same view as Tommy had. Odd' – here he smiled – 'I always think of him as Tommy, not Freeman Wheatland, which sounds too superior a name for him because to me he was a funk of a man. Anyway, to cut her long story short, and she has kept this part very short, even while keeping me amused, which is always her intention when she comes here, they worked together and they lived together. For four years they lived together. I asked her why they never married, and she answered simply, "He never asked me." What did they live on? I asked her, because they spent their days helping others. What she did tell me was that she felt he was expiating something he had done when he was young. She even says he might have been in

222

prison for a time. She didn't enquire, she just loved him. But apparently he had enough money to sustain them in ordinary living conditions, and every now and again he would give her so much to keep things going. Where it came from she never knew. His life was a mystery. But that didn't matter to her. The only thing that did was, she had him for four long years, long, happy years. And then' – now Leonard snapped his fingers – 'he goes like that. One day he was there, the next he was gone, leaving her enough money for her to carry on for six months and also a note to say he would always love her.'

'Good gracious!'

'Yes, that's what I said, John. Good gracious! I asked her if she had heard of him since, and she said, 'Never.' But what she did say was, he might have gone back to a wife and family in Ireland or somewhere out of the country. Or her earlier thoughts might have been the reason, that he had a criminal record and was living now on the results while expiating that past.'

'And she's never heard of him since, in any way; never seen a photograph or anything?'

'No, never; and just as well, I would say, for she wouldn't be living comfortably as she is today if he had stayed with her. For then she wouldn't have met her Mr Anasby . . . Mr James Anasby. You know, I've said this before, John, but her life would fill a book, and not just one. Oh no, not one, because the last episode really is fantastic. From how she told me, it should happen that she was glad to get a position as an assistant nurse. You see, she'd had no proper training, although she had nursed in that leper colony. But this day she happened to be late and was hurrying through a side door used by the staff when the door caught the end of her finger and drew her to a dead stop. And she stood holding it and exclaiming what, in ordinary English, would have been "Damn and blast it!" Instead she uttered three words in an African tribal dialect, and then was astounded to hear an immediate response in the same language. She turned to see a man in a wheelchair, flanked by two nurses and being pushed by a man in green livery. She had gaped at him for a moment, then spoke to him in the language again. What next he said was, "What is your name? Who are you?"

'She told him her name and also that she was an assistant nurse there. The latter information seemed to surprise him, and he protested strongly, "What's the Colonial Office doing, not using you in some way? How long were you out there?"

' "Oh," she had paused and said, "a number of years." And then he put his head back and looked at the man in the livery and said, "Give the lady my card, Mason." And at this the man drew a card from his inner pocket and handed it to her; but she didn't look at it immediately because she was studying the man in the wheelchair. He was elderly, well into his sixties, she surmised, as she also did that he was someone of importance. Then he said, "Will you come and see me?"

'She then glanced at the card without properly reading it, but said, "Yes, sir. I'd be pleased to." It's another long, long story, quite unbelievable, but within a month she was well installed in his expensive house as a nurse-companion. Apparently, he had spent much of his life in the area of Africa Daisy knew. He had been married twice, both wives having died. He seemed to have no close relatives. She was with him seven years and gradually knew all his business and money transactions in which he came to appreciate her judgement. When he died she was only forty-four and he left her half of his estate.'

John shook his head as he said, 'Amazing story, amazing.'

'Well, you should be used to amazing stories in your job.'

'Nothing like that, I can assure you, Leonard. Although,

224

here and there, you do get a surprise.' He now added, 'You've been talking too much; you're tired.'

'Yes, John, I am a little tired. But, in a strange way, I am happy that we've come to an understanding. At least, I hope we have.' He stared at John now, but when there was no reply immediately forthcoming from John, he said quietly, 'Have I asked too much?'

'No. No. Not at all.' But now he held up his hand, 'Don't start again. I'm going to ring for Johnson. I think you'd be wise to have an early night, because the theatre-goers will certainly not be back before eleven.'

'Oh, I had no intention of waiting up for them.'

Leonard watched John rise and ring the bell; then he held out his hand, and as John took it he said simply, 'Thank you.' But when his man entered the room, he said, 'I'm being ordered about in my own house, Johnson, and I'm not standing any more of it, so, would you like to see the doctor to the door.'

The two men smiled at each other, then went out. But there was no exchange of words: not even in the hall after he had helped John into his coat, then opened the front door, did Johnson say a word. Nor did he answer John's 'Good night'; which caused John to remark to himself, 'He's a stiff-necked fellow, that. And he has no use for me. That's plain. Well, I can return the compliment there.'

# 2

Beatrice was paying her weekly Friday visit to the town. It was a bright day, the sun was shining and the main thoroughfare was full of shoppers.

She made sure she did not always visit the same sweet shop to buy her chocolates. People talked. Oh yes, people talked. She knew they talked about her both inside and outside the house. So, sometimes she would walk as far as the outskirts of the town to a little sweet shop she knew, there to purchase the only comfort she had in life, she told herself; and they were good for her anyway; they must be, because they weren't putting weight on her.

In her tapestry-trimmed felt bag she was now carrying two pound boxes and one half-pound box of chocolates. At one time she had always put a pound box on the household order, but not since she had cut down on the kitchen requirements. Four of them there, eating their heads off, and his meagre allowance to her hardly paid their wages. She was going to do something about that, too. Two doing the gardening and Needler pottering in the yard. What did they do most of their time? Sit in the greenhouse drinking tea. Oh, she knew what went on; she had nothing to do but watch them from the windows.

Today, she had walked as far as Brampton Hill, which was almost on the outskirts. But, from the sweet shop there she had been able to buy only a half-pound box of chocolates. As the shop-keeper had said, they were only asked for pounds at Christmastime.

Seeing a post office reminded her that she hadn't any stamps, and she needed to write to that solicitor again. Oh, yes, she should indeed.

She hadn't entered this post office before and was annoyed that there were a number of people waiting to be served. When she joined those waiting for stamps, there were three people before her, and she moved from one foot to the other with impatience. She wasn't accustomed to having to wait to be served.

Her fidgeting moved the bag that she was carrying and it came in contact with the woman in front of her, so causing her to turn and stare at her, and the recognition was instant, especially on Beatrice's part. Aiming to step back from the woman, she pointedly pulled her skirt back as if from contact with her, only immediately to be admonished by the woman behind saying, 'Look what you're doing! I've got a child here.'

When, added to this, the woman in front of her also muttered something as she moved away after picking up her two penny stamps, Beatrice paused for a second before taking her place. And there, in a high and superior tone she asked for six penny stamps, which she then placed very carefully in her bag, together with her change, before turning away.

When she walked into the street and saw the woman standing as if waiting for her, she made to pass her, but the hand that came out and grabbed her arm made her turn furiously and say, 'How dare you! Let go of my arm this minute!'

'I will,' growled Mollie Wallace, 'when I've had me say, and it's this. Who the hell d'you think you are? Trying to show me up in there, pulling your skirt away as if I had the mange. You above all people, daughter of a dirty old bastard who couldn't pay for his pleasure. And I'll tell you something else when I'm on. That man of yours, he was the means of getting me put out, I'm sure of that, 'cos it was him who brought Jackie home. But I'll get me own back on him, just you wait. I'll get me own back on the lot of you. Poverty-stricken buggers that you are.' And at this she released her hold on Beatrice's arm with a push that caused Beatrice to stagger back against the post office wall.

It would appear that she had been struck speechless by the attack. But it had been only her fear of a scene, a street scene, that had prevented her from raising her hand and slapping this filthy individual, as she thought of her, across the face. But she was determined to have the last word as she said, 'Scum!' before turning away; yet even in this she was forestalled by Mollie Wallace saying, 'And if I was you, missis, I'd look out for your own man. Aye, I would that. By God! yes, I would that.' And at this she swung round and marched away, leaving Beatrice with one hand to her throat now, the other clutching the handle of her bag to her waist.

She had felt angry before, but that creature mentioning her husband in such a suggestive way made her initial anger pale against the rage that was consuming her now. Those people! That woman! How did she know what went on in the house? Oh! Oh! Why was she so stupid? Of course, servants talked. They just had to hint. She would dismiss them, the lot, the lot! She swung about now, intending to stalk away, but found that her legs appeared weak and, as was the rest of her body, were trembling. Her mind still on her staff, she cried inwardly that she didn't need them all: two in the kitchen and two in the house, and only her to look after! And three outside. She'd get rid of William Connor. But no, he was the only one who could see to the topiary; the hedge must be kept clipped, or the garden would look so unkempt, and you couldn't keep up prestige with an unkempt garden . . . or house.

Oh, dear me! Her head was beginning to buzz again. She was in for that awful feeling which obliged her to lie down. She, who until recently had never taken to reclining in the middle of the day. And when she did lie down, her thoughts would jump all over the place, and all about him. Legal separation, the solicitor had said. Well, he wouldn't get past that. Never! He was her husband and he would remain her husband until he died. But then, what did that woman mean? There was no smoke without fire. But he could do nothing there, for Helen was married. Yes, but to a sick man. And you never got rid of TB, did you? Was her dear John waiting for the man to die? Oh, yes, she could see him doing that. And then there were the carriage trips; she had watched his mother getting into Helen's carriage. There was never smoke without fire. No; that woman knew something. And if that woman knew something, others did, too.

Oh, she wished she was at home; she must lie down. She would get a cab; yes; she must get a cab.

She took a cab, and when she reached the house she went straight up the stairs, taking her bag with her. Then, having removed her coat and hat and shoes, she lay down on the bed, but not before she had gobbled half a dozen chocolates, hardly giving herself time to swallow one before stuffing another into her mouth until her body stiffened and she was unable to move hand or foot for quite some time. Yet, all the while, her brain was active, raging around the circumstances of her life, until at last the spasm in her body relaxed, and with it came the tears, and presently sleep.

It was some time later when Frances, knocking gently on the bedroom door, opened it to enquire if her mistress would like a cup of tea, and seeing her as she had done a number of times lately, lying fast asleep, her mouth partly open and her lips patterned with her indulgence from the chocolate box, she closed the door gently, shaking her head as she thought: It would be more satisfying, I should imagine, if she were to take to the bottle.

# 3

'You off tonight again to play bridge?'

John turned to his partner and paused for some seconds before he said, 'What d'you mean, *again*?'

'Well, you go over there often, don't you, and play bridge?'

'If once a week is often, then yes, I go often.'

'Oh! Once a week.'

'Yes, once a week. May I ask what you're getting at, Doctor?'

'Oh! Oh, now, laddie, don't take that tone with me. But you see I happen to know Doctor Peters. He's looking after Sir Leonard Spears.'

'Yes. Yes, he is. And I too happen to know Doctor Peters, and he is conversant with my visits and he knows I'm a friend of the family. Lady Helen is my sister-in-law.'

'Yes. Yes, Lady Helen is your sister-in-law. But I was just enquiring if you were going over tonight.'

'Why? Is your leg troubling you again?'

Doctor Cornwallis turned a flushed and angry face up to his partner as he replied tersely, 'No, my leg isn't hurting me. Nor has my tongue got a sting in it.'

'That surprises me.'

This swift reply, one which was definitely devoid of the respect due to him, caused the older man's bushy eyebrows to

231

strain towards his receding hairline. But apparently he could find no words to combat this statement for, after blowing his nose violently, he turned in his revolving chair and applied himself to some papers on his desk, and John gave a wry smile as he said, 'Good-night, Doctor.' Then, walking into the adjacent room where the young Doctor Rees was awaiting the first patient of the evening surgery, he bent towards him, saying quietly, 'Look out for squalls.'

The younger man grinned at John and said, 'Like that, is it?'

'Yes, like that.'

'Well, that's nothing new.'

'No, but it might be a bit rougher tonight.'

'Should I put my oilskins on?'

At this, John went out on a low laugh, but it disappeared as he gained the street, for inwardly he was annoyed: the old man's words had suggested much more than they had said. Perhaps Doctor Peters had made an innocent remark, because he couldn't imagine him being a gossip. He was a very nice fellow, rather reserved. But the old devil back there always put two and one together and made four. He loved tit-bits of scandal and would concoct his own version of them. Unfortunately, in many cases, he was right. Which naturally would have made him surmise he was on to something here. Well, wasn't he? No! No! The words came in loud denial. If Helen hadn't been Leonard's wife, he would still have liked the man's company, would have sought it, in fact, not only for the patient's comfort but for his own. There was something very calming about Leonard Spears's personality, which came out in his broad views and his understanding of human nature and tolerance. Bust old Cornwallis! One of *his* assets was his ability to put a damper on things. A little stir here and there and you had a topic for spicy conversation . . .

*     *     *

His mother said, 'Aren't you going to stay and have a bite to eat? Mrs Atkinson has cooked a nice meal.'

'Look, dear' – he bent over her – 'if I stay for dinner it'll be another hour or more before I can leave. And Leonard must get to bed early. But he does enjoy that game. I won't be late. I'll be back about nine.'

'Oh, don't you hurry back; Mrs Atkinson's here until ten, and as I've told you before, she doesn't mind staying on.'

'She won't need to, I'll be back.' Then, straightening up, he looked hard at her before he said, 'Are you lonely? I mean . . .'

'I know what you mean. No, I'm not lonely any more. You're here at nights, you're here at dinner-time, you're here at tea-time, so how could I be lonely? No; get yourself away. I want you to have a little relaxation.'

He nodded at her; then, his voice low, he said, 'We'll have a talk when I come back. I'm wondering if we should stay on here; perhaps I should look out for some place else, because . . .?'

'No, you won't look for some place else: I've paid up for five years; and I like it here; it suits me. And if you don't mind staying . . . and anyway—' her hands came out towards him and she said softly, 'It would only hurt her more if we moved. Here, your being in the house, or at least in a part of it, she can still put a face on things; but if we move she'll feel entirely deserted. You know what I mean?'

'Yes.' He nodded at her. 'Suits me. But I just thought . . .'

'Well, don't think for me, just think for yourself and you'll have plenty to do, laddie.' And she went to push him away but he bent and kissed her, before leaving . . .

When Hannah Worth opened the door to him and said, 'Good-evening, Doctor,' he answered, 'Good-evening, Hannah,' then instantly turned to look towards the drawing-room door, and in a mournful tone Hannah said, 'He's been coughing a lot the day, Doctor. And the mistress can't get him to stay in bed.'

Immediately he entered the drawing-room John knew there could be no bridge this night, for the deterioration in Leonard was evident.

'Hello, Leonard!' he said. 'What have you been up to?'

'Fighting off women.' The voice was hoarse and low, and Leonard directed his gaze towards where Helen and Daisy were standing together. 'The only thing those two can think about is bed . . . I thought you were going' – he was speaking directly to Daisy, and she answered in much the same tone, 'I'm going, and I'll think twice about coming back.'

'Well, before you go, tell John here about your do at the Oswalds.'

'I'll do no such thing; I'm off. Don't bother seeing me out, Helen. I'll see you in the morning . . . Hello, Doctor! and good night.'

'The same to you, Daisy,' he answered, and on this she gave a giggle of a laugh and went out.

'Sit down, John,' said Helen, drawing a chair nearer to Leonard.

John sat down and asked Leonard quietly, 'What have you been up to? Trying to trot about?'

'Of course. What do you expect?' Then turning to Helen, he said, 'Tell John about Daisy's soup business . . . She does me good, that woman.'

'Oh dear me!' said Helen; 'I couldn't tell it as she does. Anyway, to cut a very long and funny story as told by Daisy . . . short: an elderly couple, called Pratt, from the Midlands, had moved into old Swift's house on the river – it's a lovely place – and, of course, Gladys Oswald immediately grabbed at them and invited them to dinner. But, to her horror, the old gentleman slurped his soup – he was apparently holding his spoon the wrong way. Added to this, he told a risqué story about one of his mill girls and

234

so caused Ralph Bannister to splutter out his food. It was a disastrous occasion, apparently. But she made the mistake of warning Daisy about them and telling her she meant to pass round this news to her friends.

'It should happen that Daisy had already met the couple and liked them, and she told Gladys so, but she finally put her foot in it by bringing up the dreaded word and asking her how she imagined a leper would eat his soup.'

Helen held out her hands expressively, saying, 'It doesn't sound a bit funny, does it, Leonard? but when Daisy told it, it was uproarious.'

John's reaction was to say, 'You can't imagine such snobbery up this end of the country; the people seem so open and free,' only for Helen to put in quickly, 'Oh, John! you know nothing about it. For instance, apart from everything else, my father was an utter snob.'

John could have put in here, 'And his eldest daughter takes after him.'

There was silence for a moment; then Leonard said, 'We keep talking about the awful people when we should be telling you of the lovely ones. Tell him, Helen, about the wedding present.'

'Oh, yes; yes,' said Helen, now going to the head of the chair-bed and taking Leonard's hand which she held close to her chest as she said, 'Rosie and Robbie must have thought it strange that we didn't give them a wedding present. Well, you see, the trap wasn't finished. Leonard had arranged for them to have a pony and trap as a wedding present, but Mr Wilson, who was making the trap, and is a wonderful craftsman and wheelwright, as his people have been for generations, had been confined to bed with a bad bout of bronchitis, and wouldn't allow even his son, or his two workmen, to finish it. Anyway, there it was this morning, pulled by a beautiful piebald pony and driven by an absolute radiant couple. You should have seen their faces.

235

Rosie was in tears, and her rough and charming Scot was showing equally warm emotion.'

'Oh, I must go round first thing tomorrow,' John said, 'But what I am going to do now is to follow Daisy, because the place for you, Sir Leonard Spears, is bed.'

Strangely, Leonard made no objection, but he did say, 'Would you drop in tomorrow?'

John was on his feet now and answering, 'Yes; but I don't know what time I'll be over.'

'Thanks.'

The two men looked hard at each other for a moment; then John, putting his hand out towards Helen, said, 'Don't move. I can see my way out . . . Good night.'

He was glad to get out of the house, because his throat was full.

At the open barn Henry said, 'I'll harness him up again, sir;' and when John said, 'Thanks, Henry,' the man said, 'How is the master, Doctor? You never get the truth out of Doctor Peters; only the words "as well as can be expected", and not a word out of Johnson.'

'Well, the truth is, Henry, he's in a bad way.'

'Yes. Yes, I thought that. He'll be a miss. Oh, he'll be a miss. I worked for his cousin, you know, Sir Frederick, for years; and he was a good boss, but he didn't come up to this one. He treats all the staff like family, he does. Oh, he will be missed.'

Later, as John made for the annexe he thought of Henry's feeling for his employer, and that if at the end of his life a servant of his could give him such a recommendation, he would feel that his living hadn't been altogether self-centred. But he doubted that would happen. He wasn't made in the same mould as Leonard. And every day he could understand more and more the extent of Helen's love for the man, and love him, she did. And her sorrowing would be great. So, what hope could he hold in that direction, even if he had

236

been free of Beatrice? If he was brave enough to tell himself the truth, he would have to say, little or none.

The first words his mother uttered when he got in were, 'My! you're back early. Well, how did you find him?'

'Poorly. Going down hill rapidly.'

'How long d'you think he's got?'

It was some seconds before he replied, 'A few days.'

'Poor soul,' she said. 'Poor soul.'

# 4

Leonard died at half-past three on the Saturday morning. John had seen him the previous evening, but only for a moment because Doctor Peters was with him, as was Johnson. As he stood by the bed he had been unable to speak but he had taken the long white hand in his and held it for a moment. It was then between gasps that Leonard said, 'See you . . . tomorrow, John,' and he had answered, 'Yes, Leonard. Yes, I'll pop in tomorrow.' And as he went to release his hold on the hand and move from the bed, Leonard, looking at him with that penetrating gaze, said, 'Thanks, John. Thanks.' And John knew that the thanks wasn't referring to his calling on the morrow, but a final goodbye.

He met Helen in the hall, but he felt unable to speak to her, and she spoke no word to him: they exchanged a look, and then he left the house . . .

But here he was, again standing in the hall, but facing Rosie now. When she said, 'He died at half-past three,' he offered no rejoinder, except to ask, 'How is she?'

For the second time Rosie rubbed a handkerchief around her face, then gulped before she said, 'Calm, strangely calm. Since Leonard was seen to, she has sat by him – but it isn't wise. And she hasn't shed a tear.'

No, she wouldn't cry; there were some pains that could not immediately be relieved by tears.

He said to Rosie, 'Tell her I shall call later.' . . .

He did call later, and the next day, and the next, and on each occasion found he was slightly nonplussed by her demeanour, for she seemed fully in command of herself. As Rosie said quietly to him, 'It isn't right. She's acting as if every day was an ordinary day: giving orders to the servants and seeing the undertakers and such. It's strange. The solicitor came and said he would see to things, but she thanked him and told him she could manage.' . . .

Leonard was buried two days later and Helen broke the custom that it wasn't suitable for a woman to attend her husband's funeral; moreover, she remained standing by the open grave after the others had moved away. But she still remained dry-eyed, which of course was remarked upon by the mourners.

Many people had attended the funeral and a number had returned to the house, about some of whom Daisy had remarked, 'They'll get short shrift from me; they've left their visits a little late.'

It was she who dared to stand in the hallway and give polite messages to those visitors who had earlier been afraid to come near the house, using such phrases as, Lady Spears thanked them for their attendance; but she was sure that they understood she now wanted to be alone. Only one lady dared to press her right to see the bereaved, and to her Daisy spoke more than plainly. Leading her firmly to the door, she pressed her through and onto the step, saying frankly, 'Claire, you're years too late. She doesn't want to see you now or at any other time. Am I making myself plain?' And that lady had rejoined, 'Yes, as plain as your face,' and, comforting herself that she had had the last word, she marched away to her carriage.

Two days after the funeral Rosie returned home. She was

239

not a little perplexed at Helen's reaction to her husband's death and she said as much to John; also, that Helen seemed to be more at ease with Mrs Wheatland, and she had asked if John didn't think that Mrs Wheatland was a rather strange woman, for at times she never stopped talking, while at others she would sit and not open her mouth. But Helen did not seem to mind her either way.

John understood that Rosie was a little peeved that this strange woman should be more acceptable company to Helen than herself. And he understood them both: Helen would prefer Daisy's company, for Daisy, even when she was being amusing, emanated life, painful life; whereas Rosie had, in a way, regained the joy of living which could not be entirely hidden by the tears of compassion or comforting words, or by the unnatural solemn expression.

Johnson met him in the hall and said, 'Her Ladyship is in the drawing-room, sir.'

'Thank you, Johnson.' Then John paused for a moment before he said, 'What d'you intend to do now? I mean, are you going to look for another position in your own line?'

'Oh, that's been all arranged, sir. Her Ladyship has asked me to stay on and look after the establishment while she is away. I'll inform her Ladyship that you're here, sir.'

He'd inform her Ladyship that he was here. This was the first time he'd had to be announced. But, of course, it had been usually one of the girls who opened the door to him. He realised now that he really disliked this man: something about him got under his skin. But she had made arrangements and apparently everything was settled, at least with regard to the running of her household. Like Rosie he felt slightly piqued.

When Johnson said, 'Doctor Falconer, m'lady,' he had the urge to thrust the man aside.

Helen was sitting on the couch. He walked slowly up the room towards her, saying as she made to rise, 'Don't get up.' He did not immediately sit down beside her, but as he had not previously taken off his overcoat and was carrying his hat in his hand, he now laid these both on a chair, saying ironically, 'Your butler needs training, madam; he has omitted to divest me of my outer garments.'

'Oh.' She moved her head slightly. 'He's not my butler, John; quite candidly' – she gave him a wan smile – 'I don't know what to call him.'

'No? Well, he informed me almost before I got across the step that you have arranged for him to be in charge of the house whilst you are away . . . It's all arranged then? You're going away?'

'Sit down, John.' She motioned to a chair opposite her. And when he was seated, she said, 'It's all been done in a hurry. I had a letter yesterday from Leonard's cousin in Paris. She's the old lady; I think he mentioned her to you as someone who has never lifted a finger for herself in her life. Well, she wrote to me apologising for being unable to attend the funeral – she's in her late seventies – but expressing a deep wish that I should visit her. It's a very nice letter, very moving. And so, well, I wrote straight back and accepted her invitation because—' she now leaned forward and made a motion of appeal with her hand towards him as she said, 'John, I must get away. I'll . . . I'll break down completely if I stay here. It will only be for a time.'

'What d'you mean by a time, Helen?'

She closed her eyes as she said, 'I don't know. A few months. I . . . I won't admit his loss, John; I can't, not while I'm here.'

'So, you're going away to get rid of him, and his memory, to wipe him out as if he had never been?'

He had expected her to deny this vehemently, but she surprised him with her answer: 'Yes. Yes, something like that, because I can't put up with this pain. I knew it would be bad. For a long time I had faced up to what it would be like, at least, I thought I had; but now I'm in this vast . . . vast emptiness. There is nothing or no-one I can reach out to.'

'No-one?' His words were deeply sad, and she turned her head away from him and drew her lower lip tightly between her teeth before she said, 'I . . . I thought you would understand.'

His tone changed now as he murmured, 'Yes. Yes, I do, dear. Yes, I do. I, too, am feeling the pain of his loss, but of course it's nothing compared with yours. Yes, I *do* understand.'

She lay back on the couch and, taking a handkerchief from her cuff, she wiped her lips. There was no sign of tears in her eyes: they were dry and bright and they fixed on him now as she said softly, 'If there's anyone who could keep me here, it would be you, John . . . and Daisy. The rest' – she gave a contemptuous lift to her chin – 'they flood in daily now that the danger of infection is passed. But as I pointed out to dear Gwendoline Fenwick, I wasn't sure if I had contracted it; that it was a very contagious disease, and I could actually see her shrinking within her voluminous gown. Well' – she nodded – 'she's one I'll not be seeing again.'

'When d'you intend to leave?'

'Within the next day or two.'

'And you're travelling alone?'

'Yes. Yes, John.' She nodded. 'It's done these days, you know.'

'I . . . I know that.' His tone was sharp. 'But . . . but I wondered, what about Daisy?'

'Yes, I thought about asking her, but her life is well arranged, with her leper committees and good deeds. Now, in no way am I ridiculing those. What's more, she has never come anywhere near to suggesting that she should accompany me. Yet, I know that had she done so I would readily have accepted her company for, as Leonard used to say about her, "She, tight-corner fellow." The saying goes back to Leonard's Indian corporal; when men had to be chosen for a dangerous mission, he would say, "That one, tight-corner fellow." '

John was to remember and to endorse this description of Daisy.

There was a short silence before he said, 'D'you know Leonard asked me to . . . well, to be your friend, to help you in . . . in any way you needed me?'

'Yes. Yes, I know.' Her words came rapidly now. 'Yes, I know, John, and . . . we'll talk about it some time later. I know I couldn't have a better friend; and he knew that, too. Yes' – her head was bobbing now – 'We'll talk about it later, some time.' She rose quickly to her feet now and he could see she was disturbed, and he said, 'Will I be seeing you before you go then?'

'Yes. Yes, of course. It will be another couple of days or so before all arrangements are made.'

'And you are leaving Johnson in charge?'

'Yes.' Her eyes widened now and there was an appeal in them as she said, 'What else can I do? I can't just walk out and expect either you or Daisy to come and keep an eye on the staff. As good as they are, and they are wonderful, they need to have someone in charge, someone who is used to arranging and giving orders.' She paused before she added, 'He's a little bumptious, I know, and very conscious of his position. I think it is far better to have someone of that nature, one whom you can trust, than the alternative, which is to engage a housekeeper. Don't you think so?'

'Yes. Yes, I suppose you're right. Yes, of course you are.'

Again they were facing each other; and now she began nervously to straighten the narrow hem of the handkerchief in her hand, and she had brought it into a complete square before she said, 'I'd . . . I'd like to say this to you, John – I've . . . I've wanted to say it before – it's just that I'm

243

. . . I'm so sorry that your life . . . marriage, went awry. You . . . You deserve a happy home.'

He knew his face was flushed; and it was as if his voice had suddenly taken on the depths of a baritone as he muttered, 'I have a good life with my mother.'

'Oh, John, I'm . . . I'm sorry I've spoken about it; I just wanted you to . . .'

The colour was now ebbing from his cheeks and he thrust out his hand towards her, and when hers lay in it he said, 'Don't worry, Helen, I understand. And one could say it was my own fault, for my marriage came about through my indulgence in home-made wine.'

He had hoped to make light of the matter for he was smiling at her; but the next moment her eyelids began to blink and her lips to tremble, so he said swiftly, 'Please! Please! Don't distress yourself. Look! Believe me,' and now he proceeded to lie gallantly, 'my life is just as I want it. I have made it as it is and I'm content with my handiwork. I am not troubled by her, not at all. We don't see each other, so there is no irritation on either side. Now look, I am going; I'll pop in tomorrow.' He let go of her hand now and went to pick up his hat and coat from the chair as he said, 'And if you're all ready and packed, I'll see you to the station. That's if—' he was now shrugging his arms into his coat and he repeated, 'that's if you promise to write to me.'

She swallowed deeply before she said, 'Oh, yes, John. Yes, I'll write to you.'

'D'you intend to stay in Paris?'

'Oh, I won't know until I get there and meet the old dame, as Leonard used to call her.'

'And if you don't like the old dame you'll go on?'

'Yes. Likely I'll go on.'

'Have you any place in mind?'

'I'd like to go to Italy; Rome. And Austria intrigues me.'

'And all on your own?' He sounded anxious now: looking

as she did, she would be a prey to men of all types. But, he could do nothing about it.

His voice sounded quite ordinary as he said, 'I'll see you tomorrow then?'

'Yes, John.'

Without further word, he left.

He had a number of calls to make, but as he drove into the town he recalled that he had made up a bottle of medicine for a bronchial patient, but hadn't put it in his bag. And he was surprised when he opened the door of his surgery to come face to face with Doctor Cornwallis.

'Oh! Oh! I thought you were on your rounds.'

'Yes, I am on my rounds. Were you wanting something?'

'Yes, I wanted the loan of that . . . this.' He held up a syringe. 'Doctor Rees is ham-fisted; he's broken two during the last month. I'm taking it out of his salary. I've told him.' He went to pass John, but then stopped and, looking him fully in the face, he said, 'Had to visit your wife early this morning.'

Doctor Cornwallis seemed to be waiting for some comment, and when none was forthcoming, he said, 'Did she ever complain of feeling unwell when you were . . . well, living with her?'

'I wasn't living with her, Doctor, I was married to her.'

'Oh well, we won't split hairs.' And there was a touch of anger in his voice as he said, 'I'm asking you, did she have turns, as it is colloquially put?'

'I wasn't aware of any "turns", specifically.'

'Well, I wasn't there when this one happened, but it looked like a fit. And, all I know is, she was as stiff as a board when I did get there.'

'What do you mean, "as stiff as a board?" She's not dead?'

'No, she's not dead. But if my diagnosis is correct, she's suffering from a form of neurosis, all to do with the mind.'

245

John repeated to himself, 'All to do with the mind.' The man was explaining neurosis as if to a layman. Nevertheless, he hadn't experienced any real surprise.

'Do you know what I think?'

'No, Doctor; but I'm sure you will tell me.'

'Oh—' Doctor Cornwallis turned a red face towards John and retaliated, saying, 'That manner of yours annoys me, do you know that? Sometimes I'm for you because I know you're hooked up to a woman whose behaviour seems anything but normal; but at other times, as now, when you're acting like a young whipper-snapper, I'd like to kick you in the . . . arse, and not metaphorically speaking either, bad leg or no bad leg.'

John bowed his head and bit on his lip. He had a great desire to laugh as he watched his superior turn his limp into a march as he made for his office. And after closing his door, he leant back against it and put his hand over his brow as he repeated to himself, 'Metaphorically speaking, bad leg or no bad leg.' He couldn't help it, he liked the old boy, Nosy Parker or not. What had he really come into this room for? There was nothing he could find in here, except that which had to do with his profession. And yet he had been clever enough about the syringe. Oh, he was a devious old boy.

He now went into his dispensary and picked up the bottle he had forgotten. He did not, however, immediately leave, but leaning against the marble slab, he stared ahead as he muttered quietly to himself, 'Neurasthenia? Turns? Stiff as a board?' Well, he wasn't surprised. She had likely had what seemed like a fit before the seizure took hold. Unbalanced, he had implied. Oh, he would endorse that; but that wouldn't be neurasthenia. He gazed down at the bottle. How long would he have to remain tied to her? A legal separation was, after all, just a separation. What was he going to do with his life? Was it to be spent every day but one in a week between that room there and this little cubby hole?

And what was left of his evenings? Sitting with his mother. No longer would there be any visiting.

From tomorrow or the next day he would not even be able to glimpse her. France, Italy, Austria. And men, everywhere men, and she was only human. She didn't think she was, for she was convinced that the pain of her loss would never leave her. But love was a disease, and, like some diseases, it could be cured and the patient be given a new lease of life. And it could easily happen to her if she met up with some sympathetic smart alec . . . Oh, for God's sake! let him get out of here and do some work.

As he was stepping into the passage, the door opposite opened and out stepped . . . *that woman*. She looked haggard and bedraggled. He recalled he had noticed an item in the paper last week, reporting that she had been charged with soliciting and had been given the option of a fine of five pounds or ten days in jail. She had paid the fine. He thought of her husband and her son and of the effect on them.

He hadn't seen her since the night her husband had put her out of the house. Yet, as he looked at her now, he felt sorry for her. She was a pitiable creature. If it had been the demands of her body that had brought her low, then he could couple her with Beatrice, for if anyone was crazed with her body's desires, it was his wife.

He stepped back to allow her to pass him and as she did so she turned her face fully towards him, and her heavily painted lips moved into a smile when she said, 'Thank you.'

The words were simple but he knew their intent wasn't. They had not been said in courtesy, but rather in mockery. He waited some time before following her into the street.

As he lifted the horse's reins from the iron post he was aware that she was standing watching him, that enigmatic smile on her face; and as he mounted the trap her voice taunted him, as she called, 'Happy days, Doctor!'

247

# 5

Seven weeks had passed and he'd had three letters from Helen, one from Paris and two from Italy; but it was a fortnight since the last letter had arrived. However, during these weeks he hadn't been entirely without company, for Daisy had invited him to her home, and they had come to know each other very well. At this moment, he was sitting in her conservatory and she was answering a question he had posed, although not truthfully: 'Oh, perhaps once a week,' she was saying; she could not say to him 'I get two letters from her regularly every week,' for he had just said it was two weeks since he had last heard from her.

He put out a hand now and stroked the broad leaf of a plant as he said, 'Do you think her travelling is helping her?'

'No, I don't.'

He turned sharply towards her: 'You don't?'

'No, not at all. She can't ease her pain or erase her feelings by jumping from one train to another, one country to another, one hotel to another. The only way she will ease herself is to find a purpose, a purpose for living. An equivalent of my leper colony.' She grinned at him now. 'But as I see it, she is not going to experience a carbolic bath from which she will emerge at a jump.' The grin had now spread into laughter in which he joined; and then she added, 'But I'm not worrying about her: something will show her the way she has to go. It always does if we wait long enough. Some have to wait longer than others. Like you, John, for instance.'

His head went slightly to the side as if in enquiry, but he did not ask her what she meant, for he was slightly startled by her next question: 'How long have you been in love with her?'

Strangely, her directness did not disturb him as it might have done had it come from someone else. Daisy was a very perceptive woman, for behind all that jollity there was a sage. But, nevertheless, the question had caught him off his guard and he found that he couldn't look into that rugged face and those knowing eyes. So he turned his head away from her and gazed up the length of the beautiful conservatory, only turning to her again when she said, 'You needn't worry, it isn't that evident, except that Leonard knew.'

The legs of the basket chair scraped on the mosaic tiled floor as he twisted around sharply. She was holding up her hand now, saying, 'It's all right. Don't get on your hind legs. He never voiced it. But I knew from the way he talked of you, and with affection, let me tell you, yes, with affection, that he was aware of your feelings, and apparently had been for a long time. Even, I think, before he settled here. So now you can answer my question: When was it you fell in love with her?'

He drew in a long breath before looking down at his feet and saying, 'The very first time I saw her at Beatrice's twenty-first birthday party. We spoke for only a few minutes because Leonard had just arrived. Then, one afternoon we met on the top of Craig's Tor. I had fallen asleep in the sun, and when I woke up there she was. She had been sitting watching me. And we had a kind of picnic together.' He paused, running his fingers through his hair, before he said, 'It was from

249

that day onwards I became sick at heart, only to have to face facts once she was married. And when I married her sister, I thought I had got Helen out of my system.' He now turned and nodded emphatically at Daisy, saying, 'That was the biggest mistake of my life. But we won't go into that.'

Silence fell between them and lasted for some seconds before he asked quietly, 'How long do you really think she'll stay away?'

'I don't know, John. If she doesn't meet up with a carbolic bath, she could decide to come home tomorrow.'

He did not say, 'Really?' but waited for her to go on, and she nodded at him, saying, 'There's an unrest in her letters, well, the ones she sends to me. I don't think her travelling, so far, has eased her feelings very much. You know, she never cried when Leonard went, and there was no sign of tears during the days following. It's a bad sign when people can't cry; their feelings become like a canker, eating into them. And I shouldn't think that she's given way in any strange bedroom on her journey. It's going to be a long time, John, before she really returns to life. You know, the feeling she had for Leonard was very deep. I don't know what it was like when she first met him. I'm sure she really knew nothing about love then; at least, not the kind of love he had to give. But she soon learned.'

She now leaned her head back against the padded cushion of the wicker chair and stared up at the glass-domed roof as she said, 'I used to envy people like Helen who would create such love as she does; but I envy them no longer and haven't done for many a year, because such love as you have for her, John, is, you must admit, mostly pain. As for me, I didn't catch leprosy, but I did catch a form of love, in my case made up of mixed ingredients. I have substitutes now, such as the feeling one gets from both receiving and giving kindnesses, as well as a feeling of deep affection for a few people. But I must admit, it could

250

have slipped into love where Leonard was concerned. Anyway, will you stay to dinner?'

He had risen sharply to his feet and was looking down on her as he said bluntly, 'No! I won't, because I know what that means, I'd be stuck for the night, and there would be Mrs Atkinson standing with her hat and coat on waiting for my return. And so, good-night, Mrs Daisy, until we meet again, which in all likelihood could be tomorrow, or the next day,' to which she answered simply, 'Good-night, John, and thanks.'

# 6

It was a week later. He had just examined a woman in her late fifties and had made up a bottle of medicine for her.

Now looking at her across his desk, he said, 'You're a stupid woman, Emily Green. Now you go home and get yourself straight to bed, and I'll be along there in the morning to see you. Now I'm telling you,' – he wagged a finger at her – 'forget about that man of yours. He's not half as bad as you are.'

'Oh! Doctor, don't say that.'

'I'm saying it. He has a little silicosis, and most men in the mines have to put up with that. But I'm going to talk to you plainly. You have bronchitis all right, but it could become something else much more serious if you don't do what I say. Now you stay in bed.'

'But who's going to look . . .?'

'They can look after themselves. Your man still has his hands and feet, and he can walk down to the pub, can't he?'

'Oh, Doctor! What life has he? I mean . . .'

'Never mind, what life has he? What life have *you* had? Where are your daughters? Can't one of them come along and see to the cooking?'

'They both have families to see to, Doctor. And they do; they are good girls; they do pop in.'

'Yes. Yes, they pop in so their mother can make them tea and bake their bread for them. Oh, I know what goes on in your house: I've been visiting it long enough.'

He now rose to his feet and more quietly he said, 'I'm serious, Emily. Get yourself to bed and stay there. If you don't you're going to end up in hospital, and you could be there for some time. D'you get my meaning?'

Her head drooped as she muttered, 'Yes, Doctor.'

Yes, he knew she had got his meaning: she had lost a son of twenty-six with tuberculosis and, recently, her youngest, a nine-year-old girl.

She pulled herself to her feet and, smiling wearily at him, said, 'I'll do what you say, Doctor, and let them get on with it. To tell you the truth, I've been saying just that over the past few months, that one of these days I'll let them get on with it.'

'Good, Emily. Now it's only a touch and it could be put right. I'll have a talk with your husband when I call in tomorrow. And don't worry about him. It's amazing what men can do when they have to. And you know what they say, a hungry belly trains a cook.'

Her smile widened, and then she said, 'Thank you, Doctor. Thank you. You are a very good man.'

After she had left, he sat down again and shook his head. Women and their men. Her man wasn't half as bad as she already was. He coughed and made a great play of spitting. There were many worse with the same disease. He sighed, then pressed a bell to his hand. But when he heard a commotion outside the door, he rose to his feet again and was amazed when the door was thrust open to see Daisy standing there. 'I won't be a moment, I promise you,' she was saying to a waiting patient. 'I've just got a message for the doctor.'

'What on earth's the matter?' he demanded of her.

'She's back!'

He was silent for a moment, then said, 'Helen?'

'Well, who else would come back? Has anybody else been away? Helen? Yes, of course, Helen.'

'When?'

'Last night. She came around to me at about eight o'clock in the evening. I couldn't believe it. Walked in, just like that.' She stepped back from him, saying softly, 'I thought you would like to know.'

'Oh, Daisy.' His hand went out and he caught her arm, saying, 'Something's brought her back.'

'Yes, of course something has. But whatever it is, she hasn't told me. Perhaps she'll tell you. You'll be looking her up, I assume?' and she grinned at him.

'I'll call immediately after my rounds.'

'Good! But now I must go: that fellow outside will hit me if I stay a minute longer. He snorted so much I nearly suggested he should have a ring through his nose.'

She pulled open the door and smiled at the man who was much shorter than herself, and in a sweet voice said, 'Thank you very much. It was very kind of you. I'm greatly obliged.'

In answer, the man said in a conciliatory tone, 'That's all right,' then watched the odd-looking woman almost skipping along the corridor, before he entered the surgery. And there, he made a statement that John found impossible to answer: 'Queer-looking card, that.'

He had so many urgent calls upon his time during the morning that he did not get to Col Mount until around three o'clock in the afternoon.

Johnson opened the door to him and, after a moment's pause, said, 'Oh! Good afternoon, Doctor. You . . . you wish to see Lady Spears?'

The man's superior manner was too much for John at this moment, and so he said, 'Well, Johnson, I didn't come this far to call on you. Tell me, where is Lady Spears?'

254

The man drew himself up to his full height, and in an arrogant tone said, 'Her ladyship is in her room.'

'Then will you kindly tell her she has a visitor? I'll be in the drawing-room.' And with this John walked across the hall and into the drawing-room. He deliberately left the door open; and when he reached the fireplace he turned and looked back into the hall to see Johnson still standing where he had left him, then flounce his shoulders as if in a huff, as he made his way towards the stairs.

John was annoyed by the man's manner as he had been before; but at the same time he wondered why he didn't laugh at him.

Presently he heard Helen's footsteps on the stairs, and she entered the room and closed the door behind her before he walked towards her, his arms outstretched. She took his hands and smiled at him, saying, 'How good to see you, John.'

He found himself speechless for a moment; then all he could do was to repeat her words and say, 'And it's good to see you, my dear.'

She smiled widely at him, saying, 'Come and sit down and start asking me questions.'

She sat on the couch and he sat on a chair near her, and he said, 'I'll have to get my second wind; I'm rather knocked out by surprise. But, all right, I'll begin. Where have you come from?'

'Paris, my starting point.'

'I thought you were to go to Rome, then on to Austria?'

'I was in Rome and I went on to Austria. Then I returned to Paris.'

'To stay with the dame?'

'Oh no! I had thought such characters existed only in novels. But she was painted and powdered every day, with two maids seeing to her constantly.'

'How old is she?'

'Oh, about eighty, and with a razor-sharp mind, still ruling her establishment. She wanted me to stay with her. No, not wanted, demanded that I stay with her; she didn't like her secretary's voice; the poor soul had to read to her for most of the day. And that's what she wanted me to take over, and when I dared to laugh at her she flew into a tantrum. Oh my!'

'You didn't stay on, then, at the house?'

'Oh no! No, thank goodness. I went to a nearby hotel.'

'Well, what did you do with yourself?'

'Oh, I did the usual rounds, just like every tourist: the Louvre, Versailles, the Tuilleries, and of course Notre Dame, and the markets. Oh yes, the markets.'

'By yourself?' There was a note of surprise in his voice, and she said, 'Yes, sir, by myself, assisted by a very helpful cab driver, whom I hired from one day to the next during my stay, a fortnight. He would suggest what I should see the next day. He was a very nice, helpful man. He called himself my protector, for he couldn't understand me being alone.'

'Did you need protection? Although that's a silly thing to ask, really.'

'Yes, I did, in a way.' She actually laughed now as she said, 'There was one particular gentleman who became rather insistent until the day my protector, who was waiting for me after one of my educational visits, said to me, "We must hurry, madam, to the station, otherwise your husband will have arrived, and Monsieur is not famous for his patience." At least, that's how I roughly translated his suburban French. I say suburban: he was from what you would call the deep end of Paris. But there was nothing he didn't know about gentlemen . . . and, from his conversation, ladies of all types, I should imagine.' Her smile faded as she now remarked, 'You know, Leonard didn't wish me to go into black, or to have the house in mourning; but I think the former might have helped on my journeys abroad. By the way' – she was smiling

256

again – 'I didn't realise until my protector and I parted that evening, that the name he had given to my husband who was getting off that train and not known for his patience was that of a well-known boxer.

'Anyway, that took place the day before I left and I was sorry to say goodbye to him. You know, he left his cab and saw me to the train.'

'Was he a fatherly man?'

'No, John, he wasn't. He wasn't much older than me. I would say in his middle thirties. But he had a wife and five children.'

'Oh. They are a romantic race, the French.'

'Yes, they are, John.'

And now he asked the question: 'Are you glad to be back?'

The smile slid from her face as she said, 'I don't know yet. I know only that I had to come.'

'What do you mean, you had to come?'

'Again, I can't give you a straight answer, but something happened. You mightn't believe this. Imagination, you will say, or subconscious desire erupting. But it happened when I was sitting at the little desk in front of the window of my room. The scene outside was very pleasant. The hotel was on a main road but the sun was shining on a row of plane trees and there were a lot of people busying about. Everything looked bright and gay.' She looked fully at him now. 'I can remember thinking: it's a lovely city, so why don't I stay here instead of going on to Spain? It was as I pulled my Baedeker towards me – I had all but made arrangements, at least in my mind, that Spain would be my next experience – when—' she stopped and looked down at her hands clasped tightly in the lap of her brown skirt and said, 'it was so real: I . . . I felt Leonard behind me. I felt that I could put my hands up like this' – she now raised her arms quickly above her head – 'and touch his face. He often used to stand behind me while I sat at the dressing-table. But I knew he was there and I felt cold from head to foot, until it seemed that his hands came on my shoulders, and' – she paused again – 'his voice was as clear in my head as if he had spoken aloud. "Go home," he said. "No more trailing about. You won't forget me by trailing around." And, you know—' She blinked her eyes tightly now before looking squarely at John and saying, 'You know, John, I spoke aloud, I mean I answered him aloud. I said, "I don't want to forget you. I never want to forget you." And he said, "I know, dear, and I don't want you to forget me. Time will ease the pain, but only if you go home and . . . and stay there.' And then, John, you can believe me that his words were definite when he said, "Whatever happens to you, stay there." In a way, it was frightening as . . . as if something really was going to happen to me.'

John had hold of her hands now, saying, 'Nothing's going to happen to you that is in any way bad. But I believe what you have said. Such were his feelings for you, he was aware of your efforts to escape the pain of his loss, and that by doing so you were keeping him earthbound; and you know what the saying is: there are more things in Heaven and Earth than this world dreams of.'

She drew her hands from his now and rose from the couch. But he did not move. He watched her walk towards the fireplace and stretch her hand out and grip the mantelpiece and he strained to hear her whisper, 'You are quite right: there *are* more things. It was so real, I . . . I turned round expecting to see him or his ghost, or something that would actually tell me that he had been there. There was nothing; but from that moment I was filled with the urge to return.' And now she turned towards him, and she added, 'So here I am. And, you know, it's so good to be back, to see you again, and Daisy. You're the only two friends I have, real friends, that is. I can be myself when I'm with you or Daisy, but with no-one else; not even with Rosie. No, I can't be myself with

Rosie. I . . . I couldn't have told Rosie what I've just told you. I love Rosie because she is my sister, and although she is married now I still look on her as someone very young. Yet, in a way, she too has been through the mill.'

'Yes' – and he nodded – 'Oh, yes, she went through the mill all right, and she is no longer the young girl, but the young matron, and I don't think it will be long before her figure will announce she is going to be a young mother.'

'Really! Really! Oh! that's wonderful.'

'Yes, and she thinks so, too. And, of course, he . . . well, there is no other young married woman, to his knowledge, who has ever carried a child: his wife is the first who is experiencing this process.'

She smiled now, saying, 'Oh, I must go and see her.'

'She would like that. Yes, she would. You just want to pop in. I know you have written to her once or twice but, like me, this time yesterday I thought you were in Timbuktu, or Borneo, or the Congo or some such place.'

She now said quietly, 'Would you like some tea?'

'I would. Yes, I would.'

She pulled on the bell-rope and when Johnson opened the door, she said, 'We'll have tea, Johnson, please.'

To John, the man's manner was forbidding, and after the door had closed behind him, he said, 'I must confess, Helen, I can't stand that fellow.'

At this, Helen laughed, saying, 'Yes, he is a bit pompous, isn't he? But he was very attentive to Leonard. And, of course, he had been in Frederick's service for some time. But not all that long, now I come to think of it, because he took the place of Beecham, who was a lovely old butler. Now *he* had worked for the family since he was a boy. Anyway, I have had to rely on him, being away so long, and he's looked after everything very well. And the accounts are all in order. He practically insisted that I go through them this morning—' her voice dropped now as she said, 'He wanted me to see that he had saved on the housekeeping, which I'm sure hasn't pleased Cook, for Mrs Dolly Jones likes her food, as they all do. And because they work for it and I feel they should have it, I had to tell him, very politely, of course, that there was no need to skimp and to let Cook do her own ordering as she has always done. It's been rather a trying morning. And I suppose it is because of him I was welcomed with open arms by the staff, inside and out.'

'Well, I'm glad to hear I'm not the only one who apparently can't stand him.'

Johnson did not deign to push in the tea trolley, but Hannah Worth did, smiling, and when she said, 'Good-day, Doctor,' he answered her, 'Good-day, Hannah. How's life?'

'Fine. Fine, now that we have' – she glanced towards Helen – 'the mistress back. Oh by! yes, fine.'

Johnson's back became straighter, if that was possible, and he spoke now to the maid, saying, 'Leave it. I will see to the pouring.'

'There's no need, Johnson, thank you.' It was Helen speaking.

The man seemed to sigh before he turned and with measured tread left the room.

As Helen poured out the tea she said, 'Would you like to bring your mother over some evening, John? She used to manage the journey in the carriage all right.'

'Oh, she would like that. Yes, you tell us the time and we'll be here.'

'Oh, make your own time – I don't intend to go visiting. And the only other one I want near me is Daisy. So whatever time you're free from surgery, just send word and Henry will be over with the' – she laughed – 'conveyance.'

He could hardly believe he was actually sitting here drinking tea and munching delicate sandwiches with her. Daisy had said it would be a long road before Helen came alive, but her present demeanour suggested to him that she had already started along it, only for him naturally to ask himself in what way her coming back to life would affect his life, because Beatrice still loomed large; and beyond her, the law.

# 7

The last of his patients had gone. He drew together the papers on his desk and put them into a folder before standing up and breathing deeply, as much as to say, 'That's that!' Then he went into the dispensary, washed his hands, and stood for a moment staring into the small mirror above the sink as he straightened his tie and stroked back his hair.

Of late, he had lost flesh: his face looked drawn. Was he really only thirty-two? If he were to meet himself in the street he would guess his age as forty.

When he heard the outer door open and his partner's voice calling, 'Are you there, John?' he hesitated a moment before answering, 'Yes. Yes, Doctor; in here.'

Old Cornwallis had called him John, which was rare. Perhaps only twice before could he remember him using his Christian name: once had been when thanking him for having seen to the practice single-handed for three weeks while he was in hospital having his leg attended to. But that was shortly after he had first arrived, within the first year, in fact. Another occasion was when he had commiserated with him over his estranged marriage. This was after he had been called to the house to see to Beatrice.

When he strode back into his surgery, it was to see the doctor seated in the patients' chair.

'Can you spare a minute?' Cornwallis said.

'Yes, of course.'

'Well, you'd better sit down,' his partner said, and indicated his chair across the desk.

John sat down and waited.

'D'you know if anyone has it in for you, besides your wife?'

It was an odd question. John turned his head one way and then the other as if thinking before he replied, 'Likely there are a few, but they haven't come to the surface. Why are you asking?'

'Because of this.' The doctor pulled from his pocket a letter and handed it across the desk.

John saw that the envelope was addressed to Doctor Cornwallis, and he paused before extracting the sheet of paper from it. Then his eyes widened as he read:

Dear Sir,

I think it should be brought to your notice that your assistant, Doctor John Falconer, is bringing disgrace on your practice and is losing you patients. He has for some time been causing comment in the town by his over-frequent visits to a widowed lady. As is well known, he is a married man. But to make matters worse and to make the situation worse in the eyes of decent people, this lady is sister to his wife. It is known in some quarters that the lady has tried to repulse him, and that his insistence is causing her distress. Moreover, as I said in the beginning, sir, your practice is going to suffer, for women especially will be deterred from being attended to by an immoral man.

Signed, A well-wisher.

John peered over the top of the letter at his partner as Doctor Cornwallis said, 'That doesn't sound like Beatrice.'

'No! No! This is not from Beatrice.'

'Have you any idea of who could be in the know as regards your personal life, such as that indicates?' He nodded towards the letter that John had laid on the desk, and it was a full minute before he was given an answer. And then John said, 'I have a strong suspicion. But still, you can't pin this kind of thing on anyone unless you have proof. I do, however, agree with you that this isn't Beatrice's style at all: she would have it out face to face, probably in public.'

'Yes, that's how it struck me.' Doctor Cornwallis pulled himself to his feet now, leant over, picked up the letter from under John's hand, saying, 'One can't do much about this, except talk it over with the lady in question. Has she any personal friends in whom she might have confided?'

'Only one, and you know her: Mrs Daisy Wheatland.'

'Oh yes. I know Mrs Wheatland, and you can rule her out straightaway. And anyway, to my mind, this is a man's hand. Too clinical, so to speak, to come from a woman.'

'A man's hand. Yes.' John was nodding to himself: he felt certain he knew to whom the hand belonged. And he was made to ask himself what that man could hope to achieve more than he had done already.

'Well, now you know where you stand I'd be on your guard. How is Lady Helen, by the way?' And Dr Cornwallis gave a short laugh now as he said, 'I'm asking the road I know because I was talking to Peters last week, and he seems to think she's under a great strain. Apparently, she's never given way since she lost her husband, and he thinks that's bad, and I do, too. Tears are a saving grace to both body and mind. Bottle them up and you're asking for trouble. I'm always happier when I find women crying their eyes out.' He grinned now, saying, 'There's a paradox for you. Medically speaking, tears are good medicine, but you shouldn't take such medicine for too long. It can become a habit.'

264

He walked towards the door now, saying, 'I'm being very philosophical this morning, you'll notice, Doctor.'

When John did not reply, the older man turned sharply towards where he was standing gazing down at the table, and he said, 'Did you hear what I said? I'm being very philosophical this morning.'

'Yes. Yes, Doctor, I heard what you said, and I endorse your philosophy.'

'Good! Good! Well, I must away; but don't take this business too much to heart. If you want my advice, don't change the pattern of your life. Now, that's strange, isn't it? I think that the person who wrote that letter has got an axe to grind, and if you bide your time he'll come to light with the axe in his hand . . . Oh, I'd better go, else I can hear myself saying I saw him fell the tree. And what would that indicate? My! My!' He went out, pulling the door noisily behind him.

John remained standing near the desk, telling himself that he wouldn't have to bide his time to find out who had thought up that screed. Oh, no! Then he looked towards the door. The old fellow was being very decent. He was a kindly, thoughtful man at bottom, although that was covered with a thick layer of selfishness up nearer the surface. But one could overlook that. He had again called him John. That showed he was concerned for him, and for that he was grateful. Yes, he felt very grateful towards him. He shrugged his shoulders. It was a nervous action but it did not represent the feeling inside him, which was one of anger.

At one time he could open the front door and walk in, but of late he'd been obliged to ring the bell. This had annoyed him, but he hadn't commented on it.

Today, when the door was opened, he saw that Johnson was very surprised to see him. And when he passed by him without a word and made for the drawing-room, throwing his hat on the hall chair as he did so, Johnson's voice said, 'Her ladyship is not expecting . . .'

He almost bounced round on the man, saying, 'I know whom her ladyship is expecting and whom she isn't.'

He was about to open the drawing-room door when Helen came out of the study at the end of the corridor. He stood aside and waited until she had entered the drawing-room. She gave him no greeting but he could see that she was upset. After closing the door none too gently, he hurried towards where she was sitting on the couch and, taking a seat beside her, he asked, 'What is it, Helen? What is it, my dear?'

'Oh, John! Oh, John!'

Her eyelids were blinking rapidly and her words were hesitant as she said, 'Someone is maligning us. At least, you through me, and . . . and I can't bear it.'

'How d'you know this?'

'The letter.'

'What letter?'

'It's in the study, on . . . on the desk.'

He wasn't surprised to see Johnson standing only a few feet away from the door and, his voice like thunder, he barked at him, 'Don't you dare go in there, man! D'you hear me? Don't you dare go in that room! I'll deal with you in a minute.'

In the study, he saw the letter lying open on the writing desk and immediately he saw that it was written by the same hand as the one to Doctor Cornwallis.

Johnson was standing where he had left him. His face was deadly white, the mouth set in a tight line; and this time John passed by him without a word, but again banged the door behind him.

Now he was sitting with his arm around Helen's shoulders while he held the letter in his hand and read:

266

Madam,

It should be brought to your notice that you are ruining the career of a certain doctor in this town. His constant visits to you are causing a scandal and his partner is greatly troubled by the effect on the practice of this man's behaviour. It would be well for all concerned, madam, if you broke off the association with this person, for your name is being bandied about like that of a light woman. I speak only through concern for your welfare.

Signed, A well-wisher.

'My God!'

'Who would do this, John? We have done nothing wrong, yet I feel so guilty. All the time I feel guilty. I talk to Leonard, and he tells me everything's all right, as it should be. But I can't believe it. Oh, John, I'm so lost, and I seem to have gone all to pieces since I came back. But your career and . . .'

'Damn! my career. And this letter means nothing; Doctor Cornwallis received a similar one this morning, obviously from the same man.'

'You . . . you know who?'

'Yes, I know who; and it's going to end,' a statement which obviously affected Helen further, and her hands went to her throat as she pleaded, 'It won't stop you coming, John, will it?'

'Why ask such a thing! Nothing or no-one will ever stop me being near you.'

'We've done nothing wrong. Nothing. Leonard told me what I must do, before he died. But I wouldn't listen, I couldn't listen . . . John! John!' His name was erupting from her mouth like an actual wail: it was high, penetrating, as if wrenched through agony. And her face was awash, the tears spurting from her eyes and down her nose, the saliva running from her mouth. He put his arms

267

tightly about her and held her closely, saying, 'Cry! That's it, cry, my dear. Cry, my love.'

He had been unaware of the door opening, but he was aware of the voice saying, 'How dare you! sir. You've upset madam.'

He was almost choking himself as he turned and screamed at the man, 'Get out! before I' – he almost said, 'kill you'. And the man backed away, pushing past the two maids now standing at the open door; and John yelled at them: 'Hannah! Bring your mistress's smelling salts; and Betty, fetch me my bag from the trap.'

A few minutes later, after he had wafted the smelling salts under Helen's nose and had made her swallow a pill, he again turned to Betty, saying quietly, 'Make some coffee, Betty, please. And tell Henry to go for Doctor Peters and ask him if he would be kind enough to call on her ladyship as soon as possible.'

With the room to themselves, he again put his arms about Helen as she muttered, 'Who . . . who would do such a thing . . . write those letters?'

'You haven't far to look, my dear, and I think you must know it was Johnson.'

She drew in a sharp breath before she repeated the name, 'Johnson? No, I hadn't suspected him. But now I come to think of it, he's been acting strangely lately. I didn't tell you . . .'

'You have no need to, my dear; and don't talk.'

She took a handkerchief from her cuff and wiped her eyes, muttering, 'His . . . his wages are due.'

'How do you pay him, half-yearly?'

'No, by the month.'

'How much?'

'A pound a week.'

'A pound a week, indeed! and all found. He's been in clover. But the fact that he's paid monthly eases matters.

Pay him his month's salary and an added month in lieu of notice.'

'I . . . I can't bear to see him now.'

'Well, you have no need; I'll see to him. Have you any loose money lying around?'

'There's some in the bureau drawer in the study. The key—' she gulped and had to bring herself forward on the couch before she could finish, 'It's in my handbag.'

'Now lie back and don't distress yourself. Where is your handbag?'

'In the bedroom.'

'I'll get Betty to fetch it after she's brought in the coffee.'

It was when, later, he had taken the key from Helen's handbag that John noticed Johnson still standing in the hall. He passed by the man without a glance and made for the study.

But he had no sooner disappeared than Johnson rushed into the drawing-room and to Helen who, on sight of him, pressed herself tightly back into the corner of the couch. Bending over her, he said, 'Madam, you must listen to me. The master . . . the master left you in my keeping. Yes, yes, he did: he told me what I had to do, and to look after you and . . .'

As if being imbued with sudden strength, Helen thrust out her hands and pushed him back from her. And now she cried at him, 'He . . . he did nothing of the kind. You . . . you forget yourself. You were the servant to him and . . . and you have been to me, nothing more. Please! Please get out! Get out!'

'Madam, you must listen to me. That man will bring you nothing but trouble. I am here to protect you and look after you and . . .'

He was able only to turn half around before he felt himself gripped by the back of the collar and thrust with such force against the sofa table that it toppled over and the coffee tray with it. The sound smothered Helen's scream but not those of the two maids and the cook, who were crowding the doorway. And when John's fist went out and caught the man on the side of the head, and Johnson made to retaliate, Cook rushed forward and thrust her sturdy body at Johnson, crying, 'Don't you dare, mister!'

'It's all right, Cook! It's all right. Get out of his way.'

John could see that the man was showing no fear of him, in fact, that his pose was defiant. He had to draw in two long deep breaths before he could speak: 'There's your money,' he said as he threw a chamois-leather bag towards him, and when it dropped at his feet, Johnson did not immediately stoop to pick it up, and John went on, 'There's a month's wages and a month in lieu of notice. Now get your things together and get out of this house and don't you dare show your face here again. But this I'll tell you: you'll likely have to show yourself in court, because that's where the poison-pen writers find themselves.'

He now called to Hannah, 'Go and fetch the men in, please.' Then addressing Johnson again, he said, 'I'll give you exactly ten minutes to get your things together. Ten minutes,' and he pointed towards the door.

It was some seconds before Johnson stooped and picked up the bag of money, the while glaring at John; then, without any change in his defiant demeanour, he strode from the room, leaving John himself feeling dazed.

Cook and Betty were clearing up the debris as he said to Helen, 'Come along. Come out of this and into the study,' and silently she obeyed him; but he had hardly got her settled when, after a tap on the door, Hannah entered, saying, 'The men are here, doctor,' and he said to Helen, 'Lie back and relax; this will be all over in a few minutes.'

In the hall stood two of the outdoor men. Facing them, he said, 'I'll . . . I'll tell you in a moment why I've sent for

270

you,' and of Hannah he asked, 'Where's his room? He's had his ten minutes.'

But almost as he finished speaking, Johnson emerged through a far door carrying a large case and a small valise. He was wearing a grey suit and an overcoat, and his hat was already on his head. He was once again the butler and, using his imperious tone, he addressed Arthur Bell and said, 'I'll need transport to get me into town, Bell.'

'Shut up and get out!' John said grimly, 'There's a horse-bus passing the gates at two o'clock. It'll give you time to cool your heels.' And now he turned to the men, saying, 'This man is not to be allowed anywhere near this house or grounds again on any pretext whatever. And should he, in any way, attempt to see the mistress, I instruct you to call the police straightaway. In any case, I myself will shortly be in touch with them on my own account, because this individual is the author of poison-pen letters defaming my character.'

Johnson had picked up his cases and when he reached the door he swung round, saying, 'I can have you up for that. You've got to prove it.'

'Oh, I can prove it all right, and I won't even have to go to a handwriting expert.'

At the bottom of the shallow steps Johnson turned one last furious look on John and his words sounded ominous as he growled slowly, 'In any case, *you'll never win . . . never.*'

John stood taut, watching Johnson walking down the drive, and he repeated the man's ominous words, *'You'll never win . . . never,'* and although he admitted to himself they could be true, he had to wonder what that man hoped to get out of the situation he had created.

Yet why did he ask? A lone widow had come to rely on him to the extent of leaving her home in his care; and he fancied he had made himself indispensable to her and so she, naturally and with subtle manœuvring on his part, would turn to him. It had happened before: people had been put

271

beyond the pale of their class by marrying servants.

The nerve of the fellow. No wonder he had seen himself as the main object standing in his way.

Henry's voice came to him, saying, 'Don't worry, Doctor; we'll see to him. And it will be a pleasure.'

As John was about to make his way to the study, Cook came out of the drawing-room, and he said to her, 'A pot of strong tea would be very acceptable at this moment, Cook,' and when she replied, 'You'll have it in a minute, Doctor,' he added, 'And tell the girls to get the mistress's bed ready. That's where she should be.'

'Yes; yes, I agree with you, Doctor, after all this how-d'you-do, she's bound to be in a state.'

In the study, Helen was still lying, almost crouching in the leather chair. There was no colour in her face and, taking a seat beside her, he took her hand, saying, 'It's all over now. He's gone. You won't be troubled any more. I've had a word with the staff.'

She now looked at him and said, 'I . . . I realise I've been a little afraid of him for some time. When he made a statement that we should stop ordering this or that I . . . I felt, well, what does it matter? he's looking after things, even though I knew there was something not right and that the staff was unhappy. But I was so wrapped up in my own misery and guilt and . . .'

He now pressed his hand against her cheek, saying, 'Listen to me, Helen. Forget about that word . . . misery yes, but no guilt. You've nothing to feel guilty about. Although at the same time, I understand how you feel, because I'm in the same boat, as you know. You understand that, don't you, dear?'

She looked at him intently for a moment before she said, 'Yes, John. But . . . but that hasn't helped; it has only added to the feeling.'

'Now listen to me, Helen. Leonard knew this would

272

happen; at least, he knew how I felt about you. I'm sure of that. As for your feelings for him, he was sure of your love. Oh yes, absolutely sure of your love for him. But he also knew the effect his loss would have on you, not only the loneliness . . . but the aloneness, the feeling that you could never love again, that you mustn't love again. He knew all that. We talked very intimately at times, and he did actually put it into words that I should be near you, take care of you, even if it was just as a friend. He knew that my being married couldn't quench my feelings for you. And as my marriage has been a failure I have really felt no guilt in loving you. The guilt I've experienced is connected with being unable to hide my feelings, and so soon after Leonard's going. Yet again I say, I feel sure he knew exactly what would happen, and, what's more, that he wanted it this way. Believe me, dear, he wanted it to happen, because of his unselfish, undying love for you . . . Please, please! Don't cry again. You've cried enough, any more will make you ill. Ah, here's Cook's beverage.' He rose quickly to his feet and as Betty put the tray on the side-table, he said, 'I'll see to it, Betty. Thank you.' Then he added, 'Give me five minutes so I can gulp down a cup too, then come back and help your mistress up to bed.'

'Oh no! No!'

He swung round to Helen, whose head was shaking in protest, and insisted, 'Yes, yes. And I should imagine Doctor Peters will be here shortly and that's where he'd want to see you.'

When Betty left the room, he poured out a cup of tea and, taking it to Helen, said, 'Drink it up. This may not be a cure, but a couple of days rest in bed certainly will be.'

'Two days in bed! No, no, John. I'm all right now.'

'You're not all right, and tomorrow, let me tell you, you'll feel worse. That spasm of crying burst a dam in your head and the reaction will set in. In any case, you must do what Doctor Peters tells you. Now, I'm not sure if I'll be in tomorrow because Rosie is near her time.'

'Oh, yes. Yes, of course.'

'They seem to want me on hand. Not that Doctor Cornwallis wouldn't do a better job, but they've plumped for the amateur.'

After hastily drinking his cup of tea, he said, 'I must leave you to the maids now, dear.' And then in a lowered voice, he added, 'Not only for your sake but for mine.'

He took her hand and pressed it against his cheek for a moment before turning abruptly from her and leaving the room.

In the hall, his departure seemed to surprise both Hannah and Betty, because Betty said, 'You going, Doctor?'

'Yes. Yes, I'm going, Betty; I've overstayed my welcome.' He smiled at her; then addressing Hannah, he said, 'When Doctor Peters comes, will you please tell him that I'll drop in to see him sometime tomorrow?'

'Yes. Yes, I'll do that, Doctor.'

He now took his hat from Betty's hand, saying, 'Look after your mistress.'

'You'll be in tomorrow, Doctor, won't you?' It was Hannah asking the question now, and he said, 'I don't know yet, Hannah. I've a busy day before me, and I'm expecting a baby,' which brought a concerted giggle from the two women, and he said, 'Yes, you might laugh, but I'm a bit worried about it, because it's my first. What I mean is, it's *a* first.'

'Oh! Doctor.' Betty put her hand over her mouth.

This going out on a laugh, he thought, augured well, until he remembered Johnson's last words: In any case, Doctor, you can't win.

# 8

'That's it, dear. Come on. That's a girl . . . Ah, here it comes, he . . . she . . . or it. My! My! Good girl! Good girl!' As Rosie's body slumped into the bed, John handed the wet yelling infant to the midwife, saying, 'He has some lungs on him, proclaiming already that he's a Scot!'

'Oh, my! My!' Annie MacIntosh held her arms out for her grandson, and the midwife said, 'Sponge his eyes.'

'I know. I know.' Annie's voice now was a shout and to it she added, 'Robbie! Robbie!'

When the door opened almost immediately, Robbie rushed into the room, but instead of looking towards the baby in his mother's arms, he made for the bed where Rosie lay, her face covered with sweat and smiles.

He was bending over her now and she put up her hand and stroked his hair as she said, 'A boy, Robbie. You have a son.'

He made no reply. His head drooping, he pressed his face against hers and his arms went about her shoulders and raised her up and held her close. Still he didn't speak, but John did, crying at him, 'Put her down; and get by, out of the way; she wants tidying up. And she's had a heavy time. Yet I shouldn't think a first baby has come so easy before. You got off lightly, Mrs MacIntosh, d'you know that?'

Rosie now turned her face towards John as she said, 'Did I, John? It didn't seem like that to me.'

'Well, you can take my word for it. And you, sir: do you intend to look at your son, or do you want him sent back?'

There was a giggle from the midwife at that; then Annie, moving forward, handed the baby to its father.

Robbie stood looking down on the child that was blinking up at him. Its lips were moving as if it were endeavouring to speak. It had hair, too, quite a large patch across the top of its head.

'Give him me, dear. What's the matter with you?' His mother took the child from him; and in some amazement watched him hurry from the room. Then she spoke to the midwife who was attending Rosie, saying, 'That's nothing unusual. You have to remember, Mrs MacIntosh, that your son's just given birth to a baby, and for him it was very hard labour.'

They were all laughing now, including Rosie; and John said, 'You all right, Mrs McQueen?'

'Yes, Doctor, I'm all right. Just leave everything to me.'

'I'll go and clean up a bit, then,' and he left the room to go downstairs and into the kitchen, there to see Robbie scrambling to his feet from where he had been sitting at the table, and when he turned his head away, John went to him and, putting his hand on his shoulder, he said, 'Don't be ashamed of this moment, but keep it close to you, something to remember always.'

'I waited for her so long,' Robbie said, 'I never thought it would happen; and now this seems too good to be true.'

'Look, man,' said John; 'we both need something – let's have a coffee with a kick in it.'

Having washed his hands and arms, he sluiced his face under the pump over the sink; and as he stood drying himself he realised he was very tired. It had been a hectic twenty-four hours, in which he had fought with that man and seen to his

276

going. Not an hour later, he had been called upon to attend a road accident, in which a horse had run amok after being stabbed in the hind quarters by some young hooligans, and two people had been badly injured. Following this, he'd had a very full surgery and another talk with Doctor Cornwallis, putting him in the picture as to what had transpired at Col Mount. And although the older man's advice had been kindly spoken when he had said, 'I'd step carefully, John, from now on,' he had nevertheless added, 'Don't forget that Madam Beatrice is still prominently on the scene.'

It had been almost eight o'clock before he reached home, and there once again, he'd had to relate all the events to his mother and this had visibly disturbed her. And she had said, 'Could it affect your practice?' And his answer to this had been, 'What matter if it did? But it's more likely to bring the women in to inspect this Casanova,' at which she had laughed and said, 'You're right there.'

When he had at last lain down, he'd had time to think about what, to him, had been the main event of the day, which was that Helen had cried; and her tears had brought everything into the open.

Then it seemed he had hardly got to sleep before Robbie came knocking at the door. And now Rosie had a son and Robbie had a son, and Robbie, too, had cried. When would he himself cry? There was no answer to that.

# 9

Beatrice marched out of the solicitor's office, telling herself it was the last time that man would get her in there. If she took any more of his advice, the land would be dribbled away in quarter acres. This was the second time she had signed away a quarter of an acre to that builder. It didn't matter that it was rough woodland, it was still land and land was all she had, and she had told him it would be diminished no further.

When he had come back with, 'I'm glad you'll be able to manage, Mrs Falconer,' it was then she had wanted to yell, 'Why don't you get on to him? He should be seeing to the upkeep of the house and grounds. I've only one gardener now.' However, had she done so it would be telling him that she was in no position herself to put this to her husband, because they were living apart; yet at the same time she knew he was already aware of this.

Her mind was working strangely these days. She could concentrate on nothing but the fact that her husband was living but an arm's length from her. She knew the room he slept in, at least the two of which he had the choice, the third one being too small. The windows were at the back of the house and looked on to the wood. Almost below them was the low box hedge that separated the annexe garden from the grounds of the house. In this part of the woodland the trees were thickly entwined, but not for the first time had she made her way through them in the dark and looked up at those two windows, and had only just quelled the desire to throw a brick through them.

She was walking down Northumberland Street when, her temper ebbing away, there came upon her that tired feeling that often preceded an attack, and she almost said aloud, 'Oh, my God! Not here!'

Doctor Cornwallis had given her pills to take when she felt like this. She had some in her handbag.

She now stopped and, taking up a position at the end of a huge showroom window, she fumbled in her bag, and without taking the small cardboard box from it, she prised open the lid, and in so doing spilt the pills which brought from her no self-condemnation, only the words, 'It doesn't matter. It doesn't matter. Take it! Take it!'

She had a job to swallow the pill, but this done, she took in a long breath, then turned from the window and continued her walk, telling herself now that she had better get home. But . . . but what about her shopping? Oh, yes, yes. There was that good sweet shop. But whereabouts was it?

She found the shop in a side street, its window aglow with an array of boxes of chocolates and sweets.

When she came out of the shop with three one-pound boxes of Rowntree's chocolates, she was feeling quite pleased with herself. Two pounds had been her limit for some time.

Such was her feeling of satisfaction that she scurried now to the station.

The train was full. It would seem that everybody had been shopping in Newcastle. She could never afford a first-class ticket for herself, so she had to put up with sitting next to people of all types and sizes, and today was no exception.

Fortunately she had a seat next to the window, and she kept her face turned in that direction and tried to close her ears to the buzz and chatter about her.

The train was crossing the river between Newcastle and Gateshead, and the river hardly showed itself, so thick was it covered with ships and vessels of all sizes and description. She never asked herself where they might be going, or from where they had come, but her mind was making comparisons between the form of travel she was made to endure now and that which had been usual in her grandfather's time, and even for a time while her father was alive. If they wished to do shopping in Newcastle, there had always been the carriage.

She gave a little shake of her head as her thoughts added, But you were young, very young.

At Gateshead, except for herself and one other person the carriage emptied. But just as the train was about to move on the door was pulled open and a woman jumped into the compartment and sat down in the opposite window seat with a flop. The guard banged the door closed and the train now gathered speed, and as the wheels went clippity-clop, clippity-clop, they resounded so loud in Beatrice's head that she felt she wanted to put her hands over her ears as she stared at the newcomer.

The newcomer was staring at her.

Beatrice jerked her head back towards the window. Now the wheels were yelling, That woman! That woman! Clippity-clop, clippity-clop. That woman!

She now drew in a shuddering breath and warned herself to keep calm. There were two more stations to go before Fellburn. Her station was High Fellburn, and she prayed that the other passenger would remain in the carriage until then.

At the next station, the woman remained seated.

When the train re-started she kept her face turned to the window, but that was only for a time, when she was aware

280

of the woman adjusting her hat, then gathering her bag and small parcels together. And she knew that she should do the same and get out with her, and wait for another train. Yet she remained stiffly seated, hardly moving a muscle, for somewhere in the back of her mind she knew that once they were alone together, that person opposite would start talking, and she would hear things about him. Strangely it seemed that the creature must hate him as much as she herself did, seeming to blame him for her present condition in life.

It happened just as she had anticipated. The other passenger got off the train, the carriage door banged closed. The train started, and so did Mollie Wallace, quite pleasantly at first, saying, 'Funny, the folks one meets up with when travelling on a train.'

Beatrice kept her attention fixed tightly on the window, and the voice continued, 'People get talking on trains, especially them that live alone. I always feel sorry for lonely people, especially them that have been done down by their men. I know all about that because I was done down by my man. But me, I'm never lost for company. Men and me get on, in all ways we get on. But you, I hear, live the life of a hermit. Like a fortress your place. You rarely go out and nobody comes in, except tradesmen. And tradesmen . . . well! you get the right tradesmen and you don't need any newspapers.'

There was silence for a time; in fact, it went on so long that Beatrice almost turned to the woman to see if she might have fallen asleep. But suddenly her voice came again, with what another person might have recognised as a tinge of sadness, for she was saying, 'Davey, my bloke, he was a decent sort of chap. A bit soft, oh aye, a bit soft, really too soft to clag holes with; but at bottom he was a decent enough fella. And he was a working man.' Now the tone changed into almost an attack, for it had risen and was directed across the carriage towards Beatrice, as the woman went on, 'But your bloke, with his education and his career,

281

he's a snot of the first water. D'you know that? And as brazen as bloody brass, openly running two houses and definitely showing who is master in one, fighting the butler and throwing him out, all because the fella tried to protect his mistress, your dear sister, when they were having it off on the couch. She's as bad as him. Then, having all the staff in and telling them what's what.'

Beatrice felt she was about to choke. Involuntarily her hand went to her throat and she could not stop herself from staring directly at the woman, glaring at her. And Mollie Wallace bounced her head at her, as she emphasised, ' 'Tis a fact, and right from the horse's mouth, the butler himself. You wonder how I know? Oh, well, I'll tell you. I get around, but I hadn't to move out of me lodgings to hear this tale, because me landlady's daughter is in the kitchen at The Hall and she keeps her ears open. And it should happen that the second footman up there was something of a pal of your dear sister's butler. They met up in the Red Lion on their time off. And the day your dear husband battered the fella and smashed up the furniture in doing so they met up again, and the fella told the whole story. Your sister's husband had asked the butler, who was also his valet, to give an eye to his wife. And apparently he hadn't put a tooth in what he was suggesting. He was very suspicious of your dear husband right from the first time they met up. And when there wasn't a day passed that the dear doctor wasn't only on her doorstep, but on her couch, he opened up and told him what he thought. With the result that the big boy kicked him out. Oh, I could tell you, the town buzzed when that story got about. And now, they say, he practically lives there. Pops in on his mother now and again, she who's at the end of your house, but that's about all. And then, last Sunday, I suppose you know, there they were in church, her being godmother and him being godfather to your other sister's baby. What d'you think they named the baby? John.

Now isn't that nice? And then they had a tea-cum-party in that small-holding pig-sty next to you. It's a wonder you didn't hear the jollification.'

Unconsciously Beatrice found herself moving to the end of the seat, her fingers, like claws, gripping it, her whole body expressing clearly her intention, and only the woman rising abruptly to her feet, saying, 'You try that on, missis, and you won't be able to see your way out of this carriage,' checked the impulse. 'I've got it in me to get me own back on somebody,' the woman added, 'and who better than you, who's the spit of your dirty old father, because I'll tell you something now, I had to be hard up before I would let him near me. He was the filthiest swine that ever walked.'

At this moment they were both surprised when the train jerked to a halt. And now Mollie Wallace, tugging her tight-waisted coat into place, and pulling her hat more firmly on her head, grabbed up her bag from the seat, and her last words were, 'From what I see of you, you are your old man's daughter right to the core. And it's my skirt I wouldn't let touch you. D'you hear? If it wasn't that I hate his guts, I would say you're getting all you deserve. In a way you're paying me for what I had to put up with from that unnatural old swine of yours.'

The door was pulled open, then banged closed again; but the woman's face appeared again for a moment longer at the window and the hate on it could have been the expression on Beatrice's countenance.

When the train started again she fell back into the corner of the carriage. And now she was holding her face between her hands and actually moaning. She was aware she'd had to sit through that dreadful tirade because she wanted to hear about him, for no word about him ever came her way: she had been above speaking to the servants about him, so all she knew was he lived in the annexe with his mother; he did his doctoring in the town; and yes, he would visit her; and as that woman had suggested, these visits would be far from futile. But she would never divorce him. Even if she did, she had read up enough about the law to know that they could never marry. She felt she had them in a cleft stick. But this . . . filth that the woman had spewed at her: fighting with the butler who had caught them together . . . Oh God! She was going to have one of her turns. Oh, no! No! No! She must hang on. Hang on! Eat some chocolates! Eat some chocolates!

She thrust her hand into the bag and almost tore the lid off a box of chocolates, and when some of them spilt onto the floor, she took no notice; but, grabbing up two others, she rammed them into her mouth, chewed quickly on them, swallowed them, and repeated the dose.

By the time the train stopped at High Fellburn, she had eaten eight chocolates; and when she left the train she had to fumble in her bag for her return ticket. Outside, she hailed a cab and twenty minutes later she was entering the house.

Frances met her in the hall and was about to ask, 'Have you had a nice day?' when, looking at her face, she said, 'Oh, ma'am!' And she took the bag from her, helped her off with her coat and hat, then said gently, 'Come along.'

Beatrice allowed herself to be led up the stairs and into her bedroom. She made straight for the bed and sat on the edge of it, and as Frances took off her shoes she said, 'Lie down for a time, ma'am.'

Beatrice did not need any bidding and after Frances had covered her with a rug, she allowed herself to sink into the strange silence that preluded the weird feelings which led to oblivion.

# 10

'John.'

'Yes, dear?'

'I must say it; I'm worried.'

'What about?'

'It's her.' His mother nodded towards the wall. 'She's on the prowl.'

'What d'you mean, Mother, on the prowl?'

'Well, it started a couple of weeks ago. I thought I was dreaming or hearing things. But it was quite late: you had been upstairs for some time and the girls next door must have been in bed at least a couple of hours. The first time it was like a . . . well, like a dog scratching at the door. You see, the door is just along from my bedroom wall. Well, then I heard the muttering, and I knew it was her. I couldn't hear what she was saying, but her voice rose and fell: at times it was as though she were whispering. But for me to hear it she must have been more than whispering. The following night I thought perhaps I had previously been dreaming because there was no sound. But the next night, there it was again. It starts as if she is scratching the door with her nails, and during the past two weeks it's happened six times. She was on again last night. I was in the garden and I saw the little maid, Mary. She came and leaned over the hedge and asked me how I was. I said I was fine; and how was she, I asked, and she said she didn't know: all topsy-turvy, that was the expression she used. Apparently Janie Bluett had given in her notice the day before. She has been intending to leave for some time, but now, according to Mary, she can't stand things next door any longer. And it appears Cook is feeling the same; and if she goes she has promised to take Mary with her. So that's the situation.'

'D'you want to leave here?'

His mother sighed before she said, 'I never thought I would ever hear myself say so, because I loved this little house. But I must admit she's got me scared. I wouldn't believe she could have gone like this.'

He remained thoughtful for a moment before he said, 'I don't suppose I could get you a suitable place straight away, but one of the big houses on Brampton Hill has been turned into a nursing home. Doctor Cornwallis has a patient there. He says it's a fine, comfortable place. Would you go there?'

She paused before she said, 'Nursing home? Well, I've always said I would never go into a nursing home, but I think I'll be glad to get out of here, if it's only for a short while. But it must be for only a short time because I must live in a house of some kind, John, with enough space to hobble about. I couldn't bear to be tied to the one room all day.'

'I know that, dear, I know that. Anyway, I'll have a talk with the old man in the morning, then go and see the place for myself. And don't worry, please, because there's nothing to stop us just packing our bags and leaving here any minute. Now settle down. And look, I'll tell you what to do. If you hear that scraping again, take your stick and knock on the ceiling.' He picked up one of the sticks that were hooked over the end of the bed and he tried it for length, saying, 'You'll have to stand up. But do that if she starts. Now settle down. I won't be going

286

up to bed for the next hour as I have some reading to do. And that reminds me: I left a number of my medical books along in the spare room. I must try and have a word with Frances and see if she'll sneak them down for me. But I think you're more likely to see young Mary than I am Frances, so if you can catch her eye tomorrow over the hedge, give her that message, will you? Ask her if she'll bring them down and put them outside the door.'

'What if I don't see her tomorrow or the next day?'

'Well, that'll be just too bad, because then I'll open the door, go into the kitchen and if Frances isn't there, ask one of them to give her a message.'

'And risk running into her?'

'Oh, if she's keeping her visits till the night-time, I don't think she'll come along this end during the day. Still, we'll see. Now settle down.' He bent and kissed her, then went into the sitting-room, though not to read. The medical books and magazines lay unopened on the table and he sat for almost the hour pondering on the future . . .

He was a light sleeper and often found difficulty in getting off to sleep, and tonight was no exception. In fact, although he felt very tired, he had been in bed for over half an hour and was still wide awake.

It was as he stared into the darkness, his thoughts on Helen and what would be their future, when the crashing of glass and an implement that must have struck the brass rail on the bottom of the bed caused him to leap up and to stand rigid for a moment while his hand went out to the side-table to grope for matches to light the gas. But as he did so he was startled once more with the sound of more breaking glass.

He thrust on his slippers and made his way to the broken window, trudging through the glass, and he peered out of the side pane towards the other bedroom window. The light outside seemed much lighter than that of the bedroom. Then he glimpsed the dark shape of the figure disappearing into the wood.

She was mad, yet wily, for she knew that he couldn't sleep with drawn curtains and a drawn blind and, because they weren't overlooked here, that he never pulled his blind down or drew the curtains: he liked to wake up to the light of the morning.

He now made his way back to the table and the matches, and as he lit the gas he heard his mother shouting agitatedly, 'John! John!' And he called back, 'Be there in a minute. It's all right. It's all right.'

He now looked for the implement which had hit the rail of the bed. And there it was.

He picked it up. It was half a new brick, the edges sharp. As he examined it he could see her going through the wood to where they were building the house on the last quarter acre and picking up this brick.

He went into the other bedroom, where again he had to walk over glass. Here he found another half-brick, but this time it had been nearer its target, for it was lying in the middle of the counterpane. Just another yard, if he had been lying there, and it would have hit him on the head, which would have been her intention.

He carried the two bricks downstairs, where he found his mother standing leaning heavily on her sticks. And when he held out the bricks towards her, she looked at him and said, 'She's mad! she is, John, she's mad!'

He put the bricks down, saying, 'Come on, back to bed. I'll lie on the couch. Now, it's all right, it's all right. Stop trembling.' And at this, she said, 'Well, by the feel of your hand, you're not very steady yourself.'

He said nothing to this, but he helped her into bed again.

'I'll make a cup of tea,' he said.

288

Some minutes later, as he sat by her side drinking the tea, he said, 'This has put the finishing touches to it. Now I don't know where you'll be sleeping from now on, but it certainly won't be here. So tomorrow, get Mrs Atkinson to pack up all our things.'

'The store cupboard's full and there's nearly twenty bottles of wine,' she said.

If he could have smiled at that moment he would have: there was the housewife speaking. What he said, and brusquely, was, 'Leave the store cupboard. The wine . . . well if you must take them, wrap the bottles up in newspapers or odd garments or such and pack them into cardboard boxes. I'll ask Doctor Cornwallis if I can store them there.'

Taking the empty cup from her, he said, 'Now tuck down and try to get some sleep because you're going to need it; tomorrow will be a busy day,' and as he went from the room, he added to himself, 'It certainly will be for me.'

'Have a cup of tea,' said Doctor Cornwallis.

'No thanks; I've had six already; and I'm sorry to have disturbed you at your breakfast.'

'Oh, I was finished. But bricks through your window? She means business. It looks as though she's certainly becoming confused, perhaps even deranged, but . . .'

'Insane, is my opinion . . . Could she be certified?'

'For throwing bricks through your windows? Not for that, no. She's not insane. But it has become clear that she has spasms of discharging much nervous energy, which often leads to attacks of petit mal. This is what has been happening to her.'

'When did you last see her?'

'Oh, I was called to attend her about a fortnight ago. She had been out shopping and had returned in a state, so the maid said. And yet I can't really be certain in her

289

case, you know; nor, equally, can I be dogmatic and say it's hysteria, for there are many symptoms of this that she doesn't show. But there is certainly nothing I can see that would help to certify her. And like all in her state, she's wily. If I was bringing in an outside opinion, which, as you know, must be done in such cases, after hearing her talk they would find it very difficult to put pen to paper with regard to her sanity. No, you've got to find another way to get release from her. Yet, if she won't hear of divorce, I can't suggest anything. But wait—' He held up his hand and wagged his finger at John as if admonishing him, as he said, 'Just you hold your hand a minute. There's something in my mind clicking. It's about insanity in marriage. There was a case some years ago—' He now shook his head as he said, 'I'll look it up. Yes, I'll look it up. There should be a law book here somewhere. Anyway, you could go to the library. You don't happen to have any books on law, I suppose?'

'Strangely, I do. I've got three; one dating back forty years or more. I bought a bundle of books at a sale in my student days, because among them was a medical book I couldn't afford at the time. Yes. Yes, I think there's three. I'll look it up when I get back.'

'Do that. Now that's a point. Do that, about insanity in marriage.'

'And look, if you want to look around and find a place for your mother, I'll share your patients with Doctor Rees.'

'Thanks very much. I'll be grateful. I was thinking about going to that new place that you talked about in Brampton Hill.'

'Oh? Oh, there, you'll be out of luck. Yesterday when I was visiting, the matron told me they had a waiting list.'

'I'm sorry about that, it sounded a good place.'

'Where will you yourself go?'

'Not back to Mrs Pearson's, I can tell you that for sure. Oh, I'll find somewhere, don't worry.'

'Well, until you do, there's a bed upstairs if you would like it.'

John did not give any answer to this invitation for a moment; but then he said, 'That's very kind of you, Doctor. And if I can't get fixed up I'll be glad to accept.'

'Oh, you won't be putting me to any trouble. But you might have some restless nights, because when I'm not snoring, and I can snore up to high C, and singing—' he turned now and grinned at John, adding, 'I'm sober when I snore, but when I sing it's a sign that I've had my medicine.'

John was forced to smile and he came back with, 'Well, if I have a dose of the same medicine, we could do a duet, because I'm told I have a good baritone voice.'

'Oh, I doubt if that'll ever come about, because you could never carry my medicine. You're not built that way. But go on, and let me know how you get on. By the way, have you any special visits to make?'

'Three, but I can do them on the way.'

'Good.'

At this they parted and John started on his furnished-apartment hunting session . . .

By twelve o'clock he was feeling slightly desperate for his searching had been fruitless. And so, as he had been longing to do all morning, he turned the horse in the direction of Col Mount, and Helen.

It should happen that Daisy was visiting, and they were eating a light lunch, and when they pressed him to join them, he did not refuse as, other than a slice of toast, he had had nothing to eat all morning.

It was while they were sitting in the drawing-room taking their coffee that Daisy, looking hard at John, said, 'Something on your mind more than usual?'

He smiled at her as he said, 'What makes you think that?'

'Because you haven't had a decent shave today.'

His hand went to his chin as his eyes widened and he said, 'I've had a shave.'

'Yes, here and there. There are two tufts below your ears that you missed.'

As Helen burst out laughing, he too began to laugh; then he stopped abruptly saying, 'It's a wonder I shaved at all; we had rather a busy night.'

'What d'you mean?' Helen was looking towards him now enquiringly.

He didn't answer her immediately, but put his cup down on a side-table, then said flatly, 'We are having to leave the house. My mother's frightened to death. She only told me yesterday what had been happening. Beatrice has been scratching on the door in the dark as well as talking through it. Being upstairs I haven't heard her. But I heard her all right last night when two bricks came through the windows. She didn't know in which room I was sleeping, but she was taking no chances.'

'Oh, never! Never!' Helen was shaking her head now. 'She must be—' she stopped and he nodded at her, saying, 'Yes, going mad. She is mad, I'm sure, and has been for some time.'

'Does Doctor Cornwallis know this?'

'Yes. Yes, of course. But, as he says, it would be difficult to prove; he doesn't agree with me. Anyway, I've been house-hunting again all morning. I've left my mother and Mrs Atkinson packing. I imagined I would get my mother into the new nursing home on Brampton Hill; but Doctor Cornwallis tells me there are no vacancies. So I've been doing the rounds again, but so far without success.'

As Helen put her hand out towards him and was about to speak Daisy put in, 'I know of two places she could have the choice of.'

'Yes?' John's voice was high.

'Yes.' Daisy's head was bobbing now. 'Either at my place, or here.'

'Yes. Yes.' Helen and Daisy exchanged glances. Then Helen said, 'It'll be here. I would love to have her, John.'

'Oh, no; no. That would be an imposition. Anyway, she must have someone to see to her needs and she would need at least two rooms.'

'Look how many rooms there are in this house, and all empty! There are eight bedrooms upstairs.'

'But she couldn't go upstairs.' This came from Daisy. And Helen, her voice unusually loud, said, 'I know that. I know that. But there is the games room that no-one uses now. It would make a lovely bedroom. And next to it there is the smoke-room, which would make a nice sitting-room. And it leads on to the conservatory. She would be in nobody's way because the rooms are at the far end of the corridor. And I would love to have her here.'

'Oh no.' John shook his head now. 'I don't want you giving up your time.'

'Don't talk daft, man.'

He turned sharply now to Daisy, who went on, 'She doesn't know what to do with her time. She's bored to death. I've tried to introduce her to committee work, but the look on her face when sitting round a table is very off-putting to the others.'

'Oh, Daisy, how can you say such a thing? I've kept that silly smile on my face for hours just to please you. And as instructed' – she bounced her head towards Daisy now – 'talked of things I know nothing whatever about, really.'

'All right then; you do something that you do know something about, and instruct the staff to prepare those rooms; and I'll give them a hand. As for you, John, get on your way back to your mother and tell her it's all arranged, and to stop worrying. And by the way, where d'*you* propose to stay?'

293

'Oh, Doctor Cornwallis has offered me a bed until I get fixed up.'

'Well, you can get fixed up in my place any day. And that would be nice. Think about it, lad. Oh, yes, to have a man all to myself. Look, tell old Cornwallis that you're fixed up. Tell him you've had a proposal, immoral, illicit, or whatever name you'd like to put to it, but nevertheless, a proposal. And, you know' – she nodded at him – 'it isn't every man I'd make that proposal to.'

John took two steps towards her and, taking her wrinkled face between his hands, he said quietly, 'I'll tell you something, Daisy, and it's the truth: if my heart wasn't already given somewhere else, I would jump at the chance, and seriously.'

As he saw the bright eyes glisten for a moment and a tinge of pink diffuse itself over her face, he nodded at her as if in confirmation of his words. And then, turning to Helen, who stood with a soft, knowing smile on her face, he said, 'Thanks, my dear. That sounds inadequate, but at this moment I cannot tell you how relieved I am.'

And now she asked quietly, 'What time will I send the carriage for her?'

When he hesitated Daisy put in, 'It should be after dark in case Beatrice spots it. What d'you say, John?'

'Yes, you're right, Daisy.'

'Well, whatever time it goes, I'll come and . . .'

'No, no. Please, Helen.'

'He's right,' said Daisy; 'you want to keep out of it. But I'll go along and give a hand.'

'Thank you, Daisy. Thank you.'

'So, we'll say about seven o'clock?'

'Yes, that'll be fine.' He looked from one to the other now and said, 'I . . . I don't know how to thank you. I was at my wits end when I came in and now I feel—' He stopped and shook his head before muttering, 'I'll . . . I'll be away then.'

As he hurried from the room Helen went to follow him, but a gesture from Daisy stopped her. And when the door had closed on him Daisy said softly, 'He's better left alone, dear. He's at breaking point.'

It was just after six when he returned for the second time to the annexe and was surprised to see his mother sitting fully dressed for outside, and she greeted him rather tartly. 'Where on earth have you been? I've not seen you since this afternoon.' And he answered her in a similar vein: 'Mother, there are sick people out there.'

As he sat down beside her the tears began to race down her cheeks, and she said, 'Oh, my dear, I am sorry. In spite of the good news I have had a fearful dread on me all day.'

'Now don't be silly, dear; our lives are about to change, and for the better.'

She squeezed his hand, then said, 'Have you had anything to eat?'

'Woman! Woman! Listen to me! I told you earlier I'd lunched with Helen and Daisy. Now Daisy will soon be here. You're dressed, but are you all packed up?'

'Yes; except for the few books Frances promised to bring from upstairs. Mrs Atkinson had to go to the dentist; she was nearly mad with the toothache; she was going to call in on you. You must have been out. I suppose it's being by myself that's made me jittery.'

They both started when there was a distant knock on the door and a voice calling softly, 'Doctor. Doctor.'

'That'll be Frances,' he said, 'about the books.'

He hurried through the hall, unlocked the door and there was Frances. She had a number of books in her arms and she said, 'There's quite a few more, Doctor, but I couldn't carry them. Anyway, she's gone out. She must be going for a tramp; she took her walking stick with her.'

He glanced quickly over the books and realised they were mostly non-medical. He said, 'Does she usually go out at this time of night?'

'Yes. Yes, Doctor, she goes for walks round about.'

'Well, come on, I'll go up with you.'

They were both now running along the passage, through the main hall and up the stairs and to the spare room. Then he scooped a number of medical books from a shelf, but in doing so, toppled the rest onto the floor. Then turning swiftly, he made for the door, saying, 'Bring those, Frances, please.'

At the top of the stairs he stopped with the feeling that his heart was leaping through his ribs, so startled was he, for there, coming up towards him was Beatrice.

On the sight of him she paused and blinked her eyes tightly as if she didn't believe what or whom she was seeing. Then very slowly she took the rest of the stairs, lifting each foot firmly from one tread to the other.

When she was about to reach the landing he had to step back, and, like a schoolboy who had been caught in some thieving act, he almost stammered, 'I . . . I was collecting my . . . my medical books.'

'Oh yes, your medical books. I've just come back to collect some chocolates; I was hungry.' The smile on her face made him actually shudder. And when she went on, 'Something said to me, "Go back, Beatrice. You need energy." And chocolates make energy. Did you know that, John? Chocolates make energy.'

He nodded at her as he sidled round her to the top of the stairhead. He was aware that Frances was standing somewhere to the side of her. Then he turned abruptly and made to walk down the stairs. He had no way of supporting himself for his arms were holding the books.

Later, he could not recall if it was Frances's scream he heard first or his own when the foot landed viciously into

296

the middle of his back. He felt he had leaped into the air and that the books had taken wings, but he did not hear himself scream again as he hit the floor, nor the cry from Frances, nor the gasps of horror from Cook and Janie Bluett.

The screams had brought Catherine Falconer up out of her chair and grabbing her stick, before she hobbled from the annexe into the passage and towards the group of people shouting in the hall.

Frances was yelling, 'You kicked him down, ma'am; you kicked him down,' and Beatrice was wielding her stick and yelling back, 'Shut up! you, before I bring this across you. He fell! He fell down the stairs.'

'Oh, my God!' The words were wrenched from Mrs Falconer when she saw her son lying inert, one leg under him, the other at an odd angle. And there was blood seeping from one trouser leg.

'What have you done, woman? What have you done?' Catherine Falconer was screaming at Beatrice.

'He fell! He fell! He's dead!'

'No! No! He's not dead, ma'am, he's breathing.'

'Well, he won't be for long. Stay where you are, woman!' Beatrice now waved her stick towards Janie Bluett.

'You're mad! You're mad, woman! Get a doctor. I command you to get a doctor for my son.'

'Command! she says. This is my house. My house, Mrs Falconer. Your son was trespassing. And be careful what you say to me else you'll go the same way. I've had enough of you. Yes, I have, behind your closed door. But it's all over. Oh, yes, it's all over for both of you.' Then she actually screamed at Frances, who was aiming to slip past the foot of the stairs, 'I've told you, woman! You'll get this across you,' and she brought the stick within an inch of Frances's face, causing the girl to scream again, 'You're mad! You're mad! And you kicked him. You did; you kicked him down the stairs.'

297

When the stick fell viciously across Frances's arm the girl jumped back as she cried out, then hung on to Janie Bluett.

'Oh, woman! Woman' – Mrs Falconer now was pleading – 'I beg you, send for the doctor,' and in a placating voice Cook added her pleas, 'Mistress, yes; please, please, let someone go for the doctor.'

Beatrice took no heed of Cook's plea, but yelled at Mrs Falconer, 'Shut up! I've told you, or I'll knock you down off your rickety sticks,' and she was about to advance on Catherine Falconer when the sound of someone scurrying behind her turned her about, and the sight of Mary Simmons flying down the passage seemed to put her in a quandary for a moment. Then she was yelling again, 'That's it, old woman! Get down on your rickety knees. He'd be surprised to see that, wouldn't he? because you've kept him by your side for years, pretending you couldn't walk. Now I'd advise you to stay there. And you lot' – she thrust out her arm towards the three women now huddled together – 'the same applies to you, because it's going to be a long night. Three o'clock in the morning is when they die, isn't it? Three o'clock. It's very quiet around three o'clock. Have you ever been outside in the middle of the night at three o'clock? Even the birds don't rustle, and the rooks are frightened to make a sound. Did you know that? Did you know that? Because the world is dead at three o'clock in the morning and it takes the dying with it. It takes the dying with it. Oh, yes. Yes. So, like the old girl, I'm going to sit on the floor.' . . .

Mary Simmons was flying up the drive. She'd have to get help. She'd have to get help. Mr MacIntosh next door. She'd get Mr MacIntosh.

The young girl now let out a loud scream as a figure emerged round the curve of the drive and almost bumped into her, in fact, it caught hold of her shoulder. But when the voice that spoke to her was soft, her gasping breath eased.

298

'What is it? What is it!' Daisy drew the shivering girl out of the shadow of the trees into a narrow patch of moonlight. And staring into her face, she said, 'What is it, my dear?'

'Oh, ma'am, ma'am, she's . . . she's gone mad. She's killed the doctor. Kicked him downstairs and she won't let them send for Doctor Cornwallis. I . . . I was going for Mr MacIntosh next door. They are all in the hall; she won't let them pass, the cook or anybody. She's got a stick.'

'It's all right, my dear. It's all right. You go on and tell Mr MacIntosh to come quickly. But listen, my carriage is on the road. Tell the driver there's been an accident and Miss Daisy says he has to go and fetch Doctor Cornwallis. Now, can you remember that?'

'Yes, ma'am. Tell your driver to fetch Doctor Cornwallis and I'll fetch . . . I'll fetch Robbie, I mean Mr MacIntosh.'

'That's it! That's a good girl. Off you go now. Quick!'

Then Daisy herself actually ran down the remainder of the drive. The annexe door was open. She did not immediately enter, but paused and listened to a voice, its sound rising and falling. Then she was tiptoeing through the small hall and to the door that led into the corridor. Peering along it, she could just see into the hall, with a figure standing there, its arms waving. And now she could hear the voice quite plainly: 'What are you saying, old woman? You are making one last request? Oh, people who are going to die always make one last request. If he could talk, he would make one last request, wouldn't he? Oh, yes, he would make one last request all right. Your son would make one last request, and it would be to see his dear Helen. Wouldn't it? Wouldn't it now? And if he did, he'd know what I would say.' There was a pause here before the tone rose to almost a scream as it said, 'I'd say that the only way Helen will see you is over your dead body. That's how she'll see you, over your dead body.'

'He's bleeding, Beatrice. You can see he's bleeding.'

'Oh, yes, dear Mrs Falconer, I can see he's bleeding, and from the mouth now. And I expect him to bleed a lot more. Then he'll suddenly stop bleeding because dead people don't bleed, do they? Well, I don't think they do. I think I've read it somewhere that they don't bleed.'

'He's not dying; he's not!' Mrs Falconer protested loudly; 'and the blood's coming from his nose, not his mouth.'

'Well, wherever it's coming from it'll soon stop.'

Daisy bent quickly down and slipped off her shoes. And now she could have been one of the jungle animals she had become acquainted with in Africa, so stealthy was her approach.

Her appearing from the passage brought a gasp from the two women huddled together and from Cook who was now at John's other side. Then everything happened so quickly.

There was a mingling of concerted yells before she actually jumped on Beatrice, her hands going over her shoulders and under her oxters, and pinning her arms. And Beatrice herself let out a scream of pain as she was borne to the floor. She fell flat with Daisy on top of her, and it was evident that Daisy was winded, too, because she couldn't speak for a moment. But then she was shouting up at the cook, 'Something to tie her hands and feet! Quickly!'

The three women were looking around desperately when Daisy's voice came at them: 'Your apron straps! Tear them off, woman! Your apron straps!'

Cook pulled off her apron from her well-padded body and with a twist of her wrist tore the crossed linen straps from their base. And now Daisy, pulling herself up knelt on Beatrice's thrashing legs, then cried to the girls, 'Tie her wrists together!' And this they did only too willingly, and when Daisy had strapped them tight with one piece of the linen, she used the other to do the same with her ankles. Now turning Beatrice onto her back, she stood up

300

gasping, staring down at the mouth opening and shutting as she repeated one word, 'You! You! You!'

'Hoist her into the chair.'

Cook dragged the trussed figure none too gently towards a carved, bog oak hall-chair, and with help from the girls pulled her up and dropped her into it, causing Beatrice to emit a groan as her bound hands hit the back of it, the while Daisy, bending over Mrs Falconer, said, 'Come on, my dear, sit up, sit up. It's all right. We've sent for the doctor.'

It must have been the word doctor that brought Beatrice fully back into consciousness, for she screamed, 'No doctor . . . no doctor's coming here! No!' She tossed herself backwards and forwards in the chair, and Daisy, looking at Frances who was visibly trembling, said, 'Does she take sleeping tablets?'

'Yes, ma'am. Yes, she does. She does.'

'Go and get them.'

This order brought forth another scream from Beatrice.

When within a minute Frances handed the box of sleeping tablets to Daisy, Daisy said, 'I hear she eats chocolates?'

'Oh yes, ma'am, yes, by the boxful. There's an opened box in the drawing-room.'

'Fetch it!'

With the chocolates to hand, Daisy approached the writhing figure and, bending over her, she said, 'Open your mouth, woman,' which caused Beatrice only to clamp her jaws tighter together, until Daisy gripped her nose and gave it a twist. And when the mouth opened wide and she thrust in a sleeping tablet, it was immediately spat out back at her. Then taking another tablet from Frances's trembling fingers, Daisy also picked up a chocolate, gave the nose another twist and inserted the two together into the gaping mouth. This time, however, she immediately clamped down hard on the jaws; and after hearing the guttural swallowing, she repeated the process.

301

Beatrice was now staring at her, and the look in her eyes was so malevolent that Daisy had to turn away, and going to John now, she looked pityingly down on to his twisted body, and her hand went tightly across her mouth. Then, her eyes closing, she muttered, 'Oh my God!' And she added, 'Oh, my dear John. Dear John. What has she done to you?'

'Couldn't . . . couldn't we straighten him out a bit?' Mrs Falconer asked brokenly now; and Daisy said, 'No, dear. Better leave him until the doctor comes. And he's on his way.'

Catherine Falconer turned an enquiring look on her, as if to say, 'How could he be . . .?' And Daisy said, 'The little maid, I told her to send my driver, and she's gone for Robbie.'

It was as if the mention of his name had created Robbie, for there he was hurrying along the passage. But at the entrance to the hall he gazed in amazement from the trussed figure in the chair to the twisted form on the floor: 'God in heaven!' he cried.

When Robbie knelt down by John's side, Daisy said, 'I . . . I wouldn't touch him until the doctor comes. He's bleeding profusely, and I don't know where it's coming from.'

Robbie nodded, then looked down on the pallid face of the man who had been such a friend to him and found himself unable to find words to express his feelings.

'She kicked him! She kicked the doctor in the back. Yes! she did. Yes! she did;' Frances's voice was touching on hysteria, and Cook first admonished her then drew the girl tightly towards her.

Looking questioningly at Daisy, Robbie said, 'He'll have to be taken to hospital. It'll need the ambulance. Have you sent for one?'

'No. No.' Daisy shook her head.

'Oh.' He got to his feet; but still looking down on John, he said, 'He can't be left like that for long. The doctor won't

302

be here for at least twenty minutes, that's if he's in; I'll go and see about it.' And with this he ran from the hall, and as he did so there came a weird laugh from the tied figure in the chair and a drowsy voice said, 'Too late, too late.' . . .

And those were almost the words that Doctor Cornwallis muttered to himself when, twenty-five minutes later, he entered the house. And as he gently cut the trouser leg and small clothes down from the bent limb, he muttered, 'Almighty . . .!' for now he was looking at the bones piercing the flesh.

When he heard Mrs Falconer's drawn-out cry of pain, 'O . . . h!' he said to Daisy, 'Take her away into another room.'

As he felt the erratic pulse on the limp wrist, he made no outward sign but inwardly he was shaking his head.

He looked up at Daisy now and said, 'An ambulance.'

'Robbie . . . Mr MacIntosh . . . has gone for one.'

The doctor now turned to look at the drooping figure in the chair and he asked quietly, 'How did that come about?'

And Daisy answered simply, 'With some effort,' and her left hand was bearing witness to this for she knew that, in falling to the floor, she had sprained it.

As Doctor Cornwallis lumbered to his feet his words were enigmatic: 'He's got all the proof he needs for his release, but it may be too late now.'

It was just five minutes later when the ambulance arrived and under orders from Doctor Cornwallis, the men did not attempt to straighten the twisted leg as they laid John gently on the stretcher.

'I'll follow you there,' Doctor Cornwallis said to them; but before doing so he turned to Beatrice, whose chin was now resting on her breast, then enquiringly to Daisy, who said, 'I've given her a couple of sleeping tablets.'

'Oh, wise, the best thing. Yes. Two, you say?'

'Yes, two.'

'Well, she'll sleep till tomorrow morning, when I'll be along to see her; but I won't be alone. Oh no, I won't be alone. And whoever else is here, I want that girl' – he pointed to Frances – 'to remain as a witness to what happened,' to which Daisy said, 'I'll be here, too.'

He nodded, then said, 'Good,' before leaving.

When Daisy saw Mary sidling along the passage towards her, she called to her, 'It's all right. Everything's all right now, dear.' And then she patted her shoulder, adding, 'Good girl.'

Emerging from the drawing-room and seeing her helpmate, Cook said to her, 'You did well, Mary;' then turning to Daisy, she added, 'We've made the couch ready for her, ma'am.'

'Good,' said Daisy. 'Then just before I leave I'll untie her. But what are you going to do, Cook?'

'I'm away this very night to my sister's, ma'am, and I'm taking Mary and Janie with me. We had already decided to leave, and Janie's got herself a job; she can walk into it tomorrow. That only leaves Frances.'

All attention was now set on Frances, who was standing shaking her head, and it was Catherine Falconer who put in quietly, 'If you have no other plans, Frances, I'd be glad of your help: I need someone with me' – she now turned to Daisy – 'that is, if Lady Spears will agree to the arrangement for the time being.'

'Oh yes; yes, I can give you her word on that,' Daisy answered immediately. 'So that's settled; and as Cook says, it's the outside man's day off, and he always makes for his little stable rooms at the far end of the grounds; so he won't know anything until tomorrow morning. And neither will she, once we leave her on the couch; so we can lock up and go.'

# 11

Dawn was just breaking when Beatrice came to; although she remained curled up on the couch for some time, for she was feeling distinctly odd; only gradually did she become aware of her aching head, also of the pain in her body, particularly in her arms and ankles. Slowly, she pulled herself up into a sitting position to discover that she was in the drawing-room and that the gas chandelier was still alight. What had happened?

Then, as if a gate in her mind had suddenly swung open, realisation of all that had taken place came to her, passing like a series of pictures before her eyes, one rapidly falling into the other. She had killed him. Her foot had landed right in the middle of his back. Oh, that had given her a feeling of joy, as had seeing him lying there, his life's blood ebbing away. There returned to her a moment of elation, quickly blotted out by the feeling of that strange creature jumping on her and tying her up. She suddenly put her hand to her mouth, for she could feel the woman stuffing in the chocolates in order to make her swallow the pills. They had been sleeping pills, which is why she had slept so long. But why hadn't Frances taken her upstairs and put out these lights?

She pulled herself up from the couch and staggered down the drawing-room and into the hall. Where were they?

305

Where were the servants? Oh, it must be early. Yes, it must be early. But she'd waken them. Yes, she would. She needed a drink; she was dry.

Still walking as though drunk, she entered the kitchen, there to be met by a dead fire. She went from the room shouting, 'Cook! Cook! Frances!' and when she received no reply, she staggered to their quarters, only to see open doors with the early light revealing empty rooms and here and there a cupboard with drawers left open.

Back in the hall she walked round in a circle, then came to a stop at the foot of the stairs and peered at the polished boards, where large dark patches showed here and there. As she now bent down and ran her fingers over a large patch of the dried blood, she again experienced that ecstatic feeling. She had killed him! Well, she had known she would sometime. He had died in her house. What time they had moved him, she didn't know. But she knew from the look on his face and the way he had been lying with his blood flowing out that his body was wrecked; the body that he wouldn't give to her. And now because she had done it, they would come and take her away. They would say she was mad. Well, perhaps she was a bit mad. But she wasn't so mad that she would let them have the last word as to what she would do with her life. Her life was her own, and this house was hers. Oh, yes, this house was hers. But what would happen when she was dead? Because he wouldn't inherit now, would he? Oh no. But her sister could. Oh, yes. Yes, Dearest Helen could. The very thought sent her running into the drawing-room again and there, throwing herself onto the couch, she beat her hands into the cushions, yelling aloud, 'Oh, no! No! Never! Never!' For what would she do with it? Knowing that she herself had loved it so much, Helen would take a delight in selling all this lovely furniture, and then the house; or turning it into flats for common people; or . . . or . . .

She was on her feet again, running now from one room to another: the dining-room, the study, the billiard-room, the smoke-room that had been her father's room, and sacrosanct. And she repeated to herself, the smoke-room, the smoke-room, as she ran up the stairs and into her bedroom, where she stood panting as she held on to the rail at the foot of the bed. She was sweating. Her body wanted release, it wanted to be free. Free. She tore off her clothes until she reached her whalebone corsets and, looking down on them, she said, 'After, after; do the shutters first.'

She now ran down the stairs and, starting in the drawing-room, she tugged hard to release the shutters that were packed and pressed close against the side of the deep bay window. They hadn't been drawn into place for years, and she was panting heavily by the time she had covered the three windows.

It took her a full half hour to go through the rest of the ground floor of the house. The only windows without shutters were those in the kitchen; and with the exception of one, these were barred on the outside.

Only the cracks in the shutters let in the early morning daylight; the whole of the downstairs was dark, except for the drawing-room where the gaslight was still glowing.

She now sat on the third step of the stairs and, as a child might have done, she hugged her knees as if she had succeeded in doing something clever. And then she started to laugh; but the sound was not of childish laughter, for she was yelling in her head that she was going to fool them, fool them all, especially *her*. *She* would never get this house, her beautiful house, her child. And it had always been her child: when she was very young the house had been her doll's house; in her 'teens, through her mother's death, her goal had been achieved, and from then she had tended it with pride. This house was hers and would always remain hers. It would never belong to her sister, whom she had disliked in her 'teens, then hated in her womanhood.

She now got to her feet, then stepped down into the hall. She felt gay, she wanted to dance. She had been dancing on and off of late. The bedroom restricted her, but here there was plenty of room. Not yet though. Not yet. There was something she must do.

She now ran into the kitchen. They kept paraffin somewhere. Yes; yes, in the boot-room; it had been kept there following a gas leak, when they'd had to light the lamps.

The can was full and heavy, but she managed to carry it into the kitchen and to heave it up onto the table. And there, she grabbed two wide-mouth brass jugs from the mantelpiece and filled them from the can. Then, as gaily as if she had been carrying jugs of ale, she hurried into the drawing-room and sprinkled the paraffin over the curtains, moving from one window to another. This done, she did the same on the couch and chairs. She dealt similarly with the other rooms, not forgetting the annexe. Oh, she sprayed the annexe well.

The last jug of paraffin she used on the stairs and on the bedroom curtains.

Had she locked all the doors? Yes.

It was still not fully daylight when, downstairs again, she made a number of torches from tightly rolled paper, and now, starting with the annexe, she went tripping from one room to another, setting them alight.

Lastly, amid the strange patterns of flames and smoke she ran up the stairs and into her bedroom. There she tore off her corsets and her chemise, then her shoes and stockings. And now flinging her arms above her head, she pranced round the room. Of a sudden she stopped in front of the cheval mirror and put out her hand towards her reflection, crying, 'It's a good body, a young body, but he didn't want it, did he? I should have given it away to someone else. Just as Mrs Wallace did.' Strangely at this moment she was

308

feeling no animosity towards that woman, rather a feeling of sorrowful envy. And she didn't want to be put away like Aunt Ally. She put her hands above her head and started to sway as in a dancing movement; then she was overtaken by a fit of coughing, and she whimpered, 'I'm cold; I must put on my dressing-gown.'

She was making for the foot of the bed on which her dressing-gown lay when the whole house was rocked by an explosion. She was lifted off her feet and flung flat onto the floor under the window.

By the time Robbie returned with the fire brigade, the house was ablaze from end to end, with Rosie and Tom Needler standing helplessly by. Crying bitterly, Rosie rushed to the fire chief as he jumped down from the engine and she cried, 'My . . . my sister, she . . . she must be in there. Please! Please!'

'All right! miss. All right!' He turned and gazed at the house, then shook his head. 'We'll do what we can.'

It was the following day, as the house smouldered, that the body of Mrs Beatrice Falconer was found beneath the window of her bedroom. She was lying across a number of charred beams.

The newspapers used big headlines to report the tragedy of husband and wife. The reporter, waxing eloquent, also revealed that while the house was burning Dr Falconer himself was lying at death's door in a hospital.

# 12

Helen and Rosie stood by Beatrice's grave. Although they were both dry-eyed, they were full of pity for Beatrice and the way she had died. But that she had planned her own death was now evident. As Dr Cornwallis had said, the love of her life had been the house, and she had taken it with her; but not before she had, as she imagined, killed her husband. The evidence given by the four staff had verified this fact, together with that of Mrs Freeman Wheatland, who had apparently had to wrestle with Beatrice to bring her under control.

As they both turned from the grave, Helen put her arms around Rosie's shoulders, for she knew that this young girl, or woman that she was now, had more reason to hate Beatrice than had she. Beatrice had heartlessly aimed to ruin her life, and in the process had changed the course of that of the man who might now have been her own husband. Yet there was no-one happier than Rosie now, with her lovely baby and the doting affection of Robbie.

Outside the churchyard they stopped and looked at each other and Helen said, 'I . . . I must get back to the hospital.'

'Robbie says he's fully conscious now.'

'Yes; yes, he is.'

'I'll look in tonight,' said Rosie; and Helen answered, 'Yes, do that, dear. Do that.'

And they turned together and joined the mourners gathered at the door of the church.

Dr Cornwallis was standing near John's bedside and he was not talking to him, or with him, but at him. 'Now you can hear what I'm saying, laddie, so take it in. You're all right, as I've told you. Your back was unscathed. Badly bruised, yes, but no bones were broken. You were lucky. By God! you were lucky. Your leg is smashed, but after they have operated again, it'll likely be all right. The other leg is healing fine. Now you listen to me.' He bent closer to John, his voice soft and insistent now: 'You've got to make a stand. You know as well as I do what I mean. In seventy-five cases out of a hundred, you can make your mind up to go or stay. Now you've got a lot to stay for. There's that girl out there, that woman, that lady becoming ill herself because of you. You understand what I'm saying? You must, because your head's all right. You were concussed, but no serious damage was done. But this dead-pan attitude isn't good enough. You've got the idea into your head that you won't walk again, haven't you? Well, you'll walk all right. Oh, it'll take weeks, perhaps months, but you'll walk. And anyway, I want you back on the job. Young Rees is all right, but he's not you. And I didn't realise that you were more popular than I am: all those people coming in and asking for a run-down on your condition. I'm very jealous of my practice and my patients, but there they are in streams. So, do as I say. You'll make a stand and if my latest piece of news doesn't do the trick, nothing will.' His voice dropped lower still. 'I've been into it and so has my solicitor. A law has recently been passed enabling a man to marry his deceased wife's sister, so everything could be plain sailing that way.'

John's eyelids fluttered. He felt they were gummed. He looked at this man, this dear friend, but said nothing. Matters were not registering properly in his mind. Vaguely he recalled someone telling him that she had burned the house down and that she had died with it. But he hadn't seemed to be able to take it in, because there she was, as she had been since he had come round, standing at the top of the stairs staring at him, and he could still feel her foot in his back. As long as he lived, which wouldn't be very long, he would feel that foot in his back. But now Dr Cornwallis had been saying that she was dead, and the house was dead, and he was free. But what was he free for? Not to live like this, a cripple, at best in a wheelchair and a burden on Helen. Oh no. She'd had one sick man and she wasn't going to have another through him. Dr Cornwallis had just been saying it was up to him: he could either stay or go. Well, he had made his choice.

# 13

Daisy looked across the hospital bed towards Helen and asked, 'Did you know that they can cure ingrowing toe nails with cigar bands?'

Helen closed her eyes and bit on her lip, lowered her head and as she did so she squeezed John's hand. And it was he who replied, 'No; I've never heard that one, Daisy.'

'Well, nor had I until I was sitting on the upper deck of one of those new-fangled electric trams. There were two women sitting in front of me and one was telling the other about the cigar band.'

'Yes,' said John, with a tremble to his voice, 'and what happened to the cigar band? What about the cigar band, Daisy?'

'Well, I'll give you it word for word, it's true, honestly. One said to the other, "Eeh! that ingrowing big toenail of mine's nearly driven me mad," and the other one said, "Well, I told you, you should go and see one of those foot men about it." "And pay them half a crown?" said the first one; "not on your life. But I'm going to try May Thorpe's remedy. She says it works. All you've got to do is to cut the toenail straight across – not fancy round, you know – just straight across. Then, you take a piece of cigar band, just a little piece, and it must be a cigar band, because there must

313

be something in it that helps, like nicotine or something. You cut a tiny bit of that and you wedge it under the edge of the nail, where you've cut it square across like." Listen. Listen,' Daisy broke in now; 'it's true, I'm telling you. Listen, as she said, you cut the nail right across, then you take a small bit of a cigar band and press it under the nail between that and the flesh. And then, quite candidly, I nearly burst out laughing meself, because the other one said, "Then you set light to your big toe." '

As the bed shook, John pleaded, 'Daisy! Daisy! Please!'

'I'm not making it up. Believe me that's what happened.'

It was Helen now, tears running down her face, who said, 'But how do all these funny things always happen to you, Daisy? They never happen to me or anyone else I know.'

'Well, you don't listen. That's the point, you must listen.'

John laid his head back on the pillow and closed his eyes. For all the side-blessings in this world, Daisy was one. It was she who had, over the painful months, brought some lightness into the situation. And strangely, too, some days when the pain had been excruciating, the touch of her hand had brought him some relief; in fact, this dear individual, besides being a laugh-maker, possessed, in some strange way, the power of a healer.

'I must be off. There's a lot to be seen to. I'm attending a wedding tomorrow.'

'A wedding? Do I know them?'

Daisy paused, then screwed up her eyes before saying, 'Well, not really. No, not really;' and looking across at Helen, she said, 'I'll be back for you in half an hour. And mind, I'm not coming in here again; just be at the gate. He takes up too much of your time' – she nodded towards the bed without looking at John – 'and you've got other things to do.'

At this Helen smiled, saying, 'Yes, dear, I've other things to do, especially today.'

314

As Daisy went out laughing, John looked at Helen and asked, 'What do you have to do especially today?' His eyes were soft on her.

She did not return his gaze, but looked down at the hand she was holding; then, bringing it to her chest and pressing it there, she said quietly, 'Prepare for the wedding.'

'The wedding? The one Daisy was talking about?'

'Yes, the same one.'

'D'you know the couple?'

'Yes. Yes, I know the couple.'

As she continued to avert her gaze, he said, 'What is it? Something fishy here. Oh, don't tell me' – he drew his chin in – 'Don't tell me old Cornwallis has proposed to Mrs Newton.'

She lifted her head quickly, 'Doctor Cornwallis and Mrs Newton? No; no. I didn't know they were even friendly.'

'Oh, they've been friendly for years; at least, they meet once a week for cards and wine. She can put it back as much as he can.'

'Really?'

'Yes, really.'

'Well, if it isn't him, who is it?'

Now looking him straight in the face, Helen said, 'No, John, not Doctor Cornwallis, but another doctor. You.'

'M . . . m . . . me? What on earth are you talking about, Helen?'

She was now pressing him back into the pillows, her hand on his shoulder, saying, 'Don't excite yourself, please. Listen to me. I've waited long enough, and let's face facts, you could be in here another three months or more before you're on your feet and able to walk down an aisle. So it has been arranged.' She now smacked his shoulder, saying, 'Be quiet and let me speak. I've listened to your protests on this matter long enough. It has been arranged that we're to be married tomorrow in the hospital chapel. Haven't you noticed there's

315

an air of excitement among the nurses? It's been going on all week. They've been petting you and pampering you; they even got you the barber twice yesterday because you were grumbling about your growth.' She now tapped his chin.

'No! Helen. No way. Seriously, this business, Helen, no way am I having it. You've already seen to one invalid in your home; I'm determined you're not having another. I'll take you to the altar – oh! so gladly – but only when I can walk out of here in some fashion.'

She suddenly sat down, then demanded, 'Why not?' And he answered, 'You don't need me to go into why not. First of all, I know I'm stronger, and I know it might sound ungrateful, but sometimes I'm sorry they kept me alive.'

'Oh! John; that's an awful thing to say, and to me, knowing how I feel.'

'I'm sorry, dear.' He took hold of her hand now. 'But look at me' – he motioned down the bed – 'let's face it, dear, I'll never walk straight again. That leg was so fractured, it's the biggest mystery to me how they saved it. But having saved it, it's not going to be much use. I'll never be able to put much pressure on it. I'll have to use crutches at first, and then hopefully, sticks. And sticks will be with me for the rest of my life. Beatrice did a good job on me. I can imagine she enjoyed it.'

Helen pulled her hand away from his, saying, 'Oh, I hate to hear you feeling sorry for yourself.'

'I'm not feeling sorry for myself; although, I seem to be stressing I have enough to be sorry for. But I am not feeling sorry for myself; I am simply stating facts.'

'And you're not going to marry me tomorrow?'

He closed his eyes tightly and his voice sounded like a whimper as he said, 'Oh, Helen. Helen.'

There was silence between them for some moments before she said, 'Everyone's looking forward to it, particularly your mother, and, of course, Daisy. Robbie's agreed to be your best

316

man, and Doctor Cornwallis is going to give me away. It's all been arranged. And the Reverend Cuthbert from Saint Giles is going to take the ceremony. Everybody's worked so hard.'

He had his head down as he muttered, 'I loved you before. I feel I've always loved you, but I never thought I could love you as much as I do at this moment.' When he lifted his head his eyes were moist, but his hands were firm as he gripped hers, saying, 'Oh, Helen. Helen.'

When she bent over him he held her tightly, and their kiss was long and hard. Then, pushing her aside, he said, 'How on earth am I going to get into a church like this?'

'That's all been seen to, sir. Every last detail. You'll be in a long basket-chair.'

'Good Lord! Going to our wedding in a basket-chair.' He was biting tightly on his lip now, his head shaking from side to side, and then he said softly, 'You know something? You're the most wonderful woman in the world. No, not a woman, a girl, a girl who sat by my side on the top of Craig's Tor and let me sleep, then drank warm beer with me before suddenly walking out of my life, leaving me devastated.'

Again there was silence between them because neither of them, at this moment, wanted to dwell on Leonard.

Presently, Helen said brightly, 'And there'll be another surprise for somebody tomorrow.'

'Who?'

'Rosie and Robbie.'

'Surprise for them? What do you mean?'

'The land. Well, it didn't legally pass on to you. Doctor Cornwallis had already started proceedings, before the fire, to have the marriage annulled, so the property did not pass legally on to you, but came to us three girls; and Marion was agreeable to my suggestion that we legally pass it all over to Robbie. He'll have nearly fifty acres now. Rosie's in her seventh heaven.'

'No!'

'Yes.' She was nodding at him.

'Oh, Helen, that's a wonderful thing to do. He always wanted a farm. He'll make a wonderful farmer.' And when his arms came out again to her, she said, 'You're more excited about that than you are about marrying me.'

And to this he replied flatly, 'Yes. Yes, you're quite right, I'm much more excited about that.'

They were holding each other again. Then, taking her face between his hands, he said, 'D'you know what I'm realising now?' and at this she shook her head, and he went on softly, 'Well, I know now that until this moment I've never been really happy in my life. My work has given me what they call satisfaction, and yet at the same time, boredom and frustration. But now I know that come what may we shall spend our lives together. Tomorrow will seal it, but it is already accomplished in my mind. Thank you, my dearest, dearest Helen.'

She cupped his face with her hands, and looking into his eyes she said, 'Do you know something? You're a lovely man.'

At this, there was a joy in him that surpassed even the feeling of love he had for her, for he was recalling the night when he had left Henry with the thought that he doubted if anyone would say of him, after his death, what Henry had implied about Leonard.

But here he was; he wasn't dead; and he was to be married tomorrow, and she had called him a lovely man.